MYLA GOLDBERG is a first-time novelist whose stories have appeared in various North American journals. She lives in Brooklyn, New York.

Visit www.AuthorTracker.co.uk for exclusive information on your favourite HarperCollins authors.

'Nothing in *Bee Season*'s first third prepares readers for its extraordinarily disturbing crescendo. Goldberg has something rare in first-time novelists – and in more experienced writers for that matter – an appreciation of the subtlest dynamics of human relationships and experience. And as a stylist she has the equivalent of a musician's perfect pitch. This is a fantastic first novel that I wanted to read again as soon as I'd finished it'
Time Out (New York)

'It is amazing how quickly a true talent can announce itself. In the case of Myla Goldberg, it is not even a matter of pages, but of sentences … A marvellous debut novel' *Newsweek*

'Myla Goldberg's *Bee Season* is a bittersweet coming-of-age in which wise little Eliza Naumann's quirky passion for spelling bees unites and divides her family while revealing universal truths about the often crippling pain of love'
MARTHA MCPHEE, author of *Bright Angel Time*

'In a story told with unique delicacy and brave inventiveness, a young girl, innocent and all-knowing, learns how much there is to lose, and what it takes to win'
ELIZABETH STROUT, author of *Amy and Isabelle*

'Myla Goldberg delicately captures one family's spinning out by concentrating equally on the beauty and the despair. *Bee Season* is a heartbreaking first novel'
AIMEE BENDER, author of *The Girl in the Flammable Skirt*

MYLA GOLDBERG

Bee Season

A NOVEL

HARPER PERENNIAL

London, New York, Toronto and Sydney

Harper Perennial
An imprint of HarperCollins*Publishers*
77–85 Fulham Palace Road
Hammersmith
London W6 8JB

www.harperperennial.co.uk

This special edition published by Harper Perennial 2007
1

First published in Great Britain by Flamingo 2001
Reprinted twice

First published in the USA by Doubleday 2000

A catalogue record for this book
is available from the British Library

ISBN 978 0 00 779131 6

Set in Bembo

Printed and bound in Great Britain by Clays Ltd, St Ives plc

For my family

Bee Season

The world of letters is the true world of bliss.

—ABRAHAM ABULAFIA

(1240–c.1292)

Are you really proud of me?

—REBECCA SEALFON, 1997 NATIONAL
SPELLING BEE CHAMPION

AT PRECISELY 11 A.M. EVERY TEACHER
in every classroom at McKinley Elementary
School tells their students to stand. The enthusiasm of the collective chair scrape that follows
rates somewhere between mandatory school assembly and head lice inspection. This is especially the case in Ms. Bergermeyer's fourth/fifth
combination, which everybody knows is where
the unimpressive fifth graders are put. Eliza
Naumann certainly knows this. Since being
designated three years ago as a student from
whom great things should not be expected, she
has grown inured to the sun-bleached posters of
puppies and kittens hanging from ropes, and
trying to climb ladders, and wearing hats that
are too big for them above captions like "Hang
in there," "If at first you don't succeed . . ." and
"There's always time to grow." These baby animals, which have adorned the walls of every
one of her classrooms from third grade onward,
have watched over untold years of C students
who never get picked for Student of the Week,
sixth-place winners who never get a ribbon,

and short, pigeon-toed girls who never get chased by boys at recess. As Eliza stands with the rest of her class, she has already prepared herself for the inevitable descent back into her chair. She has no reason to expect that the outcome of this, her first spelling bee, will differ from the outcome of any other school event seemingly designed to confirm, display, or amplify her mediocrity.

Ms. Bergermeyer's voice as she offers up spelling words matches the sodden texture of the classroom's cinder block walls. Eliza expects to be able to poke her finger into the walls, is surprised to find she cannot. She can certainly poke her way through and past her teacher's voice, finds this preferable to being dragged down by its waterlogged cadences, the voice of a middle-aged woman who has resigned herself to student rosters filled with America's future insurance salesmen, Amway dealers, and dissatisfied housewives.

Eliza only half listens as Bergermeyer works her way down the rows of seats. In smarter classrooms, chair backs are free from petrified Bubble Yum. Smooth desktops are unmarred by pencil tips, compass points, and scissors blades. Eliza suspects that the school's disfigured desks and chairs are shunted into classrooms like hers at the end of every quarter, seems to remember a smattering of pristine desks disappearing from her classrooms over spring and winter breaks to be replaced by their older, uglier cousins.

Bergermeyer is ten chairs away. Melanie Turpin, who has a brother or sister in every grade in the primary wing, sits down after spelling TOMARROW, which even Eliza knows is spelled with an O. Eliza also knows that LISARD is supposed to have a Z and that PER-SONEL needs a second N. And suddenly the bee gets more interesting. Because Eliza is spelling all the words right. So that when Ms. Bergermeyer gives Eliza RASPBERRY, she stands a little straighter, proudly including the P before moving on to the B-E-R-R-Y. By the time Bergermeyer has worked her way through the class to the end of the first round, Eliza is one of the few left standing.

Three years before Eliza's first brush with competitive spelling, she is a second-grader in Ms. Lodowski's class, a room that is baby animal poster-free. Eliza's school universe is still an unvariegated whole. The wheat has yet to be culled from the chaff and given nicer desks. There is only one curriculum, one kind of student, one handwriting worksheet occupying every desk in Eliza's class. Though some students finish faster than others, Eliza doesn't notice this, couldn't tell if asked where she falls within the worksheet completion continuum.

Eliza is having a hard time with cursive capital Q, which does not look Q-like at all. She is also distracted by the fact that people have been getting called out of the classroom all morning and that it doesn't seem to be for something bad. For one thing, the list is alphabetical. Jared Montgomery has just been called, which means that if Eliza's name is going to be called, it has got to be soon. The day has become an interminable Duck Duck Goose game in which she has only one chance to be picked. She senses it is very important that this happen, has felt this certainty in her stomach since Lodowski started on K. Eliza assures herself that as soon as she gets called out her stomach will stop churning, she will stop sweating, and cursive capital Q will start looking like a letter instead of like the number 2.

Ms. Lodowski knows that second grade is a very special time. Under her discerning eye, the small lumps of clay that are her students are pressed into the first mold of their young lives. A lapsed classics graduate student, Ms. Lodowski is thrilled that her teaching career has cast her in the role of the Fates. Though she couldn't have known it at the time, her abbreviated classical pursuits equipped her for her life's calling as overseer of McKinley Elementary's Talented and Gifted (TAG) placement program.

Ms. Lodowski's home, shared with a canary named Minerva, is filled with photo albums in which she has tracked her TAG students through high school honors and into college. In a few more years the first of her former charges will fulfill destinies shaped by her guiding hand.

Ms. Lodowski prides herself upon her powers of discernment. She considers class participation, homework, and test performance as well as general personality and behavior in separating superior students from merely satisfactory ones. The night before the big day she goes down her class roster with a red pencil. As she circles each name her voice whispers, "TAG, you're it," with childlike glee.

Steven Sills spells WEIRD with the I before the E. Eliza spells it with the E before the I and is the last left standing. As she surveys the tops of the heads of her seated classmates she thinks, *So this is what it's like to be tall.*

She gets to miss fifth period math. Under Dr. Morris's watchful eye, she files into the school cafeteria with the winners from the other classes and takes her place in a plastic bucket seat. The seats are shaped in such a way as to promote loss of circulation after more than ten minutes. Two holes in each chair press circles into the flesh of each small backside, leaving marks long after the sitter has risen. Each chair has uneven legs, the row stretching across the stage like a hobbled centipede.

Through the windows on the left wall, buses arrive with P.M. kindergartners. In the kitchen, hundreds of lunch trays are being washed. From behind the closed kitchen comes the soothing sound of summer rain. Eliza feels a sudden pang of guilt for having left a lump of powdered mashed potato in the oval indentation of her tray instead of scraping it into the trash, worries that the water won't be strong enough to overcome her lunchtime inertia.

Dr. Morris is the kind of principal who stands outside his office to say goodbye to students by name as they scramble to their buses. Administering the school spelling bee allows him the great pleasure of observing his best and brightest. The children before him are the ones whose names adorn the honor roll. They are names teachers track long after having taught them in order to say, "This one was my favorite," or "I always knew this one would go far." Eliza is the exception to this rule. When Dr. Morris spots her in the group, he is reminded of something he can't quite place. At his puzzled smile, she blushes and looks away.

The meeting between Dr. Morris and Eliza's father that Dr. Morris can't quite remember occurs on Parents' Night one month after Ms. Lodowski goes from Kathy Myers to John Nervish, skipping Eliza. Saul Naumann only learns of his daughter's exclusion through one of his congregants who, after Shabbat services, announces loudly enough for the people on the other side of the cookie table to overhear that her son has been identified as Talented and Gifted. Saul realizes that the boy is in Eliza's class. Eliza hasn't tendered Saul the congratulatory note Aaron delivered at her age, the one that made Saul feel like a sweep-stakes winner.

Saul's is one of many hands Dr. Morris shakes that Parents' Night. Dr. Morris's office contains a desk with a framed picture of his daughter, two squeaky chairs, and a window that looks out onto the school playground. On a small bookshelf, binders of county educational code bookend with instructional paperbacks devoted to several categories of child including "special needs," "precocious," "problem," and "hyperactive." Dr. Morris keeps mimeographed pages from these books on hand to distribute to the parentally challenged.

"Hello, Mr. Naumann. It's a pleasure to see you here tonight." Dr. Morris remembers the son—smart, awkward, too quiet for his own good. While he knows the daughter's face, he can't attach words to the picture. He scans her file, hoping for help and finding nothing. "Eliza is a lovely child."

"Thank you. We think she's pretty special. Which is why I was a little surprised when I learned that she hadn't been TAG-tested with the rest of her class."

Morris manages a polite smile. Every year there is at least one like Mr. Naumann.

"Well, Mr. Naumann, that's a bit of an exaggeration. Only a portion of the second grade is tested, the fraction of the class Ms. Lodowski feels may benefit from an accelerated curriculum."

"The smarter ones."

"There are a lot of different kinds of smarts, Mr. Naumann, a lot of ways for a child to be special."

Dr. Morris addresses that last part to the picture on his desk. It's too bad Saul can't see this picture from where he's standing. If he could see it, he might conclude that this is a somewhat sensitive topic for Dr. Morris. The only people who generally get to see Rebecca Morris's picture are the students Dr. Morris catches using the word "retard." He escorts these students to his office, where they are shown the picture and ordered to repeat the word, this time to his daughter's face.

"Of course there are a lot of ways to be special," Saul continues, no way to know that he really shouldn't. "But my older son was placed in the TAG program, and I just thought that—"

Dr. Morris's face has grown red. "Instead of focusing on what you think you lack, Mr. Naumann, why don't you appreciate what you have? Eliza is a caring, loving child."

"Of course she is. That's not the issue."

Dr. Morris pictures Rebecca walking unsteadily to the van that comes for her each morning, the beatific smile that fills her face at the sight of any animal, and her pleasure at a yellow apple cut into bite-size pieces. He wants Mr. Naumann to get the hell out of his office.

"So sorry, Mr. Naumann, but our time is up. I wouldn't want to keep the other parents waiting."

"But—"

"Goodbye, Mr. Naumann, a pleasure seeing you again."

From third grade onward, Eliza's class is divided into math and reading groups. Eliza's reading group is called the Racecars. She likes it okay until she learns that the other reading group is called the Rockets. The Rockets read from a paperback that has *The Great Books*

printed on its cover in gallant letters. When she asks Jared Montgomery what's inside, he tells her that his group is reading excerpts from "the canon" and Eliza feels too stupid to ask if that means something other than a large gun. She can't help but wonder if someone told her which books were great and which ones were just so-so, if she'd like reading more. While she eventually adjusts to the faded motivational posters featuring long-dead baby animals, and the fifties-era reading books whose soporific effects have intensified with each decade of use, she can't get it out of her head that, while she is speeding around in circles waiting to be told when to stop, other kids are flying to the moon.

Within half an hour all the fourth graders have been eliminated except for Li Chan, who never washes his hair and outlasts two fifth graders and a sixth grader from a fifth/sixth combination. When Li finally misspells FOLLICLE, the eliminated fourth graders chant "Stink bomb" until Dr. Morris blinks the lights to quiet things down.

Eliza gets CANARY, SECRETARY, and PLACEBO. By the time CEREMONIAL and PROBABILITY come around, it is down to her, Brad Fry, and Sinna Bhagudori.

Everyone knows that Sinna is the smartest girl in school and that Brad is the smartest boy, but probably not as smart as Sinna. If anyone knows Eliza, it is from breaking the school limbo record, which got her name on the music classroom blackboard for a few weeks but which always goes to the short kids anyway.

Sinna has blue contact lenses and big boobs. Everyone knows her eyes are fake because they were brown the year before, but Sinna insists that a lot of people's eyes change when they go through puberty.

Brad plays soccer at recess and has a lot of moles. There are rumors that he spends his summers at a camp for kids who take math and science classes because they want to, but Brad tells everyone he goes to soccer camp. No one believes him either.

A couple times when it's Eliza's turn, Sinna starts toward the podium and Dr. Morris has to remind her to wait. Waiting for Sinna to return to her seat, Eliza pretends she is a TV star during opening credits, her face caught in freeze-frame. She imagines her name appearing below her face in bold white letters.

Sinna spells IMMANENT without the second M. She is already walking back to her seat when Dr. Morris says, "I'm afraid that's incorrect." It gets very quiet, like at the beginning of a blackout before anyone has thought to fetch a flashlight. Sinna walks offstage biting her lower lip.

Brad is next, but he is so surprised by Sinna getting out that he has to ask for POSSIBILITY three times before he spells it with one S. Despite his assertions to the contrary, he also believes that Sinna is the smarter one. Which just leaves Eliza, who spells CORRESPON-DENCE with her eyes closed to avoid looking at three rows of students staring at her in disbelief.

In Eliza's fantasy she walks to the podium, which she is suddenly tall enough to see over, and begins speaking to a cafeteria suddenly filled to capacity.

A few of you might know my name, but most of you don't even recognize me. I know you, though. And what I'm about to say is as important to you as it is to me.

It's the lead-in to a speech from a particularly powerful after-school special. Eliza's always thought it made a great beginning. No actual words come after that, but Eliza's mouth keeps moving and the music swells. By the end, all the students are smiling with little tears in their eyes and Lindsay Halpern makes a place for Eliza at her table between her and Roger Pond.

Eliza stands outside Saul's closed study door, an envelope hot in her hand. She's not sure this is a valid interruption. She's not sick, nothing's on fire, and the district bee isn't until the weekend. But if she waits for her father to come out so she can hand it to him, it might be another two hours.

Eliza considers waiting anyway. Perhaps her father will need to use the bathroom, or maybe he'll get hungry for a snack. She puts her ear against the door but hears nothing. When she looks down she finds that her hands have unconsciously reopened the envelope and removed the letter. A few words are smeared now; the paper's creases are fuzzed with wear. Eliza realizes for the first time that her last name is misspelled. She feels a sudden urge to tear the letter, burn it to ash, cram it down the disposal. Instead, she folds the letter back into thirds, licks the by now dissolved adhesive on the envelope's flap, and shoves the letter through the crack beneath her father's study door.

Saul's study is smaller than Eliza's bedroom in that it lacks a closet, making it the smallest room in the house not counting bathrooms. Its perceived dimensions are diminished further by the bookshelves lining its walls and piles of notes in various stages of collapse layering the floor. Notebooks of various thicknesses and binding methods protrude above the thinner strata like steppingstones. The average paper density increases toward Saul's desk, which emerges from the tumult like a piece of flotsam tossed by the paper tide. Saul's desk spares no room for distracting doohickey or clever calendar, covered as it is by books and notes, loose and bound. On the wall directly above the desk, framed pictures of Mordecai M. Kaplan and Gershom Scholem provide inspiration. A small desk lamp serves as one of only two light sources, both unnatural. The room's lack of windows is for the best since the bookshelves leave no room for them.

In this room governed by disorder, the shelves are the exception to the entropic rule. Saul's library is arranged alphabetically, recent paperbacks brushing spines with age-seasoned leather-bound volumes. English texts adjoin Hebrew and Yiddish. In Saul's decision to mix languages, he has accorded privilege to a letter's pronunciation over its ordinal placement. Thus, Hebrew writer Shmuel Yosef Agnon is in among the A's alongside Aharon Appelfeld even though the Nobelist's last name begins with an *ayin* and the novelist's name begins with an *alef*. While the library's overall organization might cause many a self-respecting academic to blush, to Saul the study is a paper-lined nursery in which his scholarly interests may grow and blossom by the light of two 80-watt soft white bulbs.

When Saul closes the study door behind him, he closes the book of the everyday world as well, placing it upon a distant shelf until familial duty or emergency calls him back. So it comes as no surprise that he doesn't hear the quiet *foosh* of Eliza's envelope. Unnoticed, it joins the morass of paper carpeting the floor of his study, invisible to anyone who doesn't know to look.

Saul Naumann spends the first portion of his life as Sal Newman, son of Henry and Lisa Newman, decorator of Christmas trees and Easter eggs. Henry has every expectation that his only child will follow him into the car repair business. From an early age Saul has been replacing sparkplugs and changing oil. Though he dislikes the combined smells of car exhaust and sweat, the hardness of the garage floor, and the mess of wires and cold metal that compose the machines of his father's fancy, Saul fosters these associations for the sake of the rare smiles proffered by his father in their company.

Saul is thirteen when his mother takes him into the attic and shows him the box. There is a photo of a bearded man with long sidelocks and a black hat, his hand on the shoulder of a boy. At first Saul cannot believe that the curly-haired boy with the fringes hanging past his shirt is his father, Heimel Naumann, the bearded man his grandfather Yehudah. Saul learns the word "Orthodox." His mother shows him a pair of brass candlesticks and a wine cup. She describes a world ruled by the Book, a world with little room for change. She relates eloping with Heimel after Yehudah declared her not Jewish enough. Saul sees his birth certificate and learns of his father's decision to renounce the faith, the shift from Heimel to Henry and Naumann to Newman occurring after Yehudah ignored Saul's birth. Saul, who had been named for Yehudah's brother Solomon in one son's attempt to regain a father's love, became Sal.

It is Lisa who sneaks her son books, occasionally taking Saul to a nearby synagogue on Henry's Friday nights out. It is their secret until Henry comes home unexpectedly one evening to find them lighting Shabbat candles. From that point onward, Saul insists on being called by his given name.

By Saul's sophomore year of high school, he has given up any pretense of interest in cars and his father has given up interest in him. When Lisa dies of cancer, the house becomes a lonely and divided place, the last link between father and son turning to dust in a box underground. The fights begin soon after, never violent but increasingly damaging.

Saul's escape to a liberal arts college finalizes the rift. When Saul uses his student status to stay out of Vietnam, Henry officially washes his hands of his ungrateful, hippie Jew of a son.

Saul discovers LSD and Jewish mysticism at the same time, a chance concurrence that strengthens the validity of both. During his acid trips, Saul experiences the same sense of time displacement and receptivity described in the texts. On one occasion he attests to having ascended through several levels of being in a manner similar to the ancient mystics, who rode a chariot through six castles on six celestial realms to reach God at the seventh heaven. Saul becomes a campus celebrity and preferred LSD guide. At the end of his undergraduate career and with the war still on, it is only natural that he enter rabbinical school.

Saul enters Baruch Yeshiva on scholarship. His scholarship is revoked during his freshman year when, in the name of mental exploration, he convinces his roommate to place a tab on his tongue and the resultant bad trip leads to said roommate painting his naked body blue and white and running into the dean's office to declare himself the new Israeli Prime Minister.

Saul returns to his alma mater to live rent-free in the attic of an off-campus house inhabited by undergraduates who know him by reputation alone. The attic is charred from a semi-recent fire, contains no electrical outlets, and is uninsulated. Saul can stand fully erect as long as he keeps to the room's center. He illuminates the space with chains of Christmas lights running off an extension cord snaked up the narrow attic stairs from a lower-floor bedroom.

Saul spends his time in the library studying Jewish thought and history in a rigorous, self-styled curriculum that surpasses his academic efforts at any time during his official enrollment. He regularly attends religious services and adult education classes at a nearby synagogue. Alone in his attic, Saul practices the traditional songs and fantasizes about someday leading a congregation, if not as a rabbi then as a cantor.

There are drawbacks to this scavenged existence. While Saul has ample access to drugs and female undergrads in his capacity as sexual and psychoactive guide to the student body, the role has begun to wear thin. His acid trips are too déjà vu. He has worn deep grooves in the psychedelic path, falling into the same hallucinatory and revelatory ruts time after time. Increasingly, his affairs with women remind him of his age and the fact that he hadn't pictured himself at twenty three making love to clumsy teenage coeds on a dirty twin mattress in a burned-out attic. Increasingly, Saul finds himself fantasizing about his own study, a job that gives him time to pursue his interests, and the prospect of children with whom he can share his hard-won life lessons.

On Friday nights, Eliza sits with her brother in the first row of the Beth Amicha synagogue. While Aaron recites the responsive prayers without glancing at his prayer book, Eliza focuses on a spot on the *bima* between Rabbi Mayer and her father and tries to block out the robotic monotone of the congregation reading as one. It reminds her too much of aquarium fish, the mechanical open and shut of their mouths as they stare blankly through the glass.

While the congregation drones on, Eliza turns her attention to the brown-flecked linoleum floor tiles and thinks of the biblical exodus from Egypt. She transforms each fleck into a Jew in a windswept robe, trekking forty years across the desert to reach the Promised Land. She imagines blisters from uncomfortable sandals. She pictures a tribe of Charlton Hestons looking righteous and bearded and sun-creased. Her reverie is interrupted by Rabbi Mayer's voice telling the congregation to rise, which she manages to do fast enough to hide the fact that, moments ago, the floor had been the Sinai.

Rabbi Mayer is a tree trunk of a man with a broad forehead and bushy eyebrows that have gone gray even though the rest of his hair remains dark. He looks out at the congregation through disproportionately small eyes, which he has willed down in size to take in as little of the world as necessary. Beth Amicha would not have been his preference, but he was Beth Amicha's rabbi of choice. With suburban rabbis outnumbering suburban synagogues two to one, Orel Mayer chose a steady salary over spiritual affinity. A Conservative Jew, Mayer disapproves of Beth Amicha's laxer Reform tendencies. He had initially hoped to spur the congregation to new heights of observance but Saturday evenings, when he lights the braided Havdalah candle and watches the shadows flicker upon the synagogue's walls, he is often alone. Beth Amicha tends to regard Shabbat as a Friday night obligation. Most congregants have never been to a Havdalah service, have never heard the crisp *crszh* of the Havdalah flame being quenched by the wine, the true moment of Sabbath's end. Rabbi Mayer longs to lead a congregation that appreciates this sound. But a good rabbinate is hard to find. He comforts himself with the fact that his is not the life of the itinerant rabbi, reduced to performing the brisses, weddings, and bar mitzvahs of strangers.

Saul's gangly arms look particularly cartoony when he leads prayers on his guitar, strumming and even thumping as he sings. On the Judaism spectrum Saul's self-proclaimed Reconstructionism puts him left of center, an affiliation the congregation hoped would counterbalance Rabbi Mayer's, leaving Beth Amicha's services somewhere in the middle. By playing the strict traditionalist, Rabbi Mayer makes the congregants feel as if they are being the type of Jew of whom their parents would approve. By playing his guitar and turning prayers into group sing-alongs, Saul allows people to have enough fun to forget they've come largely out of guilt. Rabbi Mayer is the dentist, Saul the congregation's lollipop reward for having kept their appointment.

English prayers outnumber Hebrew ones. The *Jewish Congregational Prayerbook* attempts to compensate for this by using "thou" and "thee" instead of "you," and by adding "-est" to verb endings. "Mayest thou liest down and risest up" is supposed to feel more like the four-thousand-year-old language the book has largely replaced. There is, of course, some Hebrew. A gifted minority can parse the words without any idea of their meaning. For those who forgot Hebrew phonetics soon after depositing their bar mitzvah checks, there are English transliterations.

The foreword to the *JCP* claims that the transliterations are "for the reader's ease and comfort." This gentle lie cloaks an embittered editor's elaborate scheme to avenge the childhood he suffered while actually learning the language. SH replaces T; a K is inserted where a G would be more appropriate. As a result, it is painfully apparent who is reading the Hebrew and who is not. Misbegotten syllables collide midair with their proper cousins, making the service more closely resemble a speech therapy class than a religious gathering.

Aaron will recite the Hebrew just a little faster than everyone else, just to show that he can. He doesn't need to actually look at the *JCP;* he can recite the entire service beginning to end with his eyes shut. Since he was eight, people have been saying he should be a rabbi. Aaron is embarrassed by how much he still likes to hear this. Walking through the synagogue doors, he imagines heads turning to look, excited whispers of "There goes the cantor's son." Inside Beth Amicha's walls, he is junior class president, football captain, and star of the school musical. In Aaron's imaginary congregational yearbook he is Most Popular and Most Likely to Succeed, with the special added superlative of Best Young Jew. In Beth Amicha, he's pretty sure girls smile at him sometimes. He never doubts his clothes. He is neither too tall nor too pale.

Eliza can't read Hebrew like her brother. In the time it takes her to negotiate the first five words, picking her way right to left across the page, the prayer is halfway over. Rather than add to the aural melee, she chooses to keep her mouth shut.

For years after his summary dismissal from Dr. Morris's office, Saul entertains hopes that Eliza will prove her elementary school principal wrong. Grading quarter after grading quarter he erases all memory of report cards past, tearing open each successive manila envelope in a frightful evocation of predator and prey.

Eliza is sitting at the kitchen table so engrossed in a *Taxi* rerun that a mini-pretzel is frozen in its trajectory from the bag to her mouth. The sealed manila envelope rests on the table just beyond the pretzel bag's shadow. Jim Ignatowski and Alex Rieger are far more comforting than the sound of Saul exiting his study. Eliza can block out the sounds of her father's arrival altogether if she concentrates very hard on the openings and closings of Alex Rieger's bloodless mouth.

Eliza is seven, she is nine, she is six and a half. She is any age at all between second grade and the present.

Jim Ignatowski is bugging his eyes out at Latke Gravas, that funny little foreigner, and Eliza is right there in the taxi depot with them, can practically smell Louis's cigar as he barks commands from the dispatch desk, wants to bury her face in Latke's grease-stained overalls. Her father's hand snaps her out of it.

Eliza wishes her father's hand were on her shoulder for some other reason, generally covets all forms of his attention. She feigns absorption in the TV so that the hand will stay a little longer. Eliza has learned this trick from Saul himself, though she knows his powers of concentration are real.

Take, for example, the time the ambulance came for Mrs. Feruzza when she broke her hip. The sound of passing sirens shook the walls, but Saul swears he didn't hear a thing, reading as he was a recent translation of Pico della Mirandola. Eliza isn't convinced her father would hear an emergency knock on his closed study door. What if she was bleeding, choking, going blind, the house burning down, the escaped convict holding her at knifepoint? She has been kept awake nights wondering if her father would save her in time.

The hand on her shoulder is gone. The manila envelope, now empty, has fallen to the floor. Eliza cannot help but watch her father's eyes scan the twin grade columns. She feels compelled to watch his face fade from expectation to resignation. Math, C. Science, C. Social Studies, C. Work Habits, B. Behavior, A. Reading, B. Spelling, A. Then, the forced smile, the patting of the head. The click of Saul's door after his silent retreat to his study always manages to cut through the sound of the television. That night when Eliza glides into sleep, she sees the disappointment on her father's face behind her closed lids.

Eliza realizes too late that slipping the spelling bee notice under her father's door may have been a mistake. There is no historical reason for her father to think that an envelope from her is a good thing. When, that first day, he emerges from his office without lauding her bee victory, Eliza assumes he has saved the envelope's opening for a better mood. She decides to keep quiet to preserve the surprise. She likes picturing Saul's face the moment he realizes the envelope's true contents, mentally screens and rescreens this imagined moment to ease her anxiety.

When three days pass without a word Eliza, so accustomed to being disappointing, begins to wonder if the singularity of this, her first achievement, has caused her to overinflate its importance. Spelling, after all, is a skill made redundant by the dictionary. The steady stream of spelling A's on her report card has never inspired much praise. Perhaps her father is even a little embarrassed? That all his daughter can do is spell? His daughter, who still can't recite the Hebrew alphabet? Eliza accepts this possibility with the inherent grace of the acutely underconfident, decides not to mention it until he does.

By Friday night, Eliza's resolve has been seriously shaken. The district bee is less than twenty four hours away. Even if her father is not impressed by her victory, he should have acknowledged by now that there are transportation needs to be met. Saul has never shirked his duty as child chauffeur, is a reliable member of any carpool. But, by now, Eliza cannot imagine bringing it up. Like many things left unsaid, Eliza's thoughts have metastasized, kernels of doubt exploding into deadly certainties. She has taken Saul's silence to mean that her accidental achievement is too little too late. Friday night after services, she cannot sleep. She stays in bed until she can't stand picturing another version of Dr. Morris's rebuke for her failure to serve as the school's spelling representative. It's way past midnight. Eliza decides to visit her mother in the kitchen.

Miriam Naumann is a hummingbird in human form, her wings too fast to be seen without a stop-motion camera. The silver in her hair makes her seem electric, her head a nest of metal wires extending through her body. Eliza can only imagine the supercharged brain that resides inside, generally equates the inside of her mother's head with the grand finale of a July Fourth fireworks display. The fact that Miriam only needs a nightly three hours of sleep helps to foster this mental image. Saul has calculated, with some envy, that his wife's Spartan sleep requirements gain her two and a half months more wakefulness than the average person annually.

Eliza has never seen her mother's law office but is certain that it is kept as obsessively clean as the kitchen. Counters are waxed daily, as is the floor. The dishware in the cabinets is arranged according to precise plan, the stacks spaced exact distances apart and ordered according to a conception of size, color, and function that no one but Miriam fully understands. Miriam refuses to waste anything and insists upon maximum space conservation, such that a spectrum of containers is needed to house everything from the single remaining meatball to the half bowl of uneaten salad. The Tupperware she uses toward this end, stored in cabinets under the oven, is a vision of military precision.

Miriam cleans at night. She is working the Formica in her favorite rubber gloves when Eliza sits at the kitchen table. The room is silent except for the tick of the oven clock and the *smrsh, smrsh* of the green side of Miriam's Scotch Brite scrubber sponge pad. Eliza knows she could sit here for an hour without attracting her mother's notice. In a concentration contest, Miriam would pin Saul to the mat every time.

"Mom?"

Miriam looks up mid-stroke. "Elly? When did you wander in?"

"Just a few seconds ago. I can't sleep."

Miriam works the counter like she's massaging sore muscles. She is at her most placid in the morning's small hours. Eliza used to fake insomnia for the chance to stay up with her, a ruse Miriam became expert at detecting. For Eliza, the smell of solvent conjures up rival feelings of love and frustration.

"Are Saul and Aaron asleep?"

In Miriam's conversations with her children, Saul has always been Saul and never "father." It is a habit of speech to which Eliza, after eleven years, still hasn't adjusted. Saul's name in her mother's mouth makes Eliza feel as if her father is not actually hers, just some man who has come to live with them.

"Yeah. They're asleep."

Miriam flips the cleaning pad from green to yellow, downshifting from scrubber to sponge. The counter gleams like an ice rink, post-Zamboni. Eliza had originally intended to tell her mother about the bee, but something about the way Miriam is scrubbing makes Eliza fear that her words will be washed away upon leaving her lips. Eliza has a growing suspicion that she never won the bee at all, her father's silence proof that she has imagined everything.

Eliza decides to keep quiet. If the bee isn't real, she would like to hold on to its illusion a little longer.

Miriam turns her attention to the refrigerator. She removes a jar of gherkins, a bottle of Worcestershire, and a tub of margarine, wiping each with a Handiwipe before lining them precisely along the line in the linoleum floor tile pattern. The fridge light bathes Miriam and the foodstuffs in a soft, yellow glow. Though Eliza cannot identify the song's title, she finds herself mentally humming the opening bars of the Pachelbel Canon, the image of her mother at the fridge having tapped into a memory of the music from a light bulb commercial.

"Mom?"

Miriam jerks her head like someone caught sleeping in class.

"Silly me, forgot you were here." Miriam offers Eliza the jar. "Would you like a gherkin?" Miriam is the only one who actually eats the gherkins, drinking the juice from the jar when she's through.

"No, thanks. I've been wondering. Do you clean so much because you like to or because you have to in order to get to sleep?"

The light from the refrigerator turns Miriam's silver hairs to gold. The Worcestershire has been placed in the exact center of the middle shelf of the refrigerator door. A pint of strawberries has taken its place on the floor between the pickles and the Parkay. Miriam knits her eyebrows together until they resemble a hairy rendering of a bird in flight. Eliza isn't sure her mother has heard her question. When Eliza looks into Miriam's eyes, she sees vast intelligence and unspannable distance.

Miriam is born to wealthy parents for whom parenthood equals patriotism. Melvin and Ruth Grossman's desire for a large, boisterous family à la Kennedy is tempered, with each of Ruth's miscarriages, into steely determination. Some of Ruth's near pregnancies are cruel in their duration, allowing for hopes to be raised and names to be chosen before the painful end. This only intensifies the couple's fervency. After four childless years of marriage Ruth and Mel have become procreative partisans in the clash between will and womb. Ruth's ultimate pregnancy and delivery of a baby girl is a battle won but a war lost; Miriam's difficult birth leaves Ruth unable to bear more children. Accordingly, Miriam becomes the repository for the expectations Mel and Ruth harbored for all five of their conceptual offspring. These quintupled aspirations trickle down to Miriam through a series of high-powered nannies and tutors, money no object in insuring that their sole surviving progeny receives the best of everything five times over.

Miriam is an exceptional and obsessive child. She forbids anyone to touch her toys and insists upon her underwear being washed twice before its return to the bureau drawer. Mel and Ruth interpret their daughter's eccentricity as a sign of genius, insist she be humored to facilitate her intellectual growth.

Miriam learns the extent of her social maladjustment upon her enrollment at a prestigious boarding school at age twelve. There, her natural predilection for study is reinforced by the unremitting mockery of her peers, the library quickly becoming her only place of refuge outside the classroom.

She is a phenomenal student. In college her powers of concentration achieve mythic status when she is evacuated from the stacks by a fireman who discovers her intent upon a book despite the blaring alarm that has cleared everyone else from the building.

Miriam and Saul meet when she is finishing law school and he is working as a research assistant for a Judaism professor. Saul has abandoned drugs to devote himself to a life of mystical scholarship. He now knows that LSD was a false doorway, a simulation of an experience accessible only after years of devoted study. He looks upon his acid insights as shadowy impostors, clay pigeons that will explode at the first touch of true transcendence. Though he knows he may never share the experience of the ancient mystics, Saul has decided to spend the rest of his life trying. Miriam embodies the intellectual discipline Saul senses he will need to reach his goal. Her unconventional mannerisms seem charming indicators of her rich mental life. He is attracted by her permanent slouch, her head always slightly craned forward as if examining a book's fine print. He likes the solidity of her body, neither fat nor thin, which she carries with a charming lack of self-awareness. As their acquaintance deepens, the hidden workings of Miriam's mind beckon to Saul like a seven-veiled Salome.

Their early courtship consists of shared dinners in the campus cafeteria followed by neighboring seats at lectures with titles like "God and the Plague: Religious Revivalism in the Middle Ages," and "Unmaking Your Mind: Discerning Truth From Falsehood in the Midst of Vietnam." Saul thrills to Miriam's intellectual voracity, attends the lectures solely to observe her assiduity as she drinks in the words. Weeks later, she can alternately defend or destroy the lecturer's arguments point by point without having taken any notes.

Until law school, Miriam's entire academic career is single-sexed, boys an elective she bypasses. Though she has been on a few abortive dates, Saul is the first beau willing to indulge her interests, the first not to suggest popcorn and a formulaic comedy followed by an invitation to his apartment. Saul's experiences with the greater portion of the female student body at his alma mater have taught him to be a good listener. With Miriam he is patient, luring her with his constancy.

Miriam is grateful for the attention. Aware that her unique temperament might severely limit her relationship options, she had been willing to take on someone far more socially stunted than Saul. Though not religious, Miriam takes self-congratulatory pride in dating a Jew, on occasion even accompanying Saul to synagogue for the opportunity to analyze group religious ritual.

Into their third week of dating, Miriam scrutinizes the library's dog-eared *Joy of Sex* and *Hite Report* from the relative privacy of her cubicle. Sex, like ironing or changing a flat tire, is an essential life skill to be mastered. She is intrigued by a firsthand account of an orgasm as a giant body wave.

And so, after a month of twice-weekly dinner/lecture dates, Miriam and Saul make love. It is the longest Saul has waited to bed a woman he is wooing. While Miriam harbors unspoken reservations (she still prefers to wash her underwear twice and is well versed in the number of microorganisms exchanged during a kiss), she is intrigued by Saul's vast sexual experience and knows he represents her best chance at a good lay. Miriam is glad they go to his apartment. While somewhat willing to yield up her body, she is less certain about her sheets and towels.

Though Saul wants to undress his new lover himself, Miriam insists upon removing her own clothes, standing with her back to Saul to fold blouse and slacks, placing each neatly on a chair before proceeding. Saul marvels at Miriam's softness, at the woman inside the scholar. He loves her small breasts and wide hips, takes to calling her his hidden pear, a pet name that makes Miriam blush but which she secretly enjoys.

Miriam is intrigued by the spareness of Saul's body. She is grateful for the opportunity to examine his angles, his long limbs and fingers, this her first object lesson in male anatomy. Miriam's shyness at her own nakedness momentarily disappears with the novelty of his. She is more interested in Saul's scrotum than his penis, fascinated by the way its skin undulates at her slightest touch, how it shrinks with the cold and Saul's increasing arousal, relaxing into a loose purse after making love, when it has soaked up the warmth of the sheets and their bodies.

The two bond over their mutual lack of family ties: Saul from his disownment, Miriam from the car accident that orphaned her as a college junior. Both want children. Miriam has inherited her parents' idea of procreative legitimacy, wants to compensate for her only-childdom. She sees in Saul the househusband who will enable her parental ambitions without disabling her autonomy. In Miriam, Saul sees the means to a book-lined study and a lifestyle conducive to mystical advancement. They are both absolutely certain these things equal love.

When Eliza knocks on her brother's door Saturday morning, he is trying to abstract the reflection of his chest in the mirror. If he can pretend that his chest belongs to a stranger, he may be able to judge it objectively rather than through ugly-colored glasses. His sister's knock sparks a comprehensive blush, the pale skin from forehead to stomach turning shades of sunburn.

Aaron hesitates before opening the door. To shirt or not to shirt? He and Eliza used to see each other topless all the time. That was before being six years apart meant anything, when their small, pale chests were indistinguishable in the tree-strewn sunlight of the backyard. It was before Aaron had learned that a small, pale chest can be a liability, that six years apart is an expanding universe with a brother at one end and a sister at the other.

But Aaron wants to play Shirts against Skins without chickening out if he's picked for the wrong team. He wants to feel comfortable in just his bathing trunks. He decides he'd better answer the door the way he is.

Shirtless, Aaron looks even more breakable than usual, as if caught in an act better accomplished from within a cocoon. A thin vein descends the left side of his neck and across the skin of his upper chest like a crack in a windowpane. Eliza tries not to act surprised at the sight of it. Though she hasn't given Aaron's chest much thought, she assumed it still looked the same as the last time she saw it, which, now that she thinks about it, was a really long time ago. Since then, her brother's nipples have grown. There are curly black hairs. The hairs are sparse and thin, as if sapped by their struggle to grow so dark from such pale skin.

Aaron's chest hairs call to mind other body hairs, hairs that make Eliza decidedly uncomfortable. She shifts her focus to her brother's face. When she looks up, however, she realizes that Aaron has been watching her watching his chest. She looks down again, this time at his feet, which she notices are also hairy.

"Um, I was wondering if you could drive me somewhere," Eliza says to the tuft below the first knuckle of her brother's leftmost toe.

Years and years before hairs and spelling bees, Aaron drives Eliza places all the time. Their two modes of transport are the living-room couch and the fallen-down tree in the backyard, one for when it's raining and the other for when it's not. While both agree that the log is better for making their destinations feel more authentic, Eliza has a special fondness for the couch, where she can sit beside and not behind her brother, taking head on the dangers that come their way. And there are always dangers. In addition to being navigator Eliza is official spotter of the alien monsters and sea squids and pumas with which they regularly engage in furious and bloody battle. Eliza likes letting her brother lead the attacks. Aaron knows all the secret moves of the ninja and Jedi and has even taught her a few. Eliza takes for granted her brother's availability for these and other games, has no cause to question his lack of additional playmates, ones perhaps a little closer to him in age. It is Aaron to whom Eliza turns after a bad dream has scared her awake, the warmth of his bed assurance that she will be protected should her night crawlers return.

Eliza's first day of kindergarten, Aaron pilots her through the doors of McKinley Elementary with sixth-grade flair. He points out office, cafeteria, and library, describes a secret short-cut to the playground swings, and explains the trick to evading as long as possible the teacher's end-of-recess whistle. Eliza starts kindergarten assured that her six-years-older brother has vanquished all school-born monsters, squids, or pumas. Aaron, who can take Eliza to Neptune or to the bottom of the ocean. Aaron, who can impale an attacking mastodon with one hand while fending off a Cro-Magnon with the other. Aaron, whose sister's gilded image of him will last four more months before the real world strips it from him.

Since Aaron earned his license, no one has asked him for a ride anywhere. This is probably for the best, as Aaron is an extremely cautious driver, viewing the car as an extension of himself and, therefore, open to attack at any moment. Another person in the car might send his wariness into overdrive.

"If Dad won't take you, then he probably won't let me take you either," Aaron responds to his sister's request. Aaron started talking softly so long ago that he has forgotten it was originally a conscious choice. Though Eliza has grown used to it, she can remember running through the backyard armed with thwacking sticks while Aaron screamed, "BEWARE, Space Demon, for it is I, CAPTAIN A, who have come to BLAST you into the 13th GALAXY!"

Aaron feels too weird being in front of Eliza without a shirt, but putting one on now might only draw attention to the fact that he was shirtless before. Besides, he really wants to be able to walk around for hours naked from the waist up, even outdoors, and not think about it.

"You're not listening," Eliza complains, tossing a sock in Aaron's general direction but hitting him in the left nipple, an unintentional bull's-eye. "The bee is in Norristown this afternoon. I need a ride."

Aaron opts for a shirt after all. "What bee?" asks the blue pocket tee being pulled over his head.

Eliza is grateful for the clothing choice. T-shirted, Aaron seems less like a flip-book construction—bird head, man body, goat legs—and more like her brother again. "I *told* you already. The district bee."

"Don't you have to win your school bee or something to be in that?" Aaron's voice is a little louder now that his nipples are hidden.

Eliza rolls her eyes and smiles.

"God, Elly, how did you do *that*?"

Her face falls.

"I mean, God, Elly, that's great!"

"I guess." Eliza's voice has become as soft as her brother's.

"No, really." Aaron puts his hand on Eliza's shoulder. He's really, really glad he decided on the shirt. "I'm totally impressed. I bet Dad's in Dad-heaven. He loves that stuff."

Eliza gives a small shrug and realizes she's about to cry. She decides it's time to talk about the envelope.

Eliza follows Aaron downstairs to their father's study. Even though the door is open, Eliza feels odd stepping over the threshold. She envies the ease with which Aaron enters, as if Saul's study were just another room.

The room is dark except for a circle of yellow light over Saul's desk, which illumines an airborne sea of dust. Saul is engrossed in a leather-bound book with stiff pages that, when turned, creak like old bones.

"Hey, Dad?" Aaron's voice is swallowed up by the dust born of innumerable book pages and spines. To Eliza, the air itself seems heavy with knowledge. Aaron tries again, this time louder.

Eliza recognizes her mother in the way Saul suddenly turns his head toward the sound.

"Hello, Aaron! I was just reading about the mystics' migration to Israel. Of course, it wasn't officially Israel yet, but—"

"Dad, did you get an envelope from Elly this week?"

At first Saul's eyes are blank, as if not even his daughter's name holds meaning. "Envelope? Was I supposed to receive an envelope?" Eliza feels her stomach tighten and realizes she is unable to speak. With her eyes she implores Aaron to continue.

"Elly says she won the spelling bee."

Saul's face lights up. "Why, that's wonderful! The class bee. You know, when I was thirteen—"

"*No,* Dad." Eliza's voice is impatient. "Not just the class bee. The *school* bee." Eliza watches the dust ride the currents of her breath.

"Well, that's just. . . ." Saul looks at Eliza as if she has suddenly borne a delicious fruit from her navel. "This is quite a surprise!"

"But I already *told* you. You've known all week." Eliza spits the words. "And you haven't said *anything.*" She feels the pressure of tears against her eyeballs but forbids herself to cry.

"Eliza. Elly-belly. I didn't know. How could I have known? When did you tell me?"

Eliza's face is pink. "The *envelope.* I put it under your door on *Monday.*"

The room is silent. For the first time Eliza notices the papers that cover the floor like snowfall. Saul grins.

"Then it must be down here somewhere."

Saul, Aaron, and Eliza sort through the drifts of paper. It is Aaron who finds the envelope, smudged from Eliza's hands and taped where she had torn it.

"Is this it?"

For a split second Eliza pictures opening the envelope and finding nothing there, the letter having been absorbed into the dense piles of paper around it. She stifles the urge to snatch the envelope from her brother.

Aaron realizes that his standing mental image of Eliza is three years out of date; in his mind she is still a shy second grader quietly insistent upon matching her socks with her shirt every morning. He wonders when she started parting her hair on the left and if she's always had the nervous habit of sucking in her cheeks.

The way Saul reaches for the envelope reminds Eliza of first-time Torah bearers, stiff-armed with their fear of mishandling the sacred burden. She likes that he uses a letter opener instead of his fingers. The smile that appears momentarily erases years of report card trauma.

"This," Saul says in a reverent voice, "is a beautiful thing."

Eliza is halfway through kindergarten when she sees her brother get beat up. What was thought to be a drill has, with the arrival of the McKinley Fire Department, been elevated to the level of a small, real fire. Though the tray of chicken fingers was extinguished long ago, certain protocols need to be followed, granting the students at McKinley a spontaneous recess while the fire department goes through the mandated motions. Eliza, as an A.M. kindergartner, was not expecting to experience recess until first grade and feels particularly lucky to have been given a sneak preview.

Eliza is waiting her turn at the swings. She is fifth in line, but the BONG BONG BONG of the alarm has been off for a while now, the firemen are returning to their trucks, and she is beginning to doubt that she will get a turn before everyone is sent back to class. She decides to abandon the line to investigate the noises coming from behind the line of evergreen bushes across the grass.

She thinks it may be Holly Ermiline and Gina Gerardi, whom she thought she heard talking about collecting red berries from the bushes in order to paint their fingernails, which Eliza thinks is a pretty stupid idea since she's heard that the berries are poisonous. Even though she doesn't really like Holly or Gina, she should at least tell them to wash their hands when they're done.

As Eliza nears the bushes, she realizes there is too much sound and movement to be Gina and Holly. In fact she gets a sort of sick feeling in her stomach that tells her she probably doesn't want to get any closer to the bushes at all. But it's the kind of feeling that also tells her in a soft, persuasive voice to keep going, the same instinct that guides young, naive hands to the pretty red stove burner even though they've been told it is very, very hot.

Eliza can make out two figures standing over a third. Eliza's first thought is *dog*. She's seen boys throwing stones at a stray that hangs around the school. The dog, named Sucker by the stone throwers, slams into trees in its frightened attempts to get away but is always there the following morning, waiting for the next cycle of torment to begin. Eliza bristles at the thought of the dog being caught, momentarily forgets her size and age, and ups her pace to the bushes, ready to battle even Marvin Bussy for the sake of Sucker's protection.

She is steps away from the bush when she sees a flash of skin and realizes that what she thought was a dog is not a dog, despite the whimpering sounds. She is close enough now to recognize the two standing figures as Marvin Bussy and Billy Mamula. They call themselves the B.M. team, which Eliza thinks is really gross but which Aaron tells her just confirms their place in the world as pieces of shit, which is the only time Eliza has ever heard her brother swear. Like most of the school, Eliza fears Marvin and Billy, but being both younger and a girl places her low enough on the elementary school food chain to allow her to call them names behind their backs.

Eliza's willingness to face a conceptual Marvin Bussy evaporates at the prospect of encountering the actual one even though she knows she'd have to do something really bad to get him to pick on a kindergartner. She has never witnessed Marvin's malice first hand. His cruelty, like sex, is something she has only heard about, something that only happens in places she doesn't go.

Eliza is staring at the scene a few seconds before she realizes that the thing that is not a dog looks a lot like her brother. Aaron has a shirt like the torn one of the boy on the ground; Aaron has skin that would contrast that disturbingly with the deep brown dirt. Marvin and Billy, backs turned and engrossed in what they are doing, haven't noticed her but there is a sickening moment of clarity when Eliza realizes that the boy who almost looks like Aaron has been watching her the whole time. His eyes, wide with fear, are the exact shape of Sucker's when the dog is running in a blind panic, slamming into trees to the sound of jeering children.

For what seems like years, Eliza stands staring. Almost-Aaron's face remains frozen, not once leaving Eliza's, his body passively accepting its punishment. It is as if, having been thrown from a window, he has realized that relaxing every muscle will reduce the damage upon his inevitable impact with the ground.

Marvin and Billy can't afford witnesses to such a suspendable offense. Eliza could call out for Gina and Holly, pretending she is just nearing the bushes to look for them. Marvin and Billy would be forced to stop and the poor boy would be saved. Eliza mentally loops the scenario, looking for flaws and finding none. It would work.

Bestial joy beams off Marvin and Billy like cold light. Eliza is mesmerized by the incongruity of action and reaction, reluctant to relinquish her stolen glimpse of such rare animals. Ultimately, however, her inaction is spurred by the revulsion that sweeps through her at the sight of the boy on the ground. His absolute stillness, his silence, his wide-open eyes. Even a half-blind stray dog would be struggling. Even Sucker wouldn't lie there, soundlessly accepting his fate. If Eliza intervenes, she will have to touch her almost-brother. He will need help getting up. And there's no way she'd be able to help this boy who can't possibly be Aaron. Aaron, who knows all the secret moves of the ninja and Jedi. Aaron, who saves Eliza from bad dreams. Aaron, who would never allow himself to be reduced to this.

Eliza will never mention that Marvin and Billy are grinding berries and evergreen needles into almost-Aaron's chest, laughing that they are curing his paleness once and for all. Or that pricks of blood from the evergreen needles are indistinguishable from lumps of berry pulp on his almost-skin. Eliza doesn't know what her almost-brother is thinking as, without a word, she returns to the swings, stubbornly facing away from the bushes until the whistle blows and she returns inside without looking back.

The calm voice of the school nurse ("Your son has had an accident. He says he's all right, but he needs a change of clothes. Could you please come in?") evokes Norman Rockwellian images of mud puddles and torn pants. When Saul arrives at the school to find a pale marble statue of a son with a bandaged chest, he demands answers.

"What the hell happened here?" he growls at the nurse, face red, eyes bulging.

"I fell," Aaron says too soft for anyone to hear.

"He says he fell," says the nurse, who is constructed like a high school gym teacher and not at all intimidated by Saul's presence.

"Aaron." Saul spins around to face his son. "Tell me what really happened. Who did this to you?" Fall definitely doesn't cover it. Though Saul can tell there's no serious damage, the scratches and bruises—already purpling—are too specific to have come from a benign source. Aaron's explanation is as unlikely as his insistence that the tack he sat on last month fell off the class bulletin board halfway across the room from his desk.

"Aaron," Saul says in a softer tone that he hopes will prove more persuasive, "it's okay to tell who did this. They need to be taught that this kind of behavior is unacceptable. You deserve to be able to play at recess without worrying about being bullied."

But Aaron knows better than that. Aaron knows that telling now will haunt him later. If not this year, then the next, or the one after that. Aaron knows that he's stuck with Marvin and Billy until high school, by which time they will be shunted into either reform school or shop class, removing him from striking range. His best strategy for now is to keep quiet and stay out of their way as much as possible.

"You're not going to tell me, are you?" Saul sighs. Aaron shakes his head, keeping his eyes on the floor. Underlying his righteous parental outrage, Saul takes peculiar pride in his silent son. A voice, not quite his own, *My son's no tattletale,* wells up from the same amorphous source of Saul's occasional urge to read the sports page, drink a beer with dinner, or change the oil in his car. These fleeting fancies are what remains of Saul's conflicted feelings for his dead father, a man who definitely would have respected Aaron's decision not to squeal.

Saul watches his son change into the clothes he brought. "You don't have to go back to class if you don't want to," he offers. "You can come home with me." Aaron shakes his head just as Dr. Morris enters the room.

"Hello, Mr. Naumann, it's good of you to come. Aaron, I heard what happened. I'm glad you're all fixed up. Are you sure you don't want to talk about it?"

Aaron nods.

"Because I'm pretty sure I know who did this, but I can't punish them unless you tell me if I'm right."

Aaron shrugs.

"What if I asked you if it was Marvin and Billy?"

Aaron blushes. He hates that he blushes so easily. "I fell," he says. He keeps seeing the change in Eliza's face as she neared the bushes. When Aaron first caught sight of his sister he had thought, ridiculously, that the two of them could band together. That with her by his side he could put a stop to the evil B & M. He was on the verge of calling out her name when she recognized him. Suddenly she became a stranger, with a stranger's way of looking at him. He realized that the Eliza he had been picturing was as imaginary as the Aaron he had hoped she would help him become.

"I fell," he says again.

Dr. Morris shakes his head and sends Aaron back to class. He invites Saul briefly into his office, where he assures Saul that an eye will be kept on Aaron, as well as on Marvin and Billy, to prevent further trouble. As Saul is leaving, Dr. Morris offers two stapled pages. "The Vulnerable Child" simpers across the top page in curving, sensitive letters. Saul offers a stiff smile and a reluctant arm, this his parenting booster shot. The ghost of Saul's father is gone. Pride has been replaced with the desire to protect his smaller, paler, and smarter than average son from the B.M.s of the world. When Aaron comes home from school that day, Saul is ready.

"You're smarter than them, you know," he says, catching Aaron by surprise as he walks through the door. "In the long run being smart wins out over just about everything else." Before Aaron can say anything, he gestures to him. "Follow me."

Saul leads his son to his study. Aaron hesitates before stepping over the threshold. This has always been a room for quick entrances and exits, a place to ask a question or to deliver a message and then to be gone. It falls into the same territory as his parents' bedroom, a room in which grown-ups do grown-up things.

"Do you know why I like it in here?" Saul asks, gesturing to his desk and the shelves lining each wall. "It's because this room is filled with things that make me happy. But today I realized that it would make me even happier if I could share it with you."

Saul's presence in the room is so strong that Aaron feels he has stepped inside his father's body, Saul's heart suddenly grown large enough for a door.

Saul sits Aaron down, places his hands on his son's shoulders.

"These people who are making you miserable can tell that you are something special. It drives them crazy because they know they don't have what you have. So they try to take it away from you, but you and I know they can't. You and me, Aaron, we're a team. What we do in here cancels out double whatever they do out there. Deal?"

Aaron pictures his father by his side as he, the Jedi ninja, attacks a legion of Marvin Bussys. Together, they can make the world safe for Aarons everywhere.

"Deal," Aaron says.

Saul is unable, on such short notice, to accompany his daughter to Norristown Area High School; he is already committed to helping Adam Lubinsky prepare for his date with Jewish manhood next month. Miriam has already left the house, Saturday often as not a workday. Aaron and Eliza are sitting beside each other in the car, this the first time she has ever sat in the front passenger seat. Eliza is un-used to the shoulder strap across her chest or a view of the road unobstructed by the back of her father's head. When she looks to her left, the sight of Aaron behind the actual steering wheel of an actual car strikes her as somehow absurd. The last time they were in a similar position, he was piloting a spaceship headed for Pluto.

Which, as far as Elly is concerned, isn't so different from where they are going now.

"What's Norristown High like?" she asks, trying to sound casual. Eliza really hopes Aaron's answer will fill in the huge empty black space that enters her head whenever she tries to think about the area bee.

"I don't know," Aaron says to the car in front of him. "It's bigger than Abington."

Aaron doesn't understand how anyone can look away from the road while driving. When Saul drives, he darts his head between the road and his conversational partner as though he's watching a tur-bocharged Ping-Pong match. This didn't make Aaron nervous until he got his own license and realized how much could happen in the split second a head was turned. Aaron wonders if he should explain to Eliza why she shouldn't expect him to look at her. A deer could rush into the road, or a car could suddenly stop or change lanes, and then he wouldn't be able to get her to her spelling bee which, the more he thinks about it, the more he doesn't understand how she got into in the first place.

You're not helping, Eliza wants to say. She knows that this is no big deal to Aaron, who does Olympics of the Mind and Science Fair, which have been at Norristown before so she knows he could tell her what it was like if he really wanted to.

Eliza remembers the first Saturday Aaron stopped playing with her. Her selective memory has isolated this event in her mind, removed it from its larger context. She no longer connects it with the fire drill earlier that same week, halfway through kindergarten. All she remembers is walking up to her brother and asking if he wanted to play and Aaron rolling his eyes. "What's the point?" he says. "You're too little. It's stupid. I've got better things to do," at which point he walks right into Saul's study like it is no big deal. They've been told over and over not to bother their father in there unless it is a real emergency, but Aaron walks in and he stays. That first Saturday, Eliza tries to play alone, making herself pilot, monster spotter, and head Jedi ninja all rolled into one but it isn't the same. "It's stupid" keeps repeating in her head.

Aaron is thorough in absenting himself from his sister's life. When not with Saul in the study, he practices guitar in his room or, occasionally, goes to the park. Eliza isn't invited on these outings. She initially mourns her exclusion, but her growing distance from Aaron allows her to observe more clearly his humble rung on the social acceptance ladder. The few times Eliza spots Aaron in the lunchroom, he is eating alone. When she secretly follows him to the park, she watches his attempts to join pickup basketball or soccer games with a combination of fascination and dread. If he is picked at all, it is reluctantly. Once during a basketball game the ball is slapped out of his arms so soundly that he falls sideways onto the pavement, his arm skidding against the asphalt. No one seems to hear him say foul. Eliza tells herself she is lucky to have learned the truth before her brother's social standing rubbed off on her. The only really hard part is weathering her nightmares alone.

At a stoplight, Aaron looks over at Eliza. He tries to regard her objectively, the way he examined his chest, to determine if she looks intelligent, but she looks the same as always. He remembers what the smart girls looked like in his fifth-grade class: Denise Li and her purple plastic glasses frames, Jenny Howlitzer with her corny decal T-shirts. Eliza doesn't look like those girls.

"Are you nervous?" he asks, neck craning toward the windshield, hands clawed onto the steering wheel.

"I don't know," she answers. "I wasn't sure I'd be going until this morning."

They've been stuck behind a truck for a while now, but Aaron won't switch lanes even though Eliza's checked a few times and it's been completely safe. Underneath a cartoon picture of a grinning chicken wearing ear muffs and a scarf are the words "The Smart Frozzen Parts People," and Eliza can't help but think it's a bad omen to be in such close proximity to such a stupid spelling error.

Aaron shakes his head in disbelief. "I can't believe you thought Dad knew about the bee and was *ignoring* it. I mean, Elly, he's been waiting for something like this to happen ever since—"

Eliza knows he is about to say, "since you got skipped for TAG," before he stops himself. After her father's fateful visit to Parents' Night, TAG became a word no one said in front of her, just as the word "puberty" became scarce when, by ninth grade, Aaron's voice still hadn't changed. When everything happened all at once for Aaron a year later, the p-word magically reintroduced itself into common parlance as if it had never been banished. TAG, however, has remained taboo. Aaron manages to switch to "since you started school" in time to think that Eliza hasn't noticed, but Eliza hears "stupid" in her head as clearly as if her brother had spoken the word aloud.

Aaron is eight years old when he sees God. He is on a night flight home from his grandfather's funeral, a man he never met while living. He has a window seat and has spent the entire flight staring at the tiny lights below which, intellectually, he knows correspond to buildings but which seem more like sequins on an endless black blanket. When the plane flies into a cloud, Aaron's sense of unlimited span and distance disappears. His window is swathed in white. A pulsing red light emanates from the cloud's whiteness. Aaron stares, awestruck. With each pulse of light the cloud is transformed into something magical. Aaron wonders if God lives in all clouds, or if his plane just happened to pick the right one. The experience is so intensely personal that it never occurs to Aaron to share it with anyone, thus extending his belief in an all-knowing, all-present God five years longer than if someone had had the opportunity to inform him he'd only witnessed the red blinker of the plane's wing.

The spelling bee registrar's face has a worn-out shoe leather softness to it specific to upper middle-aged women. She holds Eliza's library card in her hands. "Eliza Naumann." Her eyes scan her list. She crosses through Eliza's name with a red pen. The soft folds of her neck remind Eliza of turtle skin. "Do you happen to have a picture ID?"

"A picture ID?"

The registrar's glasses have slipped to the end of her nose, magnifying the age spots on her cheeks. One of them is shaped like Ohio. "You didn't hear about Bucks County?"

Eliza shakes her head.

"A boy takes fifth place and it turns out he wasn't even on the list. Turns out he lost his school bee but Mom wanted him to try again at the district. So I'm supposed to ask for a picture, but it's okay if you don't have one. What kind of little kid carries a picture ID? Besides, I can tell you belong."

She winks. The air current created by her arm as she points Eliza in the direction of the auditorium smells of cigars and talcum powder.

The auditorium has cushy seats, a balcony, and a large stage concealed by a heavy purple curtain. Aaron chooses a seat toward the back, figuring it will be easier to make a quick exit without attracting notice. He expects they will be leaving early.

The bee contestants are split according to gender between two backstage dressing rooms. The girls' has large mirrors along one cinder block wall, each mirror framed by light bulbs. A thick layer of dust has settled along each bulb, few of which are actually lit. One flickers like an amorous lightning bug.

A group of girls crowds around one mirror, mechanically brushing and rebrushing their bangs. One of the smaller girls seems to be praying. A few stand frozen as their mouths form strings of silent, hopeful letters. The only adult in the room is a badged bee chaperone. She sits ineffectually in the corner, splitting the silence at irregular intervals to remind the girls to pee.

Eliza is the only one not wearing a skirt or a dress. She sees word booklets and spelling lists from which girls are quizzing each other. She can't believe she wasted the week waiting for her father's nod when she could have been studying. She is suddenly grateful for Saul's absence, realizes that having him here would have meant watching his face fold into disappointment on a larger scale than ever before.

When it is time for the bee to begin, the children are led onstage and told to take their seats according to their numbers. It's a much bigger stage than the one in McKinley's cafeteria, the first real stage Eliza has ever been on. She grasps her number tightly in her hands and gazes at the *Times-Herald* Spelling Bee banner for reassurance.

Children shuffle to their seats like convalescents who have hopelessly strayed from the hospital grounds and are waiting to be retrieved. A small boy in the back row quietly hyperventilates. Two rows up, a girl tears her cuticles with her teeth. Another energetically sucks her hair.

The curtain opens with a whoosh of heavy fabric, the creak of rusty pulleys, and isolated gasps from startled children. The impression of the audience as a wave about to crash over them is heightened by the sound of applause. One startled fifth grader cries out, "Mo-," stopping himself before the incriminating final M, his gaffe mercifully concealed by the clapping. The same woman who moments ago had been exhorting Eliza and the others to urinate approaches the microphone. Her voice sounds like a soft-focus greeting card cover.

"Hello. I'm Katherine Rai and I'd like to welcome all of you here today to the *Times-Herald* District Spelling Bee." More applause. "The spelling bee is a truly American tradition, one that encourages learning and greater familiarity with our language. Each young person sitting on this stage is a winner. Each is here because he or she has exhibited superior abilities and knowledge. Each is an example of the best and brightest in our area. We are not competing *against* each other today. This is not a competition. It's a celebration. Of spelling and of achievement. Parents, remember that no matter what place your child comes in today, he or she is a winner. Spellers, be proud. Be proud of yourselves and be proud that you are here."

More applause. Eliza isn't sure if people are applauding because they feel they should or because they actually believe this woman's lies.

The woman continues, her voice the live embodiment of gently curved Hallmark lettering in a gender-appropriate pastel. "I'd like to introduce our word pronouncer for today's bee. Mr. Stanley Julien, Norristown Area High's own principal, has graciously volunteered his time and vocal talents to these youngsters. Stan?"

Mr. Julien walk-jogs onstage like a late night talk show host with his own theme song. More applause. Mr. Julien smiles and waves his way to where a book, a microphone, and a gavel are waiting.

"Thank you, Kathy. Ms. Rai is our school's resource counselor and she does a great job, a great job. I also understand she was once a spelling bee contestant herself, isn't that right, Kathy?"

Every year, the same script. Katherine still remembers the mortification of having to pee midway through the sixth round. By round eight, when she could hold it no longer, she misspelled her word just for the chance to get offstage. She smiles too broadly at Stanley in response, her teeth luminous in the stage lights.

In the wake of his airplane wing experience, Aaron becomes an avid sky watcher. Saul sees in his son's ardency a precocious appetite for astronomy, but Aaron's favorite nights reveal the fewest stars. More clouds mean more places for God to be. When Aaron lifts his eyes to the sky, he looks for a soft pulsing glow, nothing too dramatic or everyone would notice. He knows not to expect too much. Even Moses only got to see God once in a while.

During the Silent Amidah, the time of the Shabbat service meant for personal prayer, Aaron tenders up his own question, too shy to more than whisper the words inside his head: *There were a lot of people on that plane. Were You showing Yourself to me or did I just happen to be looking out the window as You were showing Yourself to someone else?*

He decides that maybe God can only be seen from the sky. He begins saving his weekly quarter until he learns that it would take sixteen years of saved allowances to afford even a cheap round-trip fare. If there is to be another sighting, God will have to come to him after all. He widens the scope of his God-watch accordingly. If God can be in a cloud or a burning bush, there's no reason to think God can't be in a car or a cookie. The intensity with which Aaron begins looking at the world gives him headaches. Concerned, Saul takes him to get his eyes tested. Aaron is a little disappointed to learn that his vision is fine. He had begun to hope that all he needed to see God was a pair of glasses.

As Ms. Rai lowers herself into the seat beside Mr. Julien, her fuzzy demeanor and calligraphic voice are replaced by a primal predator hunting its next meal. Ms. Rai's manicured hand becomes a bloodied talon, her gavel rising like a guillotine blade waiting to descend upon the trembling, outstretched neck of the next spelling victim. When the gavel comes crashing down and Ms. Rai growls *"Incorrect,"* all sweetness and light are gone from her voice. Her victims sometimes limp offstage as if the gavel has smashed the smaller bones of their feet.

But not Eliza. From the first time she steps to the microphone the words are there, radiant as neon. She hears the word and suddenly it is inside her head, translated from sound into physical form. Sometimes the letters need a moment to arrange themselves behind her closed eyes. An E will replace an I, a consonant will double. Eliza is patient. She is not frightened by Ms. Rai's gavel hand. She knows when a word has reached its perfect form, SCALLION and BUTANE and ORANGUTAN blazing pure and incontrovertible in her mind.

By the time it comes down to Eliza and Number 24, a small boy in a blue shirt the color of deodorized toilet water, time itself is measured in syllables. The sounds of chairs scraping, footfalls echoing on the stage, and the screech of the improperly adjusted microphone are all transformed into letters, the world one vibrant text spelling itself before her. There is no hesitation in Eliza's voice as she tackles LEGUME and PORTENT. Her pre-bee trepidation is forgotten. She stands confident, no longer caring that she is the only girl in pants. Each turn at the microphone, she spells to a different person in the audience, as if that word is the person's most secret wish.

Eliza wins the district bee with VACUOUS. Her trophy is crowned with a gold-tinted bee figurine wearing glasses and a tasseled mortar board. The bee clutches a dictionary to its chest and holds aloft a flaming torch. Eliza poses for a photographer from the *Norristown Times-Herald* alone, with her fellow runners-up, with Aaron, and with Mr. Julien and Ms. Rai. Eliza learns that if she dies or becomes too ill to attend the state competition, she is to inform the Spelling Board as soon as possible so that they can notify Number 24. She learns that Number 24 is named Matthew Harris and that he has a defective pituitary gland, but that he is going to be starting growth hormone therapy in a week. She is too happy to notice that Aaron doesn't talk much on the way home or that he spends his time at stop lights observing her as if she is a formerly passive dog who has killed its first small animal. Elly spends the car ride silently spelling the words she hears on the radio, her trophy clutched tightly in both hands.

On the day of his bar mitzvah, Aaron attends to each button on his new blue suit with geriatric care. His new shoes, professionally polished, are the first he has ever owned requiring a shoehorn. He slips his feet into them with underwater slowness. He gets his tie perfect on his first attempt and without any help. The day is a Tootsie Pop he must try to lick without giving in to the urge to bite through its chocolate center. He is determined to make it last longer than any other day of his life.

Aaron's regular visits to his father's study segued so seamlessly into studying for his bar mitzvah that Aaron isn't exactly certain how long they have been preparing. It seems that bits and pieces may have been around as early as sixth grade, when Saul first opened his study doors. Aaron remembers playing games in which he learned the *trup,* the special symbols indicating how the ancient words of the Torah and Haftorah are to be chanted. If Aaron had any doubts about becoming a rabbi, the time spent studying with his father has erased them. His father's pride in him seeps into his skin, infuses his blood, and whispers his future.

The service is flawless. Aaron acts as cantor and rabbi, leading the congregation through both the prayers and responsive readings, chanting the *Hatzi Kaddish* like a pro. He is self-assured. He doesn't slouch. As he recites each prayer from memory, his gaze moves confidently between the faces assembled before him. When he chants his Torah portion, Rabbi Mayer doesn't have to correct him even once.

Aaron's earlier habit of looking for God in everyday objects has devolved into a less focused sense of anticipation. Though Aaron no longer whispers questions to God during the Silent Amidah, part of him has never stopped praying for revelation.

Aaron is on the *bima,* speeding through the final *brachot* after completing his Haftorah portion when a warm flush starts at his toes and spreads, opening like a feather fan, to the top of his head. Suddenly, every particle of him is shimmering. He can sense each part of his body, down to each hair on his head, but at the same time feels he is one fluid whole. Though his mouth keeps moving, he is no longer focused on the prayers before him. They have become body knowledge, so deeply ingrained that they flow as naturally as air from his lungs. Aaron can sense the approach of something larger, a sea swell building up to a huge wave. Then, in a moment so intense Aaron has no idea he is still standing, it hits.

Every person in the room becomes part of him. He can suddenly see the temple from forty-six different perspectives, through forty-six pairs of eyes. He is linked. He feels the theme and variation of forty-six heartbeats, the stretch and release of forty-six pairs of lungs, the delicate interplay of warm and cool air currents on a congregation of arms, hands, and faces. For one breathtaking moment, Aaron is completely unself-conscious. He feels total acceptance and total love.

The moment passes. Aaron realizes he has finished the *brachot* and that his father is presenting him with a twelve-string guitar. Already the transformative moment feels distant, a dream he must struggle to recall upon waking. Rabbi Mayer proclaims this to be the most impressive bar mitzvah he has ever attended and presents Aaron with *The Jewish Book of Why* on behalf of the congregation. Everyone adjourns to the back room where the kosher caterers have set up lunch. Politely ignored is the fact that some of the broiled chicken breasts were not thoroughly defeathered.

A DJ is spinning Duran Duran, Eurythmics, and Flock of Seagulls, songs to which Aaron does not listen but knows are popular. When Aaron dances with Stacey Lieberman, he doesn't worry that she might only be dancing with him to be polite. When he asks for a second dance, he can tell that she's really sorry her heel hurts too much to say yes. He decides he will call her next week to ask her to a movie.

Aaron accepts congratulations and a fat slice of cake. He is contemplatively sucking on a sugar flower when he decides that what he experienced on the *bima* was God. His early years of whispered prayer and the cloud and cookie watching have been rewarded. He knows it was really God because there was no booming voice, no beam of light. His experience was something as momentous and private and unexpected as seeing a red pulsing light inside a cloud. He keeps it to himself.

When Eliza arrives home, Saul's first thought is how nice it is that the district bee gives away such huge consolation trophies. It takes him a few moments of hearing his daughter's *"I won! I won!"* and feeling her arms wrapped around his waist to comprehend that the trophy is no consolation. He scoops his little girl into his arms and tries to hold her above his head but realizes, midway, that he hasn't tried to do this for at least five or six years. He puts her back down, silently resolving to start exercising.

"Elly, that's fantastic! I wish I could have been there. I bet it was something else, huh, Aaron?"

Aaron smiles and nods, tries to think of what a good older brother would say. "She beat out a lot of kids, Dad. You would have loved it."

"I know, I know. And I didn't even think to give you the camera." Saul shakes his head. "But now I get another chance. You're going on to the next level, right?"

Eliza nods. "The area finals are in a month. In Philadelphia."

Saul claps his hands. "Perfect! We'll all go. A family trip. A month should give your mother enough time to clear the day. I'm so proud of you, Elly. I knew it was just a matter of time until you showed your stuff. A month. I can barely wait."

At which point Eliza realizes that she has only four weeks in which to study.

Studying has always been a chore on the level of dish-washing and room-cleaning, approached with the same sense of distraction and reluctance. Eliza fears that studying will leech her of spelling enthusiasm. The days following her spelling win, she resolutely maintains her after-school schedule of television reruns, pretends not to notice her father's raised eyebrows at the sight of her in her regular chair, nary a spelling list or dictionary in sight. More than her father's unspoken expectations, it is Eliza's growing suspicion that she has stumbled upon a skill that convinces her to break out the word lists. She realizes she has never been naturally good enough at anything to want to get better before. She renames studying "practice." Spelling is her new instrument, the upcoming bee the concert for which she must prepare her part.

Within a few days Eliza has developed a routine. After two TV reruns, she retreats to her room. Though she knows there is little chance of anyone disturbing her, she closes and locks her door. She likes the idea, however unlikely, of Saul or Aaron stuck outside, reduced to slipping a note under her door or to waiting for her to emerge. After dinner, she allows herself one prime-time show and then, with Aaron and Saul playing guitar in the study and her mother either cleaning the kitchen or reading her magazines, she returns to her room. The click of the bedroom door becomes one of her favorite sounds, filling her with a sense of well-being.

When Eliza studies, it is like discovering her own anatomy. The words resonate within her as if rooted deep inside her body. She pictures words lining her stomach, expanding with each stretch of her lungs, nestling in the chambers of her heart. She is thankful to have been spared from fracture, tonsillitis, or appendectomy. Such incidents might have resulted in words being truncated or removed altogether, reducing her internal vocabulary. Elly contemplates growing her hair long; it could give her an extra edge. When she closes her eyes to picture a word she imagines a communion of brain and body, her various organs divulging their lingual secrets.

Eliza starts walking around with the kind of smile usually associated with Mona Lisas and sphinxes. *I am the best speller on this bus,* she thinks on the way home from school. After a few days of studying, when she's feeling more daring, she goes as far as *I am the best speller at the dinner table,* Saul, Miriam, and Aaron innocently eating around her. Eliza knows that something special is going on. On Wednesday, she remembers the words she studied on Monday and Tuesday. On Thursday, she remembers all the old words, plus the new ones from the day before. The letters are magnets, her brain a refrigerator door.

Eliza finally understands why people enjoy entering talent shows or performing in recitals. She stops hating Betsy Hurley for only doing double-Dutch jump rope at recess. If Eliza could, she would spell all the time. She starts secretly spelling the longer words from Ms. Bergermeyer's droning class lessons and from the nightly TV news broadcasts. When Eliza closes her eyes to spell, the inside of her head becomes an ocean of consonants and vowels, swirling and crashing in huge waves of letters until the word she wants begins to rise to the surface. The word spins and bounces. It pulls up new letters and throws back old ones, a fisherman sorting his catch, until it is perfectly complete.

Eliza can sense herself changing. She has often felt that her outsides were too dull for her insides, that deep within her there was something better than what everyone else could see. Perhaps, like the donkey in her favorite bedtime story, she has been turned into a stone. Perhaps, if she could only find a magic pebble, she could change. Walking home from school, Eliza has often looked for a pebble, red and round, that might transform her from her unremarkable self. When Eliza finds this pebble in her dreams, her name becomes the first the teacher memorizes at the beginning of the school year. She becomes someone who gets called to come over during Red Rover, Red Rover, someone for whom a place in the lunch line is saved to guarantee a piece of chocolate cake. In the dream, Eliza goes to sleep with this magic pebble under her head. The dream is so real that she wakes up reaching beneath her pillow. Her sense of loss doesn't fade no matter how many times she finds nothing there.

After a week of studying, Eliza begins sleeping with a word list under her head. In the morning it is always there, waiting.

Saul and Miriam have a very small wedding, as neither has relatives they wish to invite and most of Saul's friends belong to a portion of his life he is trying to put behind him. Miriam invites a few of her law professors, who are surprised but pleased to witness the marriage of their most brilliant, if eccentric, graduate. The couple is wedded under the *chuppa,* with the traditional breaking of the glass to seal their bond. As Saul stomps on the cup from which he and his wife have just shared wine, he imagines it is his past he is smashing into unrecognizable bits. He emerges from the synagogue reborn.

Their life together begins auspiciously. They find an area with a need for both an estate lawyer and a cantor. Miriam's contract allows for a down payment on a home. Saul is proud to show Miriam off to his new congregation. The fact that he is married and planning a family quells the loudest concerns of the cantankerous rabbi he seems to have been hired to offset.

The hippie in Saul enjoys their untraditional household roles. Miriam, as chief breadwinner, handles the finances with an efficiency Saul could never match. Saul handles the cooking and shopping. He relishes having dinner waiting when Miriam returns from the office, revels in the question "How was work, dear?" asked in a fluttery falsetto. As the novelty of their responsibilities fades, Saul sometimes forgets that theirs is an unusual arrangement, is surprised by Miriam's singularity among the battalions of suited and briefcased men grimly disembarking from the commuter train.

Miriam informs Saul she prefers to keep her professional life private to counterbalance the fact that the rest of her life is now shared. She does not take Saul to the firm. There are no holiday parties or business dinners to attend. Saul tells himself it's not important to see his wife's office, that he can respect her need for independence. At dinner they watch the TV news and discuss current events during commercial breaks. Sometimes they watch "Jeopardy," competing with each other by keeping score on scraps of notepaper. Saul excels in the Bible and Mythology categories, Miriam in almost everything else.

The first years are busy ones. In addition to Saul's scholarly pursuits, which he takes as seriously as a professor angling for tenure, there is the issue of the synagogue, with its need for an adult education curriculum and a bar mitzvah tutorial program. When Saul isn't at the synagogue, he is in his study. He is grateful for a wife with enough interests to allow his return to work after dinner. He tells himself there is companionship in their discrete activities, togetherness in their occupation of adjoining rooms. Saul decides that if he only needed three hours of sleep a night he too would resent being asked to come to bed any earlier than necessary. He is often deep asleep by the time his wife slips between their sheets. Occasionally she accompanies him to the bedroom, but once they are done she leaves again. On these nights Saul feels as if he is back at the university, carefully wooing a skittish law school student.

Aaron's appearance on the scene is a supernova, illuminating Saul's life with a degree of clarity generally reserved for hindsight. Saul keeps waiting for the light to reach Miriam as well. *We've gone too far from each other,* they will tell each other. *We've got to find our way back.* But while Miriam appears to take great pride in Aaron's birth, she relates to it more as a goal attained than as a personal revelation. Birth of Son seems to occupy a similar part of her psyche as Earning Law Degree, another check-off on a lifelong To Do list. Unprepared for the care and maintenance that attend this particular milestone, Miriam delegates late night feedings and sodden diapers to Saul, who revels in the intimacy these duties afford. It becomes clear to Saul that his supernova has occurred in his personal universe rather than the rapidly expanding one of his marriage. He relishes the sense of possession this gives him. This is *his* son, *his* baby boy; Aaron fills the very gap his birth reveals.

It starts feeling natural, even beneficial, for Saul to go to bed alone, allowing him to focus on his goals for the following day. Saul realizes that Miriam's sexual prowess hasn't improved markedly since their first time together, when he perceived her as an untried pupil who would grow to mastery under his carnal tutelage. Saul grows less mindful of his wife's late night arrivals to bed, less often awaits her with eager tongue and upturned palm.

As it slowly becomes clear that theirs is a marriage of mutual utility, Saul's feelings of love ebb into gratitude. He realizes, sheepishly, that he likes his low-maintenance marriage, privately admits that he might not be suited to a more conventional situation. After Eliza's conception, their rare lovemaking tapers off even further. Saul rationalizes that the infrequency of their intimacy prevents him from taking sex for granted, a shortcoming he associates with his ignoble college days. By banishing sex from his mind, he can turn his full attention to his scholarly pursuits, exactly as he had hoped Miriam would inspire him to do. Besides, he can always masturbate to his memories. The attic is uncharred and filled with sunlight, the mattress is a queen-size box spring, and the young coeds know just which buttons to push.

Saul has noted with approval the time Eliza now spends in her room. He tells her how happy he is to see her taking initiative. Though he offers to help, Eliza feels protective of her practice sessions, takes a certain pride in studying alone.

This evening, as with every evening, Miriam is ensconced in her brown velour recliner, shoes off, prowling through magazines with diametrically opposed titles like *Neo-Proletarian Review* and *Armed Christian Family*. She will stay rooted in her recliner, still except for the movement of her hands, until she finds what she is looking for. When she finds it, she laughs.

Miriam laughs like a happy chicken. It is a joyful, uninhibited cackle entirely out of place with the rest of her, which is why Eliza loves it so much. As Miriam laughs, she flies up from her recliner to her electric typewriter, turned on in anticipation of just such a moment. She types, "Gray's quixotic implication that the Moral Majority holds exclusive stock to the country's future imperative powers. . . ." or, "I find the whole concept of 'centralized opposition' oxymoronic even from a neo-communist perspective. . . ." Miriam signs each of these gleeful invectives with a pen name composed expressly for the occasion, then stuffs them into linen envelopes addressed to editors in Freedom, North Dakota, or San Francisco, California. Though she doesn't talk about the letters with her family, she makes no secret of their writing or of the photo album she keeps beside the family encyclopedia set. They have all read the letters Miriam has carefully snipped from the editorial pages of these magazines. The first clipping is dated not long after newlyweds Saul and Miriam moved in together. It never occurs to Saul or to Miriam that the magazines have replaced the lectures they used to attend together, the arguments she once presented to Saul now addressed to others. Miriam's transition to letter writing is so automatic that she doesn't notice the substitution, her quick mind filling in the gap before she recognizes its presence. Drifting away from her husband is less a conscious choice than a series of unconscious ones.

Eliza feels invigorated by her rejection of Saul's offer of help. Her power to cause her father's emergence from his study in the name of spelling is made all the sweeter by her decision not to employ it. Rather than block out her father's and brother's guitar music she now incorporates it into her own pursuits, her words gliding on the muted chords rising up through the air vents. Even her mother's solitary habits have lost the feeling of a party to which Eliza is not invited. Miriam's typing lends Eliza's studies rhythm and tempo.

Paging through the dictionary is like looking through a microscope. Every word breaks down into parts with unique properties—prefix, suffix, root. Eliza gleans not only the natural laws that govern the letters but their individual behaviors. R, M, and D are strong, unbending and faithful. The sometimes silent B and G and the slippery K follow strident codes of conduct. Even the redoubtable H, which can make P sound like F and turn ROOM into RHEUM, obeys etymology. Consonants are the camels of language, proudly carrying their lingual loads.

Vowels, however, are a different species, the fish that flash and glisten in the watery depths. Vowels are elastic and inconstant, fickle and unfaithful. E can sound like I or U. -IBLE and -ABLE are impossible to discern. There is no combination the vowels haven't tried, exhaustive and incestuous in their couplings. E will just as soon pair with A, I, or O, leading the dance or being led. Eliza prefers the vowels' unpredictability and, of all vowels, favors Y. Y defies categorization, the only letter that can be two things at once. Before the bee, Eliza had been a consonant, slow and unsurprising. With her bee success, she has entered vowelhood. Eliza begins to look at life in alphabetical terms. School is consonantal in its unchanging schedule. God, full of possibility, is a vowel. Death: the ultimate consonant.

Toward the end of the silent *Amidah*, Aaron and Eliza play a game called Sheep that both claim to have invented. At the Amidah's beginning, Rabbi Mayer tells the entire congregation to rise. The congregants are supposed to remain standing for as long as they wish to pray, sitting down when they have finished. A lot of people actually do begin by praying, but most stop soon after they start. They become distracted by thoughts of the evening's prime-time television lineup or by how awful the perfume is of the old lady with dyed hair who always sits in the seat under the air duct so that the smell of her goes everywhere.

Because of this, knowing when to sit down is a problem. People want to appear prayerful, but they also want the service to end in time for "Remington Steele" or "Dallas" or "Falcon Crest." After a period that is short enough to move things along but long enough to seem respectable, they look for a cue. That is what Sheep is all about.

The best nights to play Sheep are bar mitzvah Fridays. The synagogue is filled with people whose nephew or cousin or boss's son is becoming a man the next morning. These people occupy the back half of the synagogue even though there are seats available up front. When they stand for the silent *Amidah* they never know whether to focus on the prayerbook or upon a distant point, looking thoughtful.

The key is to make scraping noises. When Eliza or Aaron chooses the moment they feel represents the perfect prayerful/let's-get-on-with-it ratio, they rattle their chairs and rub one or two of the chair legs against the floor to make it sound as if more than one person is actually descending. Their efforts carry to the back where it is determined that if the front rows are sitting, the other rows are allowed to sit down as well. Once Eliza timed it so around three fourths of the congregation followed her into their chairs like an elaborate chain of dominoes. Even Aaron had been forced to admit she'd set a new record.

This Friday night not being a bar mitzvah, neither Aaron nor Eliza nets any followers, the regulars making it a point of pride to have a unique time to reseat themselves. Three prayers, a Mourner's Kaddish, and two responsive readings later come the weekly announcements, which precede the final prayer. It's the same as usual—Sisterhood meetings, Sunday school classes, and singles retreats—until Saul includes a special announcement.

"Eliza Naumann has won the honor of representing our district tomorrow in the bee finals for our area. We wish her mazel tov and best of luck."

Then he moves on to something about adult education, as though what he has just said is the most normal thing in the world. Eliza starts smiling so hard her cheek muscles hurt. Aaron makes a point of not looking at her.

After the last prayer, everyone proceeds to the back room for *oneg,* where a table is waiting with tea, coffee, juice, and cookies. Eliza loves *oneg* even though the juice is watered down and there are better cookies at home. On the cookie plate are always a few chocolate wafers, but the majority are chalky shortbreads that crumble into little pieces unless the whole thing is ingested at once. On someone's birthday, there is a store-bought cake sparsely decorated with candy flowers.

The trick is to get one of the wafer cookies or, if it is a birthday, a slice of cake with a flower. This takes practice. Eliza and Aaron can't just race to the back room after the last prayer and grab what they want. They have to wait until Rabbi Mayer has come to the table and said a prayer over the food. In a way, this is lucky because sitting in the front row would put them at a distinct disadvantage if it were first come, first serve, especially with the Kaplan kids, who always sit in the back.

The key to snagging a good cookie is placement. Eliza puts herself nearest to the side of the cookie plate with the good cookies on it, then casually rests her hand by the edge of the plate. As soon as the prayer is over, her hand is in prime position.

Getting a flower is trickier. An adult always cuts the cake and there is a line. Eliza never knows what slicing method the cake cutter will use, so it is hard to anticipate where in the cake line she should be to net a flower. It is generally smarter to notice which adults get flowers and to casually ask for one. This is especially effective with women, who usually make a show of handing over their flowers in the service of the diet of the moment. With men, it isn't as sure a bet. They may hand over their flower to prove what great guys they are, but they are just as likely to make a joke about not giving over their flower to spotlight their lingering youthfulness in the face of galloping middle age. Eliza has a standing cake agreement with Mrs. Schoenfeld, who doesn't have children of her own and likes to think that giving Eliza her occasional flower gives them a special bond.

The pre-bee service happens to fall on a birthday week, so there is cake. When it is Eliza's turn Mrs. Schwartz, who is the de facto slicer and prides herself on not playing favorites, actually cuts a piece out of sequence in order to give Eliza a flower, saying that it will bring luck.

Aaron tells himself he isn't jealous. Dad's announcement is no big deal. Eliza deserves the attention, she doesn't usually get any, and the state bee is important. Except that Aaron has been to the state science fair a few times and Saul has never told the congregation about it. When Mrs. Schoenfeld offers him her flower he declines. He's too old to care about such things.

Once Eliza loots the *oneg* table, she generally drifts outside to play tag until it's time to go home. Usually this is no problem, but tonight grownups want to talk to her. Mrs. Lieberman corners Eliza by the Siddur table and kisses her on both cheeks. Eliza wonders if her lipstick has left pucker marks.

". . . is a wonderful thing that can open doors to wonderful places."

Eliza misses the first half. She has been watching Aaron, an *oneg* pro, walk outside with neither cake flower nor good cookie, a sure sign that something is amiss. She feels a strange mixture of anxiety and pride at the thought that she may have something to do with it.

Mr. Schwartz announces he is going to quiz her, one spelling champion to another. Up close, he has a brown front tooth and more wrinkles than Eliza thought. He sips his tea so loudly that she has to repeat NEIGHBOR three times before Mrs. Schwartz comes to her rescue, admonishing Phil for tiring Eliza out before the real thing. The sound of Mr. Schwartz's until now unknown first name allows Eliza to picture Mr. Schwartz in some place other than the synagogue, wearing something other than a brown-striped tie with a stained tip.

Eliza is steps away from freedom when George finds her. George, who lives in the apartment complex nearby, isn't Jewish but comes to services every Friday and attends Saul's adult education classes. Eliza once overheard him talking to her father about religious conversion, and George's belief that if he is going to do it, he wants to "go all the way," but that he isn't sure he is "strong enough." Eliza has no idea what George was talking about even though Aaron has told her he was once in the bathroom when George was peeing and saw that George was uncircumcised.

George tells Eliza she will be representing not only her district tomorrow but Her People. George holds Eliza's shoulders as he speaks and spits in his earnestness, the wetter syllables arcing harmlessly over Eliza's head.

"For centuries, the Jewish nation has been persecuted and exiled. Tomorrow is your chance to manifest the same spirit that has kept the Chosen People alive and faithful through their wanderings in the desert. What you're doing is courageous."

Eliza's eyes are at the level of George's zipper. She squelches the urge to shout "Uncircumcised," though still unsure of its meaning. Instead she silently spells the word. She smiles and nods at George as the letters dance and swirl inside her head until they are perfect, the word that is George's secret spelled out in all its mysterious glory.

The Philadelphia Spectrum serves as concert venue, hockey rink, basketball court and, every so often, books the Ice Capades. Aaron has not attended a Flyers game since learning first hand that blood bounces on ice.

The morning of the area finals is the closest the stadium comes to the best-of-breed tent at a county fair. Friends and relatives scan the spellers, trying to predict the blue ribbon winner. Eyes travel between contestants, gauging preparedness, intelligence, and spelling savvy. Some parents attempt last-minute changes to their entries. One speller stands frozen beneath a hand smoothing a cowlick. Another melts into the floor as his mother rains words like hailstones upon his slumped shoulders. A morbid camaraderie has arisen between spellers, numbered placards drooping from their necks like turkey wattles. Shared smiles and briefly held gazes acknowledge mutual doom.

This is lost on Eliza, who is too excited by her family's presence to notice. The singularity of their collective appearance outside the house lends a holiday air to their actions. They walk the stadium concourse as if beyond lies Disneyworld or Mesa Verde, this the closest they have come to the family vacation Saul has been promising since Eliza was born.

As far as Eliza can remember, this is the first time she has ever held both parents' hands at once. She swings her arms back and forth, penduluming them the way she's seen happy children do on Kodak commercials. Miriam wears the smile she usually reserves for discovering one of her letters to the editor in print. Saul whistles a klezmer tune between snapping pictures with film that has been in his camera since the Iranian hostage crisis. Even Aaron is talking a few levels louder than usual. When the time comes for Eliza to journey backstage, she is reluctant to go. She would be content to pass by the statue of Rocky Balboa, circling seating sections A–Z until the sky turned purple if it meant they could keep looking the way TV families look by the end of the show.

The area finals can be distinguished from the district bee in the details. The folding chairs for the contestants are cushioned. There is a bell instead of a gavel. The introductory speeches, while of identical content, are given by local politicians instead of school administrators. Three minutes after the applause for the stageful of winners dies down, the first speller—a thin girl with limp hair and large, sad eyes—is eliminated. Her sigh as she leaves the stage, more than the raising of the curtain, signifies that the bee has truly begun.

Tension runs between the spellers like an invisible steel cable. When one rises to approach the microphone, everyone in the row feels the pull. Many are unconscious of the fact they are spelling along with each contestant. As their mouths form the letters, the effect is that of a choir of mutes accompanying every word.

From the third row, it is impossible for Eliza to see anything but the backs of other spellers' heads. The tights Miriam picked out for her itch horribly. Eliza uses the relative privacy accorded by her seat to scratch.

Spellers can ask for word pronunciation, definition, etymology, and use in a sentence, but once they start spelling, there is no turning back. A misspoken letter is irreversible, the equivalent of a nervous tic during brain surgery.

The hardest to watch are those who know they have made a mistake. Sometimes they stop mid-word, the air knocked out of them. Even then they are expected to continue until the word is finished. They flinch their way to the word's end, mere shadows of the child they were before the mistake was made. Finally, the misspelled word is complete, its mistaken A or extra T dangling like a flap of dead skin.

There is a pause, like the split second between touching the thing that's too hot and feeling the burn. Then, the bell.

Ding.

It is the sound of an approaching bicycle, harmless as a sugar ant, but here it takes on atomic, fifties sci-fi proportions. Just as in the movies, its hapless victim stands immobile while the correct spelling, monstrous with huge, flesh-rending jaws, comes at them from the pronouncer's mouth.

It is worst when the speller stands there, nodding like a spring-loaded lawn ornament. A couple times, the fatal moment functions like some kind of psychological glue trap: even after the pronouncer completes the word, the speller remains frozen in place. One boy stands with his hand in front of him, thumb pressing an invisible button on what appears to be an invisible remote control, willing the world to rewind.

Eliza begins to wish she were closer to the front. The wait is like the slow *tic-tic-tic* of a roller coaster climbing to its summit before the stomach-plunging drop. She would gladly trade the ability to scratch at her tights unseen for a shorter ascent, a briefer fall. She is most afraid that some fatal blockage will occur between her brain and mouth, preventing the word from emerging whole. She can hear it happen with other children. She can tell they know the word by the way they intone it, but then some kind of home accident occurs. The word trips over the edge of the tongue and plunges headlong into a tooth. A letter is twisted, I into E, T into P, or there is a pause and the last letter is repeated. Eliza knows it could happen to anyone, that possessing the right spelling is only half the battle.

By the time it is her turn, Eliza is ready for the worst. Instead, she gets ELEMENT. She practically sings the word into the microphone.

Aaron didn't want to come but knew better than to say anything. There are certain times when it's easier to go along with what his father says. When the words "as a family" are used is one of those times. Saul gets a look in his eye, like that of a dominant lion, that means either act like one of the pride or prepare to be attacked by the alpha male. Aaron is grateful for these irregular demands on his filial devotion. They reinforce the idea that the four of them are bound by more than a shared roof.

With that in mind, Aaron puts on his most attentive, brotherly face as he tries to discern his sister among the rows of preadolescents squirming in their chairs like insect specimens that weren't asphyxiated before being pinned. He wants to be able to support his sister's newfound spelling abilities. It's silly, he tells himself. It's immature. But he can't help but notice the way Saul's gaze has been fixed upon the stage ever since enough spellers were eliminated for Eliza to become visible.

Even when it's nowhere near her turn, Saul sits at attention, immune from the monotony of each round. The pronouncer's voice, the heavy pauses as the children buy time at the microphone, the recurring requests—"Please repeat the word, please repeat the definition"—have no effect. Saul's gaze is fixed on Eliza. He is looking at her the way a parent looks at an infant too new to be taken for granted.

Aaron remembers that look. He is six years old. Baby Eliza is fresh from the hospital. As Saul introduces Aaron to his new sister, he cannot believe anything that small could actually be alive. He grasps one of his sister's doll hands and examines the tiny fingers. Aaron is not even aware of putting the finger into his mouth, of testing it with his teeth. His sister's scream interrupts his reverie. Saul snatches the tiny hand away. Aaron is terrified, expects the bitten finger to fall off onto the table in a shower of blood, his fragile sister forever fractured. He can barely believe his eyes when the hand emerges whole, the skin unbroken, only a slight ring of indentations left by his teeth.

"NO," his father commands, the menace in his voice a physical presence.

Aaron flinches, expecting reprisal. Instead, his father's voice suddenly softens.

"Be gentle. Your sister needs your love. Look how small she is. She will never be as big or old as you. Will you help me look out for her? She needs us both."

Aaron nods, his eyes large from the shock of his actions and his unexpected reprieve. Marvin Bussy and Billy Mamula are years away. He is still a boy who believes he has the power to protect.

A lot of time is spent raising and lowering the mike stand between contestants who have hit puberty and those still waiting to grow. Eliza wishes that those who didn't know their words would just guess instead of stalling until they're asked to start spelling by the judges. In the time it takes some spellers to get started, Eliza has spelled their word a few times, fought the temptation to just take off her tights, and repeatedly sung through the theme from *Star Wars* which, for some reason, she is unable to get out of her head.

Without realizing it, she has developed a routine. Three turns before her own, she blocks out the sounds of the bee and closes her eyes. Since she was very small, Eliza has thought of the inside of her head as a movie theater, providing herself with an explanation for the origin of bad dreams. Nightmares are rationalized away with the private assurance that she has accidentally stepped into an R-rated movie and needs only to return herself to the G-rated theater to remedy the situation. Using the mental movie theater construct, Eliza pictures the inside of her head as a huge blank screen upon which each word will be projected.

It doesn't occur to her to be self-conscious about closing her eyes at the microphone. How else is she to see her word? Not having observed the others' faces, she is unaware that most spell with their eyes open after a brief period of face-clenched concentration indigenous to constipation and jazz solos. Eliza opens her eyes only after uttering the last letter, the word inside her head as real as her nose and just as unmistakable. She has no fear of the *ding*. It's not meant for her.

By Round 7, the words have gotten serious. Eliza has a moment's hesitation with CREPUSCULE, but when she closes her eyes a second time, the word is there, waiting. After she spells it correctly, she spots her father in the audience when he is the only one standing during the applause. She considers waving but decides that it is too uncool. She tries a droll wink but is unable to manage the eyelid coordination and looks instead as if she has something stuck in her eye.

Though they haven't spoken, Eliza has developed an affection for the speller next to her, an intense and careful girl whose numbered placard lies at an upward tilt because of her boobs. When the girl is eliminated with SANSEVIERIA, Eliza feels a loss. After the girl is gone Eliza avoids touching her empty chair.

Though Miriam is glad to be sitting here, a parent among parents, she cannot help but feel there is somewhere else she should be. Miriam knows this feeling well. It is rare not to feel the amorphous pull of some nameless, important task requiring her attention. She considers herself at her best when doing three things at once. The book she has brought lessens her sense of urgency, but Saul and Aaron are paying such single-minded attention to the bee that she feels guilty whenever she starts to read.

She is startled by the sight of Eliza onstage. Though certainly cognizant of their biological connection, Miriam has grown to view Eliza as not quite her child. She had always assumed any daughter of hers would excel in school, distinguishing herself early and often from the rabble of her peers. Eliza's utter failure to do so, along with her apparent disinterest in cerebral pursuits, placed her beyond the ken of Miriam's experience. Miriam came to consider Eliza a gosling born into a family of ducks, loved and accepted but always and forever a goose. Miriam has never expressed this thought to Saul but can tell he senses it and duly disapproves. She begrudges him his disapprobation, feeling he is equally at fault for so obviously favoring Aaron, leaving her the child to whom she has the least to say.

Eliza's performance onstage shatters Miriam's private metaphor. It is not that Eliza is spelling the words correctly. It is that when Eliza stands at the mike, concentrating on the word she has been given, she looks *exactly* like Miriam when she was a girl, so absorbed in a book that not even a burning building could distract her. There is pain in this recognition. Because Miriam knows that such powers of concentration come from years of being alone, of needing to focus so strongly on one thing because there is nothing else. By keeping her distance, Miriam realizes too late that she has made her daughter more like her than she ever intended.

At the beginning of Round 12, the surviving spellers are consolidated into the front row. Eliza sits with Numbers 8 and 32, two serious-looking Pakistani boys, and Number 17, a red-haired girl with dark circles under her eyes. They are all older and Eliza keeps having to readjust the microphone. Between turns, the red-haired girl whispers a mantra which sounds to Eliza like, "My bear, my bear, my bear." Number 8 alternates between sitting on his hands and chewing his cuticles. Eliza stares into the audience, trying to find her family, but is blinded by the stage lights, which make identifying individual spectators impossible. In quick succession, 17 is dinged by DAGUERREOTYPE and 8 by CZARINA. It is down to Eliza and Number 32, the shorter of the Pakistanis.

He carries himself like a middle-aged businessman forced into early retirement. He wears blocky glasses with tinted lenses. Before starting his words he runs his fingers through his hair as if he's collecting letters from his scalp. He and Eliza avoid eye contact. When Eliza accidentally brushes his thigh with her hand as he sits down and she stands up, he jerks his leg back as if he's been burned.

Time stops sometime after PHARMACOPOEIA. Eliza knows Number 32's body as well as her own: the inflamed hangnail on his left index finger, the two gray hairs near the back of his head, the way he walks heels first when approaching the mike. He has the annoying habit of grinding his teeth, a quirk that intensifies as the rounds continue. By Round 20, it has become so loud Eliza is sure it can be heard by the spectators in the back rows. The bee has become a war of attrition. If nothing else, Number 32 will turn fifteen before Eliza, at which point he will become too old to qualify.

Despite the incredible tension, despite the fact that Number 32 has obviously been doing this longer than she has, and despite the fact that her stomach is about to tear itself into tiny pieces and explode in a bright cloud of confetti from her mouth, Eliza feels overwhelmingly, intensely alive. She can feel her lungs expanding, the rush of blood traveling from her heart to her fingers. The words hit her at a level of cognition that outpaces conscious thought, resonating somewhere where spelling doesn't need to happen because it already has, each word exploding upon entering her ear. She loves it. She loves everything about it. And she is fully prepared to spend the next year of her life on this stage, trading words into the microphone with Number 32 until his fifteenth birthday finally arrives, the judges forcibly remove him from the stage and announce Eliza to be the *Times-Herald's* Greater Philadephia Metro Area Spelling Champion.

Saul doesn't know what he is expecting to happen in Philadelphia, but it certainly isn't the realization that his daughter is a mystical prodigy. And yet, with Eliza standing over the exact spot where Dave "The Hammer" Schulz pummeled Dale Rolfe's face, that is exactly what happens. He watches, stunned, as Eliza stands at the microphone, eyes closed, body perfectly relaxed, waiting faithfully and patiently for the next word to materialize. Round after round—while the other children nod, shake, or bounce, their hands scratching and picking—his Eliza stands perfectly centered, in complete concentration, employing the techniques of the ancient rabbis.

Saul wants to jump to his feet and dance where he stands. He wants to sing, raising his hands in gratitude and humility. Even Isaac Luria needed a teacher. Even Shabbatai Zvi and Rabbi Nahman of Bratzlav required instruction to reach mystical greatness. Saul learned long ago that he was not meant to be another Abulafia. Instead, he has been hoping to encounter a student of whom history is made.

But that it should be Eliza! His own quiet, unassuming Elly-belly who does little more than go through the motions of the Shabbat service every Friday and who, until the day before the district bee, had never set foot inside his study. He would like to think he has kept his distance in order to protect his daughter from his unfulfilled hopes. He did not want Eliza to sense paternal expectations as unrealistic as they were immutable. Saul—who chose books over cars, Naumann over Newman—knows too well the feeling of becoming something a parent does not intend. *At least,* Saul had told himself, *if I cannot prevent myself from inheriting my father's faults, I can protect my daughter from their effect.*

As Saul watches his daughter go head to head with the serious-looking boy two years her senior, he realizes something with illogical and unexplainable certainty: his daughter is going to surpass his greatest expectations. She is going to win.

When Number 32 stumbles over GLISSANDO, the audience gasps as if the missing second S has left them short of breath. The ding causes the boy's body to go rigid. For everyone but Saul, who suddenly feels as if he is watching his destiny unfold, it is like witnessing an execution.

Number 32 doesn't leave the stage. If Eliza misspells her word, the bee will continue. As she approaches the microphone, every muscle in Number 32's body is tense, his teeth by now surely reduced to blighted stumps.

"Number 26," the pronouncer intones with the solemnity of the keeper of the Book of Life, "your word is EYRIR."

"Ay-reer?"

"Ay-reer."

Doubt hits Saul like a cold wave. His certainty, so strong seconds ago, seems more space than substance. He can already feel disappointment cooling his blood. He wants to run to his daughter standing so completely still onstage with her eyes closed and yell, before it is too late, *Quick. Open your eyes. This is what I look like when I believe in you.*

EYRIR is a supernova inside Eliza's head, unexpected but breathtakingly beautiful. The lights transform the audience into a sea of vague shapes, the alien syllables echoing in the auditorium's corners. It is strangely quiet. The word fills Eliza's mouth with a sweet, metallic taste.

Suddenly, it is as though she is living underwater. Light wavers on its course to her eyes. The stadium ripples as if painted in ink on a lake's surface. EYRIR is a dank thing exuding heat and threat, its dark fur tangled from years in the forest. EYRIR is the nameless, shapeless fear that haunts sleepless nights. Eliza wants EYRIR to disappear like a fever vision at the touch of her father's hand. Instead, she asks for a definition.

"It's a unit of currency," the pronouncer explains, eyes unreadable. "Used in Iceland."

"Ay-reer." Eliza pauses. *A? AI?* She closes her eyes. She doesn't think about Number 32 glowering behind her or about the fact that she will be required to start spelling soon or about her family somewhere in the audience. She waits patiently, faithfully, for the word to reveal itself. Then, as her eyelids glow red from the stage lights, it does. Eliza takes a deep breath to give the word strength.

Y, the slippery snake. Y that can change from vowel to consonant like water to ice.

"E-Y-" She lets out her breath. "R-I-R. Eyrir." She waits.

Resounding, palpable silence. Nothing moves. Eliza wonders if death is not a sleep you can't wake up from but life reduced to one inescapable moment.

The pronouncer's voice cracks the silence, a thickened shell protecting sweet meat.

"That is correct."

Applause pounds the stage like colored pebbles. An internal mute button that Eliza didn't even know existed disengages. It is like hearing the ocean after years of watching waves silently crash upon the sand.

And then Eliza sees her father. Saul is not walking but running to the stage. He is oblivious to the rows of chairs, to the clusters of people and journalists, his body reminding Eliza of a bumper car as he bounces off them on his stageward trajectory, eyes locked on her. His face is like a page from Eliza's illustrated Old Testament: Jew beholding Promised Land. Eliza feels like Moses. She feels like Superman. She holds her trophy aloft, the stage her Mount Sinai, Saul her Jimmy Olsen. When Saul reaches the stage and lifts her into a hug like manna in the desert, Eliza is flying.

The first time Perfectimundo finds Miriam, it is a complete surprise, a game of hopscotch in which the stone falls into the perfect center of square 3. It is a magic moment. The absolute rightness of the stone's placement in the square opens something deep inside Miriam that had, until this moment, always been shut. Miriam can feel the release. Her body fills with warmth at the sight of the stone, beckoning like a talisman to another world. It is this other world that Miriam wants to inhabit, this other world to which she really belongs. Miriam stops the game, infuriating her play partner, a frilled neighbor whose father is big in pork belly futures. Miriam insists upon staring at the rock, and then upon tossing and retossing other rocks until they land in the exact centers of squares 1, 2, and 4–8, respectively, an activity which has not ended by the time Miriam is called in for dinner, the frilly neighbor having long ago fled in self-righteous boredom back to Mummy.

Later that same year Miriam receives a kaleidoscope as a gift. When she first puts it to her eye, she forgets to breathe. It is a window into the world of the perfectly thrown stone, the land of Perfectimundo. Miriam wishes she could squeeze through the eyehole and into the tube, joining the flawless symmetry. Failing that, she decides she is fully prepared to spend the rest of her life holding the cylinder to her face. When a well-meaning adult rotates the cylinder, Miriam screams so loudly her nanny fears a piece of colored glass has lodged in her charge's eye. The kaleidoscope is grabbed away just as Miriam realizes that the movement did not destroy perfection, but created it anew. She demands the present back, spends the rest of the day frozen except for the rotation of one hand, the kaleidoscope pointed toward the sun. By the time Miriam goes to bed, the kaleidoscope clutched to her chest, she has decided that where there is a window there has to be a door. That night Miriam vows, with the solemnity of all seven of her precocious years, that even if she must spend her whole life searching for the door to Perfectimundo, she will find it.

Saul comes to breakfast with multiple copies of the *Norristown Times-Herald* and the *Philadelphia Inquirer.*

"Good morning, star," he says, presenting the papers to his daughter.

The *Times-Herald's* front page proclaims HUNTINGDON GIRL SPELLS HER WAY TO V-I-C-T-O-R-Y while the *Inquirer* places its more sedate "EYRIR" TAKES METRO AREA SPELLER TO NATIONALS in its Neighbor section.

The *Times-Herald,* with its photo of Miriam, Saul, and Aaron joining Eliza in the winner's circle, holds Eliza's interest longer, it being one of the few family pictures ever taken. Eliza's face is a still life of suspended disbelief, her trophy a baby she didn't know she was about to have. Saul grasps her shoulders, his face glowing with pride and possession. Miriam stands to their left, her hand caught midway to Eliza's arm as if unsure whether it is safe to touch. Aaron stands at the frame's edge, face out of focus, largely concealed by the people around him. Everything is much smaller than it seemed at the time.

It is not the photo Eliza was expecting. Her family doesn't look anything like the stuff of photography studios. Theirs is no pearl-finish portrait of interlocking hands and matching smiles. Instead, they more closely resemble odd puzzle pieces, mismatched slots and tabs jammed into each other to force a whole. Eliza examines the picture with the detachment of a stranger, seeing for the first time the way her father and mother avoid contact, her brother's perpetual old woman slouch, and the way she freezes at Saul's touch as if immobility will preserve the moment. Eliza spots unfamiliar hard lines around the man's eyes, a strange emptiness to the woman's face. Even the girl starts to look unfamiliar, her eyes a little too bright, her face a little too eager. Eliza struggles to convince herself that when she looks away from the picture she will be surrounded by familiar figures and not the strangers in the photo. Looking up from the newspaper is like walking into a darkened room from the noonday sun. It takes a moment for Eliza's eyes to readjust. But there is her father, whistling one of his morning songs as he pages through the paper. There is her mother, head tilted to one side as she scours the pan Saul used to scramble eggs. She knows these people. She turns the *Times-Herald* photo side down.

Saul, beaming like a new father, hands out papers like cigars. When he suggests they take turns reading aloud, Aaron says something about a sore throat, gets up to make himself a cup of tea. Between mouthfuls of egg, Saul does his best sportscaster imitation.

" 'After four hours, only two remained. Chopak Singh, a three-time area champion, held his ground for a grueling ten rounds, but finally lost out to first-time speller' "—Saul performs a drum roll on the table with his fingers—" 'Eliza Naumann!' "

Miriam appears at Eliza's side, something gift-wrapped in one hand.

"This is for you," Miriam says.

The room goes silent as Eliza stares at the present. Saul feels ashamed of the sudden spike of jealousy he feels toward his daughter, tries to bury it in bites of toast. Miriam gives sensible presents at sensible times: birthdays, Hanukah, their anniversary. In eighteen years, she has never surprised him.

Miriam hands her daughter the gift as though she's relaying a baton, her face concentrating entirely on the exchange. For an extended moment, both Eliza's and Miriam's hands hold fast to opposite ends of the gift and Eliza fears she has done something to change her mother's mind. When Miriam finally releases her grip in a sudden flurry of fingers, it looks as if she is waving goodbye.

In addition to Miriam's gaze, which weighs Eliza's every move, Eliza can sense her brother's and father's stares. Her initial thrill at the surprise has dulled into a vague dread. She suspects she has been given a pop quiz that will be evaluated three different ways, guaranteeing at least one failing grade.

Eliza carefully unwraps, flinches when part of the paper pulls off with a piece of tape. When she uncovers the old kaleidoscope, she mistakes it for one of those fancy tubes that tights are sometimes sold in, maybe ones that aren't so scratchy.

"No," Miriam says perhaps a little too harshly when Eliza tries to pull off the top, freezing her daughter like an animal sensing it has been sited in crosshairs. Miriam catches herself, softens her tone. "It doesn't come apart. It's a kaleidoscope. It was mine when I was a girl."

It's nothing fancy. Once bright blue cardboard is muted by age, sun, and wear. Inside, the standard beads and baubles. Eliza holds it to the light, gives it a few turns, tries to imagine what she's supposed to say.

"Um, thanks, Mom. It's neat." Miriam is staring at her so intently that she puts the toy to her eye again. Maybe her mother stuck something special inside the tube. She turns it a few more times, but no. It's just a kaleidoscope.

Miriam can taste her disappointment, goes to the sink for a glass of water. She needs the distance to stop herself from grabbing the gift back. They're all three watching her as she returns to the table.

"I should have given it to you sooner. I suppose you're too old now." She ignores Saul's continued stare, the questions in his eyes.

Eliza's face brightens. "No, Mom, it's good you waited or I might have messed it up. I mean, this is *old,* right? You had it when you were a girl."

Miriam's last hope of recognition dies.

"Yes, Eliza, it's old. Almost as old as me."

Eliza smiles, pleased. She carefully places the kaleidoscope on a cushion of wrapping paper, as if it were spun glass instead of cardboard. Miriam can already envision its internment on a dusty shelf in Eliza's room, never to be used again. Saul shakes his head and laughs.

"That's right, Elly, it's a real artifact. From long, long ago before there was Atari." Unlike Eliza, who is afraid to look, Saul can see that the excitement is gone from his wife's eyes. Even as he wonders what it was Miriam intended, he knows she won't tell him.

Soon after the area finals, Miriam starts coming home at six forty-five instead of six o'clock. Her six o'clock arrivals had been so routine for so long that Saul could anticipate where, in the opening theme music to the NBC "Nightly News," he would hear the jangle of Miriam's keys and the click of the front door. The first time six o'clock passes without her appearance, Saul can imagine nothing less than a critical accident to have caused the delay. When she finally arrives, Saul enfolds her in his arms, surprised at the strength of feelings he had thought faded.

"Are you all right?" he asks, all concern, ready to turn whatever Miriam says into a rebirth for them both. He is ready, he thinks, for a new beginning.

"I'm fine," she says, bemused. Saul releases her from his arms. His outburst has passed through her like a band of invisible light. "I'll be coming home later now. Do you mind waiting dinner?"

She says it has to do with work, but there's a flush to her face now, a barely submerged heat.

When Eliza arrives at school, the showcase in the front hallway features Sunday's articles. Eliza avoids looking at the family photo, focusing instead on her name in print. She remains there after she has finished reading, pressing her face against the glass and uttering a few well-timed *Huhs* and *Wows* with the arrival of buses in an attempt to lure admirers. She nets a few first graders but is frustrated by having to read the articles to them and gives up.

After the pledge of allegiance, Dr. Morris announces Eliza's name over the P.A. and Mrs. Bergermeyer makes the class applaud. Kids who have been in her class since second grade start looking at her differently. She feels the way Billy Mauger must have felt when he came in bald from chemotherapy and everyone stared even though they had been told not to.

Outside of class is more comfortable than in. At recess, Eliza is approached by a few of the girls who don't wear designer jeans and quietly make straight A's each quarter. Sinna Bhagudori is among them.

"What was it like?" Sinna asks, eyes bright. The other girls nod, glasses frames bouncing on their noses.

"It was like being in a movie," Eliza replies. "It was like being famous."

In class, Eliza feels like a specimen: this is how a spelling champion walks to class, this is how a spelling champion enters the girls' room, this is how a spelling champion chews her pencil eraser.

The stares she receives are resentful. *You're supposed to be one of the stupid ones,* their eyes say. *You're supposed to be like us.*

Eliza is walking to the bus when she is approached by Carrie Waxham, a stick of a girl with pinched, closely spaced eyes and stringy blond hair.

"Snob," Carrie mutters.

She pokes Eliza in the back with her finger. Hard.

"Stuck-up."

Eliza feels stupid about the tears that suddenly appear, wipes them away while pretending to scratch her nose. Carrie sits a row behind her and chews her gum just loud enough for the kids around her but not Ms. Bergermeyer to hear. She can't do fractions at all. In the class bee, she got out on PURPOSE.

"It doesn't matter," Eliza whispers to herself, then freezes. They are the same words she has heard Aaron mutter so many times, walking angrily home with a new bruise or scratch. Eliza had promised herself she would never say them, never put herself in a position where she was forced to comfort herself with that lie.

Saul has spent the day rehearsing speeches in his head, playing out entire scenes between himself and his daughter. He knows the enormity of what he is taking on and knows that if it is to work at all, he must take things slowly. He must not frighten Eliza with the scale of his plans, the height of his ambitions. As much as he'd like to, he can't start out with his bee epiphany. If Elly is to realize her enormous potential, she must realize it on her own terms.

They will start by focusing solely on spelling. Eliza must have a strong foundation from which to jump if she is to have any chance of flying. The dictionary will be their foundation. The ancients advised thorough knowledge of the texts before undertaking the

Kabbalah. The national bee is approaching. They will prepare for it together.

While Eliza is at school, Saul purchases *Webster's Third International Dictionary,* the English language spread among three hardbound volumes.

He is waiting for her when she gets home. He pretends not to notice her look of surprise, as if his presence at the kitchen table upon her arrival is the most natural thing in the world.

"You look as if you could use a snack," he says before she has a chance to say anything. "I cut up an apple for you and a little bit of cheese. You can have a cookie if you want, but too much sugar will make you crash later on, which is bad for sustained concentration. If we're going to do this right, we need to start taking things like that into account."

"Huh?" says Eliza, and Saul realizes that he's already strayed from his script, so caught up in his excitement that he skipped over the part where he lets Eliza in on the plan.

"Here," he says, leading Eliza to his study door. The far corner of the room has been magically cleared of papers and notebooks. In their place is a small wooden worktable and two chairs. The three volumes of the *Third International* are stacked on the table's center.

"I thought this would work well as a study area. We don't have as much time as I would like, but I think we can get through a lot in two months. I've drawn up a sample schedule that covers daily practice as well as a rough syllabus for the entire period, but it will all depend on what we find works best for us."

He stops for breath, notices the confused expression on his daughter's face, and shyly smiles. "So, Elly-belly, you want to give it a whirl? Can I help you study?"

For a moment, Eliza catches a glimpse of her brother in her father's face, the dogged determination and unflagging hope of a boy waiting to get picked for the team. Though she knows it is not an option, not something she would ever dream of doing, she is filled with momentary giddiness at the idea of saying no.

"Are you sure it won't be boring for you?"

"Elly," Saul replies, placing his hands on her shoulders, "you have no idea how exciting this is."

Elly nods. She manages an "Okay" in place of the jubilant "YES!!" that is inside her, fearful its intensity might scare him. She can hardly believe when Saul motions to the table and says, "This is your space, Elly. You can come here whenever you want." When she hesitates, he insists that she be the first to sit down, the first to open a volume of the dictionary. She feels the book's weight, smells the new paper smell bought for her nose alone.

Eliza is amazed by what she sees inside. The dictionary's words are the exact size of those she has pictured lining the inside of her head, chest, and legs. The dictionary is her body's knowledge made manifest. So that, as Eliza reads the words, she feels as if she has done this before, is merely ghosting with her hand and eye what her brain has been doing all along.

They study for five hours each weekday and seven hours on weekends. It is not about rote memorization. Saul wants Elly to understand these words: their origins, their roots, their prefixes and suffixes. He presents the dictionary as a book worthy of commentary and discussion, a Torah of language.

When Eliza studies, she travels through space and time. In COUSCOUS, she can sense desert and sand-smoothed stone. In CYPRESS, she tastes salt and wind. She visits Africa, Greece, and France. Each word has a story: a Viking birth, a journey across the sea, the exchange from mouth to mouth, from border to border, until *æpli* is *apfel* is *appel* is APPLE, crisp and sweet on Eliza's tongue. When it is night and their studying complete, these are the words she rides into sleep. The voice of the dictionary is the voice of her dreams.

Miriam does not remember this, the first time she steals. She is exactly eight years and six months old. She has been brought to Berman Toys by Miss Vanderhooven to choose her half-birthday present. The Dutch nanny precedes a Swiss and follows a French, part of Melvin and Ruth's attempts to add an international flavor (No Germans need apply, so what if Hitler is dead?) to Miriam's continuing education. Miriam walks down the aisles as if in a trance, the sight of untouched toys filling her with profound well-being. If she could, she would spend every moment surrounded by the brand new. She loves to run her fingers down the surface of an unopened game, stroke the cellophane skin of a prepackaged baby doll. She loves the smell of freshly minted rubber and plastic, the factory cleanliness, the machine-bred sterility. When she chooses a three-story dollhouse with electric lights and an enclosed front porch it is not to pretend at future housewifery, but to arrange and rearrange the Happy Porter Family and their to-scale furniture into varying patterns of orderliness until she arrives at Perfectimundo.

Since the propitious hopscotch game and the revelation of the kaleidoscope, Perfectimundo has been Miriam's favorite word, state, and pastime. The toy store, in its factory-fresh pristinity, is Perfectimundo. Miriam's room—when she has aligned every last building block, squared every spine of every book, and evenly spaced every garment in her closet—is Perfectimundo. The front lawn covered in untrampled snow is Perfectimundo. Miriam cannot go to sleep until she is Perfectimundo, her body centered on the mattress, her head centered on the pillow, her sheets centered on the bed. Sometimes it takes Miriam a very long time to determine this to be the case.

Miss Vanderhooven is having the dollhouse rung up at the front desk when Miriam wanders into an aisle lined with buckets of nickel and dime toys: jacks and plastic soldiers, yo-yos and baby doll brushes. Miriam is drawn to a bin of Spalding rubber balls, bubblegum pink and large as her palm. One in particular beckons to her, is particularly Perfectimundo, lying as it is atop the others, illuminated by the overhead lights. Suddenly the truth becomes clear, as irrefutable as arithmetic: the ball is a part of her from which she was senselessly separated. Luck and instinct have combined to bring her to this aisle on just the day when her missing piece could make itself known.

She easily has enough change in her pocket to purchase the ball. If she wanted to, she could keep her pennies and give it to Miss Vanderhooven to buy and bag with the dollhouse. But the idea of having to pay for something already hers is much too silly to consider. Miriam's hand reaching out and slipping the ball into her pocket is as much a given as her beating heart. The ball tingles against her palm; she is filled with the same warmth as the moment of that first, perfectly thrown stone. And then, as quickly and intensely as the moment is born, it ends. When the ball enters her pocket, it exits her thoughts.

Later, when Miriam finds the ball in her pocket, she is genuinely surprised. Then she remembers. Even as Mr. Berman wished them a nice day, the ball was hiding in her dress. No one had said a thing. The memory confirms that the ball is important, a manifested sign of her special place in the world. Miriam puts the ball in a shoebox she lines with shelf paper. She places the box on the floor beneath her bed exactly below where her head rests on her pillow. Sometimes in dreams Miriam sees the ball grown large as a house, rolling over green hills or through fields of rustling wheat. Sometimes the ball takes the place of the sun, shining on her with a special pink light. Sometimes the ball intones her name, *Miriam Grossman,* over and over with a voice like a bell that shakes the world and tickles her insides.

Every night before bedtime, Miriam checks the box to assure herself that the ball is still there. After confirming this, she whispers her favorite P-word five times. From across the room, to someone like Miss Vanderhooven who entertains thoughts of introducing the lonely girl to Jesus' love (a notion that will get her fired when she presents Miriam with a rosary on her actual birthday), this looks like prayer.

If Aaron wants to pinpoint the moment things began to change he's got to look back, before the Sunday Saul brought newspapers to the breakfast table, to the day he gave Eliza a ride to the district bee. That is when suspicion first seeded itself, when he found himself secretly scrutinizing his sister at stoplights. He has never had reason to view her as a rival. Even the clamping of her baby fingers between his six-year-old jaws at the beginning of their acquaintance was more experiment than confrontation, an early attempt to understand what little sisters are made of. Though he can remember shared games in the den and imaginary journeys in the backyard, the six years since then have expanded significantly, making their mutual past feel twice as distant. From within his father's study, Eliza has been as much a nonentity as the rest of the world on the other side of the door.

Lately, that has begun to change. Since Eliza came home with the area trophy, Aaron has sensed her presence even from within the sanctuary of the study's walls. This has been less due to him than to Saul, who has started playing softer than usual to make sure their guitar music doesn't disturb Elly's studying. Sometimes Saul interrupts a song to ask Aaron how he thinks a certain word is spelled, refraining from playing again until he has consulted a dictionary.

So that when the piles of paper start to diminish in one corner, when a table and chairs appear where no table and chairs have been before, Aaron can't help but feel a creeping sense of doom. He had hoped he was overreacting, but since Monday there has been no guitar. For days, Aaron has been arriving at Saul's study at the appointed hour, guitar case in hand, but the door has been closed. If Aaron stays by the door long enough, he can hear them studying. Sometimes he stands there a long time.

On Thursday, Aaron decides he's just going to knock. Saul can get caught up in things, he can forget the time, for example the alarm clock every day to cue him to start dinner. His father just needs to be reminded. It's silly, really, the way Aaron has blown this out of proportion. It's his turn, that's all. Elly can understand that. Aaron practices what he's going to say.

"I just thought I'd remind you . . ." *No. It's like I'm blaming him.* "Hey, did you want to practice guitar today?" *Yeah.* Grabbing the guitar case and heading downstairs feels a lot like walking to the park knowing he'll be the eleventh man at the basketball game.

The door is the same as it ever was. For a few seconds Aaron just stands outside it, the sweat from his palm making the case handle slippery. He can hear Dad and Elly inside. He sets the guitar down and wipes his hand on his shirt. His smaller, younger self is yelling at him not to do it, not to knock unless it's an emergency 'cause that's what *Abba* says. *Abba,* Aaron's first Hebrew word, *Ima* never bringing a smile to Miriam's face the way *Abba* brought a smile to Saul's. Aaron swallows the saliva that's been flooding his mouth, brings his hand to the door.

It's an old rule, the no knocking rule. It was for when he was a kid and didn't know any better. This is not a big deal. It's about time he knocked on this door, it has been sixteen years already. Aaron can hear Saul's voice on the other side. Aaron knocks. The voice stops. The sound of a chair scraping and quick steps. Saul yanks the door open.

"What's wrong? What's happened?" Saul's face is flushed, his eyes wide with concern and Aaron knows that he has made a mistake.

"Uh, *Abba*?" *That sounds stupid.* "Dad. I was just wondering . . ." Aaron's voice trails off. He holds up the guitar case.

Saul is in emergency mode. He looks for blood or a broken bone, sniffs the air for signs of smoke. The flush fades, his eyes grow puzzled. "You're okay?"

Aaron nods vigorously, trying to convince himself. "Oh, yeah. I'm fine. I just, you know. We haven't played in a while." Aaron's voice is high, as though puberty never happened. The sense of entitlement that filled him upstairs in his room now trickles out in a thin, feeble stream.

Saul is confused. "Aaron, you know about the door. Elly and I—" He opens the door wider.

Eliza watches her brother come into view. Unlike Saul, she has been fully aware of the hour. On the first day, when it was time for guitar practice, she had gotten out of her chair, certain that their study session was over. Saul asked her what she was doing. Eliza heard steps outside the door, knew Aaron was waiting on the other side. "Just stretching," she had replied, guilt and glee competing for space in her heart. It wasn't as though Aaron couldn't practice by himself, she told herself, feeling like a thief.

So that now, when Aaron looks at her, it is very difficult for Eliza to look back.

"Aaron, you know how little time I have to prepare Elly for the nationals. This is a fantastic opportunity for her. I don't think it's too much to ask that you respect this door, do you?"

Aaron shakes his head. All the extra height from his growth spurt disappears. He is the size of a shoe.

Miriam enters stores two ways. When shopping, she leads with her upper body, all purpose and direction. She doesn't linger long enough to attract perfume spritzing. She looks straight ahead, as if her goal is perpetually in sight. She's the kind of shopper salespeople call a homing pigeon, from whom the only commission will be from whatever it is she came for, generally an item so inconsequential that they might as well leave her for the cashier.

All that changes when Miriam is a thief. She luxuriates in the store's atmosphere, lingering over a blue silk scarf, admiring a garnet stickpin. She stands still as prayer as she is anointed by the day's sample fragrance, drawing the floral scent in deep, reverential breaths. When a thief, Miriam is often mistaken for the ideal customer. Salespeople fight among themselves for the chance to ply her with a flattering smile and a honeyed "Can I help you?" Miriam is patient, tiring their enthusiasm by feigning slight interest in everything, committing to nothing. Eventually the salespeople demote her to the rank of window shopper, one among a legion of bored suburban housewives who comb the aisles daily, fantasizing about what will be theirs once their husbands start making more money.

Miriam sometimes spends hours combing through floor after floor, intent as a pig sniffing truffle. She's seeking what she is meant to find, the singular item waiting for her swift hand. She and this object are intimately joined, its discovery a matter of attuning herself to her body, sensing the size and shape of the internal gap meant to be filled.

Miriam treasures this inevitable moment of communion. Nothing is as certain as the instant the object reveals itself. She can practically feel the click as the internal dislocation is corrected.

Miriam has learned not to anticipate what she is meant to find. She once browsed a store for hours to discover that her intended was a set of ceramic corn cob holders. She has reclaimed a faux eelskin belt, a pair of plastic baby shoes, and a silk shirt, size 18. The very unpredictability of her quarry, its existence outside the confines of aesthetic and monetary value, confirms the nobility of her search. She is no petty thief. She is compelled by a force far superior to material gain.

The incident at the study door goes so utterly unremarked upon that if it weren't for the guilt-ridden look Eliza gives Aaron every dinner, it would almost be possible for Aaron to believe nothing happened. Aaron's first instinct is to work toward this erasure, striving toward a future that more closely resembles his past. But as Aaron puts increasing distance between himself and his fateful knock, he realizes something that makes this impossible. He no longer enjoys the guitar.

When Aaron first sits down to play post-study door, he has no reason to think it will be any different. He has often practiced for hours alone, past the endurable blister phase to the unendurable blister-bursting phase in an attempt to get a song right. In the past, he has loved getting lost in the music, going beyond time and the pain in his fingers to a world that is the sound of his guitar. But now, with the sound of Elly and his father rising through the air vents to his room, he can't keep his mind on the music. He finds himself thinking about the hangnail on his pinky, about the ambiguous color of his bedroom carpet. As Aaron's fingers struggle through a song, Aaron realizes that he hates bar chords, has never been able to do them properly. His father's assurance that inflexible fingers pose no impediment to playing is, if not an outright lie, the idealism of a man who has never dealt with inflexible fingers himself. Saul's fingers are ridiculously long and agile. They are fingers that Aaron realized Eliza inherited when he recently saw her fiddling with her dinner fork in an attempt to avoid looking at him. Aaron puts down the guitar. He tells himself he'll play later when he's in the mood. He never seems to be in the mood.

Approaching the synagogue doors the following Friday, Saul squeezes Aaron's shoulder as if nothing is different. Aaron wonders if Saul is ignoring the fact that he hasn't been playing or if his father actually hasn't noticed that the house has been guitar-free for an entire week. Neither option appeals.

Aaron claims his customary seat and flips to the front of his *siddur* to check the name. Every inside cover has a light blue bookplate with the words, "This prayerbook is dedicated to the memory of _____," or, "This prayerbook is dedicated in honor of _____." Weddings, bar mitzvahs, and births get "in honor of." Funerals get "to the memory of." Divorces don't get anything, but sometimes Aaron comes across an "in honor of" for an obsolete marriage, like the book for the Kaufmans who he heard split up because Mrs. Kaufman ran into her high school boyfriend in the grocery store and never came home again. Aaron considers these *siddurim* bad luck. Whenever he picks an "in honor of" for a marriage, he only keeps it if he knows the couple is still together.

Aaron snaps out of his siddur reverie to find himself in the middle of *L'cha Dodi*. His hard-wired knowledge of the service has taken him through two responsive readings and three prayers as his thoughts wandered. Though Aaron can identify a few Hebrew words, his knowledge of the language is largely limited to the ability to parse letters. Aaron realizes that there's no way for him to know he's welcoming in the Sabbath bride as the English translation claims. For all he knows, the entire congregation could be chanting *Green Eggs and Ham*. At the idea of Rabbi Mayer and George and Mrs. Schwartz all solemnly intoning, "Would you, could you, in a box?" Aaron almost loses it, has to stop singing to keep from laughing. Eliza notices this and turns. There was a time when Aaron might have let her in on the joke, but he only smiles distantly and stands with everyone else to recite the Shema. At the Silent Amidah, he doesn't even glance at Eliza, sitting down early and quietly enough to make it very clear that, tonight, she's playing Sheep on her own.

Aaron is still musing over his Dr. Seuss realization when he remembers his father's early lessons in consumer consciousness. Ever since Saul dissected a Snoopy Snow Cone Machine commercial for Aaron at age seven, Aaron has been aware of the manipulative powers of advertising. "Never buy a product just because you've seen it on TV," Saul instructed at an age at which recognizing characters on cereal boxes made leaving aisle three empty-handed tantamount to abandoning a friend. As a result, Aaron has grown to mid-adolescence with an eye for label reading. It is at the service's completion, while munching an *oneg* cookie, that Aaron realizes he's bought Judaism without consulting the side of the box.

Miriam has designed a special outfit, a collection of pockets concealed within an otherwise normal skirt, blouse, and coat. Pockets sewn into the blouse's sleeves serve for small items. The lining of the skirt doubles up into one giant pocket for larger ones. Inside the coat are pockets accessible through false seams lined with wire so that they may be pinched open and shut like change purses.

When Miriam has pocketed an item, she experiences the ideal pregnancy. There is no round-belly reminder of something inside, feeding upon her in order to grow. There are no sickening turns and kicks, proof of the stranger soon to emerge from between her legs. Though an only child, Miriam grew up knowing about her mother's not-borns: the boy with the misshapen heart, the girl with the tiny head. One was neither boy nor girl but a lump that grew at such frightening speed the doctors called it cancer and misdiagnosed death within a year. Miriam grew up seeing these almost-babies in her mother's eyes. Initially Ruth had to be coaxed into touching her baby girl, afraid of passing on to Miriam whatever had poisoned the others.

The first time Miriam's belly grows, her mind fills with visions of monsters: something premature and malformed, something late and soft-brained. After Aaron is born, Miriam's fear shifts toward herself. Breast-feeding Aaron, Miriam senses some vital part of herself escaping into his tiny, sucking mouth. She resents that her body must continue to give after nine previous months of suckling. She hates her breasts, grown voluptuous with milk. She ends breast feeding early, citing the work of an outdated child development specialist.

When Saul and Aaron are alone, Saul dips his pinkie into the bottle, offering his finger to his son until his skin is pruned from milk. Sometimes, when it is very late, Saul presses the bottle's bottom to his chest. Once, sitting like this, he awakens to the warm bottle pressing against him, moving in concert to the feeding rhythm of his milk-contented son.

"Amanuensis," Saul reads, poised above the word, the honeybee to its flower.

"Where's it from?" Eliza is already taking the word apart, dissecting the junctures between syllables, weighing each vowel and consonant on her tongue. She bets the word spells like it sounds; all the syllables stand out in her head instead of blending together.

"Where do you think it's from?" Saul asks with a smile, his eyes flitting between Eliza and the dictionary.

Eliza loves this game almost enough to forget that Aaron isn't really talking to her anymore. Saul turns the words inside out with her, spurring her to venture inside each one. Even though he holds the answer in his hand, it is like he is learning with her, the two of them traveling through time and across the world to trace a word's beginnings.

Amanuensis. All the -is words are usually the same. Eliza looks to Saul. He is waiting, entirely focused on her, time measured by the movement of her lips. Sometimes Elly takes longer than she needs just to see if he will keep waiting. He always does.

"Is it from Latin?"

Saul's face lights up. "Exactly! Now what do you think it means?"

"Is it some kind of disease?" *Some kind of awful skin thing. Like that boy in Ms. Paul's class who's always scratching.*

"Let's see," he says, peering into the dictionary. "*Manu-* means hand. It comes from a Latin phrase, *a manu,* meaning secretary. Amanuensis means someone who takes dictation or copies a manuscript, like a Torah scribe. Here's a riddle. What do you and a Torah scribe have in common?"

Eliza no longer minds that her father's riddles are never riddles but things he wants her to know. Sometimes she wishes he'd just tell her instead of making her guess, especially when it's something that she'd never know in a million years.

"Um . . . we're both Jewish?"

Eliza watches Saul's mouth for the slightest upward curve so that she can make it seem as if they are breaking into smiles at the same time.

"Well, yes, but you have something bigger in common, something that has to do with you being in the spelling bee." He looks at her like he actually expects her to know.

Eliza shrugs. After one failure, he always tells.

"Both spelling bees and Torah scribes share the idea that a word should be constructed perfectly or not at all. A little mistake and you're beeped off the stage. If a Torah amanuensis makes even one stray ink mark, he's got to start on a brand-new piece of parchment."

"It's called getting dinged out."

"Huh?"

It's gotten to the point where she expects to have to say things twice. She wonders if Aaron also had the problem of only being listened to when Saul expected something.

"When you mess up," Eliza repeats patiently. "They call it getting dinged out."

Saul nods, but he's already looking through the dictionary for the next word. Eliza reminds herself how lucky she is. Most kids have to study alone.

Aaron used to enter the synagogue at his father's side feeling like a prince beholding the kingdom he stood to inherit. But he's older now. Adults are no longer impressed by his ability to recite the service from memory. He can no longer fool himself into believing that Stacey Lieberman has or ever had a crush on him, especially since she got breasts and became an alternate on the pompon squad. Most bothersome, however, is the fact that after three years of patient waiting, Aaron's bar mitzvah experience has yet to repeat itself.

Aaron had not expected to commune with God on a regular basis. He knows that what he felt on the *bima* was an experience denied to many. But he had hoped that after becoming a man, Judaism-wise, he would occasionally be able to sense God's presence, even if only a pale glimmer of what he had felt as a bar mitzvah. Instead, compared to that magic moment three years before, the synagogue has become yet another place where he doesn't fit in. He's too old to want to be seen playing tag after *oneg* and too young to want to talk to the adults. And so, guitar gathering dust in the corner of his room, his father's study barred to him, Aaron decides to apply his father's lessons about advertising to religion. He decides to visit a church.

Aaron tells himself that his decision is an empirical one, that he will grow to appreciate his given religion by testing others. Lurking beneath his empirical spirit, however, is a thrilling sense of fear. Aaron cannot even begin to picture what would happen if his father found him out.

Christianity has always existed in Aaron's head as an unvariegated whole, Christian a handy, all-purpose term used to describe anyone for whom a cross signified more than a lower-case *t*. Suddenly, upon fingering Church in the yellow pages, Christianity explodes into a jigsaw of Apostolic, Baptist, Christian, Episcopal, Lutheran, Methodist, Pentecostal, Presbyterian, and Roman Catholic. Of them all, it's Roman Catholic that sparks Aaron's imagination.

Aaron knows about Catholics. Catholics don't just sit around and say prayers. Catholics stand and kneel. Catholics go to confession and take communion. Confession and communion have intrigued Aaron for some time, but until now seemed forever beyond his grasp. Aaron is torn between feeling like an intrepid explorer and an intractable sinner.

Aaron chooses a Catholic church in nearby Norristown. He considers disguising himself, briefly toys with the idea of dying his hair, but decides that a bleached-blond Jew will look even more conspicuous than a regular Jew and then there'd be the problem of explaining his new look to his father.

Aaron parks in the parking lot of a neighboring strip mall: a congregant could live in the area and recognize the car. He surveys the mall parking lot twice to assure himself he sees no one he knows, then as casually as possible exits the car and approaches the church. Halfway there, Aaron begins to worry that he left a car door unlocked. If the car gets stolen, he'll have to call someone and then will have to explain what he is doing at this strip mall when Huntingdon Valley has strip malls much bigger and nicer than this one. Except that Aaron always worries he has left a door unlocked, always checks, and always finds that he hasn't. If he turns around, it will just create further opportunities to be spotted. Aaron continues toward the church. And when he steps inside, his paranoia really kicks in.

The minute he sits down and takes a hymnal from the pew before him, Aaron expects a siren to go off with a mechanical voice that skreaks *JEW JEW JEW JEW* until the entire congregation turns and the priest shambles toward him in that slow but inevitable *Night of the Living Dead* way. Failing that, Aaron is certain all the standing and sitting and genuflecting at impossible-to-predict intervals will earn him scorn, especially since he doesn't even know what side to start crossing himself on, something he is sure Catholics are taught around the same time *mohels* are slicing off Jewish foreskins. But then, when Aaron incorrectly anticipates a kneel and a woman sitting near him actually turns and smiles, Aaron begins to think that maybe these Catholics are okay. Perhaps there is a reason this was the first brand of religion he picked to taste-test.

During the English prayers Aaron reads out loud with everyone else. His natural tendency is to say "Cheese and Rice" whenever the name of God's son comes up. It's what Saul instructed him to do during Christmas carols to avoid having to impugn his beliefs for the sake of a school winter recital or the Boy Scouts of America. But this isn't a holiday assembly, Aaron isn't singing the tenor part to "God Rest Ye, Merry Gentlemen," and his father is nowhere to be seen. It is a sunny morning. Faces and hands are patched in the saturated blues, reds, and greens of the church's stained glass windows. They bestow upon the congregation a Technicolor otherworldliness that has never graced Schwartzes, Liebermans, or Mayers. As Aaron intones the forbidden J-word immediately followed by the forbidden C, he looks toward the crucifix hanging behind the altar, about where the ark would be in a synagogue. He tries to imagine the thorns, the nails, and the crushing weight of the world's sins.

The big issue, of course, is whether or not to take communion. Since his decision to test-drive Christianity, Aaron has been doing some reading. He is alternately fascinated and disgusted by the wine-as-blood, bread-as-flesh concept. He also knows that even Catholics are supposed to have been baptized, confirmed, and recently penanced in order to receive the host, not to mention the little detail of believing that the blood and flesh they're consuming are those of the Messiah and the Son of God. And while Aaron has no desire to disrespect or blaspheme the Catholic faith, he feels that he has to do it all to get the full picture.

To distract himself from the fast-approaching big decision, Aaron fixates on the confessionals at the far end of the church. They remind him of telephone booths, which he realizes, in a way, they are. Once inside, via a priest instead of a wire, you get to talk to God. This is a comforting thought until Aaron pictures the terrifying way Saul's eyes bulge out when he gets angry. The idea of regularly causing that kind of reaction on a cosmic level is about as appealing as visiting the dentist knowing you have a jaw of rotting molars.

The front pews begin to empty out. The time has come. As Aaron exits his row, he reasons that it would be just as easy to turn left instead of right, to return to his car, and to forget he ever heard of St. Patrick Church. But then the same woman who smiled at him before smiles again. Aaron remembers his profound sense of mission when first deciding to give religion a second look. He turns right instead of left. He is Marco Polo, Christopher Columbus, and Lewis and Clark all rolled into one intrepid Jew ready to see if, when he reaches the front of the church, he will fall off the edge of the world.

Aaron's feet are shaking as he walks down the center aisle. If he wasn't holding onto each successive pew for support, he'd probably twist his ankle and then someone would take him to the nearest hospital and stay with him despite his protests until his father arrived looking fresh off the cover of *Hadassah* and then the shit would really hit the fan. The blood has drained from Aaron's head. He is seeing spots and hearing that buzzing sound he heard just before fainting at age eleven in anxious dread of the Presidential Fitness Test. Luckily, by the time Aaron's fear has grown taut as a trip wire, it is time for him to kneel.

He is certain the priest can tell. It's not that big a congregation. The man has heard these people's sins for years and years and there's a bond there, something you can't just fake because you're young and God-curious. While lightning is probably not about to strike him, it's entirely possible that the priest will take a long hard look at Aaron and pass him by. But he's here, he's on his knees, and the flesh and blood are two mouths away so he can't back out without looking just as bad. More importantly, like a wave cresting over Aaron's fear is an intense excitement, an electrical charge that has switched every pore and hair to the On position.

Aaron closes his eyes and opens his mouth. As he waits for the wafer, he visualizes scenes from the New Testament. For Aaron, this means recalling the 7 A.M. puppet shows he used to watch on television for lack of Sunday morning cartoons. And so, with the father two open mouths away, Aaron pictures Jesus as a low-budget marionette, standing between two cardboard pillars, preaching to an audience of hand puppets with googly eyes.

Because his eyes are closed, the moment the host is placed on Aaron's tongue has all the intensity he hoped for, the surprise of unexpected contact sending warm tingles down his spine. However, as his saliva starts to work and the thrill of initial contact fades, the stale breadness of it hits. This isn't helped by the wine, which is actually worse than Manischewitz, which he didn't think was possible. The idea of finding God here dissolves with the wine-soaked communion wafer, turning to soft mush in his mouth.

Aaron stays for the rest of the service. His initial disappointment that the service is not in Latin fades as he realizes that Latin would pose the same parsing problem as Hebrew. At the service's end, he leaves through a side entrance to avoid shaking the priest's hand. He feels like a game show contestant who has to leave with the set of dish towels instead of the new car because he picked Door Number One instead of Door Number Three. It's as he is nearing the parking lot that Aaron realizes God's inherent value is reflected in the fact that there are so many doors to choose from.

Saul unknowingly gifts Miriam with a rationale for her lifelong acquiring habit midway through their courtship. It takes the form of an impromptu lesson after they have made love. Saul is on his side facing Miriam, trying to keep her in his bed until she grows too impressed with him or too tired to leave for the night. The white sheet is a stark contrast to the dark hairs curling tightly against Saul's chest, which continue to surprise Miriam long after his naked body is no longer novel. Clothed, Saul gives the impression of a smooth-chested man, his intellectualism surely having defeated his animal nature long ago.

"The mystics believe that in the beginning of the world God's Divine Light, containing all that is good, was enclosed in sacred vessels," Saul whispers, one hand cupping Miriam's breast, the other stroking her belly and gliding gradually downward. "But because there was already sin in the world, these vessels could not contain the Light and shattered into countless pieces. The Light was dispersed and the shards fell upon the world, becoming poverty, hatred, cruelty, and all the other forms injustice takes. According to the mystics, it is our job to locate these shards and to mend them through good deeds, so that God's light can be whole again. This is called *Tikkun Olam,* or the fixing of the world."

It is a concept Saul has described in similar words and with similar motions to previous lovers, though generally in an attempt to get them into bed and not to keep them there. When Miriam's face lights up, Saul has no idea it is because his words have revealed to her the reason behind that first pink rubber ball and all the objects to follow. Miriam realizes she is a broken vessel, pieces of her scattered everywhere. She has been finding these pieces, in their many forms, and bringing them together so that she can be whole again. Miriam can feel Saul's words falling into place inside her. She knows then and there that they will marry.

Saul had been hoping Miriam would stay the night but had not dreamed they would make love again. As they do, he has no idea that his words are the reason, that by opening herself up to him she is reclaiming her newest missing piece.

Aaron is in the library, ostensibly studying for the SAT, but actually reading *Eastern Religions* from behind a copy of *Sports Illustrated.* Though he knows Catholicism is just one color in the veritable Christian rainbow, he has decided against Christianity. In addition to the Son of God factor, which a lifetime of Judaism has made difficult to swallow, Aaron has trouble accepting that life is merely a testing ground for heaven or hell. It's too much like a video game, proceed to the next level. The proverbial nail in the Christian coffin is Aaron's realization that, in a country of shopping mall Santas and plastic manger scenes, everyone is Christian by default. Even people who know he's Jewish are surprised to learn there's no tree in his living room come December. Switching to a religion already assumed of him would feel too much like climbing onto a diving platform to jump off rather than dive.

Even the words "Eastern religion" are alluring to Aaron. They feel like a tropical island or a far-flung mountain range which requires several layovers and a spectrum of transportation to reach. Aaron has decided he will fly, he will sail, he will ride camelback, but he will reach Eastern religion. He will dip his toes in and, maybe, he will take a swim.

As Aaron reads on, he becomes so engrossed that he allows the *Sports Illustrated* to drop an inch or two, he stops tapping out a frenetic rhythm with his left sneaker on the carpet and frees his lower lip from the clutches of his nervous teeth. It is as if his entire life up to this point has prepared him for this book. His too pale, too skinny body, the grade school bullying, and the unforgettable moment at his bar mitzvah all fit into a larger plan. The outer world is a fiction. His own body, with all its failings, is immaterial. The spark of True Self lies within, an essence of the divine shared by everyone. Perhaps it was True Self he recognized on the *bima* three years ago. Perhaps that moment was a brief glimpse into what could be his if he found the right path. Perhaps the path begins with this book. Perhaps, like Buddha, he will experience enlightenment. Perhaps through *karma* and *bhakti* he can achieve liberation. Perhaps he should figure out the differences between these religions so they stop blending together, Buddhindutaoconfusedism, inside his head.

Eliza knows they whisper about her behind her back. She's gotten caught a couple times studying words when she was supposed to be doing math worksheets or reading history. The first time, Ms. Bergermeyer is amused and pats Eliza on the head, suggesting that she budget her time. After that, Bergermeyer starts taking Eliza's spelling sheets away and sending her home with notes for Saul to sign. Saul advises Eliza not to let spelling interfere with her schoolwork, but as far as Elly is concerned the approaching national bee requires that she adjust her priorities.

She gets better at hiding her word sheets. She can make it appear as if she's listening to Ms. Bergermeyer drone on about the life of the cell when she's actually looking at h-words. She starts spending her recesses under a tree near where the swings used to be. Sometimes Sinna Bhagudori joins her there and they review the words together.

"It's good practice for when I start studying for the PSATs," Sinna explains, seeming, if not enthusiastic, then pleasantly resigned.

Since Eliza won the area finals, Sinna has been known to save Eliza a seat at a lunch. The table is occupied by serious children who discuss the pros and cons of sharing homework and how to protect their test answers without really seeming like they are. All of them want to be doctors or lawyers or both. They eat healthy, balanced lunches brought from home in which dessert is invariably a piece of fruit, making Eliza feel the need to apologize for her occasional pudding cup. If Eliza eats with them more than once a week, the gravity they attach to every aspect of their lives begins to weigh her down.

The week before the national bee, a reporter and a photographer arrive at school. They seem disappointed to learn that Eliza doesn't play an instrument or participate in any sports, isn't in Girl Scouts or 4-H, and doesn't know what she wants to be when she grows up. They settle for a picture of Eliza with Ms. Bergermeyer and Dr. Morris at the school entrance, teacher and principal posed beside Eliza like fishermen showing off the season's record-breaking tuna.

On an evening when Saul is teaching an adult education class at the synagogue and Eliza is studying alone, Aaron goes into the den. He isn't actually interested in watching TV. He cranks the set loud enough that Eliza will either have to close the study door or ask him to turn it down. He really wants her to ask him to turn it down.

He feigns nonchalance as Elly enters the room, fakes total absorption in a "Three's Company" rerun featuring Don Knotts, whose eyes give him the creeps. He wants Elly to stand in the doorway while he continues to ignore her. He wants her to sound self-righteous so that he can deliver the speech he's been practicing, the one in which he tells her how stupid spelling is and how she's turning herself into a performing monkey just to get Dad's attention. But instead, Elly walks quietly into the room and sits next to him on the couch, sliding her leg next to his the way she used to when she was small.

"Aaron?" she says in a quiet voice that cuts through the sound of the laugh track even though he's got the volume at 6. "Why don't you play guitar anymore?"

Aaron opens his mouth and then closes it again. He sometimes looks at the guitar case in his room and forgets what's inside. He can still picture Eliza at the area finals, the look of utter joy on her face as they handed her the trophy.

"I don't know," he answers. "Why?"

"I was just wondering," she says, wishing he would turn toward her.

Aaron keeps his eyes on the rerun. "Dad's a better musician."

"He's done it longer," she replies even though she thinks Aaron is right.

Aaron shakes his head. "My fingers are too stiff. I can't really do bar chords."

They sit in silence. Suzanne Somers roller-skates through the apartment in a bathing suit.

Eliza talks to the TV. "Um, Aaron—"

Aaron is surprised at the calmness of his voice. "I don't have a gift for music, Elly. It was just something to do. It's no big deal."

Elly tries to catch Aaron's eye, but he is too intent on the TV screen. She leaves feeling as though she doesn't deserve what he has given her. Aaron is amazed by how easy it was to give.

In Eliza's dream she is taking her seat with the other national contestants when a voice rings out through the auditorium. The auditorium is Beth Amicha on a gargantuan scale, its *bima* reaching twenty feet into the air. The spelling contestants are seated across it, numbered placards attached to prayer shawls hanging around their necks. Elly cannot see to the back of the room, which is lined with endless rows of chairs. The spectators have small, predatory mouths filled with unnaturally sharp teeth.

"Number 59," the voice booms, seeming to emanate from everywhere at once. *"Number 59."* The room, which had been pounding with noise, is suddenly quiet. It is the silence of Moses approaching the burning bush, of the sealed ark afloat upon the rising flood.

Eliza realizes that everyone is staring at her. The faces of her fellow spellers are featureless except for glinting eyes. Eliza senses their impatience. By remaining in her seat she has stopped the grand mechanism of the bee, which is straining to carry the rest of them forward.

Eliza knows the inevitability of what is about to happen. Ever since she first rose from her seat in Ms. Bergermeyer's classroom she has felt defeat brush past her on its way to someone else. Each of its passings sent a ticklish chill down her spine, leaving a stone in her stomach. Looking into the eyes of the other spellers, she knows that her time has arrived.

Eliza rises from her seat. The weight of her body has doubled. Her footsteps pound and echo against the stage. The distance to the microphone stretches and stretches until it is longer than Eliza's memory of why this journey began. Her vision narrows until she faces a dark unending passage thick with the smell of her sweat. Then the light appears. Eliza quickens her pace. The weight lifts. She is sure she is nearing the sun itself. For a brief moment the pure joy of having reached her goal overwhelms her. Relief salves her body. Then she realizes where she is.

She is at the edge of the *bima,* the epic distance between microphone and empty chair now absurdly small. The sun is gone, transformed into a spotlight. The silence is leaden. A single sound rips the air. It is at once fragile and vicious, the almost ticklish sting of a sharpened razor first slicing into skin.

Ding.

Eliza's legs begin to tremble. The blood rushes from her head. Her number is torn from her neck and she is tossed off the *bima* into a teeming sea of heads and hands, where her mouth is held open, her old teeth are ripped out, and a set of smaller, sharper teeth is shoved in.

Aaron is the only small person in the front lobby of the funeral home, which is sparsely populated by men who look uncomfortable in their suits. There is a fountain in the middle of the room with a cement angel trickling water from his mouth, a sound that makes Aaron have to pee. He wants to tell his dad this, but even though Saul is holding his hand very tightly, Aaron is pretty sure he's been forgotten. When people come over, they keep saying, "You're his son, aren't you?" and it takes Aaron a few times to realize they aren't talking to him. They say, "You look just like him," or "I haven't seen you since you were a pup," to which Saul nods and grips Aaron's hand even tighter.

A man with jowls and shiny black shoes says something to Saul about a viewing. For a moment Aaron thinks they're going to see a movie that will explain everything about his mysterious dead grandfather, but then it is just him and Saul and the shiny-shoes man walking down a hallway and Aaron gets a bad feeling in his stomach that has nothing to do with the fact that he really, really has to pee.

"Dad," he whispers, because this seems like the kind of place where only whispering is allowed, "where are we going?"

Saul answers in a strange, tight voice that Aaron has never heard before. "We're going to say goodbye to your grandfather."

Aaron does not like this idea. He does not like the idea of saying goodbye to a dead person, especially one to whom he has never even said hello. He pictures a big room with a chair and his dead grandfather sitting in it. He pictures having to shake his dead grandfather's hand.

"Dad, why do we have to say goodbye?" and now Saul's lips are pressed together so hard all the red has gone out of them.

"Because—" Saul says and then stops. The man in the shoes guides them into a small, silent room with a curtain at its front. When Saul squeezes Aaron's hand again, Aaron squeezes back. Saul looks down at Aaron with teary eyes. Aaron realizes that the whole reason he has been brought to Cleveland is to help his dad in this room. He wants to tell his father that it's okay. Together they will shake the dead man's hand. But by the time Aaron starts to try to say these things, they are already walking toward the curtain.

As soon as Aaron sees his grandfather in the coffin he feels stupid for thinking he'd be sitting in a chair because of course a dead person would be in a coffin. The skin of his grandfather's face looks loose, as though it is made of slightly melted wax. Aaron briefly wonders if it's fake.

But Aaron knows it can't be fake because his dead grandfather looks exactly like his dad as an old dead person, which is much scarier than the idea of his dead grandfather sitting in a chair. Aaron's dead grandfather has Saul's nose and eyebrows and lips and maybe even eyes but the eyes are closed, thank goodness, so there's no way to know. But now Aaron is clearly picturing his dead grandfather opening his eyes and revealing Dad eyes in a dead grandfather face. So that when Saul leans over the coffin Aaron is positive that it will be his grandfather *and* his father who are dead and he starts peeing.

He is crying and he is peeing and he is pulling on his father's hand, but he is not making a sound because this is a funeral home. He doesn't want to make his dad any madder than he is sure to be already since Aaron was brought here to help and he isn't helping at all. But when Saul turns and sees what has happened, his face looks grateful. Just for a second. Maybe so fast that Saul doesn't even know it himself. But Aaron does. Faster than Aaron thought possible, they are out of the room with the coffin and in a bathroom to clean up. The man with the shiny shoes lends Aaron a pair of pants that smell a little funny but fit just fine. And when they go back to the room, the curtain is open and the coffin is closed and the men in their uncomfortable suits are there and neither Aaron nor his dad ever sees his dead grandfather again.

Even though it's days before she's due to get on the plane, Eliza is packing. She's got every piece of clothing she owns on her bed but keeps returning to her drawers for the perfect shirt. She doesn't know what she wants the shirt to look like, whether it's supposed to make her look pretty or smart or cool. She just knows she doesn't have it. So far, she's managed to pack underwear and socks and the dress she'll wear for the actual competition. It's not a great dress, but it's the only one she has that she doesn't feel stupid in. She would much rather wear her velour pants, but the spelling bee rules specify that girls are to wear dresses during the competition. Which is why it's even more important that she have the perfect shirt, so that she can wear it with her velour pants when she's not wearing the dress to show what she's really like.

"Mom?"

Miriam is filing her nails in the bedroom while sorting laundry into light and dark loads with her feet. The television is tuned to "Jeopardy," but Miriam doesn't notice that the horizontal hold isn't right, is only listening to the sound.

"Eliza, Saul said he'd do the laundry—What is the French Revolution?—when he got back from class, so why don't you bring your hamper in here and add your clothes to these baskets?"

"Sure, Mom. Um, would it be okay if we went shopping for a shirt—"

"Who is Stanford White?"

"—before Dad and I go to D.C.? I don't really have anything to go with my black pants."

"What is the cotton gin?"

Since the kaleidoscope incident Miriam has kept her distance. She is embarrassed both by what she had imagined was possible between herself and her daughter and her quick rejection of that possibility. As consolation, Miriam has been telling herself that Eliza is more Saul's than hers, focusing on Eliza's straight hair and long fingers for proof. She knows that Saul has done a wonderful job helping prepare Eliza for the nationals, displaying a selflessness Miriam knows she lacks, but she cannot help wondering how it might have been different. Miriam briefly pictured herself and Eliza poring over word sheets together, matching expressions of deep concentration on their faces. In these imaginings, Miriam focused on the shared slope of their noses, the common curves of their mouths.

"You want something special for the trip?" Miriam asks.

Alex Trebek informs America that he'll be right back after this commercial break and Miriam unconsciously nods in response. Miriam is situated between Eliza and the TV, her head framed by the glowing screen. Things with her mother have seemed different lately. Eliza can't help but feel it has something to do with the kaleidoscope. She knows she messed that up. She should have been more excited, even if it only was a little kid's toy. Thinking back on it, Eliza is pretty sure that it's the only time she's ever seen her mother look disappointed, which makes Eliza feel even worse about the whole thing.

"You should be a contestant," Eliza says.

Miriam shakes her head. "I can only answer the academic questions."

"But you get all of those right. Besides, if you sneak me on with you, I could help you with the other ones. I could hide behind the podium thing and whisper answers."

"Elly"—which really grabs Eliza's attention because Miriam never calls her that—"when you're trying to think of a spelling word, what happens?"

Eliza stays silent for so long that Miriam thinks her daughter didn't hear her, but that isn't it. Eliza is quiet because she wants to get this right, wants to make sure that, this time, she gives her mother what she wants.

"It's kind of hard to explain," says Eliza and Miriam nods, ignoring the $600 Constitution question in favor of her daughter's voice. "I start out hearing the word in my head in the voice of whoever said it to me. Then the voice changes into something that's not their voice or my voice. And I know when that happens it's the word's voice, that the word is talking to me. Everything else becomes quiet. Even if there's other noise, I don't hear it, which is one of the reasons I keep my eyes closed, because otherwise it's too weird seeing things around me and not hearing them. But the main reason I keep my eyes closed is so that I can see the word in my head. When I start hearing the word's voice, the letters start arranging themselves. Sometimes it takes awhile for them to look right, but when they do, they stop moving and I know that that's the right spelling. So then I just say what I'm seeing and that's it."

Eliza looks at her mother, bracing herself once again for her mother's disappointment. But instead Miriam is looking like what Eliza said is exactly right.

"You know," Miriam says, "I have a box of clothes from when I was about your size in the attic. I can't remember what's up there, but there might be something you'd like."

Eliza's face lights up.

Miriam forgoes Final Jeopardy to climb into the attic with Eliza where, inside a steamer trunk, amid the scents of mothballs and dust, Eliza finds a shirt with big green buttons and her mother's name sewn into the collar. In the privacy of her room, Eliza dons the shirt, pressing the collar into her neck until she is sure she can feel each individual letter of her mother's name upon her skin.

For dinner, Saul makes noodles shaped like letters and Aaron has to struggle to keep his appetite. Eliza spends the meal spelling out increasingly longer words, for which Saul lets her dig through the pasta bowl to find what she needs. When necessary she improvises, biting off the curve of a P to form an F, turning an N sideways to form a Z.

Aaron's legs hurt from an hour of trying to assume the lotus position. He finally gave up and settled for Indian style, very aware of the fact that his robe was unable to cover his crossed legs and that if someone were to enter his room they would get an eyeful of him sitting on his floor with his pubic hair, which no one in his family has yet seen and which Aaron would like to keep that way. This recurring thought was not helpful in his efforts at meditation.

According to Buddhism, Aaron's pubic concerns are illusory, but it's difficult for him to get such thoughts to act as insubstantial as Buddhism claims them to be. Not that he wouldn't prefer it. Aaron can think of nothing more attractive than merging with a spiritual continuum by sloughing off his corporeal self. Aaron pictures himself under a huge bristle brush. There is no pain, only a feeling of release as his skin, muscle, and bones are worn away to reveal a shining light like a small sun.

"Earth to Aaron. Come in, Aaron."

Aaron realizes he has been sitting at the table with his fork midway to his mouth.

"So, how about it?" Saul continues, smiling at his son's abstraction. "You think you can survive a week without me and Elly?"

They leave for the nationals tomorrow. It will be the first time in over ten years that Saul hasn't taught his weekly adult education class or led the Shabbat service.

"It won't be that much different, really," Aaron says, immediately wishing he hadn't.

Eliza blushes.

"We'll be back in no time," Saul says as if he hasn't heard.

Miriam is putting Eliza to bed, having interrupted her regularly scheduled magazine reading to do so. Eliza has asked for a glass of water and an extra blanket just to prolong the rare event. For the first time in her life, she wishes she had long hair so that she could ask her mother to brush it.

"Are you all packed?"

"Yes." Under the covers, Eliza is sliding her legs back and forth to soak up the sheet's coolness. A moss-green suitcase Saul retrieved from the attic stands packed beside the door. Eliza has checked her alarm clock three times. The suitcase is made of worn, soft leather that looks like it has traveled.

Miriam sits on Eliza's bed, the edge of the mattress sloped with her weight. Eliza surreptitiously slides her leg over until her knee rests against her mother's calf, only the bed sheet between them.

"I thought I recognized that suitcase," Miriam says. "It's part of a set my parents bought for me when I was starting boarding school. I didn't know I still had it."

Eliza looks at the suitcase with renewed interest. She tries to imagine Miriam at her age but can only manage her mother's adult head on a ten-year-old's body. Eliza assumed her mother had attended a public school like her. She realizes that everything she knows about her mother's childhood—a kaleidoscope, a shirt with green buttons, and a suitcase—she has learned in the past few weeks.

"Were you scared?" Eliza asks, the question one of thousands filling Eliza's brain.

"When?"

"At boarding school."

Miriam looks at the suitcase for a long time. Eliza tells herself the longer she stays silent, the more worthy she is of receiving her mother's answer. But when Miriam turns back toward Eliza, it is as if they have already moved on to another topic.

"This is what you do," Miriam says. "When the plane takes off and the pressure starts building up in your ears, plug your nose and gently blow. Like this." Miriam pinches her nose. "Until your ears pop. Then swallow. Gum keeps saliva in your mouth. Start chewing as soon as the plane starts down the runway. Swallow as often as you can. Swallowing might equalize the pressure on its own and you won't even need to plug your nose. Landing is usually worse than taking off." She reaches into her pocket. "Here." She hands Elly a pack of cherry Bubble Yum.

Eliza resists the urge to put the gum under her pillow, puts it beside the alarm clock instead.

"I'm proud of you," Miriam says. After moving the covers back and forth as if she's trying to even them out, she tucks Elly in.

"I love you, Mom," Elly says, soft, only after Miriam has turned out the light.

An electronic billboard fronting the hotel doors spells out WELCOME NATIONAL SPELLING BEE CONTESTANTS AND THEIR FAMILIES in white lights, letter by letter. Saul has a porter take a picture of himself and Eliza standing beneath it. At the moment the shutter clicks, W-E-L-C-O-M-E N-A-T- blazes above their heads.

The hotel lobby is glass and faux marble, lined with trees containing live birds. One uniformed man strides back and forth with a moist cloth, removing bird shit from the lustrous surfaces upon which it lands. Light-studded glass elevators emerge from a blue-lit pond in which real fish swim beneath fake lily pads.

Only in the elevator does the realness of what is happening hit. Elly and Saul share the elevator with another child and his mother, the boy clutching the same welcome packet Elly was given at the reception desk.

"What's your number?" the boy asks.

"I don't know," Eliza says. The hotel is huge. She feels like she's in line for the twirly rides at the annual Boys and Girls Club carnival, knows what she has been eagerly anticipating will make her sick to her stomach now that it has arrived.

"I'm 82. Last year, I was 132. It's interesting, because 8 minus 2 equals 6 and the digits comprising 132, multiplied, also equal 6."

"We think it's good luck," says the mother. She is wearing a grinning bee lapel pin.

Eliza opens her welcome packet. "I'm 59," she says.

"Oh, it's very lucky to have a two-digit number," says the mother. "The finalists are usually two digits."

"Aren't there only 151 contestants?" Saul asks. "There will be more two-digit numbers than anything else."

"Exactly!" says the mother.

Elly is very impressed by the complimentary fruit basket containing oranges wrapped in red cellophane and a preprinted greeting with her name handwritten in the blank between *Welcome* and *!* The bathroom has a towel warmer and a shower head with adjustable settings. The fresh paper sash across the toilet seat, announcing sanitization, reminds Eliza of her mother.

Her bed is the size of her parents' and is firmer than her bed at home. She resists the urge to jump on the mattress, instead sitting on its edge with her best grown-up posture. She looks at herself in the mirror over the bureau, behind the drawers of which she finds nothing. She decides she definitely looks older than fifth grade. Her face could maybe pass for eighth now that she's a national spelling contestant with her own room in a hotel. If only she were a little taller.

Saul has come in from the adjoining bedroom. Though the rooms are identical, Eliza was pleased when Saul allowed her to choose the room with the bad print of a sailboat rather than the bad print of a girl in a long white dress.

"How does it feel to be in a grand hotel?"

Eliza raises her chin in what she thinks is a dignified manner, suppresses her giggle. "It feels very nice," she says in her most grown-up voice, imagining a closet full of evening gowns and shoes with narrow straps that circle her ankles.

Saul sits on the bed and hands Eliza a map of D.C. "Look at this."

Eliza unfolds the map until it covers her lap and drapes her legs. She's not sure what she's supposed to look for. Then she starts reading the street names.

"Pretty neat, huh?" Saul is wearing Eliza's favorite grin, the one that makes him look like a kid instead of a grownup.

"Are they all here?" She traces her finger along the lines of the streets, trying to get a sense of them through her skin.

{ 100 }

Saul places his arm around his daughter's shoulders. "Most of them. You've got to admit it's a pretty perfect place to have a spelling bee."

Eliza looks at the city laid out before her. C Street. K Street. U Street. Practically every letter of the alphabet is represented. From the shape of each on the map, its straightness or curve, Eliza tries to see a little of what each letter has revealed to her—its consonantness or vowelness, its sturdiness or unpredictability. The city is a reflection of her own body and the words contained within it. She lets out a breath she had not known she was holding. She's got the map on her lap, her father by her side, and her mother's green-buttoned shirt. She's not afraid of anything.

The first night of Saul's absence, Miriam marches into their bedroom at 3 A.M. without avoiding the squeaky sections of floor, turns on the light, and closes the door behind her with an audible click. She is tipsy with the freedom of not having to tiptoe, the cause of such time-honored considerations hundreds of miles away. She hums as she brushes her teeth, leaving the door between the master bath and bedroom ajar. When she is done, she throws herself onto the bed so hard the headboard knocks against the wall. She cannot remember the last time she went to bed naked. She stretches her arms and legs until she is a giant X obliterating his side and hers, marking the spot as her own.

When Miriam awakens, she forgets at first the freedom of the night before, sits up carefully to avoid setting off the box springs. Looking to her left and seeing the smooth expanse of sheet where Saul isn't, she remembers. She feels like her insides have been recalibrated. Her heart beats a little looser. Her lungs stretch to take in more air. Saul's absence has served as a trigger for something growing inside her, waiting for the right moment to make itself known.

She almost doesn't put on her work clothes, overcomes the urge to slip into pants instead of a skirt. *If I wore pants all the time, I wouldn't have to shave.* She is surprised by the thought. Miriam has always resisted Saul's attempts to persuade her to be "natural." The hair on her legs and under her arms is particularly thick and dark and has, from its first appearance when she was twelve, made her feel unclean. She feels the same squeamishness toward the sparse dark hairs around her nipples. She is unsure whether they grew in during her first pregnancy or if she merely noticed them then. She did not even attempt to put Aaron to her breast until she had plucked them, her natural disinclination toward breast feeding magnified into revulsion by the image of a hairy breast giving suck to a child.

But this feeling born of a night's solitude has made the need to shave less urgent. *Forget it,* says her looser heart. *You've got more important things to do.* Miriam strokes the very beginnings of black stubble along her shins, taking pride in her body's persistence. By silently vowing to free herself from the bonds of Lady Bic, she feels she is proving her loyalty to a higher cause, her mission demanding the rejection of such petty bodily concerns in favor of a larger goal. *Tik-kun O-lam, Tik-kun O-lam,* beats her heart's steady rhythm.

Still naked, Miriam opens the blinds, allowing the early morning sun to warm her skin. She wants to feel this day on her body, wants every part of her to feel this new phase of her lifelong mission. She remembers a girl who held a pink rubber ball in her hand. She remembers a perfectly thrown stone. She is ready to heed their new call.

The four days preceding the competition itself are packed with edifying tours of the Smithsonian, the White House, and the Library of Congress, followed by carefully engineered ice cream socials, barbecues, and beach parties at which getting-to-know-you games are played. Eliza, along with her fellow contestants, wears her name tag at all times and is paired with a different speller at each planned event, an accelerated summer camp experience in which she is encouraged to forget that in a few days' time she will be pitted against her new friends until only one is left standing.

In the evenings she and Saul study. Saul has brought the three-volume dictionary, packing it in his carry-on to guard against lost luggage. Eliza doesn't like the sense of urgency their sessions have gained. At home, Saul's absorption in each phase of their studying erased all sense of an outside world or an end goal. Now Eliza feels her father is forever looking past her in anticipation of something bigger. Eliza cannot help but remember she is here to mount a stage with over one hundred other children, a roomful of strangers counting on her to make a mistake.

Saul is torn. Part of him thinks he should continue as if word lists and spelling bees are all that matter. There will be plenty of time after the nationals to reveal his true intent. At this point, new techniques and ideas might only distract, possibly causing more harm than good. He cannot risk deterring Elly from what he knows to be her true calling.

On the other hand, what better time than now to provide her with new tools? More than ever, Saul feels she is ready to receive what he has to give. The nationals present the perfect opportunity to demonstrate her incredible potential.

Eliza stands at one end of her hotel room, Saul at the other, the TV volume turned up. Both bedside lamps have been directed toward Eliza's face to simulate the lights of television cameras.

"Number 59, your word is GEGENSCHEIN," Saul says in the most officious voice he can muster.

The television is tuned to "That's Incredible." Cathy Lee Crosby is interviewing a man who has just eaten a chain saw.

"Would you pronounce it again?"

"Gay-gun-shine."

"What's its derivation?"

"It comes from the German."

"Can I have a definition?"

"It's a faint, glowing spot in the sky, exactly opposite the position of the sun."

Eliza nods, begins to chew her lip.

"Elly?"

Eliza looks up. "I thought you said you weren't going to say anything this time. You're being the judge."

"I know, I know, just this once. Tell me what you're doing."

"I'm trying to figure out the word."

Elly isn't happy with the TV, isn't happy that she isn't sure how to spell this one. She doesn't know what her father wants, only that she isn't giving it to him. There's a movie she wanted to watch on HBO, they don't have pay stations at home, but Saul wouldn't let her, insisted there'd be plenty of time for movies after the bee.

"How are you trying to figure it out?"

"What do you mean, how? I'm thinking! Okay? I'm trying to think."

Laughter and applause from the television. It's been like this every night. A look comes into Saul's eyes when they finish dinner and he stops paying attention to anything she says until she suggests they start studying. She's the one who has to suggest it. There are other kids who don't have to study at all. One girl's father even took away her word sheets, told her it was more important that she enjoy herself.

Saul turns the volume on the set way down.

"Don't," he says.

Eliza has stopped looking at him. "Don't what?"

Saul smiles his mysterious smile, the one Eliza is growing to hate. "Don't think," he says.

Eliza blinks back tears and bites the inside of her cheek. "I don't know what you mean." She wonders if Saul is ever like this with Aaron, if maybe her brother secretly treasures his newfound freedom.

Saul crosses the room, squatting so that he and Eliza are at eye level, and places his hands on his daughter's shoulders.

"You *do* know," he says. "You're stuck on this one, aren't you?"

Eliza nods, frustration written in the lines of her face.

Saul's voice is calm. The time has come.

"Thinking is good to try at first, and it will work with a lot of words, but you're going to get words like this one where thinking doesn't cut it. This is a tough word, Elly. It makes sounds that could be spelled a lot of ways."

Elly nods again, has no idea where Saul is trying to lead her.

"You might not know this particular word, Elly, but you know all the letters in it. You know them."

"So?" Eliza can hear laughter in the hallway. She wishes herself to the source of the sound, to anywhere but this hotel room.

"So?" Saul replies, a huge grin on his face. "So let the letters do the work for you!"

"I don't know what you mean," Eliza says, voice shaky. For the first time, her father's face looks ugly, like something she would like to wipe clean.

Saul sits Eliza on the bed. "Elly, honey, I know it's getting late and you're probably tired, but just listen to what I'm saying and then we'll stop for the night, okay? I'm going to suggest something new, something we've never done before. You've done a super job studying the words and their derivations. I'm amazed by how much you've been able to learn. But time has been short, Elly, and it's been impossible for us to study everything we would have liked. Because of that, you're going to come across words for which all you've learned about suffixes and prefixes and etymologies will be useless. And when that happens, I want you to try something special. I want you to try opening yourself up to the letters. The letters can lead you to the word if you let them. They have a power all their own. Take *gegenschein*. What letter does it start with?"

"G." She hates that the more frustrated she gets, the calmer he becomes, hates that when she wants to shake things up he talks like everything in the world is in its place.

"Right. Start with G. I'm going to turn the television back up, which we are going to pretend is the sound of the audience, and which you need to try to block out. I want you to go back to the other side of the room, and I'm going to be the judge again. I want you to open yourself up to G, Elly. Let G tell you what comes next. And then, when it tells you, let the next letter show you what comes after that."

Elly knows that if she doesn't at least pretend, her father is going to keep her at this no matter how late it gets. She walks back to her spot in the room and closes her eyes.

"Gegenschein," Saul intones from the other end of the room.

In her head, Elly is standing alone on the Independence Ballroom stage, chewing three pieces of Bubble Yum at once. She keeps swallowing, but nothing happens.

"Gay - gun - shine," Eliza says. "G . . ." She pictures a G with narrow eyes and an unfriendly mouth. *G for the gerbil in second grade that ate its babies.* " . . . E . . ." *I before E except after C or when pronounced "ay" as in neighbor and weigh.* " . . . I . . ." *This part is easy.* " . . . G-E-N-S-H-I-N-E. Gay-gun-shine."

Saul gently taps a pencil against a hotel drinking glass. "That is incorrect. The correct spelling is G-E-G-E-N-S-C-H-E-I-N. Gegenschein."

Eliza wants to jump at him, claw him like a cat whose tail has been pulled once too often. How can he keep smiling when his stupid idea didn't even work?

"Can I get ready for bed now?"

"You're pretty tired, huh?"

But Eliza is already in the bathroom, the door closed behind her. Saul talks over the sound of running water.

"It was a hard word, Elly-belly. You came close. It must have been tough to concentrate when you're so tired. Remember what I said, though. If the word's a stumper, don't try to think it through. Let the letters show you where to go. If you really concentrate, if you turn yourself over to the letters, they won't let you down."

The water is turned off. Eliza's voice is barely audible through the door. "But they just did let me down, Dad. The letters didn't help at all."

"Elly, the letters were there. It's just that you weren't. You weren't *really* concentrating. And that's okay. It's very, very hard to concentrate fully. All I'm asking is that you try. You didn't really try tonight. But I want you to really try tomorrow. Will you do that for me?"

Elly opens the bathroom door. "I'm sorry," she whispers, failing to blink back the tears that start dripping onto the nice hotel carpeting.

"Elly, Elly, please. I'm not angry with you." Saul gathers his daughter up and walks her to the bed. She is stiff in his arms.

"Elly, you and I are a team. I'm here to help you, but only if you want me to. If you don't want to do this, just tell me, honey, and we can stop. I'll put the dictionaries away and we won't study anymore. Come Friday, you can do your best with what you've got."

But Elly knows this isn't really an option, knows that there's only one way to answer.

"I want to do it, Dad. We can work more tomorrow. It's just that I'm really tired. I really need some sleep."

"Of course you do. Let me tuck you in. I don't want you to worry about this, kiddo. You're doing a terrific job. I'm proud of you. Good night, sleep tight, don't let the gegenscheins bite."

She dreams a sky black with swarming letters. They fly with thick, stubby wings barely able to hold their fat bodies aloft. They brush against her skin, nest in her hair. They crawl up her nose, into her eyes. The ground is covered in torn and broken letters that crunch beneath her feet with every step. The sound of letters fills the air, making thought impossible. The letters squeeze themselves between her lips and flutter their terrible wings inside her mouth. With her arms and legs, Eliza struggles against the crawling black swarm that coats her in her sleep, kicking and thrashing to wake up cold from the hotel air conditioning, the bedsheets at her feet.

On his first fatherless night Aaron actually removes *A Buddhism Primer* from the book sandwich of *Eastern Religions, Faiths of the World,* and *Are You a Hindu?* under his mattress and places it on his night table where anyone can see it. In the morning he tries meditating completely naked for the first time. He's been wanting to do this for a while. He knows he'll have to conquer the urge to touch himself, rejecting the physical world with all its false enticements. The idea of failure is as enticing as the idea of success, but he pretends that this isn't the case, sits cross-legged on the carpet and begins to work on clearing his mind. He can feel nubs of carpet pressing against his buttocks and the soft skin of his thigh. He feels cool air on his penis and realizes he's a little hard. He tells himself this makes sense since he never allows himself to be naked, not even in his bed on hot summer nights. His body is just reacting to something new. Then he pictures himself sitting naked on the floor of his room and this turns him on even more. He begins whispering a mantra in an attempt to erase the image, reprimanding himself for thinking of his body just when he should be escaping it, and before he knows it he's completely hard. *I will not touch myself,* he vows as his hand reaches between his legs. He strokes himself with each *Om,* chanting faster and faster until it is a struggle to speak at all, his words more gasps than words, and then with one final *Om* it's all over and he has to clean up the carpet fast with a sock and a glass of water he happens to have waiting so it won't stain. Luckily his carpet is tan.

By light of day the evening study sessions are shadows, fuzzy as half-remembered dreams. There is the noise of the hotel and the distraction of scheduled activities. In the east wing of the National Gallery of Art, Eliza finds herself drawn to the oil portraits, the bee having strengthened her appreciation for what it means to sit so still for so prolonged a period. The frozen faces with their glinting eyes remind her of hummingbirds above flowers, wings all movement, going nowhere.

The spellers tend to group by experience and seriousness. The two- and three-year veterans maintain a cool distance from the rest, returning to friendships formed in previous years, renewing old envies. Eliza gravitates toward the more intent first-timers. There is an inherent distrust of the home-schooled competitors, who can study as much as they want without the distraction of other subjects. One night Eliza sees a home-schooler at the hotel restaurant, her dinner plate untouched as her parents quiz her at the table. She is an eighth grader who has made it to the finals for three years running. This is her last chance to win. When Eliza sees her next, being walked by her parents back to her room, Eliza realizes things could be a lot worse than Saul's strange new talk about letters.

The press arrive on Friday morning. In each press kit, spellers are listed by number, their names and vital statistics printed below their photos. They come from Neptune, New Jersey; Gallup, New Mexico; and Kokomo, Indiana. They come from Fairbanks, Alaska; Naples, Florida; and Rome, Georgia. Their local papers featured them in last Sunday's human interest column. Between them they have 276 siblings, 89 dogs, 54 cats, and 108 fish. Sixty five have dreamed of accidentally attending Friday's competition in their underwear. Forty four have churches praying for them. Twenty nine have been constipated for the past two days. Twelve are afraid of vomiting onstage. Five have been wagered upon by overconfident parents.

One will win.

When Miriam entered her car she had no idea she'd find herself on the interstate, driving toward an unknown destination. It doesn't feel like she's going to a mall or a department store. It feels like she's heading somewhere new and more significant, her recalibrated body directing her toward the external manifestation of her internal change.

One exit sign looks different, as though it was put there just for her, and she takes it to an unfamiliar street. Though she is a woman of maps and explicit driving directions, for some reason this strange road in a strange town is a calming thing. Her looser heart and larger lungs settle into a new rhythm, *Tik-kun Tik-kun Tik-kun,* that she can hear in the pulse in her ears. It sounds like a promise, a whispered pact between herself and the future. *Come, come, come with me.*

She passes grocery stores and churches, a liquor store and a restaurant. She doesn't know the name of the street she turns onto, only that she is meant to turn. It is a neighborhood of diminishing returns. The houses are old, small, and disappointed. Retouched El Caminos and Dodge Darts rest over oil patches that rain can no longer wash away. Sprinklers remain on lawns from forgotten summers long past, the grass beneath them brown.

When Miriam spots the house, she automatically drives a few more blocks before parking. Only while walking back to it does she realize that this approach is less conspicuous, that an unfamiliar car in the driveway might solicit unwanted attention. She finds herself walking as if she is a neighbor about to borrow a cup of sugar, a friend making a spontaneous visit. She walks as if she knows the street well enough to navigate it in her sleep. Dark windows and an empty driveway tell Miriam what she needs to know.

In ten years things will be different, alarms will have been installed, people will have become more cautious, but even then there will be neighborhoods like this one that are their own insurance against theft. Miriam finds a key under the doormat, fits it into the lock, and walks right in.

The house smells of floral deodorant spray and grease. The front door opens onto a small living room with a matted carpet. Everything in the room is clean but tired. Miriam circuits the house once before examining any details, passing from living room to kitchen, hallway and bedrooms. In the back of her mind, a distant voice whispers *Wrong*, but it is barely audible. Miriam knows, technically, that she doesn't belong here, but neither does the object she has come to rescue. As long as it stays in this house, the world will remain slightly misaligned. By reclaiming it and becoming more whole she is working toward the correction of a larger imbalance. She is carrying out *Tikkun Olam*.

Her body confirms this. Inside this strange house, looking for her missing piece, she feels intensely, acutely alive. Her senses fine-tune to appreciate small details. From the master bedroom she can hear the *tick tick* of the oven clock in the kitchen. From the far side of the bed she can see a dropped earring embedded in the carpet across the room. Her missing piece beats like a heart beneath the floorboards. It pulses with its urgency, drawing her closer. Each minute she and it remain separate, the pulse grows louder and the whispering voice grows even quieter, until *Wrong* is barely a memory, a half-forgotten dream.

Miriam knows the instant she sees it that she is here for the blue ceramic dish holding spare change beside the kitchen telephone. She carefully pours its nickels, pennies, and dimes onto the weathered counter. Outside, she is careful to lock the door before replacing the key under its mat.

In exiting the house, Miriam is reborn. She has left her outer skin, like so much cracked eggshell, in the house where the dish once was, a weight she didn't know she carried until it was gone. She is more fluid and vibrant. Her new inner rhythm, born that first Saul-less night, now fits her outer body. Her looser heart beats closer to the surface than before. She can feel it just by placing her fingertips lightly upon her chest. *Tik-kun. Tik-kun.* It beats faster now, a pulse somewhere between that of woman and bird. Back on the road, the dish at her side, Miriam feels she could release the wheel and steer by looking, could press the gas pedal to the floor and soar into the air. She feels, at this moment, she could do anything.

Such a feeling of limitless possibility has found Miriam once before. Miriam is home on break during her last year of prep school, her entrance to college already assured. She is driving on a familiar back road, flush with her then irrevocable youth and the unwavering certainty of her future, when she turns off the car's headlights. She knows she has crossed a boundary, that the act of extinguishing her headlights has placed her in a world whose rules her youth hasn't mastered. Here, her presumed immortality no longer applies. This idea is both terrifying and exhilarating. She trains her eyes upon the faint gray stripe of the road divider and maintains her speed. At any moment the dark might congeal into an impenetrable wall that will accordion her car upon impact. The darkness seeps through her open windows, thick with possibility. It weights the air and coats her skin. She can stand it less than a minute before switching the headlights back on, turning the gray stripe back to yellow, vaporizing the darkness, and illuminating the two boys walking just ahead along the road's edge, close enough that, had she kept her headlights off, she might have met up with an event that would have crossed back over with her from the unlit night, rewriting her future. Driving in broad daylight with the dish by her side, Miriam feels as if she is defying her fear to push on farther and longer than ever before.

The bee is to be held the following morning in the Independence Ballroom on the bottommost floor of the hotel, three stories underground and accessed via a series of neon-lit escalators that cycle the colors of the rainbow with the descent. Each successive floor is smaller than its predecessor, the last floor housing only the ballroom. The descent recalls a deep-sea dive; the varied life forms at the upper levels nearer to the sun thin until only spellers and their families remain, the blind, albino fishes of the ocean's trenches.

After she has told her father she is going to sleep, Eliza slips out of her pajamas and back into her clothes. The muffled sound of the television from Saul's room makes it easier not to be heard. Eliza checks her pocket three times for her room key before braving the hallway, closing the door to her room so slowly and softly that even she is unsure when it clicks shut. She stifles her urge to run, afraid to draw attention to herself, settling on a very brisk walk. The hall is empty. As she passes the closed doors of her fellow contestants, she hears nothing, imagines them asleep in their beds or desperately seeking sleep, their bedside clocks ticking away the bee's approach.

The glass elevator terminates at the lobby, requiring Eliza's transfer to the escalator. At the first sublevel, grownups sip cocktails at a rotating piano bar. A sign beside the "One full rotation every thirty minutes" sign announces that bee parents get their first drink free. The conference-room floor below the bar is dark except for the cycling colors of the escalator rainbow. Eliza is exhilarated by the darkness and the strangeness of being alone so far from home so late at night, empowered by the fact that she has broken away from her expected place in time to steer her own course. To combat the fear that shadows her every movement, she focuses on centering her feet upon the escalator step.

Only the first few feet of the lowest floor reflect the escalator lights. As Eliza approaches the ballroom entrance, the dark takes on a grainy, dreamlike quality in which anything might happen. Eliza wishes she had thought to put on her mother's shirt.

She half expects the ballroom door to be locked, tells herself that she may escape the dark sooner than she thinks. When she finds the door ajar, she is surprised by the strength of her relief. It is as if the room has been awaiting her arrival.

Her eyes, having semi-adjusted to the darkness, can just make out the rows of chairs stretching back from the stage. The smallness of this stage compared to the stage in her nightmare is a comfort. From the schedule of events in the hotel lobby, Eliza knows that this ballroom housed a reception for paint salesmen last Sunday and will be filled with postcard collectors next weekend. It is just a room. Eliza closes her eyes and listens to it. *This is what I will think of tomorrow when I am onstage, of this room perfectly empty.*

Perhaps if there were a little more light or if Eliza's night vision were sharper, she would see the other small forms in the room, all absorbed in their own version of prayer, getting the last taste of peace this room has to offer. The quiet of the room feels like a held breath, its still air full of promise. Each small shadow claims one of these promises as their own, takes from the air the image of themselves at the microphone, the final winning word alive on their lips.

Saul's 5:30 A.M. wake-up call interrupts a dream in which he is making love to Miriam on the ballroom stage, naked except for a numbered placard around his neck. The suddenness of his awakening erases the vision. He will blush when he catches sight of the stage later that morning without knowing why.

Eliza is already awake, having requested a wake-up call for five so that in case she was having the nightmare she would have time to recover before starting the day. As she was not having the nightmare, the earlier wake-up call gains her thirty minutes of perfect stillness while watching the sunrise through the space in the curtains. She wonders if, back at home, her mother is awake as well. When she hears Saul get up, she closes her eyes.

Saul opens the door between their rooms slowly, creeps to his daughter's bed on the balls of his feet, and eases himself down on her mattress. Eliza has to stifle a smile, does her best to look asleep. When Saul puts his face on the sheets covering her stomach, she knows she has fooled him.

"Elly-belly," he says in his special voice, the one he uses for stuffed animals and characters in stories. "Elly-belly, the time has come. The time is now."

Eliza pops up from the mattress. "Fooled you! I've been awake for half an hour."

"I know. But did you think that on a day as important as today I would risk upsetting your delicate mental balance by tickling you? Like this?" he says, his fingers diving for Eliza's armpits. With a shriek Eliza scrambles off the bed and into the bathroom, managing not to think about the bee for a full minute.

After his failed attempt at naked meditation, a severely chafed Aaron decides he might be better off going to the park where his attempts to meditate won't face the same manner of distraction. The park is a patch of green five blocks square with a tennis court at one end, a playground at the other, and a communal lawn laced with unevenly paved asphalt paths in between. Aaron sits underneath one of the many trees dotting the grass and pretends he is about to sit for forty nine days to reach Supreme Enlightenment. He focuses on a dandelion. He pictures the world as interconnected—dandelion, insect, animal, and man all linked in karmic balance.

Aaron leans his back against the tree trunk and feels the bark press into his skin. If he puts his ear against the tree when the wind blows, he hears a rushing sound that reminds him of the ocean. *We are all water,* he tells himself. It seems like a very Buddhist thing to think. He wishes there were someone to appreciate it with him. But being a Buddhist is a lonely business in Montgomery County, where the yellow pages go from Buckets—Decorative to Builders with nothing in between.

Loneliness is not Buddhism's only problem. For all its profundity, Buddhism lacks the immediacy of Aaron's airplane wing experience. Even though Aaron knows it was only a flashing red light, he cannot forget the sense of absolute assurance that filled him with the idea that God was right there. The closer Aaron looks for God in Buddhism, the more he feels he's gazing at a trick hidden picture, where the zebra you're supposed to find isn't actually there.

Aaron has left the tree and is sitting on a bench reading *Are You a Hindu?* when a man sits opposite him on the bench. The man, a little older than Aaron, is wearing a hat and a kind expression. The man has nothing to read and doesn't seem to be waiting for anyone, but still manages to look completely at home. Aaron, who always feels he has to look as if he is doing something or at least preparing to do something to feel he belongs anywhere, is intrigued.

"So, are you?" the man suddenly says, making Aaron jump.

Aaron wonders if this is the kind of man he's heard about on the news, the kind who goes to parks to find others like him to be homos with. Aaron briefly considers saying *I am,* just to see the spark of interest that might ignite in the man's eyes. He blushes.

"No, no," he mumbles. "I'm not . . . that way."

The man nods knowingly. "Too many gods?"

Aaron stares.

The man smiles patiently, as if he has all day to explain. "In your book. Too many gods. It's why you're not a Hindu."

Aaron lets out a breath and waves *Are You a Hindu?* weakly in his hand. "Oh . . . yeah. Too many gods."

"And the caste system. To call anyone an untouchable, to say they are less worthy than anyone else . . . it's an insult to humanity and to the God who created us all."

Aaron finds himself nodding even though he's pretty sure he hasn't gotten to that chapter yet.

"My name is John, but my friends call me Chali. Are you studying religion in school?" Chali's handshake is warm.

"Um, no. I'm just doing it . . . for myself."

Chali nods gravely. "Something is missing."

Aaron blanches, fleetingly wonders if this Chali person is some kind of religious truant officer who can tell he's playing hooky from Judaism. Aaron pictures being escorted home and handed over to Saul. *We found your son studying unaffiliated religious books in the park.*

"What do you mean?" Aaron replies, hoping his voice belies his imagination.

"You feel like something's missing from your life and, rather than settle for that, you've decided to do something about it."

Aaron shrugs, still wary. "I guess so."

"And now you're wondering why a total stranger would say these things. It's because I recognize the look on your face. I used to feel the same way. I was raised Catholic, but it felt empty. I was about your age when I started reading about the Eastern religions—Buddhism, Taoism, Hinduism—and I was a Buddhist for a while, but it still didn't feel quite right."

"Yeah." Aaron's initial fear is overshadowed by the excitement of engaging an actual person in theological discussion. "I mean, the ideas are nice but—"

Chali's smile fills his face. "It feels more like a philosophy than a religion. It's not direct enough."

"Exactly!"

Aaron feels his entire body relax. Chali is looking straight into Aaron's eyes, but for some reason it doesn't make Aaron feel nervous. Aaron takes a deep breath, a breath that sends air to parts of him that have never gotten any, and tells Chali everything, starting with the airplane wing and ending with the park bench, skipping only the naked parts in between.

There are four Comfort Counselors. They appear at irregular intervals, the girl with the brown braid and the boy with no chin sometimes appearing twice before the boy with the bad skin or the girl with the disproportionately small nose. They hover at the edge of the stage like benevolent vultures, edging closer as the speller begins the descent into a word, waiting to swoop at the sound of the bell.

The counselors are college age and therefore ancient. Though it is understood by Eliza and the others that their comforters are all ex-bee participants, it is impossible to picture them seated on a stage. "The bee gets harder every year," a three-year repeater near Eliza whispers when the Comfort Counselors are introduced. "I mean, in the seventies, you could win with a word like 'incisor.' These guys have, like, no idea."

Brown Braid and Bad Skin hug. Tiny Nose and No Chin don't. It is agreed that Tiny Nose and No Chin's comfort is preferable. Nothing amplifies failure like the hug of a stranger.

The stage seethes with nervous energy. Hands grip and release seat bottoms, feet tap out frenetic rhythms, fingers tug at ears and noses, lips are chewed, foreheads scrunch, necks stretch, joints crack, teeth grind, and knees bounce. Eliza's seat in the second to last row allows her to engage in her nervous habits with some degree of privacy. In addition to biting the insides of her cheeks, giving her the look of a heavy-jawed fish, her big toe rubs unconsciously against the inside of her shoe, resulting in a blister whose origins will remain mysterious to her.

Eliza's obstructed view also saves her from the compulsion of finding and then staring at her father in the audience. Instead, she becomes fixated on the raised mole of a pale skinny girl a row ahead and three seats to the right. The mole is a nut-brown thing the size of a dime, with a surface like cream of wheat. Every time the girl's turn approaches, Eliza watches her unconsciously rub the mole with the pad of her right pointer finger, a gentle but persistent prodding that makes Eliza uncomfortable.

Tics increase in intensity with approaching turns, a wave of nervous energy that crosses the stage as each round progresses. By the time the home-schooled girl is called to the mike, anxiety has turned her into a hunchback. Her slouch combines with nervous arm-flapping to transform her, as she walks, into a huge flightless bird, its terrified eyes silently pleading, just this once, to be allowed to fly.

The pronouncer, a Midwestern English professor with the eyes and jowls of a bulldog, is in his eleventh year of force-feeding spelling words to bee contestants. The home-schooled girl doesn't look at him, focuses all her energy on the microphone stand. She hasn't slept solidly for the past three days. Her numbered placard is dog-eared from her tendency to suck its corners.

"Number 36, your word is TUBULAR."

"TUBULAR." Slight arm flap.

"Number 36, could you please speak a little louder?"

"**TUBULAR.**"

"I'm sorry, Number 36 . . . ." The judge consults a list. "Rachel?" It's the first time Eliza has heard the girl's name. "Rachel, we need you to speak louder so that we can hear you. Right now, we can't hear you at all. Your word is TUBULAR."

It's impossible for Eliza to see Rachel's face, no way for her to observe the way Rachel's mouth and eyes have tightened up, as if she needs to squeeze her voice from the very bottom of her throat. Rachel's arms go stiff and still, her wings frozen. Then her voice explodes into the microphone and out the speakers, jolting most of the audience members from their seats.

"TUBULAR. T-U-B-U-L-A-R. TUBULAR."

It is too fast, a blur of sudden sound, but Rachel knows she is right before she is told, returns to her seat in proud, hunchless strides with barely any arm-flapping. Eliza realizes she is frightened for the girl, finds herself half hoping Rachel will win just to spare everyone the horror of watching her lose.

They are all silently spelling together, a chorus of moving mouths stringing letters together in soundless prayer. Each silent spelling is a completed penance protecting against future failure at the microphone. Number 43 thanks the judge in a polite Texan drawl before being escorted offstage for misspelling MONIKER. Number 57 removes her placard as soon as she hears the ding. She holds it away from her like a dead thing that has begun to smell as CORONET is spelled back to her minus her extra R.

There is more applause for misspellings than for successes, a consolation most spellers miss at the time of their defeat, the ding absorbing all other sound. Her first turn at the mike, Eliza focuses exclusively on the pronouncer and the microphone, too intent upon ensuring her survival to locate her father. The microphone gives off a stale breath smell. There is something wedged in a section of its wind guard. It might be a piece of egg.

Between rounds, spellers are permitted to stand and stretch, but they may not leave the stage. Eliza wanders to the stage's edge with a few others to look out over the rows of seats. She finds Saul midway back, flagging her with his arms, and gives a tentative wave. Saul beams and mouths something back to her, but Elly can't tell what it is. She smiles and nods. Saul gives her a thumbs up. The judge calls for the spellers to reclaim their seats.

At a table abutting the front of the stage sits the official spelling bee recording technician. Eliza is unaware of this until Number 63, a nervous boy with tiny wrists, spells his word in a blur and, after sitting back down, is told that his word is being reviewed on tape to verify his spelling. The news causes him to start shivering uncontrollably. His teeth rattle so loudly Eliza can hear them three rows and half a stage away. After fifteen seconds that to those in chattering-teeth range seems much, much longer, the judge announces that Number 63's spelling has been verified. The shivering stops. Number 64, who has been waiting at the mike this whole time, is given HALCYON which, making sure to spell at a comprehensible pace, she spells with an I. At the sound of the ding, she bursts into tears and runs offstage avoiding

Brown Braid, who signals to No Chin for backup. The two corral Number 64 into the Quiet Room.

By college, Miriam's interactions with her parents have been reduced to monthly phone calls and an annual December visit. While they are still living, this seems like a good arrangement. Mel and Ruth have come to realize they've created a child whom, in their attempt to give the best of everything, they have never gotten to know. Christmas break is generally all they can manage of this almost-stranger without being overcome by regret or guilt. Miriam, for her part, doesn't miss something she's never had. Her annual visit home is like a trip to a favorite reference library, her parents primary sources to be examined. Through them she confirms her roots, observing enough of herself in them to assuage her general sense of at-oddness with the world. She and her parents reflect each other like funhouse mirrors, one trait stretched, another shrunk. Home is a place where her eccentricities have a clear source.

Miriam delights in the meticulous way her father arranges and eats his food, the way her mother jumps from topic to topic as she speaks. From them she inherits her tendency to group things in threes and fives. She senses her parents' discomfort around her but considers it a problem set they will eventually solve. The day they say, "But you're just like us!" she will nod sagely, a pleased professor, and reveal that she has known this all along. Perhaps it is in subconscious revenge for their inattention that she hoards this information. Perhaps she merely assumes there will be time.

Miriam's junior year roommate Martha answers the phone on the first ring. Martha has been expecting a call from her boyfriend Jerome and is reluctant to relinquish the receiver, afraid he will try to call while Miriam is talking to this stranger who isn't Jerome and is holding up the line. But Martha should have known not to worry, Miriam is not a phone person and the call is short. When Martha hears the click of the phone being replaced she turns to make sure it's completely hung up—Miriam has a tendency to leave it off the hook—and that's when she notices Miriam's face.

Miriam is generally quiet and a little strange, a good roommate in the sense that she is tidy and doesn't smoke. Miriam doesn't offer much, but she doesn't ask for much either. Martha can handle that. She's got her own life, a.k.a. Jerome, and hasn't got time for distractions.

But now Miriam's got a funny expression on her face. One Martha has never seen before.

"Are you okay?" Martha asks, even though she's pretty sure she doesn't want to know.

"It's odd, don't you think? Verbally, I mean. Is dead. Are dead." Miriam says this as if returning to a conversation already in progress. Martha is used to this, generally nods or makes *uh-huh* noises while doing whatever it was she was doing before. But this time Miriam's got that face.

"Did something happen?" Martha asks, actually turning in her chair. Miriam is sitting on Martha's bed, picking at Martha's favorite blanket, which is pilled from years of use. Martha hates it when Miriam does this and has told her so on several occasions.

Miriam has grown very pale as, funny expression on her face, she continues to de-pill.

"My parents," Miriam says. The right corner of Miriam's mouth is twitching as if being frantically tugged by an invisible wire.

"God, Miriam, what's happened?" Martha, who is good-natured at heart, rushes to the bed and puts her hand on Miriam's shoulder, an action which causes Miriam to flinch and jolt from Martha's bed to her own.

"They *were* walking alongside the road, they *were* hit by a car, and now they *are* dead. It doesn't work. Are is present tense. Dead is—well, dead is *past,* isn't it? Present tense modifying past; being modifying non-being. Language, in this instance"—and here Miriam makes a garbled noise in her throat—"fails."

Martha grabs for tissues but Miriam isn't crying. Her face looks as if it has imploded.

"Is there anything I can do?" says Martha, who has never seen or spoken to Miriam's parents, who doesn't even know their names.

"There's nothing anyone can do," Miriam replies flatly. "Time has run out."

Miriam wonders if the car had on its headlights, if the driver had tried to swerve. Perhaps the driver hadn't seen them at all, too blinded by the projected course of his own life. Miriam realizes that, by holding fast to her version of the future, she has sentenced her parents to die under the misapprehension that they were alone in the world. Miriam's punishment, she realizes, is to live knowing that she truly is.

The funeral confirms this. Miriam's parents were both only children, their own parents long dead. In making final arrangements, Miriam scrutinizes address books, letters, and the odd forgotten photo in search of a cousin or a great-aunt, anyone in whom she might find a vague familial affiliation. It is as she feared it would be. Though the service is well attended by Mel and Ruth's fellow scions of society, for whom this funeral is a must-attend event, Miriam's is the only hand for this assemblage of buffed and manicured nails to shake.

At first it is difficult for Saul to be in the room. The air is supersaturated with anxiety, leaving the taste of metal on his tongue. He is reminded of Abraham being asked to sacrifice his only son, wonders how he can possibly subject his child to this. Onstage, rows of nervous children flutter like leaves before an approaching storm. Saul finds himself holding his breath with every completed word, waiting to see if one more will be blown away. Without thinking about it, he claps harder for the losers, his palms stinging from repeated apology.

He wishes he could see Eliza but her number puts her in a back row, obscured by other children's heads. When he sees her stand up for the first time, he finds himself standing as well, barely able to stop himself from approaching the stage. As he sits down a mother beside him gives a sympathetic smile. "It gets easier," she says.

He knows she knows PROPAGATE, can even remember going over the word with her weeks before. He releases his breath in a grateful sigh.

Disappointed by the brevity of Elly's applause, he continues to clap until a father turns to stare. "That's my daughter," he explains, his voice stiff with pride.

"That was an easy word." The man shrugs, turning back to the stage. Saul can't help but grin when the man's son, a bucktoothed boy with home-cut bangs, gets dinged out on MANICOTTI.

By the third round, Saul has managed to relax. The tension of the room has become a persistent odor his nose has ceased to smell. His formerly passionate applause for the losers has become polite.

His mind drifts as other parents' children take to the microphone. He peruses the spelling bee program as if it is a mail order catalog. He skips past pages of faces and their accompanying blurbs: the girl who won a trophy for her essay on fire prevention, the boy who helps his father care for orphaned calves. He finds Eliza's photo and tries to pretend she is someone else's child. Hers is a school photo complete with mottled, soft-focus background, her smile an obliging show of teeth. Thick eyebrows draw attention to the face, but the eyes, nose, and mouth could be Any Jew. They are features which, rather than blossoming into something beautiful, will look very much the same in years to come.

Saul is so engrossed in the future life of this imagined stranger that he fails to watch his daughter spell her third word correctly, GHERKIN clearing her entry into tomorrow's spelling finals.

Leaving the park, Aaron feels he is being lit by an invisible spotlight, the kind only sensed by those who have broken through the bounds of daily existence into the realm of the Significant. He knows he has just played a part in something larger than anything in his life before. Though he didn't know it then, the airplane, the bar mitzvah, the church, and his covert research were all preparation for meeting Chali, a meeting that had it occurred any sooner, would have been meaningless. Aaron recalls Siddhartha's first journey from his father's palace, the one that compelled him to forsake his sheltered Brahmin life and become the Buddha. Even as he shies away from such lofty comparisons, Aaron cannot help but pen a line for The Life and Times of Aaron Naumann: *And when Aaron was sixteen he had a chance encounter that was to forever alter the course of his life.*

Chali has given Aaron words for his quest. God consciousness is just what Aaron has been seeking from airplane wing onward, not just a set of rituals but a living, breathing experience. Aaron was beginning to think such a thing was impossible. Ashamed of his spiritual hunger, he had been considering throwing in the God towel and resigning himself to Judaism. But now his perseverance has paid off. In their conversation and in the pamphlets Aaron received from Chali before they parted, Aaron has found what he is looking for.

It was such a simple sentence when Chali said it—"Come to the ISKCON temple on Sunday and see for yourself"—but back in Aaron's room the words become large and sharp. His father's face stares in disapproval from between the letters. Dad and Elly will be back by Sunday. Aaron will have to come up with an excuse to free him from dinner. He will invent a friend, an invitation to pizza and a movie. It doesn't stray far from the truth. Though they have just met, Chali feels like a better friend than most.

Aaron's friendships up to this point have been circumstantial, fellow targets and picked-lasts banding together for safety's sake. Conversations have been confined to sanctioned topics: sports, girls, television, school. Any slight departure from this limited docket could open up the potential for further singling out, a risk that none of them, already at the bottom rung of the social ladder, dared take. When Aaron was younger, a friend was anyone he played with at recess, a good friend anyone with whom he also shared his lunch. Only recently has Aaron realized that he knows as little about the remaindered boys he calls friends as they know about him. The years they have known each other have buttressed, rather than eased, their conversational boundaries. Rules established long ago have become the fabric of the friendships themselves. Aaron cannot imagine asking the religious views of Marvin, a compulsive reader of fantasy paperbacks featuring beasts and busty virgins on their covers. Or Steven, who brushes his teeth after every meal and wears his headgear in school, if he's ever felt God. He knows too well what would happen should he interrupt a cafeteria comparison of NBA coaching styles with a question about meditation—the silence, the strange looks, the unspoken excitement that one of their number had opened himself up for attack. Though the benefits of Aaron's membership in this group are limited to a regular lunch table and someone with whom to split a bucket of popcorn at the next *Superman* sequel, it is better than complete lonerdom, that lowest caste forced to scramble for unoccupied cafeteria seats, suffering the slings and arrows of the other diners. It is better than having to see a movie alone. Aaron had comforted himself with the idea that college would offer the opportunity for an improved him to gain a new set of friends. A year and a half didn't seem that much longer to wait. Having met Chali, Aaron realizes that he may not have to wait at all.

It is the morning of the second and last day of competition. Eliza is one of sixty five spellers who will be returning to the stage. She is robotically sliding home fries into her mouth, her scrambled eggs untouched.

"Don't forget to drink," Saul says.

"I don't want to have to pee when I'm onstage," Eliza replies, taking a token sip of her orange juice. She feels vaguely ill. She has seen the engraved loving cup, bigger than her head. She has pictured herself holding the trophy aloft like a race car winner on "Wide World of Sports." Last night she dreamed herself onto the TV news, waking to the sound of Walter Cronkite's voice echoing in her head: *Eliza*

Naumann, this year's national spelling champion. And that's the way it is. . . . She knows that winning involves luck, that LUGE can be followed by XANTHOSIS. She is suspicious of her father's calm, of last night's insistence that she finally satisfy her craving for HBO.

"Elly, try to eat. The world does not live on potatoes alone. You're going to need energy. Are you nervous?"

Eliza nods.

"I'm not. You know why? Because I know we did our best. And I'm very, very proud of you."

Eliza has to swallow a few times before she can get the words to come out of her throat.

"I want to win."

Saul reaches across the table and takes her hand. "You know what, Elly? I think you can—"

Eliza smiles so large and so fast her cheeks ache. She is about to regale him with her Cronkite dream when she realizes he has more to say.

"—maybe not this year, because I don't think we've done enough work. We only really focused on the dictionary. But the fact that you're here and that you've done so well proves to me that you're ready for the next stage. I've got a whole year to help you understand what I mean by getting to know the letters, to help you feel comfortable letting the letters guide you. I think by next year there's a chance you'll be unstoppable."

"Oh," Eliza says, the wind knocked out of her.

"Hey, are you okay?"

Eliza nods, pushes her plate away.

"Elly, sweetie, you look like you're about to cry."

Eliza shakes her head, forcing the taste of tears from her throat. Her mind is looping the sound of her father's voice when she shut herself inside the bathroom after GEGENSCHEIN. *All I'm asking is that you try.* If she had only listened, if she hadn't insisted on going to bed like a baby, they might have studied last night instead of watching "Comic Relief." Her father might be saying something different now. She might not be feeling as if, after all his time and effort, she has failed him.

"I'm sorry." She knows, even as she says it, that the words change nothing.

"Eliza, there is absolutely nothing to be sorry for. You are doing a super job—I mean, this is the national bee! The finals! Whether you win or not just isn't that important, not this year. Try to forget what I said. I'm the one who should apologize. I shouldn't have brought up any of that getting-to-know-the-letters stuff yet. I got carried away. Since I waited this long to take the next step with you, I could have waited a little longer."

Eliza knows her father knows this is her cue to ask what he means. Saul is looking at her expectantly, smiling his I've-got-a-secret smile. The sight of this smile in the past has left Eliza yearning to do or say anything to be let in on the secret too. Now it only makes her angry. For the first time, Eliza doesn't want to play her father's game. Instead of following the unspoken rules, she remains silent. She tries to put herself back into the frame of mind she occupied when she believed he thought she had a chance. But she can no longer picture Walter Cronkite saying her name, only hears her father's voice saying, *That's the way it is,* over and over again.

Aaron is setting the table for two. He briefly places his plate next to his mother's but cannot imagine them eating in such proximity to each other. He returns his plate in its usual place.

It is the first Friday night in living memory that Aaron hasn't entered the kitchen to find the Shabbat candlesticks resting on wax paper on the kitchen counter, their white candles waiting to be lit. It is traditionally the woman's job to handle the candles, but it has always been Saul who retrieved the candlesticks and the wineglass, who made sure there was challah on the table. Aaron knows where everything is.

He could defrost half a challah loaf, fill the kiddush cup with Manischewitz, and put the candles in their place, but he isn't sure who he'd be doing it for. His actions certainly wouldn't serve Miriam, who waves her hands over the candle flames but leaves Eliza to chant the blessing alone. None of his prospective religions employ candles, wine, or bread on Friday nights.

Miriam comes home just as Aaron is setting down silverware. He watches as she enters the kitchen to see if she notices anything strange, but Miriam doesn't even glance at the space where the Shabbat candles should be. Aaron realizes that Shabbat's occurrence or nonoccurrence tonight is completely up to him.

Dinners in Saul's absence have been courtesy of Swanson. Tonight Aaron has two turkey pot pies heating up in the oven. The air is sweet with the smell of baking crust. Aaron places a bubbling tin on each plate. The anomaly of foil on white china amplifies the strangeness wrought by Saul and Eliza's absence: the stiffness of the ritual place settings, the hollow sound of the kitchen chairs scraping against the floor. With two fewer faces to distract him, Aaron sees the lines at the corners of his mother's mouth and between her eyebrows, echoes of her face deep in concentration. Aaron reasons that, as a face loses its ability to cover its tracks, it must fall back on what it's most used to. When he attempts to picture himself old, Aaron realizes that the old man currently awaiting him has a face perpetually braced for disaster. He wonders if, at age sixteen, it is not too late to change his wrinkles.

The silence is pregnant with avoided topics. Miriam is giddy with the knowledge of the dish and of a stranger's home, is reminded of the time she tried marijuana: the giggles, the secret sense of elevation above the plodding world. She knows it's silly to think Aaron would suspect her of anything. Her comings and goings are too unpredictable for this most recent one to have merited attention. Despite this, she cannot help but inspect Aaron's face across the table, looking for signs that he has detected the change within her.

Aaron keeps glancing at the kiddush cup on the shelf above the microwave. Its very shape seems accusatory, the stem reaching up to the cup in a huge letter Y. Inside Aaron's head, Saul's voice is repeating that very question. Aaron can picture perfectly his father's disappointment, the head shaking, the downward glance, and now his mother is staring at him from across the table. Perhaps she is equally aware of Shabbat's absence. Can she tell, just by looking at him, that he isn't planning on going to services? That instead he plans to reread the pamphlets Chali gave him in the park this afternoon?

Silverware clinks. Water is swallowed. Aaron longs for Saul's meat loaf or barbecued chicken. They have only talked once so far, a stilted four-phone conversation that lapsed into silence once Eliza described the hotel and Saul the competition. For Aaron it is a preview of what family will become once he leaves home.

Miriam wonders if the dish's absence has been noticed yet and a plausible reason invented for its disappearance. Robbery certainly wouldn't be an option its former owners would think to consider. Though Miriam cannot imagine anyone seeing the dishless pile of change and screaming "Thief!" into the night, dread sits inside her like a stone, making it difficult to eat. Its weight in her belly only adds to her excitement, pain enhancing pleasure. She did not know it was possible for such lightness and heaviness to coexist, the one making the other more distinct. When Saul returns with Eliza from Washington, D.C., Miriam realizes she will welcome his weight on the bed, the tiptoeing to prepare for sleep. Saul's presence has become necessary ballast to keep her from falling up instead of down. At the thought of Saul, the phrase "breaking and entering" comes to mind for the first time.

"I'm going to get some ice cream from the freezer. Do you want some?" The words sound misplaced after the extended silence. Miriam looks at Aaron so strangely that he wonders if he has spoken gibberish. But now she's smiling with teeth, which is not her usual smile and which kind of gives Aaron the creeps, but at least signifies that what he said made sense.

A question. She only heard the last portion—"want some?"—and is afraid to ask Aaron to repeat himself because she doesn't want to act unusual. But then she is always asking people to repeat themselves, so asking what he asked would actually be a sign of normalcy.

"Ice cream," Aaron repeats. Miriam shakes her head. She has barely touched her dinner, tears into her pot pie with affected vigor. On his way to the freezer Aaron turns on the television, which he would have done earlier except that Shabbat is the one night they're not supposed to watch the news at dinner. The modulated tone of the anchorman muffles Saul's voice in Aaron's head and renders the kiddush cup harmless, but it cannot cancel out the previous silence, still waiting beneath the surface.

The remaining spellers occupy two rows of seats. Eliza, situated between Numbers 41 and 62, has a clear view of Rachel whom, having heard her name, she can no longer think of as Number 36. Eliza longs for the distraction of the girl with the brown mole, but she was eliminated by EDIFICE yesterday, leaving Eliza no choice but to focus on Rachel's nervous tics. With each round Rachel adds something to her anxious repertoire, which varies from sitting to standing. Seated, she picks at her placard with her fingers and teeth, tearing its edges as she tugs one way and then another, the string digging into the skin of her neck. As her turn nears, the tugging quickens and is joined by bouncing, making her chair creak. Eliza must stifle the urge to place her hands on Rachel's shoulders to hold her down.

More than ever, Eliza wants to win. She wants to win with a word so difficult her father will have to admit that he was wrong, that the letters are already guiding her.

When Number 127 is being asked to spell LOQUAT, Eliza closes her eyes and feels her mind empty out. L fills her head, a glowing yellow the color of molten metal. *This is what Dad meant.* She's surprised at how easy it is. Inside Elly's head, L grows longer, its edges curving inward to form an O. Her body loosens. When the edge of O grows a tail to become Q, Eliza feels the change in her fingertips. Q's top evaporates and its tail disappears, U settling warm in her belly. Elly feels a tickle as U flips and grows a line through its middle to become an A.

When A's legs slide together as its arm floats up, T fills Eliza, straightening her spine. Eliza opens her eyes. She feels as if she has just woken from a deep sleep. Number 127 is walking offstage to the sound of vigorous applause.

"I did it," she mouths to her father across the room.

Saul smiles and nods. "I love you too," he mouths back equally indecipherably.

By Round 7, there are seventeen of them. Number 14, whose perpetually perfect posture adds to the overall impression that he is an android, causes murmurs of admiration when he rips through DVANDVA without asking for a derivation or use in a sentence. When Number 22 gets her word wrong, No Chin has to pry her hand from the microphone. Number 33 decides midway through PERIPATETIC that he has made a mistake. He turns stubbornly silent, demanding to be dinged out rather than made to complete the word. He stands mute until his time runs out. The judge's spelling reveals that the boy's progress had been perfect until he had refused to go on.

Number 35 is called to the mike. Rachel almost trips on her way to the front of the stage, removes the microphone from its stand, and holds it to her mouth like a lounge singer. The Independence Ballroom suddenly seethes with the sound of her nervous breathing.

"Number 35, your word is GREGARINE."

Having been informed that a gregarine is a parasitic protozoan taken from the Latin, Rachel has no choice but to start spelling. She pounds her palm against her forehead after each letter, as if trying to knock the next one loose. Because she is holding the microphone so close to her face, each moment of contact sounds like a heavy blow.

"... I ..." Pound. "... N ..." Pound. "... E ..." Pound. "Gregarine."

Eliza finds herself bracing for the next blow, but none comes. The judge's "Correct" sends Rachel leaping back to her seat to resume picking at her placard, which is now noticeably smaller than the others.

When Number 43 is given PURIM, Eliza almost laughs out loud. Then she realizes that such an easy word right before her turn is a bad sign, almost certain to mean she's destined to get something awful. Number 43, the only contestant wearing a yarmulke, makes short work of PURIM and returns to his seat with a dazed grin. The judge calls Eliza to the mike.

As she stands, Elly hazily recalls her nightmare: the expectant silence, the feeling she is holding up time, the endless path from her seat to the microphone. She decides that if she can get this next word, whatever it may be, her chances of winning are practically guaranteed. From the moment she rises from her chair, she locks eyes with Saul, whose gaze practically steers her to the microphone.

"Number 59, your word is DUVETYN."

"Dew-veh-teen?" Eliza's heart lurches into her throat. In her mind's eye, she sees nothing.

"That is correct. Duvetyn."

Saul is staring so hard it feels like he's directly in front of her instead of halfway across the room. She wants to ask him to leave, to just get on the plane and fly back home.

"Um, what does it mean?"

The judge's voice is irritatingly friendly. "Duvetyn is a soft, short-napped fabric with a twill weave, made of wool, cotton, rayon, or silk."

Eliza whispers the word, feels the way it shapes her tongue and lips. From these movements she tries to chart the word's path through time and place. Where has it traveled? When was it born?

"What is the derivation, please?"

The judge's voice is ever neutral, revealing nothing. "Duvetyn comes to us from the French."

Eliza wants to see herself through the judge's eyes. Does he have favorites? Is she one of them? Or are they all interchangeable, one long blur of nervous hands and voices? Her placard suddenly reminds her of the stickers affixed to new underwear: INSPECTED BY 59.

She's got to focus. There isn't much time. She returns to Duvetyn, pushes everything else aside.

I know it starts with D.

"Dew-veh-teen."

At first it is a struggle to empty her mind, which keeps conjuring up fresh images: her father's face, a conveyer belt laden with tagged children, but eventually all is black and blank. *D, D, D, D, D, D,* Eliza thinks until D, proud and foreboding, appears in her mind's eye. Then, its top disappears. The letters are showing her the way.

"D-U . . ."

Dew - veh - teen. She speeds through the next few letters, which are obvious.

". . . V-E-T . . ." and now she's got the word in her head, letters re-arranging themselves into something that looks right, something French.

". . . I-N-E. Duvetine." It feels good.

Time moves so slowly. The silence lasts so long Eliza is sure it means she is correct. Her heart begins to pound faster. Walter Cronkite and the loving cup are practically hers.

Ding.

She thinks she's hallucinated the sound at first, is sure her ears have made some kind of mistake until the judge starts spelling the word back to her and it's got that Y in it, the one letter she had dared to call friend. Brown Braid comes up with her arms wide open and Eliza only real-izes at that instant how big Brown Braid's boobs are and how when she gets hugged she'll be smushed against them and how Brown Braid's boobs are incontrovertible proof that it's really, truly over.

Miriam is restless. Her thoughts are on the car, how close it is, how easy it would be to let it guide her to another house and the missing piece held captive there. She can hear pieces of herself calling from their scattered prisons like fifteen-year locusts, a constant high-pitched grating noise impossible to tune out. Once Saul returns it will be harder to pursue her new mission. She knows that part of her will wel-come this but, like a schoolgirl presented with the temporary anarchy of deep snowfall, Miriam wants to enjoy the brief obscuration of rou-tine afforded by Saul's absence.

Miriam's recent house forays evoke a larger sense of departure from law and order than her department store salvage operations. The magnified sense of infraction has nothing to do with monetary worth. Miriam has stolen silk scarves and flatware, books and appliances. The ceramic dish is barely garage salable, would fetch maybe a quarter on a generous Sunday. But Miriam is invited into the department stores. Their doors stand wide open. Music plays. Buffed and waxed floors welcome her instep. Store objects are meant expressly to be touched, held, and taken away. The only slight variance in their purpose and Miriam's is that Miriam bypasses a certain conventional exchange, a formality she feels entitled to dispense with.

The dish is different in that it belonged to an environment of objects already claimed by someone else. In taking the dish Miriam was violating not an anonymity but an entity, a discrete collection of memories and intentions with a name and a face. Though Miriam is unfamiliar with the complexities of the state penal code, her private precepts view this as the greater infraction. The ceramic dish tests her devotion to her cause. It is a challenge: How far are you willing to go? *All the way,* she wants to answer, never before having felt the urge to lose herself in something so much larger than herself. *This is passion,* she realizes, finally understanding the smoldering heat of a lifetime of love scenes, real and fictional, that have left her cold. She wants to call Saul, certain that even across a telephone wire he would sense the change. *Is this what you feel?* she would ask, not having to explain, the timbre of her voice explanation enough. *Is this what* we *are supposed to feel?* the question she will never dare to ask, afraid to acknowledge the answer.

The Comfort Room seems empty when Eliza is led in and seated before a plate of cookies and a cup of juice. A curtain separates Eliza from the rest of the room. Behind it, the silence is punctuated by air-sucking sobs.

"This is *your* space," Brown Braid says in a tone she learned in Psych 202 last semester, gesturing to the curtain, the cookies, and to an inflatable punching bag set up in the corner. "Everything is here for *you*."

Number 33, his eyes red and puffy, emerges from behind the curtain, his mother holding his arm as if trying to prevent a slow leak.

"Thank you," the mother of Number 33 says to Brown Braid as she guides her son out the door, slowing her pace to match his small, shuffling steps.

"You did a *great* job," Brown Braid calls out to Number 33, who leaves without looking back. Brown Braid's compulsive, faux-intimate word-stressing is accompanied by a look intended to seem meaningful but which instead makes her appear as if something small and calcified has become lodged in her throat.

Saul rushes in, envelops Elly in his arms. "You did good, sweetheart. You gave it your all." He kisses Eliza on the forehead.

Brown Braid nods to Saul and smiles. "You two are welcome to stay in here as *long* as you want. The curtain is for privacy." She pegs Eliza with her most therapeutic face/voice combo, subconsciously lifted from repeated viewings of *Ordinary People*. "It's okay to cry. You're *safe* here." She gestures to the corner opposite the punching bag. A three-foot-high bee constructed of wood and wire grins back. "You know," she says conspiratorially, "some of the spellers feel better after they've talked to Mr. Bee."

Eliza looks to Brown Braid, then to her father, then to Mr. Bee. She turns her attention to the juice in her plastic cup.

"I think we're going to be just fine," Saul says.

Eliza is sitting in the audience with Saul when Rachel's last competitor, Kush Thambinayagam, stumbles on BATHYSCAPHE and Rachel jolts out of her seat as if electrically shocked. She staggers to the microphone. The pronouncer gives her PIRANHA. The audience groans.

"That's it?" she asks. "Piranha?"

The pronouncer repeats the word.

"The fish? With the teeth?" Rachel bares her own teeth and chomps into the microphone. The amplified clicks remind Eliza that teeth are essentially naked bones.

The pronouncer confirms Rachel's definition, politely ignoring her characterization. Rachel begins flapping her arms with glee as she sings the letters into the mike, her final A combining with a screech of victory that sends the audience reaching for their ears. The press descend upon the stage. Trophy pressed to her chest, oblivious to the television cameras, Rachel begins a solitary dance to a private tune with no discernible rhythm, displaying a sensual grace that is all the more disturbing for its unexpected beauty and complete inappropriateness on a young girl with ragged, bloody nubs for fingernails.

Miriam has no memory of the time between backing out of the driveway and arriving before this strange house in an unfamiliar neighborhood. When she looks at her watch she learns she has lost forty five minutes.

Like her previous selection, it is not a proud home. It was built poorly and quickly by people who knew it would be sold not because it was desirable but because it was all that could be managed at the time. Even the small square of brown lawn sags in defeat, its center sinking inward so that, post-rainstorm, there is a muddy pool staring skyward like a bad eye. When Miriam approaches the front door she avoids the water, afraid to make it a witness by her reflection in its clouded surface.

This time the front door is locked, with no door mat to conceal a spare key. Miriam walks to the back, stepping through a gap in a rotted wooden fence that once held a gate. Overgrown grass brushes her thighs, soaking her pants with last night's rain. The back door is also locked but there is an open window. Miriam hoists herself up with her arms, surprised at her strength. She doesn't notice the splinter in her palm from the window frame until she is inside. She pulls it out without hesitation, unflinching at the sight of her blood.

The air smells of kitchen grease and cigarettes. Miriam stands in a dark room with a sagging couch that reminds her of the front lawn. A dog-eared *Penthouse* lies centerfold down on one cushion. A Felix the Cat wall clock with wagging tail and moving eyes loudly ticks the time, ten minutes slow. A plate of dried-out spaghetti, having served more recently as an ashtray, rests precariously on a sofa arm. It's the kind of room that should make Miriam's skin crawl, compelling her to spend five minutes scrubbing her hands. Instead, she feels as if she and the room are not occupying the same space. There are two realities: the house and the special zone meant only for herself and the object she is here to claim.

She knows immediately it is not in this first room. She moves on to the kitchen where her feet stick to the floor in places, where the sink is overflowing with dishes, and the garbage needs to be taken out. There are cockroaches. Her stomach doesn't even clench. It is as if in entering the house she has grown her own carapace, her normal sensitivities safely shelled over. With a perverse sense of pleasure, she opens the refrigerator, unleashing the smell of something moldy and revealing a half-drunk six-pack and an encrusted ketchup bottle.

She finds what she has come for in the bedroom. It's the only ashtray without cigarette butts in it, a piece of pressed copper bearing a cameo profile of a woman's face. It feels warm to her touch.

With the object in her possession, the safety of her shell cracks. The staleness of the air, the dust, and the grime seep under her skin. She is just able to make it to the toilet before throwing up. She is suddenly certain that the barest contact with any surface will cancel her out, dissolving her as surely as a snail in salt. She can smell her metallic sweat, the scent of her own panic seeping from her armpits, darkening her blouse. Drops of perspiration pool between her breasts even though it isn't warm. The house has become a crude stranger standing too close on a crowded bus. It presses against her, insinuating itself into her most guarded places. Miriam grips the ashtray tightly in her hand. In her haste to leave, she barely remembers to exit the window through which she entered.

Though Saul insists on calling their first meal back a victory dinner, Eliza's heavy silences at the table belie the euphemism. Miriam is strangely animated, peppering Saul and Eliza with questions and not noticing that Eliza's answers mirror her father's.

Aaron is much more comfortable staring at his father's hands than his eyes. In a fit of guilt-induced fear, he removed two candles from the Shabbat candle box and lowered the level in the Manischewitz bottle in preparation for Saul's homecoming. Even as Aaron performed these compensations he sensed they were unnecessary. His father is no candle-counter. Of course Saul's son, the future rabbi, would have observed Shabbat in his absence.

Aaron found himself giving Eliza a solid sympathy hug in response to the news of her defeat. He has a feeling she was as surprised by it as he, but the way she squeezed back assured him that, though unexpected, it was not unwelcome. He's pretty sure he can detect the ghost of a smile when they exchange brief glances across the dinner table. He almost wishes he could tell her about skipping out on Shabbat, has a feeling she might get a good laugh out of it. Eliza's small smile eases some of his anxiety over the lie he has been preparing all day to tell.

Both wife and son insist, over Saul's repeated questions, that absolutely nothing at all happened while he was gone. Aaron shyly mentions a new friend, haltingly asks if he might join this Charlie for pizza and a movie tomorrow evening.

Saul can't help but wonder if there is something more to Aaron's question—look at the way he's blushing—and takes great pleasure in asking, "There wouldn't be a girl involved in this pizza/movie venture, would there?"

"No, Dad, it's nothing like that. I mean I wouldn't . . ." Aaron had braced himself for the unmasking of his untruth, but he hadn't prepared for his father to be this clueless.

"Aaron, it's okay. You don't have to be embarrassed about going on a date. When I was your age, I went out with girls. To tell you the truth, I was getting a little worried—"

Aaron's voice is flat. "Dad. It's not a date." He wishes Elly and Mom weren't at the table. "I mean, girls don't even . . ." He can't say the rest. It's too obvious. The last time he even touched a girl who wasn't a relative was at his bar mitzvah, now three years past, the token dance with Stacey Lieberman whom he was stupid enough to call the week after and whose unconditional, mortifying refusal to accompany him to a movie alerted him to the fact that she had only been his dancing partner out of politeness after all.

When Saul looks at his stammering son, he suddenly sees him through a stranger's eyes. While he assures himself that this has no effect on his fatherly love, which is of course unconditional, he realizes that Aaron at sixteen is as mockable as Aaron at ten. His son is a walking target, an invisible yet unmissable KICK ME sign forever pinned to his back. Of course girls don't go out with him. Saul looks at Aaron's wounded face and reproves himself for the insult he has added to adolescent injury.

"Hey, Aaron, it's okay. Don't worry about it. I didn't mean to put words in your mouth. Of course you can catch a movie with Charlie tomorrow. What are you going to see?"

Aaron hadn't thought this far in advance.

"Uh, *Ghostbusters*?"

"Haven't you seen that one already?"

"Yeah . . . but it's good and Charlie hasn't seen it yet." Maybe he should have said something impossible like *Bambi*. Something his father would have to suspect.

"Mom, did you go on dates in high school?" It is an intentional conversational shift. Eliza can tell her brother is lying, feels the need to protect him out of a lingering sense of guilt and indebtedness. She darts Aaron a glance, but he is still too mortified by Saul to appreciate her gesture.

The question catches Miriam by surprise. "Oh. Well. No. I attended a girls' boarding school. There were occasional dances with our brother school, but I generally used the time to study."

"When was your first date?" Eliza realizes she has no idea how her parents met.

"Well . . . in college, I suppose, but I didn't . . . I was very focused on my studies." Miriam blushes. She wishes there were a book on the subject, slim as it would be, a *Mother's Dating Life* she could substitute for conversation in the tidy manner of *Where Do Babies Come From?*

Eliza, sensing her mother's discomfort, conveniently becomes uncomfortable as well. She keeps any other questions to herself.

"Dessert, anyone?" Without asking if everyone is finished, Saul begins clearing the table. He places a dish of chocolate pudding before each family member. Eliza looks at the unmarred surface of the pudding with longing, thinking she would easily trade eating her dessert for the opportunity to *be* it for a few seconds: serene and self-contained. When she looks up, she notices that Aaron and Miriam haven't picked up their spoons either, are also staring wistfully at their bowls. Saul, oblivious, sits down and starts to eat. Reluctantly, the others follow. The sole sounds for the rest of the meal are of swallowing and the clicking of spoons.

The only previous time Aaron consciously lies to his parents is on the last day of middle school. To most eighth graders the day heralds their initiation into the holy American trinity of homecoming, prom, and football. To Aaron, it signifies the end of middle school gym.

The uniform is navy blue and bruise yellow, the school colors being blue and gold but gold far too expensive a color to standardize. The shorts are completely free of natural fibers and cause Aaron's butt and upper calves to itch horribly, on warmer days causing him to break out in a rash. The shirt wouldn't be so bad if he didn't have to change into it in the locker room, subjecting himself to daily comments regarding his unnatural paleness, his lack of physique and general prepubescent state.

Aaron's expectations for the future are basic. At Abington High he can opt out of gym for all but one year, giving him the opportunity to pubertize before again subjecting himself to locker room scrutiny. That is, assuming he will ever grow, an event he no longer takes for granted despite parental and medical assurance.

It is in the spirited resentment of late-onset puberty that Aaron, upon coming home, proceeds directly to the backyard. If he is going to do this, he has to do it in the afternoon, before his mother gets home or his father leaves the study. Aaron's thirst for justice overrides his ingrained fear of getting caught. This is something he must do.

Aaron carefully places the gym suit in the patio's center. His more cautious side has already considered and rejected the idea of cutting the uniform to shreds or burying it. He wants something more thorough. He needs vengeance. He craves fire.

Fire-setting is, of course, prohibited. The prospect of unequivocally breaking a family ordinance does not appeal. Withstanding Saul's bulging stare is extremely unpleasant. All the more difficult is his father's insistence upon the preeminence of disappointment over anger, as in "I am not angry at you, I am just extremely disappointed," which to Aaron seems far worse. Anger is sea-squall temporary, its intensity something to be weathered. Disappointment is slow-acting, a poison that accumulates over time. Aaron can remember every single occasion in which he has disappointed his father. Each time he is certain that his actions have demoted him to a new and permanent sublevel of paternal disregard.

But Aaron needs to do this. He considers consulting Saul but decides against it. While his father might enjoy helping incinerate the cause of so much personal grief, this needs to be an independent statement. Never again will he allow himself to be victimized by a piece of fabric. The whole thing loses its punch if he goes asking *Abba* for permission.

It is much less difficult to get the uniform to catch than Aaron anticipated. The cloth bursts into flame with a satisfying *foosh*. The fire eats holes in the fabric, turning it a satisfying black.

Then, to his horror, Aaron realizes that the uniform isn't burning. It is melting. The polyester shorts are forming burned, black lumps that look rather permanent as they fuse to the patio. Aaron rushes for the hose. The water succeeds in both quenching the flames and smearing a layer of black ash across the white concrete. Aaron panics, his brain frozen like a rabbit in the headlights of his father's impending appearance.

Aaron goes into the house, returns with a butter knife. He uses the edge to work the melted plastic off the cement, flinching at the dental scraping sound it makes. He works until the knife is worn hot and smooth. Then he blasts the debris with the hose, sending pieces of melted gym suit scuttling into the grass. A dark burn remains at the epicenter of a larger problem, water and ash having stained the concrete gray. Aaron's joy at having witnessed the gym suit's destruction is replaced by abject fear. He retrieves a bottle of bleach and pours it on the stain. This yields the opposite effect: a blanched spot lighter than the surrounding, stained concrete.

Aaron decides the only solution is to color the entire patio an even whitish brown. He unearths portions of lawn and rubs dirt evenly across the cement. He is giving the patio one last rinse with the hose when Saul appears at the screen door.

"What are you doing?"

Aaron drops the hose. From behind the screen his father's shape is dark and indistinct, conforming to the shape of Aaron's growing fear. From behind the screen and inside the darkened house, small mercy, Aaron cannot make out his father's eyes.

Aaron is close to tears. He hasn't cried in front of anyone since elementary school. The thought of doing so now is as mortifying as the idea of peeing his pants. He swallows his initial urge to tell all in favor of reviewing possible alternatives.

It is not immediately apparent that he has been setting things on fire. The matches are in his pocket, the object of inflammation safely hidden in the grass. There is nothing technically wrong with standing on the patio with the hose, spreading dirt and water with his shoes. These thoughts flash through Aaron's brain with such incredible speed that the pause between Saul's question and his answer is barely unnaturally long.

"I was . . . playing."

Aaron immediately regrets his unbelievably lame response. He is certain Saul can see the lie as easily as if it is emblazoned across his forehead. The only thing worse than setting a fire is lying about it. Lying, as far as Saul is concerned, is the worst offense because it compromises the most important virtue, which is trust. *People make mistakes,* his father's voice reverberates in Aaron's head. *Mistakes are a part of life. Don't compound your errors by lying about them. I will always support you the best I can as long as you are honest with me.* Aaron realizes he fears the unmasking of his lie more than the discovery of what he has done.

Aaron has no idea how much time passes. He stands utterly still, afraid to regard his father's face, certain if he does he'll see the bulging eyes blazing from behind the screen door. He braces himself for the ear-popping descent to a new level of fatherly disappointment. He cannot see, from his vantage point, the bemused expression on Saul's face.

"Okay." Saul shrugs. The dark shape retreats. The study door closes. Aaron collapses onto the lawn.

Saul is clearly puzzled when Miriam follows him up to their room and into their bed hours before she usually goes to sleep.

"Are you feeling okay?" he asks. "Is something wrong?" He wonders if he should lock the bedroom door—Miriam only ever has sex if the bedroom door is locked—but then worries that while he is doing so she will change her mind. It has been a very long time.

Miriam can see the mixture of confusion and hope in her husband's eyes. She places his hand against her breast, saying nothing. How can she tell him that she needs him inside her or she fears she will float away? That she is fighting something she must struggle to want to fight? She looks at the scab left behind by the splinter with fondness. Even the sight of a ketchup bottle fills her with longing, the house's repellence eclipsed by the glory of another missing piece recovered.

Miriam tries to focus on the feeling of Saul's hands on her breasts, his tongue on her skin. *This is what people do,* she tells herself. Perhaps if she thinks of Saul as a house she can channel her passion into him, can search his rooms for something to reclaim. But it is all too familiar. She knows his chest, the hair thicker than you'd expect, the nipples laughably large. Years ago, they'd actually joked about the evolutionary absurdity of nipples on men. Years ago, she could talk with him about bodies. The memory exposes the degree to which they have changed, attesting to a time when their lives were not nonintersecting lines. She cannot pretend he is a house because she already claimed what he had to offer.

Hours into the night, Eliza is heading back to her bed from the bathroom. At first she thinks the house is settling in the wind, but the creaks are too loud and regular. She freezes in the hallway. She knows what the sounds are.

"Do you think our parents do it?" Aaron had asked, years before Eliza knew what he was talking about. He sounded puzzled and a little sad as he explained. "They're supposed to do it a lot. That's what being married is, but I never hear them, even when I listen at their door."

"Maybe they only do it when they know you're not listening," Eliza offered. Aaron had shrugged, his face reflecting his doubt. Over the years, Eliza has become pretty sure they don't do it either, can't imagine their secret parts touching when their unsecret parts rarely do.

So that now, when Eliza hears the creaks, she feels as if she has sighted a rare bird. She rejects the possibility of waking Aaron. Elly doesn't know if the creaks from the bedroom are something her brother would even want to know about anymore, now that everything seems to make him uncomfortable. Eliza stands stone still, barely breathing, afraid to alert her parents to anything that might interrupt their sound-making. She knows there's hair down there, imagines the creaks of bedsprings as crickets in the underbrush of two private forests whose tree branches are intertwining. She hears a sigh like a breeze through leaves and then it is quiet. Eliza tiptoes to bed.

Aaron wakes up nervous. He reads and rereads the pamphlets Chali gave him as if cramming for a test. For all he knows, there will be a test, only the correct answers granting entry to the temple. Aaron realizes that religion has become another team for which to be picked, another opportunity to be skipped over.

Aaron wills the day to go by quickly but only succeeds in becoming acutely aware of a minute's breadth. To divert himself from the sluggish tic of his watch Aaron walks to the park, but realizes once there that he unconsciously expected to see Chali there. The park has shrunk in Chali's wake. It is practically impossible for Aaron to distinguish the bench upon which they met, its ordinary wooden slats not nearly grand enough to signify the place where Aaron's life was destined to be changed. Aaron leaves before the park's drabness shrinks his resolve as well.

At home, Saul's open door beckons. Since his father's and sister's return from D.C. there have been no spelling sessions. Aaron could easily walk into the study and resume the roles of guitar player and future rabbi as if they had never been lost to him. One look from Saul would erase the divergent path he has begun to forge. Aaron returns to his room to reread the pamphlets. He has come too far to be so easily derailed. He remains safely behind his bedroom door until it's time to tell his parents he's going to the movies.

Saul hears his son come in from outside. Aaron has been restless all day. Even at breakfast there was a nervous quality to his actions that Saul hadn't seen before. Not that he has been paying much attention. Saul has been meaning to apologize to Aaron for the way he embarrassed him at the study door, but the time never seemed right and now such a long time has passed that it seems better to just let it be. After all, Aaron has become so sensitive lately.

Saul can hear the television from the next room. The sound prevents him from concentrating, but he wants to keep the study door open so that Eliza knows she has other possibilities. As much as he would like to sit Eliza down and convince her to continue their studies, he knows if they are to go any further it is she who must come to him. The places he wants to take her can only be reached by those who wish to go. Maybe in the meantime he should find Aaron and invite him to play a little guitar. It's silly to keep waiting at his desk for Eliza like a wallflower hoping to get asked to dance. Perhaps he should spend a little quality time with his son.

Saul grabs his guitar and heads upstairs. Aaron will be surprised; in the past it's always been Aaron who has come to him. Saul is certain his appearance will go a long way toward making amends, likes to think of himself as a man of action over words.

For some reason, Saul hadn't been expecting a closed door. Aaron's door presents difficulties in the light of their previous encounter. Saul can't very well knock when he gave Aaron such a hard time for doing just that. He's got to show Aaron the same respect he expects to be shown if he is to have any chance of being considered a cool dad under the unflinching light of adolescence. Saul descends the stairs with a grin. He'll leave his study door open. When Aaron comes back down, he'll call his son's name.

On the outside it's an innocuous brick building that could pass for the office of a tax preparer or dentist. Aaron doesn't know what he was expecting, only that he feels disappointed.

He has to ring a buzzer. An Indian woman in a sari answers the door.

"Hari Bol."

"Um, hi. Chali told me there was a service that I could, uh, come to." Aaron feels like he's come to the party of a friend of a friend who hasn't arrived yet.

"Welcome. The temple is the first door on the left. You may leave your shoes in the hallway. I'll tell Chali you are here." She smiles at Aaron before disappearing up a set of stairs.

The entryway smells of incense. From down a hallway comes the muted sound of voices. Alone in this strange place, the determination that powered Aaron to this moment leaves him. He pictures Saul storming through the door, demanding an explanation. Aaron pictures the Hari Bol woman—her brown skin, her kind eyes, her saffron robe—and can think of nothing they have in common. He has made a mistake. There is no way he will ever belong here. It will be easier for everyone if he just leaves now, before Chali has a chance to realize his misjudgment in extending an invitation. Aaron is about to back out the door and return home when Chali appears at the stairwell in a light yellow robe. Aaron's surprise at Chali's shaved head is eclipsed by the expression on Chali's face. Aaron can't remember the last time anyone looked happier to see him.

"You made it! Wonderful. I had a feeling you would. A lot of people say they'll come and then I never see them again, but I could tell you were a man of your word."

Chali's handshake fills Aaron like a hug.

Chali is smiling. "So, this is it. It's not much, but you should see the ones in Detroit and New York City. The best, of course, are in India. One day I hope to see them myself. But for now my place is here. Let me show you around."

Chali leads Aaron down the hall, toward the voices. Outside a set of double doors, Aaron adds his sneakers to a collection of sandals, feels grateful that his feet will at least look like everyone else's.

As soon as the door opens, Aaron hears the singing. The plainness of the hallway is forgotten, another country left far behind. Aaron is in the temple.

It is a large, open space filled with light, its wood floor highly polished. Instead of a place of worship, Aaron thinks of a ballroom, imagines sari-clad women swirling in the arms of lustrous-haired men. Beth Amicha seems dull by comparison, St. Patrick Church a gloomy cave. Ten people in robes, mostly men, face an ornate dais featuring a dark-eyed, dark-haired statue, adorned in gilded clothes and holding a flute to his lips. Beside him stands the statue of a woman in a vibrant gown of red and gold. The statues' necks are draped in garlands of fresh flowers that reflect the colors of the carved wooden peacocks in the wood panel behind them. An old Indian man with a face like a bullfrog sits on a platform opposite the dais. It takes a moment for Aaron to realize that the man isn't moving.

"He isn't real, is he?"

Chali smiles. "Pretty convincing, huh? The first time I came here, I thought he was alive too. That's Srila Prabhupada, our Founder-Acarya."

Aaron watches as Chali prostrates himself before the wax statue, lying flat on his stomach with his face to the floor before rising and tossing flowers at the old man's head and chest. It looks like something Aaron might see on PBS, narrated by a modulated voice with a British accent.

"Do you . . . worship him?" He knows that if Chali says yes he will have to go, knows he will never be able to bow before a wax frog-man.

Chali laughs. "Oh, no. We worship only God. To Prabhupada we give thanks and show our respect. I'm sure it looks strange to you, but don't worry. As you learn why we do what we do, you'll see for yourself how much sense everything makes. In the meantime, don't feel like you need to do or say anything you don't want to. Everyone comes to Kṛṣṇa at their own pace and on their own terms."

"Krishna?" Aaron tries to say as politely as possible. He can't believe he didn't think of this before. The orange robe. The shaved head. "As in Hare Krishna?"

Chali nods. "Kṛṣṇa is our word for God. Hare Krishna is the name given us by strangers for the words in our prayer, but it isn't what we call ourselves. I can see you've heard of us?"

Aaron nods warily.

"After you learn more, I'll be interested in hearing whether your personal knowledge matches up with your original, third-hand impressions. I have a feeling that you're going to be pleasantly surprised. Though we call God Kṛṣṇa, the name is immaterial. Kṛṣṇa, Jesus, Adonai, these different names all refer to the same Supreme force. ISKCON, the International Society for Krishna Consciousness, works in harmony with the world's established religions. Our goal is to advance our understanding and to improve our relationship with God, thus improving ourselves. But it isn't my intention to convince you of this. Let's go to my office so I can give you what you'll need to reach your own decisions."

Chali and Aaron return to the entryway and mount the stairs. Inside a small room is a desk, bookshelves, a cabinet. Aaron feels himself relax. He is in familiar territory again, no wax statues or deities to contend with. From a cupboard, Chali withdraws two books.

"I can tell you're feeling overwhelmed. That's okay. You should feel overwhelmed. Nothing in your experience has prepared you for this. Judeo-Christianity has nothing like our deities or our temples. I've had people ask me if by worshiping Kṛṣṇa we're not breaking the second commandment. But worshiping Kṛṣṇa is not idolatry because we are not expecting the deity to answer our prayers. The deity serves a focus for our worship and as a reminder of Kṛṣṇa's qualities when he was on earth—his kindness, his beauty—which inspires us to bring out these qualities in ourselves. But we don't expect you to blindly accept any of this; you need to experience it for yourself. Like the Jews, we are people of the book. The *Sri Isopanisad* will introduce you to the principles of the *Vedas,* which is our sacred text. This, the *Bhagavad-Gita,* is the most important of the *Vedas.* However, the most important aspect of Kṛṣṇa consciousness is also the easiest and you can do it without reading a single word."

From the cupboard, Chali produces a string of wooden beads the size of hazelnuts.

"These are *japa* beads. They are made from the wood of the sacred banyan tree. We use them in chanting *japa,* which consists of God's holy name."

Aaron's face lights up. "You mean like meditation? Like a mantra?"

"Exactly, but this is not just any mantra. This is God's name it-self. When we fill our mouths, ears, and minds with the sound of God's name, we free ourselves from material existence and realize our original and pure relationship with God." Chali hands Aaron the beads. "Each bead symbolizes a completed chant. There are 108 beads on this string. To complete a round of chanting is to say the chant 108 times. As a devotee, I chant at least sixteen rounds a day. If I have time, I chant more."

Aaron eyes the beads dubiously. "How long does that take?"

"It takes me two hours, but it will take you longer until you get the hang of it. Don't feel like you need to do sixteen rounds at first. Just try doing a little every day and see how it feels. Morning is the best time—before the material world has time to fill you with its petty concerns."

Aaron peers at his feet. "But do you actually *feel* God when you do it?" he asks so softly he fears Chali hasn't heard him.

Chali waits for Aaron to raise his head. His eyes grip Aaron's.

"In the beginning, no. I felt more relaxed, but I was still too in-volved in the material world to feel God. Then, as I learned to let go of *maya,* the world of illusion, chanting *japa* began to fill me with amazing happiness. God is inside all of us, but we forget this. Chanting allows you to remember."

Aaron strokes the beads with his fingers. Incense wafts up from his palm. The scented wood is cool and smooth to the touch. It feels good in his hand.

At school, no mention is made of Eliza's national defeat. Without the spelling sheets in her pocket, class drags. Eliza cannot remember how she used to make it through the day. The first of her newspaper arti-cles, "Huntingdon Girl Spells Her Way to V-I-C-T-O-R-Y," is re-placed in the school showcase by an article about a third grader whose spaniel placed fourth at a recent dog show. Though Eliza knows she is still welcome at the lunchroom's good girl table, she doesn't feel like she belongs there anymore.

Eliza tries to return to her routine of after-school television, but she no longer enjoys the reruns. Their familiarity, in which she once found such comfort, now mocks her. In every episode Eliza sees the predictability of her post-bee life. Just as surely as she knows that Blair and Jo will reconcile by the end of today's half-hour installment of "Facts of Life," she knows that each day will be a repetition of the last—bus, school, bus, home, bed—with some food and television in between. None of that comes close to the excitement of tracing a word back to its salty origins, of charting its transformations over time. Ms. Bergermeyer and her high-pitched nasal lectures are no match for her father's asides, expansions, and non sequiturs, his excitement enough to make it all relevant and alive.

Eliza knows Saul is waiting for her. Ever since the national bee, he has kept his study door open in standing invitation. But she also knows that if she returns it will be to different rules. There will be no more dictionary, no more word derivations. If she wants to continue with him, she's got to want to "get to know the letters." She isn't sure how she can pretend to want something she doesn't understand, something she'd be embarrassed to mention in front of anyone else. Getting to know the letters sounds like a game for little kids, as obsolete as Chutes and Ladders or Candyland. Yet she knows that if she walks through the study door her father will convince her that getting to know the let-ters is something she desperately wants to do. Though she doesn't have the time or personal perspective to put it into words, she senses that once she enters her father's study, she is destined to give him whatever he wants even if she isn't sure she has it.

As far as Eliza can tell, Saul has been effortlessly filling the time that moves intolerably slowly for her. Eliza doesn't know his seeming occu-pation is intended to make her feel free. Instead it strikes her as a taunt: *I don't really need you.* She feels caught out in the face of this, realizes she had come to think of herself as necessary. With the spelling bee over, she had entertained soft-focus visions of father/daughter kite-building and cookie-baking, images she doesn't realize she has lifted from an old

Hallmark commercial until she sees it again on TV. In the wake of her own loss, she finally appreciates what she took from Aaron by replacing his guitar sessions. The guilt that fills her is no longer tempered by a private sense of victory. Instead of feeling as if she has won her father from her brother, she feels as if she has lost them both.

Back in his bedroom, Aaron examines Chali's gifts. It's hard to believe that half an hour away is a place where these objects actually make sense. If it weren't for the books and beads, Aaron is pretty sure he could convince himself that his visit was a dream, that there is no Chali, no place where robed men and women walk with *japa* beads hanging from pouches around their necks. Aaron slips his own pouch over his head. He looks at his closet full of clothes, the books on his shelf, the dusty guitar case in its corner. "*Maya,* the world of illusion," he whispers.

Aaron sits cross-legged, the *japa* beads in one hand.

"*Hare Kṛṣṇa Hare Kṛṣṇa Kṛṣṇa Kṛṣṇa Hare Hare. Hare Rama Hare Rama Rama Rama Hare Hare.*"

The words are tentative, his voice self-conscious. It's nothing like what Chali sounded like. Watching Chali had been the clincher. When Chali closed his eyes and began to chant, the words ran like water from his throat. Chali's face became suffused with a joy so intense Aaron expected at any moment to see him jump up and begin to dance, could not imagine that much happiness remaining still. Aaron decided right then and there that even though the wax statue and the Kṛṣṇa deity were a little weird, it was all worth a try if it meant having a chance at feeling the way Chali looked at that moment.

Aaron closes his eyes and tries again. By the fifth cycle he's found a rhythm, stretching the A's in *Rama* the way Chali did. In his head is an image of a stone rolling down a mountain, building momentum, the chant's finish carrying over to its start so that the words are seamless, his fingers on the *japa* beads the only indication of a beginning or an end to the sounds. Aaron chants fifty cycles before he hears someone coming up the stairs and stops, afraid of being overheard. He decides that tomorrow morning he will wake up before Elly or Saul and try again.

Eliza cannot get through a day without at least one spelling bee word finding her. The word can come from anywhere: a television newscaster, an overheard conversation, a song lyric on the radio. On each occasion she gets an adrenaline rush that makes the world more intense for a few moments, the word standing out the way a random object highlighted by the sun acquires sudden significance. Life becomes filled with opportunities for discovery. Elly repeats the word inside her head. She pretends she is once again at the microphone and victory still within reach, an entire room silent save for the letters from her mouth. But she cannot maintain the moment. Invariably the word fades, leaving her with that disappointed feeling at parade's end after the last float has passed.

It is during a "Barney Miller" episode that she hears Detective Nick Yemana say LOQUAT and remembers how the word blossomed in her head, its letters inhabiting her as surely as her own skeleton. She remembers her father's words, "Next year you could be unstoppable." Remembering LOQUAT, she decides to believe him.

The next night Saul awakens to find himself hard inside his wife's mouth. At first he thinks he is dreaming, but the distinctly nondream-like detail of used dental floss on his nightstand assures him that he isn't. His dreams never feel this specific—her hands clutching his hips as if they are all that is holding her to the bed, her hair brushing the inside of his legs as she works her mouth up and down.

"Miriam," he whispers, but she doesn't hear him. "Miriam," he says a little louder, ending in a moan. Only when he props himself up on his elbows and touches her shoulder does she finally look at him, seemingly startled to discover a person attached to the focus of her attention.

She had gotten as far as the garage door before she forced herself to turn around, knew the only way to resist the car and an unfamiliar house would be to go directly to bed. When she first started and he had been completely soft, she wasn't sure whether or not she wanted him to wake up. As he became harder she realized it didn't matter. All she needed was him inside her.

"Miriam, slow down. Come here so I can touch you." He has fantasized about this, but it has never actually happened, a lover waking him in the middle of the night. A long time ago, when it still felt natural to talk about such things, he had mentioned this to Miriam. When he asked if she had any fantasies of her own, a look of utter puzzlement had been her only response.

Miriam must not have heard him. He's getting closer and closer to coming even though or perhaps because he is trying to hold himself back. Maybe he should pull away so that he can bring her with him but it feels so good and she's so *intent,* as if she's got a secret mission, he can't hold back much longer and now she's taking him between her legs and he can tell that she's dry, he can feel the resistance going in. He knows it can't feel good for her, knows she needs time, wants to pull out but she's thrusting him in so hard there's nothing he can do; it's over. He looks at her, confusion in his eyes, but she's not even looking at him, not even aware that he's come. She's still pumping up and down. He has to push her off before she stops.

Eliza's table has been replaced by two overstuffed pillows. The dictionary has joined Saul's other books. Until Eliza smells the dust and paper and crumbling leather again, she doesn't realize how much she has missed her father's study. Even as a long-absent sense of well-being overtakes her she has no idea that this feeling is contingent upon the smell, which she associates with Saul's love.

At first Eliza thinks her father's ideas are weird.

"Think of your brain as a muscle. A runner does stretches to warm up. Brains need the same courtesy."

Some days he has Eliza write the alphabet over and over again without looking at the paper, switching the pen between her right and left hands. He tells her not to think about what the letters look like or if she is writing too small or too large. She is only to focus on the motion of her hand, upon the feeling of the letter emerging. Eliza imagines the alphabet climbing inside her arm and taking her hand for a ride until she is no longer aware of her fingers' movements, only knows what she is writing after she looks at the page.

Sometimes Saul has Eliza visualize the first letter that comes into her head, telling her to make it grow to the size of a tangerine, to a melon, to a small dog, and on and on until the letter is bigger than herself, bigger than the house, stretching majestically toward the sun.

"What is a universe of A like? What's a universe of Q?" he'll say, usually not guessing the letter that's growing inside her head like a time-lapse film of seedling to flower. Occasionally she has trouble breathing, the letter grown so large in her imagination that it takes up all her air.

Sometimes they chant the alphabet together, forward and backward, in unison and independently, until the letters are a continuous ribbon of sound unwinding from Eliza's tongue. She feels most like her brother then, the ghost of his guitar entering the room. The letters become music, the alphabet their own duet.

"Okay, Elly, I want you to clear your mind."

This is the hardest part. There is so much going on. The more of her mind Elly makes quiet, the more she finds making noise. *Nothing, nothing, nothing, nothing,* she repeats as fast as she can, sweeping her other thoughts away. Eliza pictures her brain as a tunnel extending deep into the earth, *nothing* the water slowly filling it from bottom to top.

Saul can see the change. Elly's jaw relaxes, her face slackens. Only a few minutes after closing her eyes, she is in what Saul calls the Zone.

"Are you clear?"

Elly nods.

"I want you to open yourself up to a letter."

Elly has learned that this is something different than thinking of a letter. When she opens herself up, she doesn't know what the letter will be. Somehow, Saul can tell if she is opening up or thinking. The trick is to think about babies.

Eliza imagines she is floating in a warm space. She is a mere half something waiting to be made whole. Rushing toward her are all the letters of the alphabet. Each one moves in its own way, X cartwheeling over and over, C hopping forward, M and N marching stiff-legged and resolute. Each letter struggles to be the first. Some letters stumble. Others slow and then stop. What was once the whole alphabet is now only part of the letter spectrum. Elly feels mounting excitement as the remaining letters approach. One pulls away from the others. It comes closer and closer until, finally, it passes into her, filling her with its A-ness or R-ness, K-ness or Y-ness, and now she is a growing thing, the letter present in every fledgling heartbeat, every newborn drop of blood.

This is how she comes to discover that the letters feel different. She's afraid to tell Saul, uncertain what he'd think to learn that L thickens her skin, that F makes her feel liquid, that Q fills her head with beautiful glass beads until she can only hear them clicking together. Not all the sensations are pleasant. E tenses her muscles as if they are bracing for an attack. K coats her joints in sandpaper.

Saul can tell when a letter has come. Eliza's face goes from a state of relaxation to intense concentration, as if she is trying to hear a very soft sound.

"Do you have a letter?" he asks loud enough to enter her thoughts without shattering them.

Eliza nods, eyes still closed.

"Good. Now, without deliberately thinking about it, I want you to open yourself up to all the words that contain that letter. Let the words flow through you, like you're a hollowed-out log being carried by a current."

This has become Eliza's favorite part. It took awhile to make her father's instructions work. At first she was too conscious of trying to pull words from her memory: apple, acorn, around, arrest. The key is to take baby-making to its natural conclusion. Filled with a letter, she imagines growing with it. Pieces of the letter break apart or fuse together to form her eyes, her nose, her hands and feet. The letter bends and flexes, and suddenly a stream of words is passing through her, coming so quickly she barely feels each word before it is replaced by another. *Accommodatarantulassoramblastand*. A whispering noise, like the rustle of silk. Words she feels in her fingertips as she sees behind her closed eyes. Beneath the words she hears are ones she doesn't quite catch, words to which she has not been properly introduced but which hover, expectant, on the periphery of consciousness. *Next time,* she promises, remembering that for every baby there are countless neverborns.

Through it all, Saul watches. Elly's eyes dance back and forth behind her closed lids. Her fingers flutter and twitch. Inside Saul, dreams once destined to be neverborns begin to grow.

At first Aaron chants with the stereo on to mask the sound of his voice, but he soon decides that mixing the words of God's name with those of the Eagles is too large a dilution. Which is what gives Aaron the idea of the closet. He likes the darkness of the closet, the softness of his shirts against his face, cushioning and protecting him. He chants into flannel, he chants into cotton. The holy sound of God's name is absorbed by the cloth as soon as it leaves his mouth. He likes to think that by soaking up the sound, his shirts become holy too, the same way that placing food before Kṛṣṇa turns it into *prasadam,* infused with God's spirit. The word "Kṛṣṇa" still sounds alien. Aaron ups his chanting to three rounds daily in order to make Kṛṣṇa more at home on his tongue. He begins carrying his *japa* beads to school inside his left pocket. He chants to himself when class drags, when there is a mandatory assembly, when he is stuck in the lunch line. The chant becomes a looping refrain in his head.

When the scent of the *japa* beads first sticks to his fingertips, he is startled. It is a strong smell, a combination of spice and perfume that belies the paleness of the wood. Aaron discovers himself smelling his fingers at odd times, not having consciously brought his hand to his nose. The scent marks him, reminds him that the most powerful symbols of belonging are invisible. He feels a gratitude toward the *japa* beads that initially embarrasses him, a feeling of kinship that seems inappropriate toward a simple object. But when Aaron next visits the temple (another movie with Charlie, who Saul is pleased to know is becoming a close friend) and sees the devotees praying before the Kṛṣṇa deity, the idea of praying before a statue doesn't seem nearly as strange.

The first time Aaron chants sixteen rounds is a Saturday. He only intends to chant eight, tying his record for the most he's ever chanted, but instead of feeling twitchy and restless by the middle of the eighth round, he feels like a long-distance runner getting a second wind. He is barely aware of the shirts in his face or the stale air of the closet. His fingers count out the beads of their own accord, unconnected to conscious thought, which has taken a back seat to the sounds streaming from his mouth. He feels his voice resonating in his chest and belly. The feeling takes up everything. It erases time, wipes away his awareness of his moving lips and fingers. His mind empties of his boredom with school and his mounting anxiety over his covert visits to the ISKCON temple. He is only the sound of God's name coming from his mouth, too caught up to even notice that he sounds like Chali now, his words fast but precise, the chant's end and beginning blending together into a seamless, rolling whole. He doesn't realize until he has stopped that his fingers have set aside sixteen beads, signifying the completion of a full chanting cycle. He looks at his watch. Two and a half hours have passed. The warm air of the closet surrounds him like an embrace.

They do not talk about what happens at night. Because their days are the same, it is almost possible for Saul to convince himself that their nights also remain unchanged, that he has somehow imagined it all.

Ten times now she has followed him to bed. Six of those ten he has said no. Two of those six, her masturbating in front of him has changed his mind. His few unswayed refusals have led to awakening to himself hard in her mouth, in her hand, or between her legs. When he manages to pull away in time, he is kept awake by the fear that he will be awoken later to the same thing. He tries to condition himself to wake upon being touched but can't, his wife weaving herself too deftly into his dreams. A few times he hasn't woken up until the middle of orgasm, the unwanted pleasure filling him with a sense of shame he hasn't felt since the first wet dreams of his adolescence. He has never felt so divided, wonders if Miriam has secretly intended a crash course in mind/body separation.

It shames him that he cannot bring himself to talk to her because the possibility she may stop is worse than that of her continuing. He cannot remember the last time he felt that distinctive, delicious groin ache from too much sex. He imagines trying to describe his dilemma. *That's a problem?* he would be told. *You should feel lucky she wants it at all.* He tells himself this imaginary voice is right. He tries to assuage his discomfort by inventing a medical explanation based upon his own off-brand of science. Perhaps Miriam's new proclivity marks the onset of menopause. Perhaps, he rationalizes, there is a final surge of sexual energy before that part of her body shuts down; all the more reason to enjoy it while he can. But he has stopped sleeping well. He dreams of hands clutching at him and not letting go.

One dream starts so realistically Saul is uncertain whether he is asleep or awake. Miriam is on top. Perspiration dots her upper lip. She is oblivious to the fact that he is lying completely still. As he observes his lower body's mindless response to his wife's ministrations, Saul is filled with resentment. He decides that enough is enough. In a stern voice he tells Miriam to stop. Miriam pauses briefly and, without re-moving her hands, looks down at Saul and shrugs. She starts pulling at his penis. Her grip is firm but not too hard. Just as Saul wonders what she is trying to do, his penis suddenly tears away as easily and painlessly as a piece of clay. There is no blood. When Saul next looks at his body, a swath of perfectly smooth skin spans the space between his legs, delicate and overripe like a healing burn. Miriam rolls off him, completely focused on her new prize. Rather than horror, Saul feels relief.

There are four rules to follow: No gambling. No intoxicating sub-stances. No illicit sex. No eating meat. At first Aaron thinks that not eating meat will be hard. When, on Chali's suggestion, he pictures a burger as part of a cow, a drumstick as a chicken's leg, he realizes that he has never before granted meat a former life. As soon as meat be-comes something more than a plastic-wrapped lump on a Styrofoam tray, the idea of avoiding it becomes much easier.

Aaron's first test comes at dinner the day after he vows to begin fol-lowing Kṛṣṇa's precepts. Saul has made barbecued chicken, one of Aaron's favorites, cooking it on the grill mere feet away from the mys-terious light spot on the patio whose origins only Aaron knows. At the table, Aaron heaps his plate with macaroni. He can barely look at the barbecued chicken parts which, at his glance, mentally assemble them-selves into the blackened corpse of a bird.

"I'm a vegetarian now," he says to a surprised Saul when he refuses a drumstick and a breast, his former favorite parts.

Eliza looks up mid-wing and notices Aaron's plate of pasta for the first time. By so obviously enjoying her dinner in the face of his ab-stention, she has surely enacted another betrayal. She puts her wing down and takes more macaroni, hoping to demonstrate solidarity, but Aaron isn't paying attention. Elly tries to take bites of chicken only when her brother isn't looking. That being most of the time, her chicken wing disappears at a rapid pace, with her reaching across the table for more to avoid drawing Aaron's attention with the verbal request. As Eliza bites into her second wing, she knows that a good sister would have at least refrained from taking seconds.

Aaron is too focused on Saul to notice. He is less concerned with his proclamation than the questions sure to follow, senses that once again he will need to lie.

Aaron's declaration reminds Saul of the short-lived vegetarianism of his college days. His alternative lifestyle lasted as long as it took to realize that the horrific farts produced by his bean diet seriously compromised his sex appeal.

"Very admirable," Saul says. "What, may I ask, inspired this decision?"

When Aaron gets nervous he bites his lower lip. "Well, Charlie's a vegetarian, and after talking to him about it, I decided it just made sense." He wishes he could describe the delicious meals he's had at the temple, the intensity of the flavors making a convincing case for the food being suffused with Kṛṣṇa's spirit.

"This Charlie fellow sounds pretty interesting. I'd like to meet him sometime."

Aaron wonders what his father would make of Chali, can't help but think he'd like him. "Well, Charlie doesn't have a car and he lives kind of far away, but maybe someday you will."

"What do his parents do?"

Chali has never talked about his parents or anything, for that matter, not related to temple life. Everything else is *maya*, Aaron reminds himself, irrelevant. With a chuckle, he realizes that this conversation is irrelevant, even Saul is irrelevant. If he joined the temple, he could put his entire life behind him like a shirt he has outgrown.

"They're vegetarians too," Aaron says, his thoughts having made him bold. "They've invited me to dinner to see what vegetarian food is like. They said I could eat with them whenever I want."

"How nice," Miriam says, wondering what their house looks like.

Eliza is amazed that neither parent seems able to detect Aaron's lie. It's so obvious. He would chew his lip the same way during Monopoly when attempting an unfair deal, for example trying to convince her to trade Park Place for St. James because orange is so much uglier than blue.

Eliza gives Aaron a questioning look. He glares at her. She turns to the chicken bones on her plate, which she has stripped clean, and keeps quiet.

After the sticky failure of his initial meditation attempts, Aaron decides he will only allow himself to masturbate once a week and then only on a day when he has no meditation plans. He quickly discovers he likes being made to wait. He looks forward to Tuesdays with an enthusiasm only matched by Monday's exquisite proximity to the special day. With Monday's arrival, Aaron finds his entire body sensitized. Brushing against soft fabric or feeling nubby carpet on his bare feet sends chills across his body. The difficulty comes in hiding the spontaneous hard-ons that plague him through Monday afternoon. Once in the middle of math, his anticipation is so intense that the tight stretch of underwear against his sudden erection is enough to set him off. He doesn't even realize he hasn't been paying attention to the equations on the board until his body begins to shudder gently and he feels wet between his legs. He quickly turns the episode into a coughing fit, asking to be excused for a drink of water. In a locked bathroom stall he removes his underwear and buries it in his backpack, desperately hoping that the novelty of walking around without won't set him off again. The next morning, at the appointed hour, he struggles over whether yesterday's surprise counts as the week's masturbatory allotment and decides it does not since he didn't actually touch himself to make it happen.

So that weeks into his vegetarianism, when Aaron shyly asks Chali what illicit sex means, he feels a certain thrill when Chali explains that sex doesn't require two people to be illicit. This, Aaron realizes, will be his greatest challenge, the true test of his devotion. He has been chanting sixteen rounds every day except Tuesdays, but even that one day a week has been distancing him from God. Aaron privately vows to devote himself entirely to Kṛṣṇa.

The first few weeks, it is difficult to unlearn the feeling of Mondays or the excitement of waking up on Tuesday mornings before the alarm, his body still anticipating his forsworn habit. Aaron becomes a devotee of showers of extreme hotness or coldness, the shock of the water helping to make undistracted chanting a possibility. He refers to his new sense of discipline in veiled terms to Chali, who heartily congratulates him on having overcome *maya*'s strongest pull.

Though Aaron still feels conspicuous in his *karmi* clothes and unshaven head, he is no longer a stranger at the temple. Devotees are split between whites and Indian families, the whites mostly guys in their twenties like Chali, with the occasional woman or middle-aged man. Though Aaron is younger than most of the white people, there are several Indian children. There is a girl close to his age, the daughter of a guru. Sundays, she presents skits illustrating Kṛṣṇa's teachings, her faith electrifying her words and compelling even the freeloaders who have only come for the food to pay attention.

Today, the girl tells a story from India.

"Every holy day," the girl says, "an old woman followed behind the temple elephants, cleaning up their dung as they circled the temple grounds with the temple deities on their backs. The devotees, concerned with their struggle to be reborn into a higher life, did not notice her. Still, every holy day she was there at the temple with a shovel and a basket. One day a guru visited the temple and noticed the old woman. 'This woman,' he said, 'has been serving Kṛṣṇa with no thought of her own reward, and will go straight from this life to Godhead.' And, when the woman died, she left earth, passed through the heavenly planets, and went straight to Godhead where she is now at Kṛṣṇa's side."

Aaron knows, deep in his heart, that he is meant to marry the guru's daughter. This girl is the one with whom he is meant to create a new life for Kṛṣṇa. They will be married with their guru's blessing and then, a few months later, they will approach him with their wish.

The guru will smile as he grants permission. They will stand side by side as they announce their plans to the temple, their faces glowing with joy. Preceding the special meal, they will chant for six extra hours to insure they are spiritually clean enough to merit a child with a pure soul. Then they will perform the sacred act. Aaron has only pictured the girl's body in dreams he doesn't remember, prides himself on the fact that in his waking fantasies he pictures only the girl's smiling face and a baby with her eyes. After a few weeks of this fantasy, he realizes he has been erroneously picturing a white baby, retouches his imaginary infant's skin until it is a shade closer to that of his imaginary bride's. With a flush of pride, he realizes how far he has come from his father's study and the Stacey Liebermans of the world.

Filled with visions of dark babies, Aaron participates in *kirtan* for the first time, dancing and chanting with the others until he is no longer aware of his arms and legs. Before, he had been terrified he might be recognized by someone and his secret revealed. He stuck to the temple's corners while the others danced and chanted. Today, when Aaron walks to the room's center and joins the others, he can see the pride in Chali's face, a smile that affects him like an outstretched palm, pulling him into the dance. Currents of incense brush Aaron's face, the air set in motion by the twirling robes of the dancers. The sweet, spicy smell encompasses him, claiming him as its own.

For the first time, Aaron doesn't think to watch the door. Submerged in the energy of the *kirtan,* he leaves the thoughts and concerns of his old life, his *maya* life, behind. His new life is the movement of his arms and legs, the sound of *Hare Kṛṣṇa* coming from his mouth. Without knowing how it got there, he finds a tambourine in his hands, then looks at the girl and realizes it is from her. He raises the tambourine above his head, filling the air with its sound. The girl smiles. A tremor passes through him so strong his entire body shudders. He panics with the pleasure of it, prepared to make a quick exit à la math class to the bathroom. But he isn't wet. The pleasure he felt was entirely pure, uncompromised by his *maya* body. He begins to shout God's name, his intensity affecting the others like a wave, who begin to shout with him. The room resounds with their voices.

Miriam has never been drawn to a neighborhood this close to home before and it makes her nervous. She has circled the block twice now in her car, deliberately focusing on the road ahead and not the homes on either side. Each time she has felt the house's presence as she passed, its pull unmistakable. She parks three blocks away and begins a casual walk toward her destination. The neighborhood is more humble than her own, but not by much. The houses are a little smaller, a little less well kept up, but not so bad that she can't imagine having moved here if she and Saul hadn't done as well as they had for themselves. There are gardens, the occasional small boat. Wooden signs beside doorways announce O'Connolls and Waverlys.

Miriam is half a block from her objective when she hears a voice behind her.

"Miriam Naumann?"

Miriam whirls around, the blood having drained from her head. She does not know who she expected, but it is not this smiling stranger. The shock of hearing her name has made Miriam dizzy. She sits on the curb.

"Are you okay?" The woman is at Miriam's side. "I didn't mean to startle you. Madge Turner. Our boys were in Scouts together. I thought I recognized that curly hair of yours. We're not neighbors, are we? Why, I'd feel so silly if this whole time we had been living a few blocks away from each other."

Miriam forces a smile. When Aaron was a Scout, she had attended the troop's annual holiday pageant, generally a nativity play with a Chanukah song tacked on at the end. Aaron and the two other Jewish boys were invariably cast as barnyard animals. Saul was delighted when Aaron decided to quit.

"The holiday play?" Miriam asks.

Madge Turner beams. "I can't believe you remembered! I made the costumes. I always thought Aaron made the cutest little piglet. You know, I was so glad to have Aaron in the play. Jesus *was* Jewish, after all."

Miriam nods, mind numb. She can see the house from where she is standing. It takes supreme effort to keep from running toward it and pretending that she never stopped for this stranger named Madge Turner, who has gone on to describe her son's Christian youth group.

"... and, you know, it really is for young people of *all* denominations. The main purpose of the group is to encourage spiritualism and clean living, which is important for young people no matter *what* their religious background."

"Mrs. Turner—"

"Oh, please, Miriam, call me Madge. After all, we're neighbors."

"Madge, could you please help me? I've gotten horribly lost. I was meaning to take a short cut to Route 73, but I must have taken a wrong turn and I was just walking down the street looking for a house where someone might be able to give me directions."

"Route 73? But it's not even near here! You must have gotten *really* turned around."

Miriam laughs weakly. She can't tell whether Madge believes the lie. "I'm afraid I must have."

"Well, it's all for the good because it's allowed us to find each other again. Let's exchange phone numbers so that Matthew can tell Aaron about the next Young Life meeting."

Miriam takes the number, gives a slightly altered version of her own, and listens to Madge's directions on how to reach a road she has no intention of finding. She does her best to walk back to her car without looking as if she is desperate to escape. Driving past the house on her way out, Miriam can feel a small part inside herself shrivel at the manifestation of her failure.

The school year ends. Eliza's final report card overflows onto its back with glowing comments penned in Bergermeyer's careful hand. Bergermeyer calls Eliza her "little star," and waxes prosaic over the "lovely surprise she gave us all this year." Eliza's spelling A becomes an A+ and is joined by unprecedented A's in History, Work Habits, and Reading, bumping her up to Honor Roll for the first time in her academic career. Saul celebrates by baking a cake whose emergence from the oven only he and Eliza witness, Miriam working late and Aaron gone to an end-of-school pizza and movie with Charlie. If either of them notices that dinners for two have become the norm, they don't mention it. Eliza is too excited by the idea of spending entire summer days with her father ensconced in words and letters. Saul, for his part, has been waiting for summer's beginning to progress to the next stage of their studies. It's time for Eliza to meet Abraham Abulafia.

Once the cake has been sliced, Saul lifts his plate above the table.

"A toast," he says. "To the end of a wonderful school year and the beginning of a very exciting summer."

Eliza giggles, lifting her plate so that father and daughter may clink dishes.

After the first slice Eliza expects Saul to tell her she has had enough, but when she looks up from her plate she finds him deep into seconds, eating with the abandon of an unmonitored child at a birthday party. Eliza eats four more slices, each topped with a candy flower of the coveted *oneg* variety, solely because she can. For fifteen minutes, vigorous chewing and occasional giggles fill the room. When the sounds subside the cake, which had been easily large enough for four, has been reduced to crumbs.

Eliza and Saul stare at the empty plate, amazed. Saul looks up at his daughter with stricken eyes.

"We ate the *whole thing*," he whispers.

In the slight crinkles around her father's eyes, where before Eliza only saw age and authority, she now perceives youth. She can envision softer versions of those same lines in a younger face marveling at a colony of thumbnail-sized baby frogs or the blueness of a swimming pool. Now permanently reflected in her father's features, Eliza sees the boy he once was, a child whom Eliza considers a friend.

"Aaron will be mad he didn't get any," Eliza says.

"Let's not tell him," Saul stage whispers. "Or your mom."

Eliza giggles and nods. "We'll clean up the evidence."

"They would never understand, anyway," Saul says, no longer whispering, looking into Eliza's eyes.

Eliza knows he's right.

Miriam decides it's a simple matter of returning to the stores. Since her romance with houses began, what had once been an integral part of her life has faded unnoticed into obscurity. In contrast to her weeks with houses, her years with stores feel like a distant memory, a college friend from whom she has grown apart. She decides if she can wean herself off houses the previous patterns of her life will reassert themselves, overriding her unsuitable passion.

Returning to stores is more difficult than anticipated. Stepping into the car, Miriam's body demands the fulfillment of its real desire and not this wishful placebo. Miriam can already feel the pull of unfamiliar roads upon her skin. Her limbs are already gearing up for the carefully casual stride to a stranger's front door. Miriam feels literal pain when she wrenches her car into the mall parking lot, her denied craving a muscle that has been torn.

It feels all wrong from the moment she steps outside. The air feels stiff in her lungs, every breath a reminder that this is not where she is meant to be. Sights and sounds are perceived at an extreme remove. She feels she is observing her surroundings through reverse binoculars while listening to an ambient recording of suburban parking lot sounds. As she nears the mall, it is difficult to believe its doors are not part of an elaborate backdrop in the 2-D world created in the wake of her refusal to obey the houses.

She forces herself through the mall doors, past the clothing stores, gift booths, and eatery to a department store. She assures herself that once she enters she will be safe from the path she abandoned and the world will reinflate. As Miriam crosses the threshold to waxed floors and tinned music, she takes a deep breath, willing the familiar smells of perfume and air conditioning to welcome her back.

It doesn't work. Even here, where she once sought her quarry with equanimity, the sense of pervasive wrongness doesn't abate. The very aspects of department stores that used to comfort only recall her willful betrayal. The lights are too bright, the colors too sharp. For the first time Miriam feels conspicuous. Her eyes dart back and forth as if seeking escape. Her hands refuse to be still. She keeps turning, certain store detectives are lying in wait.

Miriam wanders from department to department, a sleepwalker. There is no beacon to follow, no sense of when or where to turn. She stares accusingly at each item she passes, *Are you the one?* knowing that if she has to ask, it won't answer. She tries not to think about where she should really be: a worn carpet beneath her feet, her nose immersed in the smells of a stranger's home. Here in this universe of fluorescence and packaging, it is a place as exotic and unreachable as a fairy tale.

It is hopeless, but Miriam is determined to leave with what she came for. She blindly grabs a shoe from the sale rack, not even glancing at her hands as she slips it into her purse. Sweating, she makes for the nearest exit, breaking two of her cardinal department store rules: Never leave immediately after taking what you've come for. Always go out the way you came in.

The shoe department exit deposits Miriam on the second level of a parking garage. To return to her car, she must either go back through the mall or walk across the lot and down a ramp not intended for pedestrians. She chooses the ramp. At every step, the shoe in her purse bangs into her hip, mocking her. Halfway down, there is a car and Miriam must press herself into the wall to avoid getting swiped by its side-view mirror.

By the time Miriam returns to her parking space, she feels she has been walking for miles and not minutes. Once inside the car she opens her purse. The shoe is a hideous thing, a monster in her womb. She must abort if she is to save her own life. Miriam lobs the shoe out the driver-side window. It skitters across the pavement, coming to rest under the front tire of a parked van. Wiping her palm repeatedly on her slacks doesn't remove the sense of it in her hand. With a sick, excited feeling in her stomach, she realizes that her store days are over.

Eliza has no idea how much of each day is spent in her father's study. The letters erase time with their presence. She allows her pen to slip from a word's moorings, exploring every possible combination of its letters, the motion of her hand and the release of ink upon paper clearing her mind until there is nothing else.

Her father calls it permutation and describes it as a way to get to the essence of the letters themselves. Words are barriers, necessary gates beyond which lies the larger letter universe. Most people stop at the arrangement of letters a word presents: EARTH is earth and only earth. But within EARTH, there is RATHE and THRAE. Within EARTH, there is HEART. By departing from a given word order and exploring every possible combination, the true essence of the letters can be reached. E's true identity can only be known once it has been experienced next to A and R as well as between them. Only by knowing E in all its states can E's presence be sensed in AERATE as easily as in CABOOSE.

At first Eliza sticks to smaller words. A three-letter word contains only six possible combinations; four letters produce twenty-four. She feels comfortable inside such limits, is less afraid of making mistakes. Initially, permutation is a daunting math problem. A five-letter word with its 120 possibilities seems terrifying, the 720 permutations of a six-letter word impossible. But as the weeks pass, Eliza becomes more confident. The letters' internal rhythms begin to make themselves known. Eliza's first five-letter word grants a sense of release absent with shorter words. She learns not to anticipate the letters. Instead she lets the pen in her hand guide her as she submits to the power of the word itself.

Sometimes she stumbles. Deep into five-letter permutations, she can lose her way, suddenly unfixed from the letters and their strange internal rhythms. She becomes fearful of the paper and its nonsensical letter combinations. She and Saul revert to dictionary study then, spelling drills a welcome return to apparent normalcy.

The day Eliza attempts her first six-letter word she knows she is ready. She can feel this certainty in her blood. She picks up the pen and closes her eyes. It is easy to clear her mind now. In a few deep breaths she has washed away the day and all sense of yesterday or tomorrow. She waits for the word to arrive.

MANTLE enters her pen like a gust of wind and her hand begins to dance. The letters fill the page with their lines and curves until her entire body is carried by the steady stream of letters as they come together and break apart, touching and falling away, M making way for A and N, then shifting into a solid crunch of consonants. L, T, M, and N attract and repel each other with magnetic intensity as Eliza proceeds from NTLEAM to TLEAMN to LEMANT. She can hear the dissonance and harmony of each combination inside her head. She feels no fatigue. Thirty minutes into the permutation her hand continues its frantic pace, 300 recombinations down and 420 to go, though she isn't counting. The letters are all she needs to know. MANTLE's energy wells up from deep inside her, bubbling to the surface.

After little more than an hour, MANTLE is complete, its 720 permutations filling ten sheets of paper which lie scattered about Eliza like shed skin. Saul has been watching, entranced, for the last forty minutes. He doesn't need to review her work to confirm what she has accomplished.

"You did it," he says in hushed wonder.

Eliza, exhausted but exhilarated, can only nod.

Saul realizes the time has come to tell his daughter everything.

In 1280 a Jewish mystic named Abraham Abulafia writes a book entitled *Chayay Olam HaBah,* or *Life of the Future World.* Before this book, the world of the mystic had been a closed one, the methods by which one communed with the Divine a secret combination of magic words, talismans, and Talmudic erudition. Those deemed unworthy of the journey were punished with madness, blindness, or death.

Abulafia's book changes everything. In it, he states that the key to transcendence is language itself. Creation takes place through words, a series of "And God Saids" bringing each new stage of life into being. Language is God's divine power made manifest in the world. The foundation of language is letters.

"Letters," Saul says. "Abulafia believed that, by concentrating on letters, the mind could loose itself from its shackles to commune with a presence greater than itself, what Abraham Abulafia called *shefa,* the influx. He believed that barriers separated personal existence from the larger stream of life, the Divine Intellect."

He pauses to look at his daughter, to see how she is taking all this. Eliza is extremely still, completely focused on his face. *Tabula rasa,* Saul thinks. She is his own blank slate.

"Abulafia was branded a heretic and his books denounced. Neither *Future World* nor any of his subsequent treatises on practical mysticism was published. But they survived. Handwritten manuscripts were copied and handed down through the ages. His ideas were not only discussed but put into practice. Today, Abulafia is recognized as one of the great Kabbalists.

"The steps that Abulafia outlines, the methods that caused such an uproar, are basically instructions on how to meditate. Abulafia uses language play as a way to clear the mind, to remove oneself from daily concerns and thoughts. The exercises we've been doing are Abulafia's. His methods are primarily a kind of Jewish yoga, a way to relax. For most, what Abulafia describes as *shefa,* the influx of the Divine, is a historical curiosity to be discussed and interpreted. Because, while anyone can follow Abulafia's instructions for permutation and chanting, very few can use them to achieve transcendence. I've never been able to do it. After years of failure I convinced myself that the transcendent state Abulafia described was the result of an inspired imagination or perhaps a condition made inaccessible by modern times. But when I saw you onstage at the area finals, I realized I was wrong."

Eliza starts getting a warm feeling in her stomach. It's a cross between a fluttery excited feeling and a sick feeling. She can tell that
whatever comes next is going to be big. Part of her wants to freeze
time. She would rather enjoy this vague sense of importance than have
it defined. She has a feeling that once her father has said whatever it is
he is about to say nothing will be the same.

"I think you have what Abulafia had, Eliza, something he took for
granted when he wrote his books. You have the ability to use his exercises as he intended, as a means toward achieving *shefa*. I've seen it.
You're able to go beyond simply clearing your mind. You're able to remove yourself entirely from daily life to brush against the limitless. It
happened with EYRIR at the state bee. It happened today. But these
were accidents of latent ability, the merest shadow of *shefa*. In order to
truly reach *shefa*, you must work even harder. You must explore the letters through Abulafia's methods. I will prepare you. Spelling is a sign,
Elly. When you win the national bee, we'll know that you are ready to
follow in Abulafia's footsteps. Once you're able to let the letters guide
you through any word you are given, you will be ready to receive
shefa."

In the quiet of the room, the sound of Eliza and her father breathing is everything.

"Do you mean," Eliza whispers, "that I'll be able to talk to
God?"

Saul leans forward until their heads are touching. His words are too
fragile to survive anything stronger than a whisper. "It's impossible to
describe. But from what Abulafia wrote, it seems less like talking than
a special kind of listening."

"And you think I could do it?" The question comes out louder
than Eliza intended, startling them both.

"In all my life," Saul says, not whispering now, the power of his
voice unmistakable, "you're the only person I've encountered who
might have a chance."

Every day Aaron says something different. He is going roller-skating, playing basketball in the park, seeing a movie, visiting the library. He's not sure it makes a difference. He begins saying the same thing on the same day of each week just to see if Saul notices. When Saul doesn't, Aaron tells himself he is happy. It is freedom he wants, not a father breathing down his back, tracking his every move.

Summer finds Aaron helping Chali in the ISKCON office, taking calls, keeping the shelves organized, and occasionally keeping an eye on the children of devotees. Chali has invited Aaron to accompany him to parks, but Aaron isn't ready for that yet, even with the added incentive of a commission on the beads and pamphlets he sells. The risk of recognition still looms too large. Aaron doesn't want to risk his father learning from a stranger how he has been spending his time.

Aaron spends large parts of the afternoon in the ISKCON library. After reading *Sri Isopanisad* and *Bhagavad-Gita As It Is*, Aaron moves on to *The Science of Self-Realization* and a thin volume called *Om Shalom*, which cheerfully attests to the many similarities between the science of Kṛṣṇa consciousness and Judaism. Aaron becomes known around the temple as *Chaitanya*, which he learns is Sanskrit for energy. He revels in the nickname and does his best to live up to it, participating in the temple's classes and discussions with the same vigor he used to apply to Shabbat services.

During the weekly ride to the synagogue with Saul and Eliza, Aaron's thoughts concern a different temple. By sniffing his fingers, he can conjure up the smell of the incense he knows is being lit at the feet of the deities. He pictures the camphor and ghee, the water in the conch shell. Though he knows it will be years before he can hope for such a thing, he pictures himself as the *pujari,* leading the service and chanting. He has already memorized the first chant. The pleasure this evokes mirrors that of his first Hebrew recitations for Saul almost ten years before.

Saul is at the wheel, whistling the song he always whistles on the way to services. He keeps sneaking peeks at Aaron in the rearview mirror. He is looking for some external indicator of the internal changes in his son, who seems to be spending as much time away from the house as possible and curtails Saul's attempts at conversation with short, curt responses. Though Saul knows that adolescence is marked by the increasing need for independence, he is alarmed by the speed at which Aaron seems to be asserting it. Saul can't help but wonder if the end of their guitar sessions provided an unintentionally large push in that direction. Saul misses being with his son. There were times when their music became an umbilicus stretched between them, recalling for Saul the intimacy of late night feedings when the world contracted to include only him and his baby boy. Saul wonders if their time together spurred something distantly familiar for Aaron as well: the creak of a rocking chair, the beat of Saul's heart as Saul held him against his chest. Saul fears it is a question whose time has passed.

Aaron used to love arriving early to Shabbat services. He and Eliza would fight over who got to unlock the front doors. They would take turns switching on the circuit breakers, flush with the power to transform the synagogue from a dark and shuttered thing to a place overflowing with light.

As a small child, Aaron had graced the synagogue with the same ageless, slow-flowing cognizance he granted to trees. Its windows darkened, the synagogue couldn't see them coming, could only know to prepare for their arrival if Saul parked in the more distant gravel parking lot and not on the silent street fronting the building. The sound of the gravel scrunching beneath the car was Aaron's signal to the synagogue that he had arrived.

It is a squat, brick building that shows its age. The bricks and mortar have darkened over time, dulling the crisp contrast between clay and cement. One spot to the left of the doors is a little lighter than the rest. The sand-blast scar is all that remains of the removal of a spray-paint swastika. It had appeared the day before High Holiday services when Aaron was in elementary school. Aaron still remembers the stoniness that entered his father's face as he received the call from the police. Eliza had been too young, but Saul had taken Aaron with him.

A small, anxious woman had met them at their car as they pulled in. She had spotted the twisted cross while walking her dog and had immediately called the police. Aaron can still hear the woman's soft, sad voice, belonging more to her plaintive eyes than to her ungenerous lips. "We aren't all like that," she had said. "There's no call for such ugliness in the world." The anger seething from his father had frightened Aaron more than the symbol itself, which seemed small and powerless beside Saul's fury.

Saul is fishing through his pockets for the keys to the doors as the three of them stand on the front step, the evening air just turning chill. Aaron finds himself staring at the keyhole. It looks like the keyhole to a zillion other doors, could just as easily be guarding the entrance to a gas station lavatory or a convenience store.

Saul finds the keys, producing them with a dramatic *"Aha!"* Eliza tries not to let her brother's disinterest diminish winning the temple keys from her father's hand, but it is a three-person game that loses its charm when only two are playing. There is no satisfaction in opening the door, which suddenly feels to Eliza like a pleasure she should have outgrown.

The synagogue's smell comes to Aaron immediately. In the past, Aaron has associated it with the rows of *tallith* in their holders along the wall and the lighting of the Shabbat candles at the beginning of the service. Today the smell dissects itself upon entering his nose, becoming an uninspiring blend of floor wax and dust. As Aaron watches Eliza flick on the lights he doesn't think of transformation but of the circuit breaker labeled "Eternal Light," its switch eternally taped to the On position. He sees the rows of dented metal folding chairs, the scuffed floor tiles. When he looks at the building's windows, he no longer thinks of eyes. When he looks at the walls, he forgets he ever imagined a slow-beating heart. Compared to the colors and smells of the ISKCON temple, Beth Amicha is plain and uninviting, a spinster who long ago gave up on luring a groom.

The congregation shuffle in and take their customary seats. Aaron makes a point of not looking in Stacey Lieberman's direction, instead imagining himself into a picture of Kṛṣṇa appearing to a meditating man. He is determined to keep his mind and body pure.

When Aaron was younger, his father's resonant *"Shabbat Shalom"* opening the service filled him with excitement. He would scramble from his seat with the other children to help light the Shabbat candles. Now that he has danced *kirtan,* Aaron cannot help but wonder if his eagerness reflected an instinctive awareness that God cannot be worshiped sitting down. The ISKCON temple with its open space seems so much more appropriate than the synagogue's stiff seats. If Aaron were at ISKCON, he would be chanting *japa* in preparation for bed so that God's name would be the last thing on his mind and tongue. He would not be trapped in a chair, the enforced stillness making him acutely conscious of the body separating him from God. Aaron wants to counterbalance this awareness by chanting in his head, but he is too anxious that practicing one religion in another's place of worship may constitute a multidenominational sin.

Aaron finds it impossible to read along with the responsive prayers now, but he makes an attempt to sing, trying to recall the pleasure the melodies once brought. Once upon a time he aspired to his father's place. Now Saul seems more like an organ grinder leading a troupe of trained monkeys.

Aaron's nonparticipation makes it even more difficult than usual for Eliza to concentrate on the service. She keeps checking to see if Saul has noticed his son's silence. She's pretty sure he hasn't. At one point Elly thinks she hears Aaron saying something under his breath, but when she turns to him he suddenly stops. At the Silent Amidah, Aaron ignores Eliza's attempts to start up a game of Sheep, returning to his seat in the first wave of sitters. Elly persists until she is the last one standing, until her father and Rabbi Mayer have turned away from the ark to face the congregation again. She wants to send her father a signal, to let him know that something is wrong, but instead Saul only winks.

At the end of the service, after the initial *oneg* rush has passed, Eliza follows her brother to a corner of the synagogue where he is retreating with his cookies.

"What's wrong?" she whispers even though there is no one to overhear them.

"What do you mean?" Aaron replies coolly, hoping to stay his sister's curiosity.

"I mean, you were barely even singing. Are you sick?" She knows he's not.

Aaron shakes his head. "I'm fine. I'm really good, actually." And it's true. The stifled feeling born of entering the synagogue has been replaced by the certainty of having discovered something better. Aaron looks at Eliza and thinks of the Indian children at ISKCON.

"Let me ask you something, Elly. What do you think of all this?" he says, gesturing to the chairs, the *bima,* the *siddurim* stacked like small black bricks at the back of the room.

Eliza looks at him blankly. "What do you mean?"

"I mean, how does being here make you feel?" If he had his beads with him it would be easier to explain. "Does it make you feel close to God?"

Aaron's voice is suddenly eager, his excitement plainly written on his face. Eliza feels as if she has been offered a rare backward glimpse into a time before she and Aaron became virtual strangers. She racks her brain for something to extend the moment.

Eliza is a little embarrassed by the way she pictures God. A seminal viewing of *The Ten Commandments* at a susceptible age has impressed the voice of John Huston booming from the clouds into Eliza's mental cement. Though it has been years, Eliza still remembers the power of that voice, the utter certainty. *Take off your shoes, for you are on hallowed ground.* While waiting for the right time to sit down during the Silent Amidah's games of Sheep, Eliza still occasionally listens for that voice, unsure whether it will be heard by the whole congregation or just by her but ready to whip off her shoes either way. Elly has a feeling she'll need something better than that to impress her brother.

"I used to think God was a voice that could talk to people," she says, avoiding the more embarrassing present tense. "But I don't know what I think anymore." She blushes at the small lie, her belief in John Huston shaken by its exposure to light and air but still intact.

Aaron nods sympathetically, but he's only being polite. He has remembered Chali's words: *Everyone must come to Kṛṣṇa on their own time.* Eliza isn't ready. If he were to talk to her, she would want to talk to

Saul. Aaron isn't ready to face his father, his beliefs still too fragile to survive outside the ISKCON temple.

"Yeah, well, it's a tough thing to figure out," Aaron says, his face already closing up, the moment gone.

Throughout their summer of daily studying, Saul has not offered Eliza one of his books. Saul's occasional references to his library have become an unintentional taunt, these the toys she cannot have, the doors she cannot open. Eliza has adapted to this by coming to view her father's books as framed prints or potted plants, decorations which bear no relation to the unexplored worlds Saul describes with such enthusiasm and utter disregard for her feelings.

So that when Saul does reach for a slim leather-bound volume Eliza cannot help but feel that something momentous is about to happen. There is care in the way he carries the book on the short journey from its shelf, as if it were constructed not of leather and parchment but of flesh and blood. Eliza tries to mask her excitement as Saul places the book soundlessly on his desk. He turns to the first page, the bindings creaking like aged floorboards. Saul buries his face in the book, then gestures for Eliza to do the same. The sharp, dry scent of old paper, the combined smells of dust, leather, and time.

"Otzar Eden HaGanuz," Saul says. *"The Hidden Eden.* In this book, Abulafia describes the process of permutation. There's a lot in here you already know, but some of it will be new. This book is the middle step. Once you have mastered it, you will have mastered words, and once you have mastered words, you will be ready to receive *shefa.*"

Saul passes the book to Eliza, allowing her to hold it in her hands. The book leather is cracked, but its pages are smooth and not nearly as stiff as she anticipated. She eagerly turns past the initial pages to where the text begins, then stops, trying to quell her disappointment.

"It's in Hebrew," she says quietly.

"Isn't it beautiful?" Saul replies. "It's a reproduction of a reproduction—a copy of a handwritten copy made sometime in the centuries between now and Abulafia's lifetime. There's something evocative about the arrangement of the Hebrew letters, their shapes and angles, which adds another level to their meaning and is, of course, entirely lost in the translation you'll find at the back of the book."

Eliza's face brightens.

"You didn't think I'd offer you a book you couldn't read, did you?"

Tucked between the pages toward the back, thick enough that Eliza should have noticed them before, are pages of lined paper covered in Saul's assertive script.

"I translated this a few years after college, right around the time I met your mother."

It is strange for Eliza to imagine her father's hand, so much younger than it is now, forming these confident letters, strange to be holding something her father did before she was born. It is the closest Eliza has ever come to a snapshot of her father as a young man.

Eliza spreads the pages on the desk beside the book and begins to read. There is a lot of metaphorical language that sounds silly but which Eliza knows she's not supposed to laugh at, like when the mind is compared to a horse and a person who permutes letters to a warrior. Another passage reads, "A permuter for silver, a furnace for gold, but God tests the heart," which reminds Eliza of "A stitch in time saves nine," and seems to signify just as little. Her initial thrill at having finally been given a look at one of her father's books begins to fade. Her father must have been wrong. Not only is there nothing in here she feels she knows, but there's nothing that seems even vaguely familiar. Elly wonders how to tell her father that, far from opening a new door, he has presented her with an impenetrable wall. When Saul speaks, it is as if he has been reading her thoughts.

"Don't let all the flowery language bother you. They all wrote like that, but eventually they get to the point." He points to a paragraph halfway down the page. "Read that and tell me what you think."

Make yourself right. Meditate in a special place. Cleanse your heart and soul of all other thoughts in the world, then begin to permute a number of letters. Permute the letters, back and forth, and in this manner, you will reach the first level. As a result of your concentration on the letters, your mind will become bound to them. From these permutations, you will gain new knowledge that you never learned from human traditions nor derived from intellectual analysis. It will arouse in you many words, one after the other.

The words, which before had seemed as distant and dead as Abulafia himself, are suddenly affixed in her head as if born there and not across an ocean centuries before.

"That's exactly what it's like," Eliza whispers, amazed someone could describe so well an experience she thought was hers alone.

"There's more," says Saul, skipping over the biblical quotes and pointing to a passage that a younger Saul in his enthusiasm wrote darker and larger than the rest:

You will feel then as if an additional spirit is within you, arousing you and strengthening you, passing through your entire body and giving you pleasure. You will experience ecstasy and trembling. There will be no question that, through this wondrous method, you have reached one of the Fifty Gates of Understanding. This is the lowest gate.

"That's what we're aiming for, Elly. In twenty years of trying, I've never been able to reach the lowest gate. Once you're there, the words will be yours. I'm sure of it."

Later that night when Eliza imagines this coveted gate, she drifts into dreams of her father's outstretched hand.

Saul decides that tonight will be the night. He drinks a cup of coffee just before bedtime and heads upstairs with a Leon Uris novel. At 4

A.M. the bedroom door opens and there is Miriam, her shirt already unbuttoned, one hand pulling off her skirt.

"Miriam, we have to talk."

Miriam startles at the sound of Saul's voice, instinctively covering her breasts with one arm.

"I didn't know you were still awake."

It's the first time during these encounters that she has actually spoken. Saul feels a rush of optimism at the sound of her voice. Miriam rebuttons her blouse and fastens her skirt before heading to the bathroom. Saul gets out of bed, follows her in.

Miriam is brushing her teeth. Sink is separated from shower and toilet by a door. Mirrors on opposite walls create a repeating reflection, infinite Miriams scrubbing furiously at their teeth in front of countless Sauls naked except for faded and slightly sagging Jockey briefs. Saul waits for Miriam to finish. When she spits into the sink, there is blood.

"These past few nights have been so strange," he begins. "Tell me what you really want." His voice is gentle but firm. "Tell me what you've been feeling." For hours he has been preparing, barely reading his novel at all, weighing the varying impacts and repercussions of each potential word he could say.

I want to fuck, Miriam thinks, the harshness of her language surprising her. *If I don't, I'm afraid something will happen.*

"I want to go to sleep," she says. "I'm tired."

"Miriam, please. We need to talk about this." He touches her shoulder but she moves away, begins to undress again. "Tell me what has been on your mind."

A house. A house I have never seen before but which has part of me inside it.

Saul follows Miriam from the bathroom and into bed. Miriam pulls the covers up to her chin.

"Haven't you liked it?" She is too ashamed to more than whisper the question, which is less an inquiry than an attempt to embarrass her husband into silence.

"It's not that," Saul says too quickly. "Please don't think it's that. It's just that it could be so much better if you would just allow yourself

to—if we could just—" Saul, who once took such pleasure in dis-
cussing sex, now finds himself unable to speak. "Please let me make
love to you," he whispers, more supplicant than seducer.

He strokes her hair, then cradles her face with his hands. When he
begins to kiss her, Miriam wills her mouth to respond. *Perhaps this will
work,* she tells herself, but her skin is as dead to his hands as if shot full
of Novocain. She considers feigning pleasure but knows Saul will be
able to tell, doesn't wish to humiliate him further. She analyzes his
progress down the length of her body as she might evaluate a legal argument, mentally commending him for covering all the right points.
She wishes he could be satisfied with a passing grade.

"I want to make you feel good," he whispers in her ear, breathy and
desperate. He is hard though he hasn't let her touch him, has pushed
away her hands. If he would let her, she would put him between her
legs and enjoy the blankness only possible when he is inside her. But
he is a man with a mission now, his hands and tongue stroking and
probing, a safecracker with his ear to the lock. She doesn't know how
much time passes, decides it is better not to look at the clock. Finally
he stops, his patience spent.

"What do you want? Just tell me what you want." There is a hard
edge to his voice.

"I would like sex, please." At the sound of her words, their prim
ridicule, Saul recoils.

"You don't. You're dry. Every night it's the same thing. It can't be
what you want."

"How the hell would you know?"

She says it so quietly. She turns away, wondering if sleep will be
possible. In the back of her mind she is considering waiting until he
has fallen asleep to take him. Even as she hates herself for thinking of
it, she knows that she might. But Saul grabs her, no gentleness now, and
rolls her back toward him.

"You want sex? Fine. I'll give you sex." He parts her legs and thrusts
himself inside. She feels her skull bump against the headboard, notes
the way her backside bunches up the sheet. *This is what I want,* she
thinks to herself as she feels her insides rubbed smooth and blank,

Saul's force quieting her more than any of the times she was acting alone. At first Saul looks at his wife's face, waiting for the slightest signal to stop, but Miriam's eyes are closed, her face maddeningly serene, and he has to stop looking at her altogether, focusing his frustration into his hips. He has never treated a woman this way, never. He is not cruel.

"Thank you," he hears her say and he can feel wetness on his face, trickling from his eyes. He does not understand. How can this be what they've become? He hates himself for it feeling so good, hates her for saying that she wants it and now it is over. He can stop. There is some blood. He feels sick. He rolls away from her and out of the bed.

Miriam hears the bedroom door close and realizes she is alone. Saul's footsteps sound on the stairs. She wonders if he is leaving her, pricks her ears for the click of the front door, but there is nothing. There are no sheets or blankets downstairs and she considers bringing him some, but she is so gloriously sleepy now. She hasn't felt this tired in a long, long time. She closes her eyes.

He sleeps in his study now. The children do not know. He creeps upstairs each morning to change into his clothes. One night she tries his door, but it is locked.

It seems only fitting to Aaron that, having gained his own Sanskrit nickname, he should be invited to spend a weekend at the temple. Aaron has been waiting for this all summer, knows it's the first step toward becoming a devotee. He accepts immediately.

He knows he will have to give his father some explanation for a weekend away. No matter how devoted he may seem in Chali's eyes, Aaron knows he is only playing at changing religions until Saul knows the truth. Abstention from meat and masturbation are simple games compared to revealing his newfound faith to his father.

The certainty of Saul forbidding a weekend stay is as strong as Aaron's determination to go. Asking his father's permission will only make getting away more difficult. He needs an alternate plan.

Though school seems worlds away, Aaron remembers seeing posters for Sierra Club outings. He decides there's no reason they couldn't sponsor a summer camping trip. He devotes the rest of the day to planning. Should he fake a permission slip? Should he seem excited or nonchalant? Aaron runs through the various potential outcomes to his gambit. By the end of the day he is thoroughly spooked.

Aaron hands his father the fake permission slip at dinner, the most promising of a series covertly drafted upon a typewriter in Chali's office.

"Sierra Club?" asks Saul. "I didn't know you were a member."

But if Aaron's hours of anticipation have made him overanxious, they have also left him prepared. "I'm not, but anyone can go," he answers, trying to keep his voice steady. "There was a poster at the library. I haven't gone camping since Scouts."

Saul realizes this is true. The amorphous cause of Aaron's increasing detachment suddenly solidifies into a single source of fatherly guilt: Saul has never taken his son camping. Saul calls up rustic Sears catalogue scenes of fathers and sons in plaid flannel, lighting kerosene lanterns in front of pup tents and smiling at each other in mutual appreciation of their primogenital heritage. It is the best Saul can do given his utter lack of personal camping experience.

"Maybe we could go camping together," Saul says in a tentative voice that strikes terror into Aaron's heart because, in all his interpolations of this moment, this was never a possibility.

"Uh, sure, Dad," gulps Aaron, unsure whether this sudden change bodes well or ill, but now Saul is signing the permission slip. Now he's handing it back. Aaron realizes with equal parts relief and anger that the camping trip, like the legendary family vacation, will never exist beyond his father's words.

Saul smiles and adds *father/son camping trip* to the mental list of things he really does intend, someday, to do.

Even if Aaron weren't putting all his effort into not revealing that he's about to spend a weekend wearing a robe and chanting mantras, even if Elly weren't flushed with the thrill of having met Abulafia in print, neither would notice any difference in their parents. Saul alternates between being relieved and appalled that life continues as it always has despite the fact that he and Miriam only see each other at dinner and then only if she arrives home in time to eat. Although he knows her increasingly belated homecomings are job-related, he can't help but wonder if his new sleeping arrangements have led her to seek someone with fewer compunctions about providing what she claims to want.

Neither has mentioned that horrible night. The longer Saul waits to say something, the more surreal the whole thing becomes, until it takes on the hazy quality of a partially forgotten nightmare. He begins to take comfort in the nocturnal solitude of his study. The reason for this change of venue slowly shifts until he has convinced himself that he is there for Eliza's sake. It frees him to focus entirely upon their studies and how best to guide his daughter's progress. Ultimately, his relocation to the study represents the best chance to achieve their goal. If Saul conceals this new arrangement from Eliza, it is only to avoid alarming her. He doesn't wish to burden her with his efforts on her behalf. Saul begins to take pride in his new routine, can actually look at his wife without picturing her in their bed, bleeding. His new conviction becomes so strong that he starts remembering a conversation in which he and Miriam discussed the move, complete with jokes about how they'd see each other again next June, after the national bee was over.

When, during their next study session, Saul suggests that Eliza chant each letter recombination aloud, she balks. She is used to permuting in silence. Her voice will slow her down. The strange letter combinations will trip up her tongue, so awkward compared to the grace of her pen.

"God didn't write the world into existence," Saul reminds her. "He spoke it into being. And God *said*. Eventually you won't need to write at all when you permute. It's the next step on Abulafia's ladder, the only way to reach *Keter*, the Crown, where *shefa* becomes possible. Remember, no matter how silly a group of letters may sound, that sound is intrinsic to those letters. You won't know them if you don't know every sound they make. If you feel self-conscious, just remember that chanting is only a middle step. Ultimately, you'll be doing everything inside your head."

The idea of mentally transmuting six- and seven-letter words is extremely empowering, evokes comets streaking across the universe of Elly's mind. She dreams herself astride these comets, rushing toward an illustrious destination where she will no longer be a forgotten speller, a nameless face in a class picture.

It is all Saul can do not to gape at his daughter's progress. She is soon chanting even the most awkward permutations as if they were ordinary words, their sounds smooth and flowing in her mouth. Her new powers of concentration astound him. He laughs to recall a time when she struggled to ignore the sounds of a television. He has sneaked behind her during her chanting and dropped all three volumes of *Webster's Universal*. She hasn't moved, as far as he can tell not even hearing its unabridged collision with the hard floor.

Eliza's initial reluctance and self-consciousness are replaced by impatience. Though Saul is proud of the hunger he now sees in his daughter's eyes, he knows he must be cautious. Abulafia warns of the dangers of premature transcendence, mentions both psychological and spiritual consequences: *Many great men and sages have stumbled and fallen, were trapped and snared, because they exceeded the bounds of their knowledge.* Saul doesn't want to risk overestimating his daughter. It is why he doesn't show her the books beyond *Hidden Eden*. Instead he adapts parts of them for her. This way, when she is ready, the new books will seem familiar without having been introduced too soon.

When they begin a new exercise not described in *Eden,* Eliza is skeptical. Saul promises that the new technique will speed their progress, is something of which even Abulafia would approve. He is thankful when Eliza seems to accept his assurances. It spares him from having to explain that movement and vocalization are techniques taken from *Light of the Intellect,* the next rung on Abulafia's ladder to *shefa,* a book he has deemed best not to show her.

"Consonants are the backbone of language," Saul begins. "They give words their shape. But consonants alone are useless. They require vowels to give them dimension. An H alone is barely audible, but paired with a vowel, it comes to life. That life is different depending upon which vowel it is paired with. HE is incomparable to HU."

Eliza nods vehemently. She knows this better than he does. Saul wishes he could just hand her all the books, wind her up, and watch her go.

"It's important that the body express these differences in sound. Sound, after all, is a physical thing. Instead of just knowing how these sounds make you feel, I want you to express them in movement."

"Like by dancing?" asks Eliza.

Saul chooses his words carefully, not wanting to reveal too much.

"It's like dancing, but you might not move as much. Your movements can be big or small, long or short. What's most important is that you express the sounds the way they feel to you, not how you think they should look."

Saul's first instinct is to teach Elly the movements as Abulafia describes them, but a superficial grasp of Abulafia's principles would cost them everything they are trying to achieve. Rote learning would preclude a deeper understanding. If Saul wants his daughter to have a decent chance at *shefa,* she must be permitted to develop a feel for the letters on her own.

"Start with the letter A," Saul instructs. "I want you to say the letter out loud, drawing it out so that you sense it fully. Then, when you're ready, I want you to say it again, this time moving your body to express the way the letter makes you feel."

Eliza nods. Saul can tell by her face that she's ready. It's as if she has grown a mental dimmer switch that, with one turn, can shift her from full attention to imperturbable inner concentration. It's a startling transformation, Elly turning unfamiliar as her face becomes a shuttered window, all action occurring beyond view.

"AAAAAAAAAAAAAAA."

The sound is so pure that if Saul weren't looking he'd be unable to discern the age or gender of its source. The sound envelops him, the air having taken on A as completely as it would the scent of baking bread.

Eliza stops. Saul thinks she is waiting for his approval, but another look at her face reveals that he doesn't factor into what she's doing at all. He realizes, with a flush of excitement, that Eliza is preparing to move.

"AAAAAAAAAAAAAAA." Eliza's body remains still as stone, her arms lax at her sides. Only her head rotates slowly, steadily, from right to left.

The blood drains from Saul's face. He realizes that if he doesn't sit down he may faint. Nothing Elly has read, nothing Saul has told her, hinted at this. There is no way she could have known. Yet, somehow, she is performing the motion exactly as Abulafia describes it in *Or HaShekhal (The Light of the Intellect),* a book Eliza has never read.

"Dad, are you all right? Is something wrong?" Suddenly his daughter is back, her face that of a little girl again. Her eyes are all concern and the will to please. "Did I do okay?"

"You did great," Saul manages, trying not to sound as though he's just had the wind knocked out of him. "You did just fine."

Eliza is as surprised as her father. She had pictured herself dancing across the room, the power of the letters bestowing grace and ballerina toes. But when the moment came, she knew that anything more than her head would be too much, that the letters' power arose from their simplicity. As she moved her head, each letter resonated as if she were a plucked string channeling sound waves to the small hairs atop her feet. She could feel the different vowels in her marrow, her bones chimes through which the letters blew. A sense of completion had filled her, the small movement of her head encompassing a new world.

She had expected her father to be disappointed. This, after all, was not the grand gesture she thought he wanted. When, instead, he is impressed, Eliza realizes she needs to shift her focus. The path leading toward *shefa* lies not in second-guessing her father but in following her own voice.

Which is how she knows she's ready for more. She knows about the other books. She can see them beside the gap left by *The Hidden Eden*. She keeps waiting for Saul to show them to her. Even the sound of Abulafia's name sets off music in her head. A-bu-la-fi-a. It's magic, the open sesame that unblocked the path to her father and then to language itself.

But when she asks to be shown more, Saul insists that she wait. She has to first prove her readiness by winning the national bee. Eliza doesn't need the national bee to prove this. When she permutes, each word opens up like a huge sunflower, each letter a petal with her at the blossom's center. Saul assures her that her time will come. As far as Eliza is concerned, her time is now. When she pictures *shefa,* she thinks of the red phone on the President's desk that is supposed to be a direct line to the Soviet Union. *Shefa* will be her red telephone, a direct line to God. She will get A's on everything without having to study, transmuting her way to transcendence and a perfect grade. All the popular girls will consult with her about boys and she will use *shefa* to tell them if their affections are returned. She will become so popular that Gina Whitworth will call her first when she decides to have a party. With all that *shefa* has to offer, Eliza sees no reason to wait.

The rule against borrowing books from the study has been so clear and constant from so early on in Eliza's life that it has achieved the status of natural law. Though secure in the necessity of her actions, the idea of borrowing a book without express permission makes Eliza's heart beat cold.

The best time will be this Saturday, when Saul is conducting a bar

mitzvah lesson. If Elly doesn't take the book outside the study and replace it before her father returns from the synagogue, her secret will be
safe. The trick will be to act like nothing has changed, to not let slip
that pupil has outpaced teacher. *Shefa* will erase years of average report
cards, undo seasons of unfulfilled expectations, and legitimize Eliza's
new place by her father's side. *Shefa* will neutralize the guilt she feels
when she sits opposite Aaron at the dinner table. *Shefa* is Eliza's national
bee backup plan. If she can get God on her side before bee season begins, she can be assured of avoiding dings and Comfort Counselors.
With God on her side, the national trophy is as good as in her hands.

Sleeping bag and pup tent are carried to the car in passing reference
to camping. The fact that Aaron actually plans to use the sleeping bag
helps. It seems strange that discovering Kṛṣṇa has made him a better
liar. Aaron assures himself that his newfound deceitfulness is a necessary short-term skill to be abandoned once full-blown devotee-dom
has been achieved.

It seems wrong that it should be this easy. Saul has unearthed the
family camera for the occasion, takes a shot of Aaron beside the car.
When he offers to lend Aaron the camera for the weekend, Aaron
manufactures a river-crossing itinerary that will make camera carrying
too risky. Saul deflates a little at the refusal.

"Of course," he says, but it's the same voice Aaron uses when told
there's no more room on the team.

Even though there's nothing left to say, Aaron remains standing beside the open car door, his father within arm's reach. The two resemble nothing so much as a couple concluding an awkward first date.
After refusing the camera, Aaron feels he shouldn't make the first move
to leave. The longer they stand there, the longer Aaron feels that this is
the time to say everything.

Saul's silence and immobility are linked to similar feelings of immanent and fleeting opportunity. Aaron having refused the camera,

Saul feels the need to leave him with something else, a small acknowledgment, perhaps, of Aaron's increasing independence, or an admission of his own recent preoccupation. The air between them carries an imbalance of the kind a few well-chosen words could correct.

"Dad?" Aaron says, making Saul's heart jump. "I just wanted to tell you . . ." Aaron feels how easy it could be, can actually sense the truth on his tongue.

But looking up from his shoes is a mistake. The undisguised eagerness of Saul's face frightens him. It's a face that begs to be pleased.

"I just wanted to tell you to have a good weekend." Aaron can feel the heat in his face as he blushes, digs his fingernails into his palms in disappointment.

"Thanks, son. You too." What felt like possibility has soured into awkwardness, the weight of unexplored conversations too much for the moment to bear. Saul clasps his son in a hug. It was the hug meant for words unspoken, a hug which, in their absence, feels staged.

Aaron suddenly wants to get as far away from his father as possible. "Well, I guess I'd better get going. Everyone's waiting."

"All right." Another pause, shorter this time. "I love you, son."

"Yeah, Dad. I love you too," but Aaron is already getting into the car, mumbling his words to his seat belt as he closes the door. Though he has been cultivating the ability to observe himself and the world at a spiritual remove, Aaron is suddenly mired so deep inside himself that he can barely breathe, weighed down by what he has done as much as by what he hasn't.

Watching his son drive away, Saul wishes they could back time up and try again.

As soon as the ISKCON temple comes into sight, Aaron feels lighter. He has to struggle not to speed into the parking lot. The woman at the door is familiar to him now, smiles at the sight of his arrival.

"Hari Bol. Chali tells me you've come for the weekend?"

Aaron nods, grinning. Being here reminds him how inconsequential the camping story is compared to what it is allowing him to do. He takes off his shoes, cherishing the feeling of his feet on the smooth floor.

"Chali is upstairs. He's expecting you."

Aaron hesitates, waiting for the woman to lead him. When she doesn't move, he realizes that he already knows the way.

It is only as Aaron is changing out of his jeans that the reality of what he is doing hits. Until now, the idea of spending a weekend in the temple was purely conceptual. Staring at his *karmi* clothes on the floor, Aaron realizes he is really doing it. The smell of incense wafts from the saffron cloth he wraps around himself. Aaron wills the scent to mark his body the way the beads have marked his fingertips. A phrase from the Shabbat service suddenly pops into his head: *I am anointed with fragrant oil.*

The robe changes everything. Bowing before the statue of Prabhupada and the deities feels natural. He is no longer an outsider. If someone were to walk into the temple they wouldn't see Aaron, but a devotee performing *arati*. Aaron loves how his voice blends with the others, as if they were all singing with the same mouth.

When the preliminary mantras and invocations are completed, the *Hare Krṣṇa* chant begins. It starts slowly, almost delicately, the words flower petals on Aaron's tongue. The chant is so familiar to him now, each syllable so much a part of him, that it has acquired the unconscious grace of breathing. Then, with the sound of the *mridanga* drum, the chant begins to quicken. Without looking to the others for reinforcement, Aaron begins to dance. Aaron, who at Homecoming always keeps to the wall. Aaron, who refuses to go skating. His legs and arms are moving on their own, the rhythm of the drum emanating from every muscle, the chant a synaptic message. Aaron finds himself holding finger cymbals. He throws his hands above his head and feels their reverberation down his arms. He is laughing now, his head tilted toward a ceiling painted a cloudless blue. Aaron occupies the center of a dancing circle. Every face is smiling. Every arm reaches toward him. At the sounding of the conch shell, Aaron knows he is home.

Even though Eliza knows there's no chance of anyone coming through the study door, the act of reaching up to the shelf and removing a book is terrifying. She halfway expects her father to storm into the room, his disappointment freezing her in place, prolonging her betrayal. Instead, the moment of removing the book is so completely normal as to be anticlimactic. The book slides off the shelf and into her hand like any other. In the space of a few seconds, a lifelong spell has been broken.

It is a slim volume like *Hidden Eden,* leather-bound with Hebrew on its spine. Elly is unsure she has selected the right one until she finds the notes toward the book's back. *Light of the Intellect* greets her in her father's slanted hand. The first few pages bore her with lofty language and convoluted biblical passages, but Elly knows to keep reading. She finds what she's looking for in a single sentence separate from the rest of the text:

This is the mystery of how to pronounce the Glorious Name.

The words that follow are so familiar Elly forgets she's reading them for the first time. Abulafia's instructions for preparing to chant are identical to *Hidden Eden,* save for additional Blessed Holy Ones and King of Kings along the way. It's when Abulafia gets to talking about vowels that Eliza gets really excited.

The names of the vowels are different because Abulafia is talking about Hebrew, not English, but the sounds they make are the same. Eliza knows them. *Kametz, Tzeré, Chirek, Cholam, Shurek.* A, E, I, O, U. And now Eliza realizes why her father was so pleased with her. Because Abulafia's instructions for each vowel describe what Eliza is already doing.

Standing alone in her father's study, the sole light above her father's desk casting long shadows across her face, Eliza follows Abulafia's instructions for the chanting of יהוה, *Adonai.* It is a little different than she's used to. She has to breathe at certain times and not at others. Ultimately, she's not transmuting the letters so much as exploring how each one sounds with every vowel. The first time, she has to refer to her father's translation for every successive step. Every time she makes a mistake she has to start over. What keeps her going is Abulafia's description of what happens next. His instructions are free of flowery prose and biblical confusion. They are simple as a recipe. If an image appears, bow before it. If a voice is heard, say, "Speak, my Lord," and prepare to listen. Eliza thinks back to countless Amidahs spent waiting to hear that voice. Abulafia's words speak to Eliza like a promise. She will master the breaths, the vowels, and the movements attending these four simple letters, and then she will listen. And finally, she will hear the voice she has been waiting for, the one that will explain everything.

Miriam has realized that she prefers to sleep alone. Her attempts to use Saul as a buffer between herself and the houses was just one more drain on her energy. She knows she is fighting a losing battle. It is only a matter of time.

Some nights she gets as far as putting the key in the ignition before making herself stop. Once she keeps the urge at bay by sleeping in the car. No night is complete now until she has entered the garage not less than twice, at least one of those times getting as far as opening the driver-side door.

She knows her preoccupation is causing her to miss things. Saul and Eliza's study habits are taking up more and more of their time. Miriam knows that she should probably do something to console Aaron, but Aaron has always been Saul's child. Even as a baby he seemed happier in her husband's arms. The effort required to resist the houses leaves Miriam just enough strength to ghost the motions of her daily routine. There is no surplus energy for motherly words of wisdom to a boy obviously replaced in his father's attentions.

Miriam had thought the night of her final capitulation to the houses would be presaged by something to push her over the edge, but it is a night the same as any before. Perhaps Aaron's absence makes a difference, lessening as it does the family's gravitational pull, but more likely Miriam just realizes she has nothing left with which to resist. As she gets into her car, her rational objections to what she is about to attempt—the higher risks of night entry, the greater likelihood that someone will be home—sound as far away as the sleep-time rhythms of her children's breathing. Backing out the driveway, coasting with the engine off to avoid making a sound, Miriam feels a huge internal release, as if a secret pair of lungs, frozen all this time inside her, have taken first breath. Bearing down the empty highway, the silence of the street pouring into her open windows, Miriam cannot believe she waited this long. For stretches, there are no other cars to be seen, not even the wink of lights in her rearview mirror. The world has become Miriam's empty mansion, rooms stretching to the horizon waiting to be filled. Miriam is young again, the immortal girl whose life is infinite, who can drive a familiar back road with her headlights off because she knows nothing bad can possibly happen.

With the road deserted, Miriam hears the Dopplered *phwa* of exit ramp signs rushing past her open window. More than ever, the thought that these signs speak to her makes sense, the sound reinforcing the notion that they've been guiding her all along.

Miriam ends up in a planned community, four models of home alternating in varying patterns to give the perception of diversity. It's a neighborhood devoid of streets or roads, having traded up for lanes, passes, and ways. Miriam finds herself at a house, dark save for the steady yellow illumination of its front door. She parks her car in front instead of down the street, secure in the knowledge that there is no one awake to see it.

It is late enough that the grass is filled with tomorrow's dew. Its moisture seeps through the cuff of Miriam's pants to lick her ankles. It feels to her like a benediction. The movie-set stillness of the picture-book houses and manicured lawns adds to Miriam's sense of invincibility. She is both director and star of this show, entirely in control of the action.

The fact that it is the nicest home she has ever approached doesn't deter her from walking up to its front door and feeling surprised to find it locked. She checks the mailbox and beneath the macramé doormat without success for a spare key. She is about to walk around back when she thinks to check the garage door. She is unaccustomed to houses with attached garages.

When Miriam pulls up tentatively on the door handle, she encounters no resistance. The air is cool. An occasional cricket rubbing its legs together is all that pricks the night's silence. Miriam's senses are so acutely sharpened that she imagines she can feel the slight differences in temperature resulting from the pinpoints of feeble light cast by distant stars upon her skin.

The garage door is halfway raised when there is an explosion of sound. Miriam is knocked onto her back. Her night vision collapses into itself, her senses reeling from sudden overload. She does not realize at first that she has been knocked over, tries to walk, and is confused by her legs striding uselessly through the air. There is something pressing into her, something making sound and weighing her down. The back of her head strikes the driveway and immediately begins to swell. Even as she realizes she is being attacked by a dog, a distant voice inside herself is concocting a story to explain away the emerging bump.

It is a mid-size dog but heavy. Each time it barks, Miriam's face is awash in dog breath. Its front paws press upon her chest. Miriam begins to wrestle, instinctively rolling in an attempt to slide the dog off rather than try to force it off her body. She manages to roll onto her stomach and push up from the ground. She is standing. She wants to return to the night's previous stillness just long enough to give her a chance to breathe, but the dog is lunging. She must force her suddenly leaden limbs to run. She moves quickly toward the car, not noticing the dew now as the dog runs barking behind her. A light comes on in an upstairs window before she has reached the car door. By the time a face appears she has already pulled away from the curb, thankful to have left the front door unlocked, the dog, still barking, running after her.

Miriam will never know what kind of dog attacked her, will imagine a Doberman or a German shepherd with snarling, angry teeth despite the fact she bears neither bite marks nor broken skin. It will never cross her mind that the dog was a beagle and that she was knocked over from surprise more than force. The children of the house she fled will use the incident to convince their parents to keep the dog, which had been on the verge of being given away for its propensity to shit at the slightest hint of thunder, it having been sequestered in the garage that night because of a stormy forecast. The family will never know what manner of burglar their dog deflected, will imagine a scruffy, heavy-set man with scars and a limp groping the family jewelry. It will never cross their minds that their intruder was an upper middle-class wife and mother of two who would have had eyes only for their Chinese teakettle.

Aaron's difficulty falling asleep is perhaps augmented by the knowledge that he will have to get up at 3:30 A.M., a time so exotic its possibilities seem endless. Until now, three thirty has been a time only inhabited by adults like his mother, a time suspected to harbor great secrets. By setting foot inside this mysterious temporal zone, Aaron is certain he will be making a foray into his own adulthood. He is still child enough to believe that adulthood brings certainty and self-confidence. In waking at 3:30 A.M., Aaron anticipates that the strength to face his father will sprout from an internal seed waiting to take root.

Aaron's sleeping bag does little to cushion the floor beneath him. He cherishes the hardness beneath his hip, likes feeling the temple at bone level. Having never shared a room before, Aaron is struck by the profound sense of closeness he feels to those around him: their unguarded faces and resting limbs, the quiet rise and fall of their chests. He times his own breathing to coincide with his roommates', imagines them as a single body.

Aaron is amused to discover that Chali snores.

He isn't sure how much time passes contemplating oneness and impending adulthood, too excited to sleep. He considers exploring the temple by night. Ever since Chali confided that he once saw Kṛṣṇa's arm move at the height of the *arati* chant, Aaron has felt a pressing urge to sneak behind the curtain that shields the deities between services. Alone with the deities, perhaps he can experience such a moment for himself.

Aaron doesn't realize he is dreaming when he finds himself sitting motionless on the dais, Kṛṣṇa's arm beckoning to him. As Aaron brushes the shoulder of the devotee asleep beside him, Kṛṣṇa draws him close. Suddenly Kṛṣṇa's lips begin to move: *Shema Yisrael Adonai Eloheinu Adonai Echad*. It is his father's voice, emanating from the mouth of the god.

The first *arati* takes place at 4:30 A.M. Aaron stumbles into the temple. His dream gets tangled in the spokes of his waking brain as he stands before the dais, straining to hear his father's voice. It is Chali who gently draws him toward the others. Aaron blushes. He had thought he was alone.

"It's hard to get used to at first," Chali whispers, "but after a while this schedule will feel natural."

Aaron nods. Now awake, he realizes the dream was a message. Hearing the *Shema* from Kṛṣṇa's mouth proves the truth of one of Chali's earliest assertions. In becoming a devotee of Kṛṣṇa, he is not betraying Judaism; he is growing closer to God.

The next morning is the first Aaron is able to chant *japa* without fear of being overheard. He is so used to the stuffiness of his closet that chanting in the open room feels like removing a mask. When Aaron pictures the boy who hid among his shirts, he doesn't recognize him. Aaron vows never to hide again. He chants loud enough to hear his voice bounce back at him from the walls, loud enough to feel the sound vibrating in his stomach.

The first disappointment comes at breakfast. Aaron longs for cereal and not *prasadam,* has his first pang of homesickness at the thought of Frosted Flakes with sliced banana. Saul once used a needle and thread to slice the banana inside its skin. When unpeeled, the perfectly cut slices fell into the bowl of a young and astonished Aaron. For a few minutes, Saul let him believe in a special breed of banana grown expressly for cereal bowls. Aaron wants to tell Chali, but talking is discouraged. It distracts from the holiness of the meal.

After that the day with its prayers and duties, classes and discussions sweeps Aaron up inside it. There is not a moment when he doesn't have somewhere to be, something to do. At evening *arati,* Aaron realizes he hasn't thought about the outside world since breakfast. It is difficult to accept that his house is half an hour and not half a planet away, that just beyond the temple door people are driving cars, watching television, and going shopping. The mundanity astounds him. He can't believe how much time is wasted when here, at the ISKCON temple, not a moment is lost. The temple's daily schedule appeals to him on the same base level as frozen TV dinners, each course in its own compartment. Aaron doesn't notice that temple meals are actually served upon similarly apportioned dishes, unaware of the subconscious pleasure this gives him. He ends the day more satisfied with himself than he can remember, certain he has spent the day working toward something important. He falls asleep in moments, too tired to dream.

Miriam startles awake to the sound of voices in the kitchen. She is so accustomed to being the first up that her initial thought is burglars. She turns to Saul's side of the bed to rouse him. Then, remembering she sleeps alone now, she stumbles downstairs. She is still half asleep when she enters the kitchen.

"Morning, sleepyhead," Saul says. He can't remember Miriam ever coming downstairs in a nightgown, hair unbrushed. It has been weeks since he saw his wife in anything but work clothes and even longer since he saw her so fresh from sleep. He gets a sudden flash of Miriam as a small girl, pictures perfectly what she must have looked like at Elly's age, curls piled in a wild cumulus cloud about her head, small hands rubbing at sleep-fringed eyes. He isn't sure whether to kiss the creature before him or to pull her protectively into his arms, realizes that either would mean more contact than he's had with Miriam since he took to his study. Flush with love and regret, he moves toward her, deciding to begin with an embrace.

Miriam stands stiff in his arms. "Why didn't you wake me?" she asks, her voice dull, her body unresponsive.

Saul backs away, suddenly furious. He is amazed at the speed of his anger, unsure whether Miriam's words or physical impassivity flicked the switch. *Because I don't know when you're home anymore,* he wants to answer. *Because we don't share a bed.* If he were alone with her he wouldn't hesitate to speak his mind. He forces a smile. There's Eliza to think of.

"Darling, you never sleep in. I assumed you needed the rest. Here"—he points to the table—"Eliza and I made French toast."

Spurred by the falseness of her father's voice, Eliza comes to the realization that her parents aren't sleeping together anymore. Small things she thought she'd forgotten—occasional morning stubble on a normally clean-shaven cheek, the new elongated imprint on the study's sofa, the recent appearance of dental floss on her father's desk—come together to form an image that is as irrefutable as it is unexpected. She wishes Aaron were here to confirm this sudden truth, looks accusingly at his empty chair. Her brother has always hated camping. Eliza remembers his complaints about the mosquitoes and the burned food, the pranks that can be played with dirt and a sleeping bag. Elly returns to her French toast which, moments ago, she was gleefully drenching in syrup and realizes she's no longer hungry.

Miriam isn't sure why her head and tailbone ache. Finding a bump the size of a small egg just above her neck, she remembers. She pulls away her hand as if scalded.

"Are you hurt?"

"I'm fine," Miriam says more sharply than she intended, for a moment unmasking the anger in her husband's eyes. Startled, she backs into the hallway, only turning when she is certain the back of her head won't be seen. She runs up the stairs, cupping the back of her head with her hand in case Saul is following behind.

"Dad?" asks Eliza in a small voice once the footsteps have stopped and the house is too quiet. "What just happened?"

"It'll be okay," Saul answers, still looking down the hallway, both of them perfectly aware that he hasn't answered her question.

Only specially trained initiates are permitted to prepare *prasadam,* but Aaron is allowed to help clean the kitchen and watch. The ISKCON kitchen is the cleanest room he has ever seen. Suddenly Aaron thinks of his mother. Everything sparkles and gleams. Aaron can see his reflection in every surface.

Aaron is used to the way Saul cooks, a blur of motion with breaks for tastings. The ISKCON cooks carry themselves with a solemnity Aaron has only seen in priests and nuns, a silent process of chopping and mixing, careful stirring and sautéing, with no tasting in between. Aaron closes his eyes to better appreciate the smell, a mix of spices that has never graced his father's pots, a scent full of promise. Chali gently pulls him aside.

"As devotees of Kṛṣṇa, we don't smell or taste while we're cooking. Each meal has to be completely pure when it's presented so it will be worthy of Kṛṣṇa's presence. Only then can the food become *prasadam* and filled with Kṛṣṇa's holy spirit."

"But if they don't taste it, how do they know it's any good?" Aaron thinks of his father, the last-minute additions of pepper or oregano, salt or sherry.

"Some people are gifted cooks, others aren't. Thinking of Kṛṣṇa is supposed to help, but when I served in the kitchen the *prasadam* was terrible." Chali laughs. "That's why I write a newsletter and these people do the cooking. Everyone serves Kṛṣṇa in their own way."

"Do you think I could be a cook?" Aaron imagines himself above the steaming pots, likes the idea of resisting the urge to smell or taste.

"You can practice by cooking at home. Before you go back, I'll give you a recipe book. Some devotees have their own altars in their homes so that they can offer food to Kṛṣṇa and eat *prasadam* even when they're away from the temple."

With the word "home," Aaron realizes the weekend is almost over. It seems impossible that he'll soon be getting into his car. He doesn't see how he can reinhabit a world of clothes and grades and television, where the air doesn't smell of incense and the wood of the banyan tree.

"I want to live *here*," Aaron says, his eyes tearing, wishing it was that easy.

When Chali grasps Aaron's shoulder, Aaron realizes how rarely people in the temple touch each other.

"I'm glad to hear it. When some people come for their first weekend, it's easy to tell their hearts aren't ready. It's a difficult transition that can take time. I tell them not to rush, that they will know when the time is right. But I can tell that you're different."

"When can I become a devotee?" Aaron whispers, Chali's words almost too good to be true. He's heard about the ceremony, the fire lit on a bed of sand, the special colors and dances.

"After six months in the temple, you'll be allowed to undergo *Hare Nama Diksu*. Your guru will give you your spiritual name."

"And that's what I'll be called?" Aaron remembers writing thank you notes after his bar mitzvah. It only took signing the first ten for his name to become a random arrangement of letters that had as little to do with him as the pen he was holding. He now realizes it was a sign. "Aaron" was only ever meant to be temporary.

"The moment I received the name Chali, I knew it was my true name. John was so common. I hated having to share my name with so many others. But I've never met another Chali, have you?" Chali grins. Aaron shakes his head in agreement. He silently vows to have a new name before his eighteenth birthday.

Miriam has the urge, once upstairs, to lock herself inside the bedroom. She has a few books here, enough to take her through the day. She has never viewed the bedroom as a place to spend time and realizes that the room reflects her disregard. The meager attempts at decoration—a Chagall poster and, above the bed, a nondescript print of Cupid and nymph—are Saul's. The room could belong to anyone, after eighteen years of habitation still awaits a personality. Miriam remembers talk of new sheets and a new bedspread, a lamp to replace the overhead light. At his most ambitious, Saul had mentioned sculpture, something fluid and slightly erotic to be placed opposite the bed. She had said yes to it all, but neither had the time to go looking. Saul became caught up in his studies and she in her editorials. The wall decorations are Saul's college leftovers. They were meant to be temporary. Now their presence only amplifies the room's sterility.

Miriam closes the door but doesn't lock it. She is embarrassed enough by her dramatics downstairs, doesn't wish to add a locked door to the performance. Her memory of last night pains her as much as her bump, but neither is enough to deter her from planning her next venture. Her recent failure pales in comparison to the houses still waiting. Though she may be able to delay long enough for her bruises to fade and her bump to diminish, she can already feel the houses' renewed pull, can sense the highway waiting.

She steps into the shower and blasts the hot, loving the sharpness of the water on her skin. Only in the shower has she ever felt comfortable with her body. The pursuit of cleanliness grants her time to examine her arms, legs, and breasts. As a newlywed she tried to accommodate Saul's preference for shared showers but Saul's body, sloughing off its dead skin and hair, was an invasion. Even as he soaped her back she would think about the bacteria carried by hands. She found herself staying in the shower long after he had left, making sure the drain and the soap bar were clear of all signs of him, and then starting over. Saul must have guessed her feelings. When he ceased to offer his company, she could not help but feel relieved.

His knock startles her.

"Miriam? Are you all right?"

She reaches to cover her breasts and begins looking for a towel.

The gesture is as silly as it is earnest; she really doesn't want him opening the bathroom door.

"I'm fine, Saul. I didn't mean to startle you. I must have bumped into the night table when I was asleep. I've got a real goose egg on the back of my head."

"Do you want me to bring you some ice?" The shower steam wafting up from under the door mocks his offer, but it is the only thing he could think to say to get him inside.

"That's okay. It's feeling better already. I'll be downstairs soon."

Saul knows he has been dismissed but he remains beside the door, listening to the changing sounds of the water as his wife steps in and out of the spray. He pictures her soaping an arm, a leg, scrubbing her body until her skin pinks. As if in a dream, he remembers the way the water relaxes her hair until it clings in loose, wet waves to her head. He does not even realize he is touching himself until he looks down and finds his hands at his crotch. He stops. He has become a married man masturbating to visions of his wife behind a closed door.

"Miriam?"

Her *What?* is too shrill. She had thought he was gone.

"I was hoping we could have dinner tonight. All four of us. To celebrate Aaron coming home."

It sounds right, like something they should do.

"That sounds nice."

She is about to turn off the water, but if she does she fears he will stay. She soaps up again even though the water is turning cold.

When they practice that day, the first after her covert book-borrowing, Eliza's eye keeps straying to a particular volume on her father's bookshelf. She imagines having accidentally replaced *Light of the Intellect* upside down or spine first, keeps looking anxiously at Saul for a sign that he has detected her ruse. Yet her continuing desire for the book is as omnipresent as her fear. Every moment in the study is a struggle not to make for the book, father or no father, and return to work, to attempt one more step toward Abulafia's terrifying, miraculous promise.

Because Eliza has given the discovery of her parents' secret a lot of thought since breakfast. She can picture only two potential causes. Either her mother has banished Saul from the bedroom for his spelling preoccupation or he has decided to live out of his study in devotion to their work. Both implicate Eliza as chief instigator. Both leave her determined not to let her father down.

Miriam had expected her bumps and bruises to defer her next venture. Instead, they are a constant provocation. Too many missing pieces are relying on her to make the world whole. She must prove she won't be so easily deterred.

Miriam walks downstairs. She is going to the store for typewriter paper and ink ribbon, no need for alarm, nothing out of the ordinary, but faced with the closed study door, her pretensions are unnecessary. She is unsure of her destination, knows only that she won't be returning to the site of her recent defeat. Anything waiting inside that house is dead to her now, its call silenced. It won't happen again.

Miriam rejects the highway in favor of a back road generally invisible to anyone not looking for it, a one-lane strip of eroding asphalt bounded by trees, interrupted by an occasional house. Though some of the houses are well maintained, even those betray a level of poverty Miriam has neither witnessed nor considered. Broken windows are patched with wood or cardboard. Roofs are topped with plastic tarps. Undrivable cars decay on rough gravel driveways. In the fading light of the afternoon Miriam sees a child playing in the dirt with a plastic spoon.

The house that selects her lacks neighbors, is the last before the road dissolves into a sparse trail of sun-bleached litter. Her view is impeded by long-neglected grass and shrubbery. Even as Miriam imagines a similarly unkempt man waiting in the shadows of his living room with a hunting rifle, she knows she must go inside. Fear stiffens her limbs and makes movement difficult. She feels a tightness in her stomach and the burn of sour bile in her throat. In the quiet of the late afternoon she can hear the distant rumble of the highway and, closer, the calls of small birds. Then, after a lifetime of struggle, the demands of Perfectimundo take charge. Miriam feels her arms and legs loosen, her stomach unclench as she hands off responsibility to the thing grown larger than herself, relieved to finally relinquish control.

Miriam can make out nothing of the house's interior through the few windows not boarded shut. From the porch even the highway is mute, the air cobwebbed with silence. Miriam wonders how long the house has been abandoned, wonders what could possibly be left inside to draw her to it.

The front door, half off its hinges, detaches completely when Miriam pushes it aside. It hits the half-rotten floor with a thunk that causes her to suck in her breath as if slapped unexpectedly. The front room is littered with fast food cartons, broken bottles, and old newspaper. A scorched chair is interred upon a charred portion of flooring studded with soot-blackened cans. The air reeks of mold and dust and the rankness of a still pond.

The back room is darker and mustier. A tree grows through its broken window. A hardware store calendar is pinned to the wall, October 1974 too sun-faded to betray its original color. A warped wooden bureau leans into a corner, its one open drawer choked with Chesterfield coupons. Miriam pulls at the others, but they won't budge, the wood bloated with time and neglect. What at first looks like an abandoned stuffed animal is actually a desiccated dog, white bones peeking through strips of lifeless fur. Miriam feels her stomach lurch and her bowels constrict, but doesn't retch. With a perverse sense of pride, she realizes how far she has come.

In a small side room she initially overlooked, Miriam finds a wooden chest bordered by shoe boxes of rotting photographs. She is about to heft open the chest when she spots a photo on the floor. It is a yellowed and water-distorted Polaroid of a small, dark-haired girl with serious eyes that have already learned not to expect too much. She is standing in what might have been the same room an unknowable number of years before. Miriam is momentarily transfixed by a deep sense of recognition. Even after the image resolves into its proper arrangement of unfamiliar features, Miriam's sense of connection to the photo remains. She reverently peels the photograph from the floor, careful only to handle its edges, and carries it back to the car.

As soon as she places the photo on the seat beside her, something inside Miriam shifts. The sights and smells, muted in the house's presence, hit her full force. Miriam barely reopens her door before they are spilling out her mouth—the mold, the rotten wood, the dog corpse. She hasn't quite finished when the need to be as far away as quickly as possible causes her to start the engine. She pulls away before properly reshutting her door. Her departure barely scrapes the silence of the place she leaves behind.

Aaron's return home feels like awakening from a sleep of Rip Van Winkle proportions. Everything is familiar but removed. His own memories seem like secondhand stories. Even his image, reflected in the front windows, stares strangely back, the boy in *karmi* clothes at best a distant relation. Aaron's legs, having known the freedom of robes, balk at the seams of his blue jeans, yearning to dance.

At the door, Saul wraps Aaron in a hug that catches him by surprise.

"Welcome back, camper. How was your trek in the wilderness?" Saul's voice seems too large, his smile too broad. Aaron sees Eliza hovering in the hallway behind their father, her face strained.

"Is everything okay?" Aaron asks, realizing as Saul answers that it is a question for his sister.

"Everything is fine, just fine. We're happy you're back, that's all. I'm cooking a special dinner, a family dinner for the four of us. Your mother is really looking forward to it." At which point Aaron knows that something is amiss. He looks at Eliza again.

"Where *is* Mom?" Aaron asks.

"Oh, she's out," Saul replies. "But she knows all about dinner and has promised to be on time."

Something in the kitchen buzzes and Saul grins, returning to the kitchen.

Aaron and Eliza stare at each other for a few moments before Eliza asks, "Do you want to go outside?" and Aaron knows exactly where they are going.

The tree still lies at the same angle on the same stretch of ground, having been felled by a lightning bolt prior to either Aaron's or Eliza's memory. Since they last visited it together almost six years before, one end has grown soft with decay. Even taking the decay into account, the log seems smaller, the reality of it suffering the usual comparisons with memory and the fact that both Eliza and Aaron have grown significantly since their last visit.

The mix of earth, dogwood, and crabapple activates an image previously unaccessed from Eliza's mnemonic cold storage. It is a visceral freeze-frame, a snapshot of multisensual memory powerful enough to temporarily reconfigure her surroundings. She is unsure of her age, but she is young enough that her feet, when straddling the log, do not touch ground. Her field of vision is taken up by Aaron's shirt, which is striped blue and orange. Her hands clasp her brother's waist. In addition to the evocative mix of earth, dogwood, and crabapple that fills her nose, she can smell her brother's skin, a combination of sun, grass, and sweat. For a brief moment, within the grip of this memory, Eliza can actually feel the original surge of excitement that coursed through her then, a sense of exhilaration spurred entirely by the imaginary trip they are taking. Even more fleeting, but equally identifiable, is the sense of security underlying the thrill of the journey. At that moment in time, Eliza's hands are clasped around the most solid thing she knows.

At first brother and sister circle the tree as if it is a museum piece, both afraid to break through the glass. With a shrug, Aaron then breaches the circle traced by their footsteps. Eliza quickly follows.

Rather than straddle the tree they sit beside one another facing the house, just far enough away that their hips and legs don't touch.

They can see Saul at the stove through the kitchen window. He is cooking more frenetically than usual, seems to be continually looking to add something to the pot.

"How long has he been in there?" Aaron asks.

"Awhile," Eliza says. "Ever since we came out to the kitchen for a snack and he realized Mom had gone out. She's been gone all day." She picks at the tree, focuses on a scale of bark she manages to peel away with her fingers. "I don't think she and Dad are sleeping in the same bed anymore."

A motorcycle revs its engine a few blocks away. Above them from a tree in the yard, a bird chirrs the same repeating pattern. Three chirps, then stop. Three chirps, then stop. Aaron grabs a twig from the ground and traces a circle in the dirt.

"Elly, if I tell you something will you promise to keep it to yourself?"

The question is out before Aaron realizes he is asking it, but it is accompanied by intense relief, a loosening of internal strictures in place so long Aaron had taken their discomfort for granted.

Eliza nods, afraid that if she speaks he'll change his mind.

"I didn't really go camping."

When Aaron blushes, he is not sure if it is from the shame of revealing his lie or for having betrayed his secret.

Eliza deliberately looks away until she thinks her brother's blush has faded. "I kind of wondered about that," she says quietly. Then she adds, "Where did you really go?"

Aaron focuses his eyes on the back of their father's neck through the window. He wonders if Saul will turn if he stares hard enough. "I went to a certain place," he says. Saul continues to face the stove, oblivious to Aaron's gaze.

"What kind of place?" Elly asks, braver now.

"A religious place. For people who want to get closer to God."

He looks over at Eliza then, to gauge her reaction, but Eliza's face is completely open, bears the same trusting expression it used to wear when he would pilot them through space and time.

"What do you do there?"

"Lots of stuff. You pray. You take classes. There's a special chant. You can't gamble. You can't eat meat. You can't—you know—touch yourself." He blushes again, but this time recovers quickly. "There's dancing and music. There's even kids your age."

"Is it better than Beth Amicha?"

Aaron nods. "Way better than Beth Amicha. You won't tell, right?"

Eliza shakes her head solemnly. "I won't. Not even Dad," she says. She has learned for herself that there are things Saul shouldn't be told.

When Miriam finally arrives home, Aaron's first thought is that his mother has been replaced by a disheveled twin. Aaron has never known his mother to look anything but freshly washed, pressed, and ironed. The woman who sits down to dinner has a stained shirt, a smudged face, and tangled hair. More disturbing is the odor. Miriam's nose is acutely sensitive to twice-worn shirts and unwashed hair, too fine-tuned for anything but unscented soaps. Yet she smells like she's been sorting through week-old garbage.

"Miriam?" Saul asks in a cautious voice. "Honey, are you all right?"

Miriam smiles and pulls her chair closer to the table. "I'm sorry I'm a little late. I hope I didn't worry you."

Dinner is, by now, a foregone conclusion, but Miriam eats oblivious to the cold food and startled faces.

"Miriam, did something happen? Was there an accident?"

Miriam looks at Saul as if he is an endearing but somewhat slow child. "I'm *fine*. Did something happen to you? You seem . . . strange."

"Miriam, come to the mirror." Saul reaches for her hands. She pulls them away until she remembers that Eliza and Aaron are watching.

Saul guides his wife to the mirror in the bathroom and turns on the light. For a moment there is complete silence. No one breathes. Miriam stares at the stranger looking back. It never even occurred to her to check her appearance after leaving the house.

"Oh, my God."

The voice is not quite Miriam's. It is a scared animal version of her voice. The sound of it is too much for Eliza, who begins to cry quietly, beyond Saul's hearing, but loud enough to spur Aaron to put his arm around her shoulders.

"Miriam, honey, come upstairs," but Miriam is already out the bathroom door. Saul races after her, knowing if she beats him to the bedroom he will not be allowed inside.

"Aaron," Eliza says very quietly, "what's happening?"

Aaron pats Eliza's shoulder and stares after the receding footsteps, the sound that was almost his mother's voice replaying in his head.

When Saul doesn't return to the kitchen, Eliza and Aaron start to clean. They fall wordlessly into a rhythm, their regained sibling unity expressed in the perfect timing of relayed dishes, in mutual anticipation of towel or sponge. At the slightest sound from the hall, real or imagined, both freeze and look toward the doorway, anticipating their father and parental reassurance. There is a moment of disappointment each time neither of these manifests, after which their cleaning resumes.

They take their time. Eliza inches the sponge over the kitchen table, rubbing at spots that aren't there. Aaron ignores the dishwasher and scrubs each plate by hand. The two dry together, making sure the very idea of moisture has been removed from a dish before carefully replacing it in their mother's immaculately ordered cabinets. By the time dinner is cleaned up and put away, Saul still hasn't appeared.

Aaron opens the cabinet beneath the sink for the cleansers as Eliza reaches for rubber gloves. Miriam always keeps a second pair as a backup. Eliza starts on surfaces while Aaron works sink and stove. They know from years of observation which cleanser is used where and with what implement. They relax into the sound of scrubbing and the smell of ammonia unsuccessfully masked by lemon. Lulled by such familiarity, they stop looking toward the hallway, giving themselves over to the shine of Formica and the glimmer of stainless steel.

Refrigerator door and floors are next in the litany. Eliza scrubs moldings while Aaron mops with oil soap. It is unclear who starts the whistling. Aaron harmonizes to Eliza's melodies, most of them silly television jingles or top 40 songs that neither likes. When both forget a song simultaneously, they realize the kitchen is finished, the house completely still.

"It looks good," Aaron says, and Eliza nods, thinking how surprised their mother will be when she comes downstairs and sees what they have done, how much better it will make Miriam feel.

They have no choice now but to go upstairs. It is late, past both their bedtimes. At the base of the stairs they peer toward their parents' bedroom, but the door is closed. Eliza tells herself this is a good sign; it means they are sleeping in the same bed again. She gives her brother a smile, but Aaron is staring too intently at the door to notice, as if he could see through it to the other side.

They brush their teeth together at the sink. Aaron says yes before Eliza even finishes asking if she can sleep in his bed, her traditional refuge from bad dreams. There is less room now that they are bigger, but their curled forms still fit on the twin mattress. Their backs touch mid-spine: two butterfly wings, one big, one small.

"Aaron," the small one whispers, "do you like it better there than here?"

"Elly," the bigger one whispers back, "be glad for me."

Eliza feels the expansion of her brother's lungs as he breathes, his back briefly pressed more closely against hers.

"Would you be happier if I stopped spelling?" Elly is crying a little, but she's trying to act like she's not, determined not to be the baby.

Aaron's voice is gentle. "You've got a talent, Elly. You shouldn't let it go to waste."

"Does that mean no?" Her nose is now completely stuffed up even though she was barely crying at all.

"It's not your fault," Aaron says, his voice sleep-slurred. "You'll feel better in the morning."

"Do you think Mom will feel better in the morning?" she whispers.

"Go to sleep," he replies.

Eventually, she does.

Saul waits silently outside the bathroom door while Miriam showers, the water so hot he can feel the temperature in the bedroom rise. She emerges wrapped in flannel from neck to foot. They do not speak. Instead he holds her for hours as she lies very still, neither of them sleeping. He cannot remember the last time they did that, simple prolonged touch complete in itself. It makes him hopeful enough to swallow his mentally rehearsed suggestion that she seek help, because this, he reasons, is so much better a beginning.

Miriam dreams of the house. She sees the lattice of cracks running across its ceiling, the layered dust floating above its window sills. This time, after exploring the front room with its burnt floor and trash, she goes straight to the side room. She sees the trunk but the photo of the girl isn't on the floor. Miriam rifles through the photos in the shoe boxes but they are all blank. Miriam knows her parents' bodies are inside the trunk. She runs to the back room with its Chesterfield coupons. She yanks on the warped drawers of the bureau, certain one of them contains the photo of the girl, but she is distracted. There is a shape at the corner of her eye, the body of the dog. She turns her head, but it is not the dog. It's much bigger, and there are two of them. It was a closed casket service, too much damage, the undertaker had said, but here they are terrifying in that they are perfectly intact. Their heads were crushed by the car yet their hair is in place; their skin unbroken. They are staring at her with perfect dead eyes and now there is a smell, the overpowering, sweet putrescence of decaying garbage. Miriam realizes that this is the house's stench, a stench she couldn't smell until she was taken to the mirror by her husband and shown her reflection.

Eliza awakens and returns to her own room, her sense of filial closeness now faded to an awkward blush with the coming dawn. Staring at the lightening sky through her bedroom window, she hears sounds through the wall and realizes that her brother is also awake. At first she thinks he might be calling to her, but there is no pause in the sounds that come fast and then slow, seeming to repeat. Eliza gets out of bed to hear better, creeps into the hallway, and places her ear to his door.

The only word she recognizes is "hairy," followed by ones she can't make out. She isn't sure why such strange words seem so comforting until she realizes that it is the way her brother is saying them. In the smoothness of the sounds, the way they flow from her brother's mouth, she finds echoes of her own chanting, this a secret she didn't know they shared. Their familiarity lulls her until Aaron's voice becomes the sound of water lapping at the hull of a boat. Eliza is crouched into a corner of the storage hold, trying to fall asleep in spite of her uncomfortable position. Her head knocks against the side of the boat with a thump. The water stops.

"Elly?"

She opens her eyes and she is back in the hallway, trying not to move, scared her brother will open the door and find her spying.

"Elly, go back to sleep," says Aaron through the door. Elly keeps still, torn between asking to come in and sneaking away as though she was never there to begin with. When the chanting starts up again, she runs back to her room and places her ear to the wall, letting the sound of her brother carry her back into dreams.

When school begins, Eliza is placed in Ms. Paul's sixth grade, this her first noncombination classroom since Ms. Lodowski. The desks are uncarved. The seats do not wobble. Baby animal posters have been replaced with posters of presidents. To pass the time, Eliza transforms each student into the letter they most resemble. Even when Ms. Paul moves Eliza to the first row, Eliza keeps her eye on the clock, waiting for the moment she will be set free.

She no longer needs pen or paper to bring the letters into her mouth and body. In class, the letters in her textbooks rearrange themselves at her least glance, eager to reveal their true natures. Eliza tries to explain that this is the reason she can no longer read aloud. Her explanation only gets her a note home and an appointment with the school psychologist to discuss her "difficulty separating reality from imagination." Luckily, by the day of the appointment, Saul has explained enough for Eliza to keep her knowledge of the letters from Miss Osbourne, who has her draw a lot of pictures and gently asks if anything "bad" has happened, maybe something she's been told to keep secret. Miss Osbourne is satisfied enough not to ask Eliza back. Elly works on stilling the words long enough to read them. There are no more notes, though Ms. Paul now looks at her the same way she looks at Glenn Guerdo, who stands up in the middle of class, drops his book, and says, "It's called gravity," whenever he forgets to take his medication.

Eliza doesn't mind that she sits alone at lunch now or that she is laughed at for studying word lists at recess. As far as she's concerned the day doesn't really begin until she gets home. The only thing she likes better than studying with her father is spending time in the study without him.

Alone, Eliza grapples with the 200 combinations that compose *Light of the Intellect*'s dissection of *Adonai,* working to memorize Abulafia's instructions. She will need to chant perfectly to gain her reward. Hebrew chants different than English, its letters carrying the weight of millennia. She likes the heaviness. The weight soothes her, reminds her she can take her time.

Each Friday night יהוה leaps up from the pages of her *siddur.* Eliza finds it difficult not to move her head along with each vowel, discovers herself breathing according to Abulafia's careful cadences. As she listens to the congregation sing, glossing over *Adonai* as though it is any other word, she can't believe she used to be one of them, blind to *Adonai*'s potential. She is even more amazed that her father is able to feign ignorance as he leads the prayers, his lips betraying no sign of where the word can lead.

Fall slides into winter. Saul is pleased, if surprised, to find that Aaron has taken a sudden interest in school clubs. Debate team, science club, chess club, yearbook, and the Sierra Club take up alternate weekdays and weekends, often not bringing Aaron home until long after dinner, except on Fridays when Saul insists that Aaron be there in time for the blessing over the candles. If Saul notices a certain distraction on Aaron's part at Shabbat services, he attributes it to Aaron's newly busy schedule and the intense solipsism of the teenaged. Aaron, Saul tells himself, is merely a late bloomer who has finally blossomed. The best thing he can do, as a father, is to provide room for his son to grow.

Since their night of tentative embracing, Saul and Miriam have reached a state of marital détente. While Miriam has implied that she would prefer Saul to remain downstairs for the time being, she has reverted to her 6 P.M. homecomings and tends to stay in on Saturdays. There have been no overt discussions of the evening Miriam came to dinner *not herself,* as Saul prefers to think of it, but when Saul now asks his wife how she is feeling it is with an air of tender diligence he feels accurately conveys his concern. Miriam, for her part, has shown no further sign of the stranger she briefly became. This helps to further everyone's secret hope that the longer the strange interlude goes unmentioned, the less significant it will become.

If Eliza continues to worry that her covert book-borrowing will be discovered, she needn't. In the face of the past months' familial shifts, the movements of a particular book from a shelf in the study do not register on Saul's internal Richter scale.

The day begins so normally. By the time Eliza comes down for breakfast Aaron is almost finished eating, Saul is in his study, and Miriam has left for work. Though she can't remember his ever having done it before, Eliza tells herself that Aaron hugging both her and Saul before leaving for school is normal. They are, after all, a family. When Aaron tells Elly to take care of herself too low for Saul to overhear, Eliza nods as if this is a regular request. She follows him out the door soon enough to see him back out of the driveway and down the street. Though she knows he can't see her, she waves.

After school lets out and Eliza returns home, she and Saul dive into her studies with their usual fervor, Saul breaking away only to put something on the stove. Eliza enjoys studying to the smell of her father's cooking. It makes the words seem nutritive, reminding her that she is feeding her brain.

The call comes in the middle of dinner. Dinner calls are the most common, that being the time favored by the solicitors of magazine subscriptions and long-distance services. Eliza concentrates on her food, waiting for her father's self-righteous, "You have interrupted dinner with my family," even though it's just the two of them. Instead, her father's face grows still and serious. He says lots of small words like "Yes" and "Of course" in a correspondingly small voice. Elly cannot imagine who would make her father sound just like her or Aaron when they are caught doing something wrong.

"Your mother's been arrested," Saul says quietly to Eliza after hanging up. The words are completely alien, too unlikely to possibly mean what they say. Saul's face remains expressionless, its features seemingly sprayed into place. "Why don't you stay here and wait for your brother while I go to the station? I'll call as soon as I know what has happened."

Eliza tells herself this must be a family version of a school fire drill or a test of the emergency broadcast system, a just-in-case for an event that won't ever happen. But then her father is fetching his coat, and then he is out the door, and if this is a test Saul isn't showing any sign of calling it off.

Eliza hears the car door slam. The engine starts up and then fades in the distance until the loudest sound is the tick of the oven clock. It is the first time Eliza has ever been in the house alone. She turns on the television and begins clearing the table of dinner, deliberately knocking into cabinets and rattling plates in an attempt to fill the vast space she has suddenly found herself in. The sound of the television cushions the emptiness of the house as long as she has dishes to do, but once they are done the TV laughter bounces oddly off the walls. She needs something else.

When Eliza thinks of the *Light of the Intellect,* she doesn't picture the Hebrew she has never been able to read or her father's spidery translation, but the face she has attached to its author. Abulafia has become a man with kind dark eyes and curly dark hair whom Eliza has yet to recognize as an older, male version of herself. It is this face she imagines speaking to her after she closes herself inside her room, mentally reciting the instructions she has memorized. Abulafia's imagined voice inside her head is just the company she needs to make her feel less alone.

Though Eliza has been patiently permuting יהוה for some time now, her attempts have not yet yielded the desired effect. No image has appeared before her. There has been no special voice. Every time she has completed a permutation without seeing or hearing anything special, she has managed to find some small error in her execution to explain away their absence—a slip of the tongue, a misjudged breath. The very elusiveness of her goal has inflated it in her mind. Many nights she has fallen asleep to the divine visions she is certain await her. Having cycled through the more classical images, her imagination has set out in more subliminal directions. God has become a baobab with ladybugs for leaves, a million-story high-rise that sings through its doors and windows, an umbrella that turns raindrops into candy. The voice, however, is nonnegotiable. The voice she knows she will recognize.

So tonight to block out the fact that Aaron isn't home yet, that her mother has been arrested, and that her father has left her alone to find out why, Eliza decides to try again. Sitting on her bedroom carpet, the door closed behind her, she cycles through the proper combinations of *yod, vav,* and *heh,* her voice and body perfectly attuned. Chant feeds seamlessly into movement as if these two things have always been integrally connected. There is no room left in her head to wonder where her brother is or what her mother has done. There are only the ancient letters and the sounds they make.

By the time she finishes she is slightly out of breath and covered in a delicate sheen of sweat. Never before has she chanted the letters so well, struck so perfect a balance between vocalization, head movement, and breath. She can hear the words of the book echoing in her head, Abulafia's voice an unconscious blending of her father and Mr. Clean from the TV commercials: *If you should hear a voice, loud or soft, or see any image before you, you have been received by God or His Highest Angels.*

She is poised in wait for the promised sign. She feels a sudden wave of resentment toward her father's books and their secrets, their paths persistently barred. She is on the verge of tears—over her continued permutation failure, over her unexpected and frightening solitude—when three of Abulafia's words echo back to her, the aural equivalent of a sudden beam of light parting the clouds.

loud or soft

She realizes she has been waiting for a thunderbolt, a booming presence to shake her to her marrow. She hasn't been thinking in terms of a whisper. She hasn't been considering the voices of the letters themselves, the soft voices she has known so long that she takes them for granted. The book whose door she has been pounding her fists against has been open this whole time, waiting to usher her in. She falls asleep secure in the knowledge that she is ready to take the next step.

Though Saul has never engaged in anything more subversive than rhyming "four" with "war" during a few anti-Vietnam protests and hasn't touched a drug in just as long, he can feel his heart pounding as he faces the police sergeant. Saul wishes he had brought Eliza with him. Perhaps proof of Miriam's motherhood would downgrade whatever the police have in mind to a small fine and a "Don't let it happen again." Saul has the sudden urge to own up to the grass he smoked, the acid he dropped, and the slogans he chanted, irrationally certain that the man before him knows it all and is waiting for his admission of guilt as a precondition for his wife's release.

The sergeant, a lean man with intelligent eyes, opens a file but doesn't look at it as he begins to speak.

"We got a call from a family in Jenkintown. They were upstairs when they heard an intruder. The husband wanted to go down with his gun, but we kept him on the line until a patrol car arrived on the scene. We found Mrs. Naumann in the living room. She came quietly enough, but it was pretty hard to get her to give up the vase she had in her hands. She's lucky the husband listened to us or she'd probably have gotten herself shot."

Saul pales. "My wife hasn't been feeling well. I had no idea—" But he stops, certain that his ignorance implicates him just as strongly, if for a different crime.

The sergeant gives a curt nod. "If you don't mind, Mr. Naumann, I'd like to show you something."

"When can I see my wife? Is she okay?"

"We've got her downstairs. She's fine. We'll need to hold her until she can be arraigned tomorrow morning. You're welcome to see her, but I'd prefer if you'd wait until after I showed you what I'd like to show you. You can either ride with me or follow in your car."

"I guess I'll follow in my car," Saul says, too afraid to ask if he can decline the invitation completely, very much not wanting to be shown anything at all.

They take a long road through an unfamiliar industrial district. They pass windowless warehouses with metal doors, parking lots of trucks and buses, a salt silo guarded by plow attachments waiting for the arrival of the first big snow. They pull into the parking lot of a U-Store-It with a bulging-cheeked chipmunk mascot. Large chunks of paint on the chipmunk's body have peeled away, the underlying gray sign metal looking like some kind of communicable skin disease. As they exit their cars, a squat man in a Day-Glo orange hunting cap peers out the door of a dimly lit office, sees the sergeant, and waves him on before closing himself back in.

Squat, windowless buildings with sliding metal doors line the dirt lot. Sodium lights flicker a shade of yellow that makes anyone standing beneath them appear ill. The sergeant beckons to Saul as he heads around the corner, to the second row of buildings. He waits for Saul by one of the doors, tossing a key lazily from hand to hand.

"The manager was kind enough to give me his copy," the sergeant says in a tone that makes Saul feel as if he's being tested. Beyond the occasional rumble of a passing truck and the electric hum of the nearest light, there is nothing, not even a cricket. Saul's world feels thousands of miles distant.

The sergeant scans Saul's face as if reading something there before unlocking the door. It lifts more quietly than Saul anticipated.

"Perhaps you'd like to do the honors," the sergeant says.

"What do you mean?"

"The light. Why don't you get it?"

Saul does not like the sergeant's tone. "Where is it?"

The sergeant sighs in exasperation. "Come on, you know where it is."

"Officer," and Saul can't believe he's saying Officer, remembers bravely shouting *Pig* in college demonstrations as if he didn't know he was out of uniformed earshot. "Sir, I have never been here before in my life."

The sergeant shrugs, reaches inside, and flicks a switch. White light floods a storage room the size of a small gym. The silence is immense.

"It's beautiful," Saul finally says very softly, in the kind of cautious voice reserved for libraries, museums, and cathedrals. "What is it . . . all?"

The sergeant looks at him. "You really don't know?"

Saul shakes his head, perplexed.

"I believe you." The sergeant's voice relaxes. For the first time since being in the man's presence, Saul doesn't feel impugned. "I can tell you've never been here. Sorry if I made you nervous before. Something this size, it seemed only natural your wife might have an accomplice."

"Miriam did—all this?"

"It seems she did, sir. The family who called her in wasn't interested in pressing charges. They were more concerned about her health—mentally, that is. We were actually taking her home when she said, 'I suppose you'll want to see the rest,' and took us here."

"But where did it all come from?"

"It's stolen. Your wife has been renting this space for eighteen years, always pays on time, best and longest customer. According to her, she's been taking this stuff for as long, maybe longer. We haven't had time to inventory yet, but you can see for yourself we're talking about a lot of stolen property here, more than enough to rank as a felony offense. Although, quite frankly, we're concerned for your wife's health as well. This isn't exactly what you'd call a normal theft case."

It is impossible to walk without treading on something. The most easily negotiable floor sections are the portions given over to buttons. Pearl buttons of various colors dot spaces between larger buttons of complimentary shapes and hues, grouped together in vague stepping-stone arrangements which, when taken together, remind Saul of pictures he's seen of the circulatory system. The button paths are only wide enough for one, bordered on either side by meticulous constructions of larger objects that stretch back to the walls of the room, a landscape of unending shape and pattern.

A spiral of shoes of decreasing heel heights cycles from brown to orange as it winds its way to a center of earrings whose shapes and colors form a pattern of stripes and circles in sparkling metal and rhinestone. The shoes are framed by pens and pencils stacked at careful angles to form a free-standing fence of contrasting colors and shapes, the curve of a pen's tip set off by the blunt end of an unused pencil. An arrangement of pink erasers becomes the flesh of a creature governed by laws of geometry.

The transition from shoe to wineglass is barely perceptible, the shoes as they stretch toward the glasses actually assuming shapes that reflect or contain a wineglass within them. The perimeter is composed of glasses lying lengthwise on the floor, but with the aid of marbles, beads, and shot glasses, the line arches upward in a graceful curve to join a column of stacked wineglasses, brandy snifters, and champagne flutes reaching higher than Saul's head. Occasional colors in the stems of the vessels form symmetrical patterns independent of their tower, balanced compositions of line and curve that catch and clarify the room's light. When Saul gazes at the tower, he sees water reflecting the sun, he sees a night sky of stars, he sees the patient, timeless ice of the poles. He wants to stand at the center of the tower, the glass his second skin, its light beamed directly into his body.

Farther on, a hedge of books expands into a miniature labyrinth. Books give way to picture frames, each containing its own mosaic of small objects. Beads and earrings, cuff links and stickpins create their own immaculate order, establish worlds that seem far preferable to the one Saul inhabits. Candlesticks, light bulbs, and salt and pepper shakers alternate with combs and coffee mugs to form an integrated whole, a combination of objects so commanding it is difficult to imagine the objects separate, performing the functions normally assumed of them. All around him, each object presents itself redefined, this its true function, this the reason for its creation. Saul feels the sudden urge to take off his shoes. He places them gently behind him on the button path, wanting to disturb this vision as little as possible.

Hats of felt and straw and cotton and crepe alternate with dinner, dessert, and salad dishes to form a study of circles. Their varying patterns and hues contribute to a larger design of complimentary colors that vibrates when Saul looks at it, requiring him to turn away, feeling like he has been gazing too long at the sun. Gloves and scarves become an ocean of texture and color in which Saul feels he could easily lose himself, their colors cycling so subtly it is impossible to tell when green becomes blue becomes purple.

It is impossible to put his eyes where something does not demand his full attention, a pattern that hints at something true, an arrangement of objects that suggests a forgotten order. Abstraction is equally hopeless. The room's collections of objects interlock as seamlessly as their discrete selves to form compelling geometries. They are more than patterns. They are reminders. Saul cannot look without recognizing something lost, the room a return to a state of grace he had not known he remembered, a pure existence he suspects only at a fleeting, subcellular level.

Saul is attempting to stave off sensory overload when he looks up.

At first, what he sees seems a trick of overworked eyes. As he continues to stare, he realizes it is no mirage. Suspended from a web of delicate threads hang silverware, hatpins, and peacock feathers, silk cravats, plastic figurines, and artificial flowers. They are strung individually and in groups, arranged to interact with each other as well as to capitalize upon the slightest wind current. Looking back the way he came, Saul sees a swath of motion carved by his path, innumerable objects twisting and twirling in response to his passage through the room. This space is not a passive object to be observed and left behind. It is interactive. Every person who steps inside becomes an object in its perfect order, associating with it in infinite, beautifully balanced ways.

Saul starts finding it difficult to breathe, the unfulfillable demands of the room overwhelming him until the warehouse feels like a coat closet, until his head begins to ache. When Saul starts to cry, it is out of this sense of supersaturation as well as having arrived at a new level of understanding. If he were capable of creating such a vision, he too doubts whether he could resist its pull.

Feeling ill, Saul makes his way back to the entrance.

"I've seen enough," he whispers to the sergeant, who has been waiting by the door.

"I don't blame you," the sergeant replies. "I can't stay more than five minutes without getting a headache. Still, though, it's something to see. Almost a shame we're going to have to tear it all down," the thought of which only makes Saul sicker.

Saul realizes he is still barefoot only after stepping on a sharp pebble outside the door, runs back in to collect his shoes. He feels reluctant to reclaim them, their return to his feet a diminishment compared to the prospect of remaining behind. Saul turns off the light and slides the door closed behind him. The last object to reflect his presence is a feather suspended just above the entranceway. It twirls in the ebb of the final air current left by Saul's passing. Then it is still.

They are walking back to their cars. Already, in the rocks embedded in the asphalt, in the clouds of the sky, in the way the yellow light casts a sickly pall upon everything, Saul can see a shadow of the room's order, its patterns implied the way a sculpture hints at itself from within un-carved stone.

"Let me ask you something," the sergeant says. "Does the word 'kaleidoscope' have special significance to you?"

Saul looks blankly at the sergeant, shakes his head.

"Because that's what your wife called this place. She called it her kaleidoscope."

It is only as he is driving back that Saul realizes he neglected to call home. Guilt floods him as he imagines Eliza and Aaron sitting by the telephone for hours, waiting. He ups his speed in an attempt to close the gap between himself and his children as quickly as possible.

The house is dark when Saul pulls into the driveway. He expects to find Aaron and Elly on the couch with the television for company, is surprised to find the living room deserted. Upstairs, both Aaron's and Eliza's doors are closed, but only Eliza's has a line of light beneath it. Quietly, Saul pushes her door open.

She has fallen asleep on the floor fully clothed, knees tucked into her chest, thumb in her mouth. Saul is fairly sure she is not normally a thumb-sucker. He kneels beside her, gently strokes her hair.

"Elly?" he whispers.

Eliza murmurs but doesn't stir.

"Elly, honey, it's okay. Daddy's back. Daddy's going to put you to bed."

Very carefully, as if handling a fallen baby bird, Saul eases his daugh-ter into his arms. He is surprised at her weight, surprised that such seeming fragility could be so solid. Once he has lowered her onto the mattress, he debates whether or not to change her into pajamas. He knows he would be soothed by such caretaking, feels suddenly protective of his daughter's body, this one part of the evening's disorder he can put right. But he knows his motives are selfish, suspects Elly has reached an age where she would prefer to change her own clothes when she awakens. He tucks his daughter in, kisses her forehead, turns out the light, and closes the door behind him.

It is dark underneath Aaron's door. Saul knocks softly.

"Aaron?"

He very much wants Aaron to be awake. Night often provides Saul a clarity day seems to obscure. In the darkened hallway outside his son's door Saul is filled with things he wants to say to his son. He will start by apologizing for his inattention, assuring Aaron that the change is purely circumstantial and in no way reflects a lessening of his love. Standing outside Aaron's door, Saul's heart is so full of love that he can feel his eyes fill with it, can feel love dripping down his cheeks.

"Son?" he whispers, but the house is completely silent. What he wants to say will have to wait for morning.

Saul knows not even to try to sleep. Instead, he spends the morning's earliest hours examining Miriam's belongings. He rummages through drawers he had always prided himself on not opening. He investigates Miriam's closet and bedside table drawers, searching for a sign of the woman from the warehouse and finding not a hint of anyone. Only while sorting his wife item by item does he realize the overwhelming generality of her existence: a closet of sensible clothes in practical colors; four pairs of shoes ranging from casual to dressy in either black or brown; no knickknacks; no pictures; her only jewelry that which he gave her early on, before realizing she never wore any. It is enough, in retrospect, to lead him to suspect her of living life elsewhere.

Then, under Miriam's side of the bed, Saul finds a Buster Brown shoe box. It is faded from age, the boy and his dog having long been replaced in consumer consciousness by Nike and Tretorn. Inside, resting on several layers of padding, Saul finds a rubber ball, palm-sized and bubblegum pink. Saul puts the ball to his nose, inhales a scent from his childhood. He drops the ball to the floor. For a moment it appears that it may return to Saul's waiting hand despite the laws of physics. Saul is ready to believe that this can happen, sits absolutely still, his hand outspread, waiting for the ball to come back to him. When it doesn't, Saul picks it up and tries again. It's a matter of effort and will, he decides, and he for one is willing to keep at it until the ball lands where it should have landed to begin with. He knows, if he tries hard enough, that he can make things right.

When Saul goes downstairs to start breakfast, he notices the blinking light of the answering machine.

"Hi, Dad, it's Aaron." Saul cannot tell if Aaron's voice sounds far away because of the connection or the recording. "Um, I'm staying over at Charlie's house tonight. I'll call back later and explain when you get home." The message is followed by two clicks, which Saul presumes to be Aaron hanging up on two successive attempts. Saul dials the operator, who agrees to connect him to the last person to call the house.

"Hare Kṛṣṇa, Vraja Dasa speaking. How may I help you?"

"I'm sorry," Saul replies. "I must have the wrong number."

Confused, Saul climbs the stairs. He knocks on Aaron's door, then enters. The room is empty.

"Eliza?" Saul says as Elly exits her room for the bathroom. "Did Aaron come home last night?"

Eliza is still asleep enough that last night's events remain at a safe remove. "I guess so," but now she is remembering the phone call during dinner, her father's departure, and shutting herself in her room with Abulafia to keep the world at bay. If Aaron had come home while she was transmuting, she wouldn't have heard him, but it seems strange that he wouldn't have sought her out. Perhaps he tried to come home last night but forgot his keys, was locked out, and she was too caught up in a permutation to hear him knocking. Where she felt pride the night before, she now feels hollow, her new progress merely a further sign of her own selfishness.

"Did you hear the phone ring or the answering machine pick up?"

Eliza darts into Aaron's empty bedroom. Perhaps he knows something she doesn't. "Is Aaron with Mom? Can I go too? Are they okay?" She doesn't realize she has started to cry until she tastes the tears on her lips, isn't sure if they are for her mother, her brother, or herself.

"Shh," Saul says. "Everything's going to be fine. Your brother stayed with a friend last night," he says, trying to sound as if he hadn't found this out minutes before. "And your mother isn't in jail, she's in a hospital," which while not true yet probably will be soon. "The police found her last night when she was very sick and confused and they called us."

"Can I see her?" Eliza has never looked more like her mother. There is a hopeful quality to her eyes that Saul never associated with Miriam until seeing it reflected in his daughter's face.

"I don't know," Saul replies. "Eventually you can."

He doesn't mention that he hasn't seen Miriam yet either, that last night his wife would only talk to her lawyer, that he will be attending her arraignment this morning, unsure whether she will speak to him or not.

"Some hospitals have rules about children. I'm going to visit the hospital today while you're at school. By the time you get home, I'll be able to tell you more."

"Is she going to be better soon?" Eliza asks with her mother's eyes.

"I hope so."

Saul escorts Eliza downstairs and feeds her cereal, hoping he can get her out the door in time to get himself to the courthouse without it seeming like this is anything but a normal day.

The arraignment is mercifully brief. Miriam's attorney meets Saul at the courthouse door and looks puzzled when Saul asks if he and Miriam work together. They do not have long to wait before Miriam's name is called, after which the lawyer does all the talking. The power of his words and the quality of his suit ensure that everything goes according to plan. Miriam Naumann, wife and mother of two, with no priors, Your Honor, and clear evidence of mental instability is committed to the Holliswood Center for psychiatric observation. Throughout the entire proceeding, Miriam barely moves, barely acknowledges her name. Some essential internal switch, whose existence Saul never suspected, has been turned off. In the brief period Saul is allowed contact before Miriam is taken away, he places his hand on her shoulder. It is like touching wood.

"Everything's going to be fine," he says for the second time that morning, feeling like a poorly trained parrot. Miriam looks at him, then through him, then is escorted out. Saul is thankful to have somewhere else he needs to go. He proceeds directly to Abington High.

Saul has an urge, upon entering Aaron's school, to wander. Strolling hallways bounded by the muffled sounds of class in session feels like playing hooky, reignites the adolescent joy of bending rules when rules were easier to bend. The hallways are redolent with the sights and smells of secondary education. The tang of grape bubblegum mixes with the musk of drugstore aftershave. A thin trail of precipitate left behind by the custodian's push broom winds through the corridors like a breadcrumb trail. Saul resists the desire to continue his sentimental journey. Aaron has waited long enough.

Saul enters the front office with the air of someone deserving immediate attention, an air cultivated on the *bima*. He uses the words "family emergency" and looks the secretary in the eye. The truth of these words, of his manner, doesn't reduce the feeling that he is playing a part, that he and this officious secretary, who is obviously pleased with her cameo role, have been rehearsing singly and together for this moment's drama. Saul cannot overcome his sense of removal, the events of the past twenty-four hours so much easier to stomach as someone else's story.

Saul realizes he doesn't know his son's homeroom. The secretary, disappointed, perceptibly cools as she accesses the senior class list. She makes Saul repeat the name. As she makes her way down the page, she begins to read aloud—Nassen, Nastor, Nattandi, Nauger. Saul ponders the surnames. Any of their fathers could just as easily be here. Saul turns toward the door, half expecting Messrs. Nassen, Nastor, Nattandi, and Nauger. He will exchange complicit smiles with these men. They will assure each other they are not alone.

"He's listed as absent for today." The secretary's voice dispels Saul's vision. He could have sworn he just heard the woman say that his son was not here.

"Absent? But that's impossible. Aaron stayed with a friend last night. My wife was unexpectedly ill and he stayed with a friend. I was gone until late—at the hospital—" Saying the words out loud makes them seem true. "He stayed with Charlie and then the two of them went to school together."

The secretary pictures a bed sandwiched by an IV pole and one of those beeping heart things, the name of which she doesn't know but which are always featured on "General Hospital." Last week the doctor informed Laura that the clear liquid dripping out of Luke's unconscious nose wasn't snot but spinal fluid. She really likes Luke. "I'm so sorry about your wife. What's Charlie's last name? I'll see if he's accounted for."

Saul realizes that he doesn't know Charlie's anything.

"Perhaps it's my mistake. Charlie's parents may have already taken Aaron to see her. It was crazy this morning, I might have forgotten."

Saul pretends to rack his brain for events that never happened. His own guilt quenches any small flames of annoyance at Aaron's unexpected disappearance, for doing to Saul what Saul has done to him.

"Yes, yes, now I remember. They said they'd take him to the hospital. I'm so sorry to take your time like this. I had completely forgotten," and Saul beats a hasty exit to sympathetic secretarial assurances.

Walking to his car, Saul assures himself that Aaron is fine, that he is probably home already, that he is hiding out with his mysterious friend until school ends, that he is a teenager reacting in teenage fashion to Saul's failure to handle this crisis. Saul will go home. He will tell Eliza to study on her own. And when Aaron arrives, he will take his son into his arms.

If her mother were really sick, the police would have taken her to the hospital and not the police station. Eliza knows this much. But her mother is a lawyer. Lawyers don't commit crimes.

Then it comes to her. Her parents are getting divorced. She knows that getting divorced involves going to court, so it makes sense that getting divorced would also involve the police. Her father didn't want to tell her about sleeping in his study, so he also probably didn't want to tell her about the divorce. Which is why he told her that her mother was found by the police instead of admitting that she went to the police on her own. Eliza decides that if her father wants to use the word "sick" instead of "divorced," she's old enough to play along.

Eliza knows most kids of divorced parents have to choose who to live with, but she thinks her situation will be different. Her father, after all, is already sleeping in a different room and her mother isn't home much anyway. If her mother moved out, she wouldn't have anyone to cook for her and she would never have time to see Eliza or Aaron. Eliza decides, with relief, that it will be easier for everyone if everything stays just as it is.

At lunch, she spends the first ten minutes wandering around the cafeteria looking for Sinna's table before remembering that Sinna is in middle school now.

The lawyer assures Saul that Holliswood represents the absolute best in private psychiatric care, but Saul still entertains gothic expectations of barbed wire fences, rough-hewn stone, and barred windows. Instead it looks like any other medical facility. There is a well-manicured lawn. Curved sidewalks feature an occasional nurse pushing an occasional wheelchair. A centerpiece of ornamental shrubbery and perennial flowers fronts the door. The lobby is sunlit, with comfy chairs, dog-eared magazines, and a television burbling at low volume. The woman attending the front desk smiles at Saul as he enters. Saul almost accedes to the urge to check the sign outside to confirm he has come to the right place. He approaches the front desk, face downcast, even as he tells himself to look her in the eyes. There is no reason to be ashamed.

"May I help you?"

It is the same question he is asked everywhere: a department store, a library, the produce section. It makes no difference that it is now being asked by a mental health professional, doesn't matter that the answer now involves his wife.

"Um, yes. I, ah . . ." Saul prides himself on the directness of his speech. "My name is Mr. Naumann. Saul. I've come to see my wife, Mrs., I mean, Miriam Naumann. I believe she was brought here this morning."

The nurse consults a list, confirms that Mrs. Naumann has indeed been admitted, asks if Saul called ahead to clear his visit.

"Cleared it? Are there set visiting hours? I can come back later if you'd like."

The nurse's voice is as melodious as a Disney character's about whose shoulders fly tweeting birds.

"Oh no, Mr. Naumann, the time of your arrival is not the issue. It's just that Mrs. Naumann or her doctors may have determined that she isn't ready for visitors. I'll call over to her wing and find out. In the meantime, why don't you make yourself comfortable?" which Saul realizes is actually a command and not a question. He does his best to look as if he is following orders by sitting in a nearby chair, even though he knows that comfort, in this context, is impossible.

The waiting room is deserted except for an older woman in purple leg warmers intently watching television. Her wig is crooked. Saul wonders if she is an inmate slipped out to pretend at being sane. But then an old man appears in the hallway wheeled by a nurse. The woman leaps up from the chair to kiss the man's slack cheek. The man is attired in purple silk pajamas neatly pressed, his hair perfectly combed, his face showing no sign that he has been approached or kissed by this slightly askew woman, who takes the wheelchair from the nurse to head for the door and the early afternoon. Saul is alone. He watches the sun slanting through the front windows. He cannot help but compare it to the light slanting through a certain tower of wineglasses.

"Mr. Naumann?" Saul turns toward the Technicolor voice. He is expecting to see Miriam, is ready to join the lady in leg warmers and her oblivious purple husband for a stroll of the grounds, but there is only the front desk woman.

"You've been cleared," she warbles. "Go out through the door you came in and follow the sidewalk to the left until you reach Building 3. You'll have to buzz to be admitted, but they're expecting you." Saul nods his thanks, hurries out into the sun.

When another melodious voice greets him through the intercom, Saul can't help but wonder if the ability to sound perpetually perky is part of the job description. The voice makes it too easy to imagine his wife asleep in an enchanted bed, awaiting his kiss to turn everything right again.

Saul is buzzed inside. There is no front lobby, just a nurse waiting inside the door. When she inspects the box he has brought, it occurs to Saul that he should have come with a nightgown, a toothbrush, or at least a comb and not a pink rubber ball. He follows the nurse as they pass through another door that requires her key and which locks with a foreboding click behind them.

"Your wife is in the day room, Mr. Naumann. Just follow the yellow line down this hallway and to the left."

Saul follows the line, the shoe box clutched in one hand, past doors whose windows he does not look into and past people he does not greet. The yellow line ends at a set of double doors that he at first pushes instead of pulls. When they refuse to open he fears he has unwittingly become subject to a test of his own mental fitness. Then he sees the handle that he somehow missed. He pulls.

Miriam sits alone on a nubbly green couch in a corner of the room. Until today Saul has never seen his wife without at least one part of her moving. If not accomplishing one of her endless tasks, she would be tapping a foot or bouncing a knee or twiddling a finger to maintain her body's momentum. At the sight of Miriam so still, Saul realizes that his wife's perpetual motion had become as much a personal constant as the ticking of his watch. It is her stillness, and not the events of last night or her present setting, that dispels Saul's sense of remove, forcing him to realize that this is his family and not some clever simulacrum.

"What have they done to you?" is the first thing out of his mouth. He sits down at her side but she shifts beyond his reach. "They've drugged you, haven't they? I'm calling your doctor first thing. This will not happen again. I can't believe—"

"Saul." Her voice is flat, unimpressed by his ardor. "Saul, they haven't done a thing. They wanted to put me on something, an anti-depressant, I think, after my entrance interview, but I wouldn't let them. I told them it wouldn't make any difference. What's done is done."

"You mean they haven't—you're sure you aren't sedated?"

Miriam laughs, but it is toneless.

"Do I look like I need to be sedated? You saw me in court. The police will tell you I was the same last night. I'm a model prisoner."

"You are not a prisoner," Saul insists. "You are ill. The police found you."

"Did they tell you where?"

"Yes. They said you were inside a stranger's house."

"Doing what?"

Saul's replies are slow and stubborn. "Holding a vase."

"And, according to the police, was the vase mine?"

"No."

They are both silent, Miriam daring Saul to look in her eyes, Saul looking anywhere but.

"Did they show you my kaleidoscope?" Miriam asks softly. "Isn't it beautiful?" For the first time since their visit began, Saul hears expression, senses the Miriam he thought he once knew.

"I've never seen anything like it," Saul admits, unable to keep the wonder from his voice.

"I've been searching for the proper pieces since childhood, before

I even knew what they would become. It was you who made me realize what they were for. We had only known each other a little more than a month then, but at that moment I knew you were the man I would marry." She leans closer to Saul, her eyes bright, her face alive. "*Tikkun Olam,* the fixing of the world," she whispers. "I've been gathering up the broken vessels to make things whole again."

Saul does not remember the specific conversation, was given no reason at the time to fix it in mental amber. To him, *Tikkun Olam* was merely one of many intellectual pillow talks, cerebral calisthenics performed for the sake of keeping his skittish, brainy lover in his bed. He cannot believe she began keeping secrets from him so soon.

Miriam looks to Saul for a response. He nods, afraid to do more. He doesn't know whether he wants to yell or plead, isn't sure if he should become accuser or supplicant. How could she have kept all this to herself? Was she afraid he would try to stop her? Even as Saul suspects Miriam was right not to tell, he can envision a wistful alternative. In another life, another Saul might have been her willing accomplice. Together they might have explored the mysteries of color and symmetry, creating a vision of a world more intensely unified than their own. A world in which they could have lived without secrets.

He knows it is best to stay silent. The last thing Miriam needs is the fanciful perspective of a sleep-deprived and overstressed husband. It is in his wife's best interest that the beautiful contents of her storage room be disassembled by the time of her release. It is best to put all of this behind them as quickly as possible.

"I don't expect the doctors or the police to understand," she says, her voice matter-of-fact. "You and the children will continue to be provided for. I added your name to my parents' trust long ago. Talk to my attorney. He'll provide the details."

"Miriam, don't talk like that. I already talked to your lawyer. He's sure we can get you a commuted sentence and probation in exchange for a promise of good behavior, public service, and intensive therapy. You won't even need to go to trial. You'll come home. I'll—I'll work harder at giving you what you need. We can go to therapy together. We can even take the children. You'll never need to steal again."

"I've never stolen anything in my life." Her face is resolute.

"Miriam, your lawyer says it's best to confess to everything, to admit to your problem, and to show sincere contrition."

She smiles. "But I'm not sorry, it wasn't stealing, and if I could I would do it again."

Saul tells himself he doesn't know what she means.

"Miriam, please."

Her smile is larger now, defiant. He offers her the box. The smile vanishes, replaced by something close to wonder.

"I found this." Saul shrugs. "It's silly, but I thought you might want it."

"You *do* understand," she whispers. She reaches for the box slowly, as if afraid it may be a mirage.

"It may not be what you think. It was under your side of the—"

"I know exactly what it is," she says, carefully lifting each layer of tissue paper. "Thank you." The two words are more intimate than any she has ever spoken. Saul feels as though he is inside her in ways beyond the merely physical, connected by a bond transcending flesh.

She reaches into the box, cups the ball reverently in one hand. She is about to pronounce the secret word, the one she has never spoken to anyone, when she notices the scuff marks. The ball has been indelibly and irredeemably ruined. The feel of its flawed pink surface on her skin revolts her, each scuff mark a wriggling worm. She stops herself from flinging the ball across the room, knows it will only draw unwanted attention, instead drops the small pink corpse into its coffin.

"Please go," she manages to say without screaming, without pummeling the man responsible for this blasphemy with her fists.

"But, Miriam, I just got here. We still have time."

"Nurse!"

"Miriam, please. I know you're upset."

"Nurse!"

"Miriam, talk to me. Tell me what's wrong."

A man appears in a white shirt and white slacks. "Mrs. Naumann, can I help you?"

And there's that universal question again, the one that doesn't mean a thing.

"I would like to go back to my room. Now." Miriam is already at the locked door to the day room, is trying to open it with Saul behind her.

"Please, Miriam, let me help." Saul reaches out his hand, grazing Miriam's shoulder. Miriam stiffens.

"Don't you *dare* touch me," she says in a low hiss that turns Saul's mouth dry.

"Mr. Naumann?" says the nurse in an infuriatingly calm tone. "Why don't you let me escort Mrs. Naumann back to her room and then you can talk to her doctor." Up close, he really is quite large.

"I don't want to talk to the doctor," Saul says as close to level as he can. "I want to talk to my wife."

Miriam is pounding at the door. The nurse stops her fists with his arm. "I'm going to take you back to your room now, Mrs. Naumann. Just calm down. Mr. Naumann," the nurse says without looking back toward him, "I think it would be best if you waited here for the doctor. He'll be with you shortly."

Saul wants to be furious too, longs to pound the door with his fists. He wants to be stopped by something large and impassive and led to a bed with soft sheets and a pillow large enough to block out the sound of the world collapsing. Instead he stands where he was told to stand. He waits for the doctor he has been told will arrive. He listens to the sound of his wife's footsteps receding to a room he will never see.

The possibility that no one will pick up the phone tonight is too terrible to consider. Aaron needs to be done with it, needs to get the words out, or he may explode. He knows better than to eat, knows that nothing he puts in his stomach will stay down until it is done. After getting the answering machine three times in a row the night before he could barely sleep, spent the whole time chanting to himself just to stop from thinking about it. He keeps reminding himself he is not asking his father for permission. He is informing him of a decision.

It came to him at school two days ago. Since September he had been going through the motions of his classes, filling the chairs in the various classrooms and secretly chanting *japa* until he could return to the temple, staying there for the last *arati* and then returning home in order to get up the next morning and do it all over again. Then two days ago he was changing out of his gym uniform in a corner so that no one could see, trying to block out the sound of the shower he was supposed to be taking and the guys making fun of him because he wasn't, when he realized he was going in circles. His life at that instant was no different from the life he had been living in eighth grade. And as simple as that he realized it was time to stop. He had the means to break the cycle. So the next morning he hugged his father and sister goodbye and got into his car feeling lighter and happier than he has ever felt. And as soon as he can make that phone call, his new life will really begin.

When Eliza gets home, Saul sits her down at the kitchen table. He has rehearsed in front of a mirror to confirm that his face matches his words.

"Eliza, honey, I've got some sad news. If you have any questions—anything at all—I want you to ask me, okay?"

Eliza nods.

"Last night your mother went into a stranger's house to take something she thought was hers but really wasn't. The people in the house called the police. When the police came, they could tell that she was mentally ill, so they sent her to the hospital. I visited her there today. She was very upset and confused, but the doctors are going to work with her so she can start thinking clearly again."

Eliza smiles at Saul like he's told her an inside joke. "It's okay, Dad. You don't have to say all this."

Saul puts his hands on his daughter's shoulders. "I know it's not a nice thing to think about, Elly, but telling the truth about things like this is important. Your mother might be in the hospital for a long time."

Eliza giggles. "It's okay, Dad. I know. I won't tell anyone if you don't want me to. She can come back."

Saul talks very slowly and carefully, the way one might try to coax someone down from a ledge. "Elly, honey? Can you explain what you're talking about?"

Eliza squares her shoulders and looks her father in the eyes. She puts on the most grown-up voice she has.

"It's okay that you and Mom are getting a divorce. I won't tell anyone. I told Aaron that you guys weren't sleeping in the same bed, but I won't tell him about the divorce if you don't want me to. You can tell Mom it's okay to come back. She doesn't have to pretend to be sick."

Saul's eyes well with tears. "Oh, Elly, is that what you think has been happening? That your mother and I are getting a divorce?"

Eliza nods a little too vigorously.

"Oh, Elly-belly, I wish it were that simple. It's true that your mother and I have been having problems and it's true that we haven't been sleeping in the same bed, but I'm afraid that she really is sick. She's been breaking the law—stealing things—because she's been very mentally confused, and now she's in the hospital to try to get better."

"She's a burglar?"

Eliza's voice is different now, the certainty gone, the careful calculations she made at school useless. Saul talks calmly, as if soothing a nervous animal.

"According to the doctor, she has a mental illness that makes her believe she needs to take things." He knows he's talking down to her, but he doesn't want to use the words the doctor used, words that scared him to hear.

"My mother's been stealing things because she's crazy? And she got arrested? And now she's in a loony bin?" Saul flinches. At first he doesn't reach for Eliza, afraid that she, like Miriam, will back away, but his daughter folds into his arms, grinding her head into his chest as if she wants to bury it there.

Saul strokes Eliza's hair and whispers soothing sounds into her ear. When she has stopped shaking, he tries again.

"There are a lot of ways to think about what has happened to your mother, but not all of them are helpful. Calling someone crazy doesn't describe the problem. It's a name used by people who don't understand or are too afraid to understand what's really going on. Your mother is mentally ill." It's much easier to say this in terms of Eliza's mother rather than his wife. "Being mentally ill is a medical condition like having diabetes or having high blood pressure, except that the part of the body that isn't working right is the head. Because the head is so complicated, it sometimes takes longer to figure out what exactly is wrong and how to fix it," or if it can be fixed at all, he thinks, remembering the doctor's confident use of the words "delusional disorder," his tentative mention of the term "schizophrenia."

"Is she going to go to jail?" Eliza asks, and Saul begins to wish he had waited for Aaron to get home before doing this, doesn't want to go through this a second time.

"I'm not sure yet, but I don't think so. We've got a really good lawyer who is going to explain all this to the judge and I'm pretty sure the judge is going to allow her to stay out of jail as long as she promises not to steal anymore and to get therapy."

"How long is she going to be in the hospital?"

Saul wishes he could tell someone about the way Miriam backed away from him in the hospital day room, about the beauty of the world she is being told to abandon.

"I don't know, honey. That's pretty much up to the doctors and your mom."

"Dad?" Eliza says after the two of them have sat silently not looking at each other for a while. "Can we keep on being the way we are? Can we keep on studying? Maybe if she knows that I'm still working hard it will help her, because then she'll want to get better so she can watch me spell again. Maybe this year we can all go to the nationals together."

Eliza doesn't say the second half of her idea because she's pretty sure her father wouldn't approve. Eliza can think of no better way of helping her mother than if she has God's ear. If what she realized in her bedroom last night is true, if she has heard a voice, then it's time to move on to the next book on her father's shelf, the last rung on Abulafia's ladder to *shefa*.

They are both relieved to adjourn to the study, to close the door behind everything that has been said, and to bury themselves in words. Saul warns Eliza that when Aaron gets home he is going to let her study alone so that he can talk to him about all that has happened, but as the hours pass they grow more and more willfully absorbed. Saul forgets he is waiting for the sound of the front door, forgets it should have come by now. So that when the phone interrupts them, Saul is shocked to see that it's eight o'clock, that they worked straight through dinner, and that the house is still empty.

"Dad?"

"Aaron, is that you? Thank God. Where are you? Are you all right? We've been so worried."

"Dad, I told you last night. I'm at Charlie's. I tried to call you again, but you weren't home."

"Son, I'm sorry about that. It's your mother. She's been having some problems . . . mentally . . . and she's in the hospital. I was with her last night until very late."

". . ."

"Aaron?"

"Is she okay?"

"I'll tell you all about it when you get home."

". . ."

"Aaron? Are you there? Your mother is going to be okay, son. Just come on home."

"We kind of need to talk about that. I don't really want to come home."

"Aaron, what do you mean? I understand last night, and even why you weren't in school today. It must have been scary for you—Eliza

{242}

was here, but she was asleep so she didn't hear you when you called—"

"Dad? Please just listen, okay? My friend Charlie is actually named Chali. It's a spiritual name, Dad. He lives at the ISKCON temple. I've been spending a lot of time here and what they're doing is something—well, I mean, it's basically something I think I've been looking for all my life. I mean, now that I've found it I don't want to give it up, you know?"

"Aaron, tell me where you are. Whatever it is you're talking about we can talk about at home. There's a lot we need to discuss, including your mother, but also my own preoccupation lately. You deserve an apology, son, but I'd like to do it in person, here at home. You're obviously too upset to drive, so just tell me where you are and I'll come get you."

". . . ."

"Aaron? Are you crying?"

"I don't want to tell you where I am, Dad. I want to stay here."

"Aaron, are they making you say these things? Are they holding you against your will? Aaron, son, if they're not letting you—"

"No, Dad, that's not it at all. It's completely opposite."

"Aaron, I'm going to call the police."

"No! Dad, it's not like that, I swear. Okay, I'll tell you where I am and you can come get me, and we can talk. Okay? But keep an open mind, okay? Because it's really important that you listen to what I'm going to tell you with an open mind."

"Just give me the address."

He sends Eliza to bed before leaving to pick Aaron up, but she easily stays awake until their return. She tries to guess where they will talk. She has a feeling it will be in the study where Saul thinks he can close the door and not be heard. He doesn't know about the vents and the way they carry sound.

They come into the house talking about Miriam and how long she may be away. Aaron sounds calmer than Eliza remembers being, but she knows it's hard to tell that kind of thing just from someone's voice.

There's a brief silence. Elly thinks she hears the door close. Then, suddenly, there's her father's voice very loud, completely different from a moment ago, and Eliza knows that, if it startled her a whole floor away, Aaron must be terrified.

"My God, Aaron, what have they done to you?"

Eliza wishes she knew what her father was talking about because from up here Aaron seems the same. That her brother is able to talk at all with Saul so upset impresses Eliza immensely.

She isn't able to follow everything Aaron says, but it has to do with something he saw from an airplane. Then she hears Saul say the words "cult" and "brainwashed" and Aaron say something back about India and Eastern religion. Then they both get loud enough for her to hear everything.

"You're not going to live there."

"Dad, I'm almost an adult. Soon what you think won't matter. You can make me wait, but you can't make me stop."

It gets really quiet. When they start talking again, it is too low for Eliza to make anything out. She desperately wants to sneak downstairs and put her ear to the door, but the prospect of being caught is too terrible to consider. She keeps herself awake by spelling in her head until she hears them both climbing the stairs. Once she stops hearing sounds from her father's room, she creeps into the hallway. Aaron's door is closed.

She knocks softly.

"Aaron?"

She knocks a little harder.

"Go away, Elly."

"Aaron, what happened? Please can I come in?"

In the silence that follows, Eliza stands obstinately still beside the door.

"Are you still there?" he asks after a few minutes that could have been a few hours, as far as Elly is concerned, because she was prepared to stand there all night. "Well, you might as well come in then." The door is unlocked.

He is playing his guitar very softly, nothing identifiable, just a series of wandering chords. He doesn't look at her as she sits across from him on the floor.

He's wearing an orange robe that reminds her of the togas they used to make with their bath towels when they were little. Around his neck is a strange cloth pouch.

"What is that?" she says, pointing to his neck.

"It's where I keep my *japa* beads," he says, continuing to strum.

"What are *japa* beads?"

"They're what I use to chant."

"Is that what I heard you doing that night?"

"So you *were* at my door."

"Yeah, but only because I heard you when I was in my room."

Eliza listens to the guitar chords rise and fall.

"So I guess you know about Mom."

Aaron nods, continues to play.

"You know," he says, "according to the *Vedas,* we die only to be reborn, over and over again. How well we lived the last life determines what we get reborn as next. At some point you and I were both living animal lives, but we've managed to progress to human ones. Once we're good enough humans, we can progress to the Heavenly Planets and then to Godhead itself."

She thinks he's kidding at first, but his face is completely serious. Eliza looks at her brother more closely. Except for the orange robe, he seems the same. "Do you actually believe that?" she asks.

"I'm not sure," he says with a slight grin, "but if it's true it means that our parents are only two of the countless parents we've had or ever will have. Kind of changes your perspective."

Eliza shakes her head. "What difference does it make? They're our parents now, right? If we're supposed to live good lives, doesn't that mean helping them? I mean, if there was something I could do that would help everyone—Mom and Dad and you—don't you think I should do it?"

Aaron stops playing. "Elly, what is Dad trying to get you to do?"

"Nothing," Eliza says, vehemently shaking her head. "It's just the opposite. He doesn't know I want to do it. I mean, he knows it, but he thinks I won't be doing it for a while. But I'm pretty sure I'm ready to do it now."

"Hey, Elly?" Aaron's voice is different now, more gentle. "Do you remember when we were kids and I would teach you things?"

"Like the secret moves of the Jedi ninja?"

Aaron smiles. "Yeah, like that."

And suddenly Eliza is incredibly angry. She has no idea where this anger has come from or how it could have filled her so fast, but she finds herself practically hissing at her brother, her voice pure venom. "You made it all up. You couldn't really fight. You just lay there on the ground like a beat-up old *dog*—" She can picture it for the first time since it happened, her brother so pale and still, his eyes so filled with expectation, as if saving him was *her* job instead of the other way around. Then, just as quickly, the vision is gone and the anger gone with it, leaving Eliza feeling reduced and slightly ashamed.

"Aaron, I'm sorry," she whispers.

He's still holding the guitar but he isn't playing it now, just staring at it as if it reminds him of something else.

"It's okay, Elly. It doesn't matter. And it's okay if you think I look stupid in this robe—"

"I didn't *say* that."

"—and if you think the idea of being reborn is really strange—"

"I didn't say that either." Eliza is pissed off again, he can tell, because her face is turning red and, unlike him, she never blushes.

"I know you didn't say those things, Elly, but it would be okay if you did and this is part of what I'm trying to tell you. I'm trying to teach you something I really know. I didn't make this up, okay? I know you're into this spelling stuff, but be careful. Make sure it's what you want and not what Dad wants. Because he can be pretty convincing sometimes. Okay?"

"Okay," Eliza says even though she's pretty sure he's got it all wrong.

Saul calls the number he has always thought of as Miriam's work number. *You have reached the desk of Miriam Naumann. I'm out of the office right now but* . . . It is the same message he has always gotten, the one he never doubted because she always called him back.

He calls the number listed for the law firm in the phone book and is told that Miriam Naumann hasn't been in their employ for over ten years. He calls the hospital, but she is not accepting visitors. He talks briefly to a doctor who says he will receive weekly progress reports by phone and mail and passes along a message from Miriam to contact her lawyer. Miriam's lawyer informs Saul that his name was added to a trust left to Miriam by her parents' estate and that this trust has been paying the bills Saul assumed were being paid by Miriam's pay check for the past ten years. Saul asks the lawyer if he knows anything about cults, but the lawyer says no and asks him why. Saul does not tell him.

According to Aaron, it is an ancient Indian religion that Americans call a cult because they are frightened of what they don't know. Aaron has given Saul books to read. Saul does not want to read them. Saul wants to go back six months in time and notice how little his son is around the house. He wants to ask his son questions about his new friend. He wants to let Eliza study on her own a little while he and Aaron play guitar.

Now that these things are no longer possible, Saul wants to insure that history does not repeat itself. He does not want him and Aaron to become the strangers he and his own father became half a lifetime ago. He does not want his own grandchildren to meet him for the first time at his funeral. While Saul has helped lead Aaron to this point, he may still be able to lead him back. He will read. He will allow Aaron to spend time with these people. And every night that Aaron is home, they will talk. Saul has a little more than a year to make Aaron change his mind. After that Aaron will become legally empowered to make decisions for himself. Saul comforts himself with the notion that Aaron's visits to the Hare Krishnas will become less exciting now that they are neither secret nor forbidden. He assures himself that this, like anything else, is a stage to be outgrown.

Despite the fact that it is not Sunday, Saul makes French toast, has it waiting by the time Aaron and Eliza arrive downstairs for breakfast. At the sight of the food and their resolutely smiling father, both sit down without a word and begin to eat. Eliza darts several glances in her brother's direction, but he is mechanically intent upon his plate. Saul talks about everything that has nothing to do with Aaron or Miriam. He tells himself he is fostering needed normalcy in the face of difficult circumstances, can believe it because he doesn't notice how tightly his children are gripping their forks.

"What time do you think you'll be home?" he asks Aaron, his forcible nonchalance straining against the tightness of his throat. "I'm going to try to have the first chapters of that book read by the end of this afternoon so we can discuss them after school."

Even Eliza, doing her best not to listen, can hear the command embedded in her father's words: *After school you are to come directly home to me.*

"I'm not sure," Aaron replies, and Eliza is amazed at how relaxed he seems, as if he doesn't hear the thinly veiled message they have both been so well trained to detect. "I've got to go grocery shopping after school if you want me to eat my meals here, and then it's going to take awhile to prepare my food."

"I'm happy to cook you extra vegetables, Aaron."

Aaron smiles at his father as though Saul is a young child. "That's very nice of you, but it's not that simple. There are special foods that have to be cooked in special ways. I don't have my own shrine yet, so I won't be able to eat *prasadam* here, but I want to get as close as I can."

"Prasadam." The more uncertain Saul is, the more he tends to phrase his questions as statements of fact.

"Food that has been spiritualized. Next to chanting, it's one of the most important ways to get close to God. If you'd like, I could cook enough for all of us so you can try it."

Saul nods his assent. "And after dinner we can talk?"

"Sure, Dad. I'm looking forward to it," Aaron says, terrified.

In school, Eliza thinks of the letters that could aid her mother: injections of B for steadfastness, tincture of Q to remind her of her family. Eliza imagines herself as a letter doctor, curing the world's ills with the properly administered consonant or vowel. This idea carries her through recess without one intruding thought of her father or brother or the electric tension that now crackles beneath the surface of even their most casual words.

When Eliza comes home from school, Saul is waiting. They jump into the exercises with the enthusiasm of swimmers the first day the pool is open, only coming up for air when the smell of food reaches them and they realize that dinner is ready.

They emerge from the study to the smell of incense. Aaron stands proudly beside a stove steaming with three pots. When they bring Aaron their plates as instructed, he carefully spoons food onto them, mindful not to mix the contents of one pot with the other.

"This is chick peas in *ghee,* which means butter. This is zucchini, and this is rice." Aaron is grinning so hard that it is difficult for him to speak. Eliza cannot remember the last time she saw him looking so happy. "Before we eat, I'd like to say a few words of thanks."

Faster than Saul can respond, Aaron begins.

"This material body is a lump of ignorance and the senses are a network of paths of death. Of all the senses the tongue is the most voracious and uncontrollable. But Kṛṣṇa has sent us this very nice meal to help us conquer the tongue. So let us take this nice food to our full satisfaction, glorifying his lordship, Radha and Kṛṣṇa, and in love call upon Lord Chaitanya and Naityananda to help us."

Eliza does her best not to giggle. Saul stares as Aaron begins to eat, studiously ignoring them both.

"Lump of ignorance? Paths of death? Do you hate yourself that much, Aaron?"

Aaron blushes deep red. "The body is part of the material world, Dad, which is an illusion. What's important is to get beyond the body in order to be close to God."

"But didn't God make our bodies? By scorning the body, aren't you actually scorning God?"

"Can we please eat first and have a discussion later?" Aaron's voice has leapt to a register he thought he'd left behind with the end of his growth spurt.

"Of course," Saul says, taking a forkful of chick peas and discovering as Eliza already has, that they crunch between his teeth. He quietly replaces his fork by his plate.

"Aaron?" His voice is gentle now. "How long did you cook these?"

Aaron is stubbornly crunching away, ignoring the fact that what he has cooked tastes nothing like what he has eaten at the temple. "I thought I cooked them long enough. They looked done."

The chick peas are awash in melted butter, which has started to congeal on their plates. Eliza turns her attention to the zucchini, which is overcooked but at least easy to chew. Saul has given up on dinner altogether.

"Didn't you taste them to make sure?"

Aaron explodes. "You're not *supposed* to taste them. Okay? There are rules. You don't know anything so how am I supposed to talk to you? Don't eat it if you don't like it. Go back to your meat. I'm going to eat in my room." He takes his plate, which he has just piled with burnt rice and limp zucchini, and marches up the stairs.

When the house has stopped echoing with footfalls and Aaron's door has slammed shut, Saul looks at Eliza with a sad grin.

"Will you help me clean up the kitchen? We should go ahead and save this food even if no one ends up eating it."

They clear the table in silence. When her father starts on the pots, Eliza can't stay quiet any longer.

"Dad? What do you think Mom ate for dinner?"

Saul doesn't pause in what he's doing, takes in the question as if Miriam is a completely natural topic of conversation.

"I don't know, Elly, but I bet you it was better than this. You want me to make you a hot dog before I go talk to your brother?"

"Dad? When can we see her? When is she coming home?"

Saul turns off the tap water and bends down so that his face is level with his daughter's.

"Elly, I don't know, but it might not be for a while. She's not accepting any visitors right now, not even me."

"The doctors won't let her?"

"Actually, it's not her doctors." He had decided this was more truth than his children needed, but his anger gets the best of him and it's out before he can stop it. "She's not seeing anyone because *she* doesn't want to."

Eliza makes a small O-shape with her mouth but no sound comes out. She asks her next question to the floor.

"She said she didn't want to see me?"

Saul puts his hands on Eliza's shoulders but it's like touching a small stone statue. He wants to whisk up her small body in his arms and spin counterclockwise to roll back time.

"No, Elly, she didn't say that. She just doesn't feel well enough to see anyone yet."

Eliza's voice, when it comes, is very small, could almost be mistaken for a trick of the wind.

"Is she very angry?"

And now Saul does scoop his daughter up, but she is dead weight in his arms, reminding him too much of Miriam. He quickly puts her down again.

"I don't think she's angry. I just think she's confused."

"I think she's angry," Eliza says, barely any louder, such that Saul has to kneel down again and ask her to repeat it.

"Why do you think she's angry?" he asks, trying to keep the exasperation out of his voice, but it's really hard because he needs to not have to worry about her. If he can have that one thing, he knows he will be okay.

Eliza shrugs. Saul pats her on the head and tells her everything will be fine. He suggests she practice on her own in the study while he talks to Aaron upstairs and that he might be awhile. She says okay even though she'd much rather he admit the cause of Miriam's anger. If her father

would just acknowledge that losing the people they love is the temporary price they must pay for their efforts, they could at least agree that it
is a sacrifice worth making. Because once Eliza reaches God's ear she
knows she'll be able to get her brother and mother back. She knows this
as surely as she knows that the time is now, that tonight, to drown out the
discussion that will be going on above her, she will advance to the next
book on her father's shelf.

Saul's presence a floor above puts a fluttery feeling in Eliza's stomach.
She feels certain that the nervous click-click of her teeth is Morse-
coding her intentions up the air vent to her father's ears. Eliza presses
her jaws together to will the shivering to stop, to coax her body into
her service.

Though her father's and brother's voices have been reduced to
murmurs, Eliza can read the tenor of the conversation from their
tones. She can tell her father's voice by his low-pitched certainty, his
longer, carefully measured cadences. By comparison, Aaron sounds like
a frightened bird, his voice coming in short, sharp bursts of sound that,
from below, sound to Eliza like her own fears made manifest.

It takes a moment for Eliza to steel herself to touch the book containing the last steps toward *shefa*. Its unshelving has become a test of
personal worthiness. She has convinced herself of the possibility that it
won't yield to her touch.

She half hopes for this failure. She is young enough to be discom-
fited by the idea that her father's knowledge is finite. If she has overes-
timated her abilities, she can reinstate her father as personal guide and
sage. It will be a relief to place herself once again under his guidance,
to know she is meant to follow and not to lead. When the book slides
from the shelf to Eliza's hand without fanfare or paper cut, Eliza
quickly postpones the moment of truth to the book's opening.

Because there has to be a moment of truth. This is the only way

Eliza can reasonably invest this volume with the power her father ascribes to it. In a quick revision of her expectations, Eliza decides that anyone can hold a book; the trick lies in opening it. If she isn't ready for the book's contents, her own unpreparedness will serve as the most effective of locks.

Eliza carefully grasps the front cover between thumb and forefinger. For a moment she merely holds her fingers there as if they have come to rest. She is unsure whether or not she wants the book to let her in.

When Eliza finally does open the book, its spine creaks like a volume twice its size, as if the power of its words has lent it extra weight. Its pages give off a fresh paper smell tinged with a bitter hint of ink, its innards not having been exposed to the world long enough to dull the scents of its birth. The pages remind her of the sheltered parts of her own anatomy, the paleness of her inner arms and tummy, skin that rarely sees the sun. There are no smudges or fingerprints marring these pages, none of the stray drops of coffee that had marked her father's presence in the last volume. Though Eliza cannot read the Hebrew, these letters lack the insectile coldness of the temple prayerbook, reminding her more of trees than beetles. The four letters from her most recent permutations jump off the page to greet her, as if she is viewing the book through 3-D glasses. She is comforted to realize that within this strange alphabet she has made a few friends. As Eliza continues through the book the wide, pristine margins lend the impression that she is striking out onto freshly fallen snow. Though her father has translated these words, it is clear he has never tried to follow them. He never made it this far.

The voices from Aaron's room have become more regular, regaining tones of normal conversation. Even when Eliza presses her ear to the vent, she can't make anything out, leading her to wonder if sound, like helium, is lighter than air. Realizing that this could work to her disadvantage, she covers the vent with a cushion from the sofa to prevent her own sound's escape.

Life of the Future World, though a slim volume like its predecessors, is more difficult to understand and filled with depictions of *shefa* that surpass even her father's enthusiastic representations. *Shefa*, as portrayed by the book, will allow Eliza to see all of creation, which it compares to looking into a mirror and seeing both one's own face and "the faces of all who pass by." According to Abulafia, Eliza will not only hear but see God, who may take the form of anything from a young boy to a sheik to an old man.

The actual Hebrew word she's supposed to permute to achieve all this is itself a puzzle, is in fact not a word at all. The Name of Seventy-Two consists of three Torah verses of seventy-two letters each, which she is supposed to combine into seventy-two specific triplets. Each letter is pronounced with its own special vowel, in addition to a specific head movement. While Elly is coordinating all this she must also pay attention to her breathing, Abulafia requiring a certain number of breaths for every triplet set.

It's a lot to have to do. Every skill Eliza has attempted to master, both with and without her father, is called into use. She cannot even start with the Name itself, but must first permute other words with pen and paper until the pen falls spontaneously from her hand. Eliza thinks of the Ouija board she and Aaron once used to attempt to contact the ghosts of their grandparents. *I Don't Know* was the pointer's answer to their every question, leading Aaron to wonder if ghosts suffered from amnesia and leaving Eliza to concede the possibility of moving something without meaning to. The *Future World* makes it clear that unintentionally releasing her pen will have much graver consequences than putting words into the mouths of imaginary ghosts:

> If you are unworthy, your mind will become confused, your thoughts confounded. The power of your imagination will overwhelm you, weakening your intellect until your reveries cast you into a great sea.

Even if she manages to drop the pen when she is supposed to, her reward for doing everything right seems even scarier than her punishment for doing something wrong:

After you have cast the pen from between your fingers, the divine influx will begin to prevail in you, and will weaken your external and internal organs. Your entire body will begin to tremble until you think that you are about to die. This is because your soul is separating itself from your body as a result of the great joy that you experience when you perceive and recognize these things.

Eliza is beginning to wonder if she shouldn't seek her father's help after all when she reaches the only words with the power to sanction her highest ambitions. She has always known that these words would be the sign. Their presence in the middle of the page, as if they have been waiting for her all along, validates both her secret book borrowing and her desire to continue as she has been, alone. They are the words she has been praying to hear through years and years of silent *Amidahs*:

Remove your shoes from your feet, for the place upon which you stand is hallowed ground.

At which point she loses her trepidations as quickly as her sneakers.

Though the cushion over the air vent now does little to muffle the increasing noise from her brother's room, Eliza is blissfully unaware of the angry voices upstairs. She is so engrossed that she wouldn't notice Saul were he to burst through the study door, wouldn't hear the sirens if the house were aflame. Hundreds of hours of study and practice are finally coming together into a synchronous whole. The only thing now standing between her and transcendence is the memorization of the Name of the Seventy-Two in its triplicate complexity.

By the time Eliza finishes, she feels as if she has eaten a large meal rather than read a small book. Before returning *Future World* to its shelf, she copies down the triplets and their accompanying vowel sounds, her concentration now lessened enough to hear the ongoing argument above her. She hears Saul yell something about Aaron ruining his future, Aaron stridently insisting that Saul doesn't understand. By the time an upstairs door slams and footsteps sound on the stairs, Eliza has finished her copying and has replaced the book on its shelf. Saul yells something about Aaron trying to avoid the issue by leaving, forbids him to take the car keys. Eliza sticks her head into the kitchen to see her brother standing by the door to the garage.

"Our discussion is over," Aaron yells loud enough for Saul, still upstairs, to hear. "If you don't get out of my room right now, I'm gone."

The floor above them creaks. Footsteps sound on the stairs. Before Eliza has a chance to say a word, Aaron scoots through the kitchen and into the living room, easily bypassing Saul en route through the hallway. When Saul reaches the kitchen, there is the sound of feet scampering up the stairs and a door slamming.

"I hope we didn't disturb you too much." Saul's voice has deflated. His face sags in places it hasn't sagged before.

Eliza sticks the paper with the triplets into her back pocket, pulls her shirt down over her pants.

"What were you guys fighting about?" she asks, more to distract attention from her own actions than out of any desire to know, fearing that proximity to the conflict may be interpreted as enlistment.

"We weren't fighting," Saul says, unconvinced. "We were holding a theological discussion. Your brother has been exploring other religions."

"What do you mean?" Eliza asks, wide-eyed. "Do you mean he isn't Jewish anymore?" She can't believe she didn't think of this before.

"He will never stop being Jewish," Saul replies in a steely voice that makes Eliza inadvertently recoil.

"I'm going to go to bed now," she says.

"Elly-belly," Saul says too quickly, "it's okay. Your brother and I are just having a difference of opinion. I'm trying to help him see things straight, but he's at an age where nothing I say can possibly be right. We'll work it out."

"Is he moving out?"

"As soon as legally possible," comes Aaron's voice from the stairwell, surprising them both.

Saul immediately starts into the hallway, Eliza forgotten. "Aaron, come into the kitchen."

Aaron stays where he is. "I'm going to bed, unless you want to try to forbid me to do that too."

"How do you expect us to carry on a rational discussion when you are acting like a child? I'd have more luck talking to Eliza."

"Of course you would. She'd agree with everything you said. Talk about brainwashing; you're an expert."

Eliza starts back toward the study where she can at least close the door behind all this but Saul, red-faced, motions for her to stay.

"I demand that you come into the kitchen right now and explain yourself. You at least owe your sister an apology. She's been working extremely hard. She doesn't need your crap."

Eliza cannot imagine having that voice directed at her and surviving. When Aaron's voice comes to her from the stairwell, she can tell he is crying.

"I'm sorry, Elly. It's not your fault. You don't know any better. Sleep well." The stairs creak and a door clicks shut.

In her outside-the-house life, Eliza feels as though she has been given special eyes to see the secret world hidden inside the regular one. She cannot look at a poster or a book without smiling. *I know what you're really like,* she wants to sing out to the letters, so innocently frozen on signs and on television, in newspapers and on T-shirts. It is as revelatory a feeling as the time she looked through the class microscope to see a universe of tiny creatures inside what had seemed a simple drop of water.

At school, Elly can generally get enough of a head start on a permutation to block out the questions people have started to ask her, like why isn't her brother wearing normal clothes or is it true her mother is in the loony bin and won't come out. She supposes she can't help it if someone's older sister has seen Aaron in his robe, but she'd like to know how they found out about her mother being sick. Elly doesn't like hearing "Like mother, like daughter" just because she has better things to do than play at recess. A good day is when the school bus catches all green lights on the ride home.

Once the study door closes behind her, the world beyond is just as Eliza wants it to be. Her mother is no longer in the hospital, but in the living room writing one of her letters. Aaron and Saul are getting along.

The few hours Saul now has with Eliza before dinnertime are the spark of his day. He secretly returns to bed after seeing the children off in the morning, setting the alarm to wake him in time for Eliza's return. It has gotten to the point where he needs to set alarms on both sides of the bed to insure his timely revival, having developed the habit of unconsciously turning one off. Asleep, he wanders the bed, waking up on Miriam's side or with his head where his feet should be. He has not changed the sheets since she left, not wanting to lose her scent.

He keeps the weekly reports from the hospital under the bed with the rubber ball. When the children ask, he tells them that their mother is making slow progress. He tells them she has begun taking medication to help order her thoughts and keep her grounded. He refrains from giving them any idea of when they might see her again.

On weekends, he lets Aaron go. It is a break they have both come to require, the accumulated tension having, by that point, become unendurable. He tells himself that Aaron is a phone call away, that the Hare Krishnas are more reasonable than he first feared. He has spoken with Chali briefly. The man thanked Saul for allowing Aaron the freedom to explore his beliefs. Somehow, Saul does not find this gratifying.

He reminds himself that greatness is impossible without suffering. Abulafia was rejected by the rabbis, disappointed by his students, and persecuted by Jew and Christian alike. Ambition has its price. None of this would be happening if his daughter weren't worthy. On Fridays when congregants ask him where Aaron is, he tells them his son is trying out a different temple. It does not feel like a lie.

She memorizes the letter triplets to the tune of "Oh, Susannah" to keep them all straight. She's got to sing it three times to get through them. She's mostly able to keep the song to herself, but a few times Ms. Paul has told her to stop humming and Elly reminds herself to be more careful.

Ms. Paul has warned Eliza that if she doesn't start paying more attention she won't let her participate in the class spelling bee, but they both know she's bluffing. Dr. Morris has already told Eliza how excited he is for her about a hundred times and even the cafeteria ladies are saying how much they're looking forward to watching her on the lunchroom stage so they can say they saw her when. The closer the bee gets the less Eliza gets teased, as if even the other kids recognize that what's about to happen is larger than them all.

She can feel her father getting nervous. When they practice together, any little sound that breaks the silence makes him jump. He asks her how she feels a lot. She generally doesn't tell him. Even when her back is turned, she can sense where she is in relation to *Life of the Future World*. She holds her progress with the book responsible for the fact that she barely has to concentrate now to spell perfectly any word her father gives her.

She's come to covet her time alone, doesn't know what she would do if her father and brother called off their nightly skirmishes. Saul's adult education class at the synagogue provides Aaron his only weeknight respite. Those nights, Elly can hear her brother chanting in his room as she works a permutation. She feels closest to him then, his sounds blending with hers in the shared space of the air vent.

At dinnertime, if Saul gets up to use the bathroom, Eliza tastes whatever Aaron cooked for himself that evening. At first Eliza only did it to be nice, but lately he's been getting much better and she can mean it when she says he's a good cook. Aaron tells her he plans to work in the temple kitchen once he becomes a devotee.

Elly thinks of her mother even more now that she's stopped sleeping. It happened gradually. For a while, Eliza only needed an extra half hour to wind down from the buzz of a permutation, a feeling similar to having drunk too much sugared tea at *oneg*. In the time it takes to wind down, however, she has become increasingly aware of a rising tide of questions her brain can't seem to stop asking. They aren't the important ones like *How is Mom?* and *What's wrong with Aaron?* and *Will I be able to win the bee?* Instead she thinks long and hard about whether her left or right side is better to lie on, having once heard something about one putting more pressure on the heart. Then she will think of her heart, beating all this time, and worry if it ever gets tired, beating like that. She will press her hand against her chest, but it will only make her scared, so she'll start thinking about the letters and singing her triplet song, which has become the only thing that can make the other thoughts go away. So that now at least four hours pass between being put to bed and closing her eyes.

In the day the repeating questions are different, but the feeling is the same. It's like the time she went to the bathroom and two tall girls followed her in to stare over the kid-sized stall door as she tried to pee. She had to pee really badly, her bladder hurt because it was so full, but the staring girls made it impossible. Eliza has started to feel that way all the time now, as though she needs to do something so much it hurts but she can't. She can't answer the small, stupid questions filling her brain. She can't get to sleep. She can't get hungry. She finds herself eating as quickly as possible to get it over with, putting food in her mouth and chewing because she knows it's what she's supposed to do.

When she is alone with the book, she tries not to think about how much she wants the pen to spontaneously leave her hand. Thinking about it only breaks her concentration. But she can't chant the triplets she's finally memorized until her stupid pen does what it's supposed to do. Time is running out. Eliza wanted to be able to stand up at the class bee with God on her side, but she has come to accept that God might take longer. This realization has allowed her to relax more during her nightly attempts at transcendence. She has become less focused on the state of her hand and more on the temporary escape the words provide.

Lately there has been less and less to escape from. Saul and Aaron's debates have degenerated into tense silence. Though Saul still insists upon spending the after-dinner hours with his son, Aaron has become more spectator than participant in their relentless discussions, having determined their pointlessness. Saul is less willing to concede stalemate, interprets his son's prolonged silences as a sign that he is beginning to listen to reason. The illusion is shattered when Saul notices how resolutely Aaron's hand stays in his pants pocket when they talk. Finally he asks Aaron what he's got in there. When Aaron won't answer, Saul makes a sudden lunge for his son's arm, manages to extract the hand before Aaron knows what is happening. Dangling from his son's fingers is a string of wooden beads.

"What the hell is this? A rosary?"

Aaron shakes his head, too weary to be upset. "They're *japa* beads, Dad. Each bead has been carved from the sacred wood of the banyan tree."

The scent of cheap incense fills Saul's nose, reminding him of the incense he would burn in his college days in preparation for a coed seduction. A smell that might otherwise have made him nostalgic, it now transforms the ISKCON temple into the seducer, Aaron into the coed about to be duped.

"What do you do with them?" Saul asks, his attempt to sound objective canceled out by the look on his face.

"You *chant* with them, Dad." Aaron doesn't go on to say that Saul should know this by now, that he has already been told this in the course of the "discussions" that Aaron has abandoned.

"And is that what you've been doing the whole time I've been talking?"

Aaron is proud to have turned their nightly scrimmage into something worthwhile. He nods, not masking his grin. Saul pockets the beads.

"What are you doing?"

"There are appropriate and inappropriate times for prayer. Since you don't seem to be able to distinguish between the two, I will help you."

Aaron can't imagine school without his beads. If, as Prabhupada writes, the true devotee should glorify Krṣna at all times, Aaron needs the beads to stop school from being anything but a giant waste. He comforts himself with the fact that the beads his father has confiscated are only a practice string. His guru will give him his true *japa* beads once he becomes a devotee. He will get another practice set this weekend from Chali. And from now on he will be more careful.

On a calendar in his study Saul has marked the dates of all the bees from class to national. At the end of each study session he and Eliza strike through the day together, each X edging them a little closer to their shared destiny. Saul has gained special permission to sit in on Eliza's class the day bee season begins. As recently as last year Eliza would have been mortified at the prospect of a parent in her class. The girl she's become accepts that her father has worked hard for this moment, has as much a right to be there as she.

Saul makes his daughter promise to use Abulafia's method even when the words are simple.

"If the word is CAT, I still want you to wait for those letters. Let each one fill you before you let it out. It's the only way to avoid making a careless mistake."

Eliza doesn't need convincing. She is all too aware of how easily it could end, their ambitions shattered by a letter spoken too fast. She can picture her future clearly now. There will be television interviews, speaking engagements, a trip to the White House. She will be taken out of school because everyone will be forced to concede that her attendance has become superfluous. She will be buffeted with questions from all sides of the world, called upon to resolve conflicts, invent cures, fight famine. There are certain things she will not do. If the President asks her to develop a weapon against the Russians, she will refuse. She will only use her powers for good. At this point her imaginings lapse into cartoon, she the caped superhero bringing liberty and justice to the world between commercial breaks.

Which is why it is so important not to make any stupid mistakes. Which is why she would really prefer to have *shefa*'d by now. Barring that, she is more than willing to honor her father's precautions. It is impossible to be too careful.

Aaron waits until the evening before the class bee to drop his bomb.

"She's not even in the hospital, is she?"

He says it so quietly that at first Saul and Eliza, sitting across from him at the dinner table, aren't sure they heard correctly.

"Son?" Every word between them now is fragile, could fragment into shrapnel at a moment's notice. "What are you talking about?"

"I'm talking about my mother," Aaron says loudly enough that the sound bounces off the walls. "I'm talking about the story you and Elly have made up about her being in the hospital. It would have been easy enough to do. I wasn't home. You could have come up with anything you wanted."

Aaron's voice makes Eliza feel sick. If she weren't watching him speak, she would swear it was someone else talking, someone whose life had turned to poison.

If Saul feels the effects of his son's voice, he doesn't show it. "And what do you propose really happened?" he asks wearily.

"I think she *left* us." Aaron slams his glass down so hard it cracks. Water runs in a thin stream down the side of the glass and across the table, dripping onto the floor. No one moves to clean it up. "I think she got sick of you and Eliza playing your little games. I think she got tired of hearing you and Elly laughing together and knowing that if she knocked on your door it would stop. I think she got tired and got the hell out. And I think you covered it up because you knew it was your fault. Tell me the truth, Dad. Why can't you live your own stupid, lonely life? Why do you have to pull me and Eliza into it? Why can't you just leave us alone?"

The only sound is the water dripping onto the floor. When Saul stands up from his chair, the table shudders.

"All right, Aaron, you want to know the truth? I'll tell you the truth. Your mother has been lying to you your entire life. The most fundamental things that you take for granted are false. Your mother's a lawyer, right?"

Aaron nods warily.

"*Wrong*. She hasn't had a job in ten years, Aaron. The whole time we thought she was at her office, practicing law, she was stealing. Stupid things that weren't even valuable or pretty. For ten years we've been living on her dead parents' money while she stole things she could easily have paid for. She was very good at what she did, Aaron. She was never caught. You know what finally did her in? She started breaking into houses. Houses, Aaron. That's when the police arrested her and took me to where she'd been storing it all. But that's not the whole story."

"Stop it."

"She *arranged* it. Into the kind of patterns only a crazy person would make. It made me sick to look at it, Aaron."

"Please stop."

"So, for your information, your mother *is* in the loony bin and she's there because she *is* completely crazy, and I have no idea when or *if* she is ever coming out."

Aaron is crying silently, the tears incongruous with his deathly still face. Eliza has dried up, her body an empty husk. The moisture is gone from her mouth and eyes. Her tongue is pasted to her teeth; her lips are sealed shut. Her skin has become so fragile she knows it will crumble away at the slightest movement, reducing her to bones and reddish dust that was once her blood.

"It's not true," Aaron whispers, but Eliza knows it is, knows that her mother has always been a stranger.

"Not true?" Saul says, and begins to laugh. Not in a nice way. Not so that others would want to join in. "God, Aaron, if you want proof, just look at yourself. Like mother, like son. For the past few weeks you've been going around in an orange robe telling me about heavenly planets and rebirth and sniffing the hand you use for your prayer beads like it had been touching a woman, not that you know what *that* would smell like. Why can't you just be like me, Aaron? When I was your age, I had friends. Real friends, not religious freaks who only saw me as one more body to sell flowers in an airport—"

At which point Eliza begins to scream. At first there is just sound, like the sound a small child might make if it were trying to run away from a frightening animal much bigger and faster than it was. Eventually there are words.

"Please stop it, please stop, please, Daddy, just leave him alone," but the words are slurred. It is somewhat difficult to make out.

Saul emerges from his indignation to shattered glass, the dripping of water, and the faces of his children.

"I'm so sorry," he whispers, moving to take them both in his arms, but Aaron is all motion, his palm slicing through the air to slap his father across the face before his long legs propel him from the table and into the hallway. Eliza can feel her father's arms crushing the dry shell of her body, can feel herself disintegrating in his grasp. He holds her so tightly she can feel the pulse of his veins, can hear the tide of air feeding his lungs. Somehow, when he asks her if she is all right, Aaron's hand outlined in red against his cheek, she manages to find the strength to tell him what he wants to hear.

Saul has gone to bed early, advising Eliza to get a good night's sleep to prepare for her big day tomorrow. Aaron has been chanting for hours now, the words fast and dangerous, each one honed to a sharp point before leaving his mouth. Through their shared wall Eliza can hear him, a bicycle without any brakes. When she knocked on his door, he just kept chanting, an endless tape loop without a stop button. It was at that point that Eliza decided to go into her father's study, to fetch the book, and to bring it back to her room.

She doesn't worry that her father will miss it; he is too distracted to note its absence. Besides, the comfort the book provides outweighs her fear. Eliza strokes its cover with the unconscious tenderness of a mother. Its soft leather is soothing to touch. Its Hebrew no longer intimidates. The angled alphabet beckons like the fairy tale forest in which her happy ending lies.

The sound of her brother's chanting fades as Eliza empties her mind. Tonight, instead of closing her eyes to await the word that will guide her into permutation, she is drawn to the pages of *The Life of the Future World*. The columns of Hebrew erase time, their own shapes unaltered by history. Eliza could be in 500 B.C. Jerusalem, in the shadow of the Second Temple; she could be in the stone city of Sefat in the 1600s, in a synagogue with a ceiling the color of the sky; she could be in thirteenth-century Spain, Abulafia at her side. In all those places the word she chooses would be the same, its angles and curves unaffected by diaspora, inquisition, or age: אור, Hebrew for light. Eliza is drawn to the word's last letter, resh an ancient signpost pointing the way toward transcendence. She begins to explore its combinations with her pen, chanting with the vowels Abulafia has taught her, his gift across time.

Ah-va-reh, va-reh-ah, reh-ah-va.

She watches her hand move across the page. Her hand and voice are working in such harmony that it seems her mouth is extending through her arm to the very tip of her pen, the letters the physical embodiment of her voice. She is not consciously aware of how many letter combinations she has written, or how many remain. The exploration of אור is a journey across rolling terrain, traversed to the rhythms of her breath and blood.

Her voice has never been so sure of itself, so grounded in every syllable. As she continues, she is no longer certain whether she is chanting aloud or in her head, too filled with sound to tell. Her body has become a network of invisible strings, each letter resonating according to its own secrets. Sympathetic vibrations set off by the letters in quickening succession build within her until her entire body is humming. Eliza can sense her skin producing sound through its pores, a frequency so low she can only feel it, music that sets every nerve tingling until she is no longer aware of the floor, the air, her clothes, her room, the pen that has dropped from her hand.

Warmth floods her body until she glistens with sweat. Sweat pools at the corners of her eyes, the cleft between her nose and upper lip, the hollow of her neck. It runs down the line of her spine and the curve of her stomach. It fills her belly button. Were she to taste it, she would find it thick and a little sweet, her body turned honeycomb.

The buzzing of the letters fills her head with light. She can feel her eyeballs vibrating in her skull as words beam at speeds too great to hear, making themselves known at the center of her chest instead, within each beat of her quickened heart. There is no possibility of extraneous thought, no mental distance with which to regard what is happening at a safe remove. Each passing moment composes Eliza's entire universe, no room for the contemplation of past or future. Eliza's body begins to tremble. Her body sinks to the floor, the convulsions of her arms and legs completely separate from those of her neck and torso, each part of her an instrument played by a different set of frantic hands. Eliza begins to know fear.

The words that start streaming into Eliza's head come from a source beyond her recognition, at speeds too great to control. She is no longer producing the words but receiving them, a mute vessel scarcely up to the task. Every language that is or ever was resounds in the small chamber of Eliza's skull, the syllables of long-forgotten words beating against her brain like something buried alive. Somewhere deep inside her head, in a place far beyond the realm of ordinary sensation, Eliza feels something collapse.

Pain arcs from her scalp to the soles of her feet and carves inward until it strikes marrow. As tears stream from the corners of Eliza's eyes, she feels certain she is dying, but even this knowledge drowns in the torrent of words in her head, calling to her, shouting at her, pleading to be heard. The words are all abrasion and rough edges. They grate at the back of her cranium, steady as sandpaper. She can feel the convolutions of her brain being smoothed away, reduced to a warm, thick liquid that plugs her ears. Something heavy and hard is taking its place, something that isn't the right shape for her skull.

Eliza is unsure whether her eyes are open or closed when she sees the unfolding. A shape, its surface teeming with figures and images, is growing steadily larger, devouring the space around it as it spreads. Its surface shifts at speeds too fast to catch. Eliza thinks she discerns animal and human forms, crawling insects and crashing waves, but then realizes these are only meager attempts to lend familiarity to shapes that defy experience or sense of scale. What seems like a tree could just as easily be a feather, a lung, a network of rivers stretching across a continent. The shape expands until Elly is just a speck in its shadow, it having grown too large for her to see anything but blackness.

It becomes impossible to discern sight from sound, the two senses melding at an impossible pitch. The heavy, hard thing that came into her head too large has taken root. Desperate to get it out, she begins to shake her head violently from side to side. She cannot feel the movement, only hears a slight sloshing sound: a cup of sea water inside a plastic bucket.

Even as Eliza continues to chant, she can feel the muscles of her lower face clenching and unclenching as she chews her tongue. She can feel her jaw straining as it opens and shuts. There is a metallic taste in her mouth. The pain in her jaw muscles and the pain in her tongue become indistinguishable. Eliza no longer hears the sound; she inhabits it, lives in a small, neglected room that has been all but forgotten inside its massive bulk. She thinks she feels liquid trickling from her ears. She can feel each tooth as it bites into her tongue, but her tongue feels nothing. Her tongue is that of a dead cow, lying huge and slack upon the kitchen counter. She does not feel the urine pooling beneath her and mixing with her sweat. Its heat is canceled out by the impossible heat of her skin. She is willing to die for this to end, wishes she could die so that it would be over. As if in answer to her desperate prayer, the words soften, turning first into the clatter of insects, then to the rustling of leaves, then to water seeping through soil, and then to nothing.

The quiet is a benediction. The world, and she within it, is still.

It is the stillness of an uninhabited coast at ebb tide, of the womb in the moments presaging the first beats of a tiny heart. In gratitude, Eliza finds herself pronouncing the first six triplets of God's name.

The sounds are drawn out of her slowly, molten glass at the end of a glassblower's pipe. She expands with every syllable. Slowly, delicately, she stretches beyond her bones, beyond her skin. She had never perceived the extreme confinement of life before, when she was smaller than mountains and oceans, contained by her impossibly tiny body. She has grown large as the shape that dwarfed her with its expansion. She knows that the shape has a face, that everything depends upon the glory of that face's unveiling.

Eliza can feel the rise and fall of her breast above her heart, the stretch of her veins as they pulse with her blood. These are the manifestations of her body's desire. She exists only in relation to the face and its eminent appearance. She is halfway through the first six triplets. The knowledge that she will behold the face only after she has spoken the eighteenth syllable of God's name does not cause her to quicken her pace. Each letter must be born of her breath with the same slow inevitability of water carving stone. Part of the joy of each interval is this delicate slowness, the miracle of the final moment having been brought imperceptibly closer.

She never knew how much one syllable could contain. Each sound is ecstatic with possibility, an element from which all else springs. Pain has been replaced by a sense of release, locks and fastenings at last unbound, her body an infinite sail finally unfurled. A lifetime ago the shape seemed too large. Now she and the shape appear before each other as she speaks the final syllable.

Time stops.

In the split microsecond that follows, it is impossible for Eliza to see as much as she does. The shape's face is every face ever formed. Its surface teems with infinite human and animal possibilities, waves of flesh that crash against each other, consume each other, overflow and replace each other in perpetual transformation. The faces of the young, the old, the dead, and the extinct. Beautiful faces and faces deformed. Fur and flesh and feathers and scales. All simultaneous, all fulfilling the best and worst of their natures. She is mauled and licked clean by a lion. She is bitten by a cobra even as she feels the wonderful coolness of its skin. She is choked and crooned to, slashed and kissed, stung and cuddled, fed upon and fed. It is impossible to discern pain from pleasure, sensation devouring sensation. It is a microsecond that lasts a million years. Every cell is taxed to its limit, synaptic messages exploding along passageways blown clear away, the dam broken, sensation flooding the towns and drowning the townspeople, carrying away forests and herds and babies in their cribs.

There is no moment of reprieve when the face disappears, no blessed silence in which to heed the flow of her breath. The face is gone. As far as Eliza has expanded, filling all of space, she begins to contract, her impossibly small body rushing up to meet her at enormous speed. There is immense heat and immense cold. She knows she must, somehow, prepare herself for this corporeal reclamation, but it is impossible to do anything but disintegrate. She can feel parts of her burning and crumbling away. Eliza realizes that a return to her old self is impossible. The thing she has become and the body she left behind will cancel each other out upon impact. For this, she is thankful. There is the sensation of drowning, of suffocation, her lungs filling with a substance that is both thicker and thinner than air. This is the pain of creation, of life emerging from void, of vacuum birthing being.

When Eliza's alarm wakes her up the next morning, she is afraid to open her eyes. At the sight of the sun streaming through her bedroom window, she breathes a sigh of relief. *It was only a dream,* she thinks until she realizes she is lying on the floor, in damp clothes that smell of urine. Her jaw muscles ache. Her tongue hurts to move and feels three sizes too big for her mouth.

She sees the book lying open beside her. Afraid to touch it, she uses a shoe lying near her right hand to flip it shut. Then she locks herself in the bathroom and rinses her clothes in the tub.

When Saul sees his daughter enter the kitchen, she is pale, with dark circles under her eyes. She doesn't respond to his question about trouble sleeping.

"I want to apologize for last evening," he says. "I said a lot of things that I didn't mean. The past few weeks have been very hard. Your brother and I are going through a difficult time and your mother being sick makes it tougher on everyone. I love you both very, very much and I'm sorry all that had to happen the night before the bee. I hope you can put last night aside and enjoy today. You've worked too hard to let anything spoil it."

When Eliza nods, Saul kisses her on the forehead. "You're a real trooper," he says.

Aaron does not join them for breakfast. He goes straight from his room to the front door, managing to back the car down the driveway before Saul, who has run outside after him, can recite his apology.

Eliza watches her father run out the door as if in slow motion. She watches his legs extend, his arms swing back and forth. He returns slightly out of breath, face flushed. For a brief moment Eliza thinks she is still in her room, still trapped in the dream that wasn't a dream that she can't remember, because her father's face is suddenly several faces at once in a way that feels very familiar. She can see the faces of multiple men and women lurking just beneath his skin like afterimages, like long-lost relatives whose pictures she might have been staring at just prior to looking at her father's face. And though it all happens incredibly quickly, so quickly that Eliza isn't sure whether or not she is imagining it, she can't help but notice the way some of her father's features match up with the other faces and the way some stand completely apart, uniquely his own.

Perhaps Saul catches Elly staring at him funny, because he asks if she is all right. When she answers that she is, she realizes that she's not just telling him what he wants to hear. She can feel the truth of her answer deep inside herself, at a level where she used to think the words resided but where she now knows there is just her heart and stomach and lungs.

She spends the bus ride to school puzzling the previous night together, alarmed and relieved at the profusion of missing pieces. She remembers taking her father's book. She remembers beginning to chant. She seems to recall feeling a moment of utter clarity, her life suddenly coming into absolute focus. After that, the blanks begin. She remembers her head pressing against the carpet and feeling that it was being held there. She remembers being afraid. The memory of the pain is more tangible, manifesting itself in the soreness in her muscles and her tongue. She knows that whatever happened last night was her fault. She knows she'd like to be forgiven. Looking into the bus window, Eliza sees Miriam reflected in her own face. "Hello," she whispers to the window. When she smiles, her mother's reflection in the window smiles back.

By the time Eliza gets to school, she is no longer the girl who had to wash her clothes out in the bathtub. She has become someone wiser, perhaps that other girl's older sister. She likes the way this new someone walks past the school showcase without checking for remaining newspaper articles. She appreciates this new girl's calmness, focusing extra hard on the chalk in Ms. Paul's hand when a memory of last night, a bad one, tries to claim her attention. She is especially proud of the way the new Eliza barely ever checks the clock to see how much time is left before the bee begins.

Saul arrives at ten forty-five sharp. He is showered and shaved and wearing a tie. Though his face is haggard, he cannot stop grinning. As he enters, he tousles Eliza's hair, whispers, "This is it, kiddo," into her ear. The students point and giggle. He is led to a chair on the other side of the room but cannot stop staring. He is a man in love.

Looking at him, Eliza feels incredibly old. Old like she is his grandmother, like they are in a doctor's office and he is here for his shots. She wants to take him aside and tell him that it will be okay, that it will only hurt for a little while.

At precisely 11 A.M. every teacher in every classroom at McKinley

Elementary School tells their students to stand. Eliza stands up no more eagerly or reluctantly than the rest. There are a few giggles, a few pointed stares. Though Eliza doubts that what she is about to do will affect her mother much, she wishes Aaron were here. She's pretty sure he would like to see it.

Ms. Paul works her way down the rows and it's words like MANAGER and GHOST and MARSHMALLOW. Saul is beaming; Eliza can feel his excitement from across the room. If this small thing weren't part of something so much bigger, she would love to give it to him. By the time Ms. Paul gets to Elly, Saul is straining at his seat like a tethered helium balloon waiting for the slightest excuse to soar into the sky.

"Eliza, your word is ORIGAMI."

Saul's smile is contagious. Ms. Paul is smiling now too, her words curving to fit her upturned mouth.

"Origami," repeats Eliza, the word inspiring an image that has little to do with paper cranes and boxes. Instead, "origami" conjures its opposite, a shape created by a seemingly endless unfolding, leaving room for nothing else. The image serves to validate a decision Eliza realizes she has already made. She feels suddenly queasy, as if a small earthquake were occurring inside her. Her legs begin to shake. Then she focuses her eyes at the front of the room, on the artificial wood grain of her teacher's desk. The feeling fades. She is ready.

Eliza had thought that once this moment arrived she wouldn't want to look at her father, but now she realizes that she must. Saul's face is frozen in expectation, his body completely still. Eliza is reminded of Aaron, of the look in his eyes in the schoolyard so many years ago. There was a time when either Eliza would have had to turn away from that look or give it whatever it wanted.

Eliza doesn't close her eyes. She doesn't empty her mind. She doesn't wait for the letters to come because she's already picked the letters she wants. She faces her father as she pronounces them one by one.

"Origami," Eliza says. "O-R-I-G-A-M-Y. Origami."

Everyone in the room breathes in at once. For a moment it feels as though there isn't enough air. Saul is covering his mouth as if his hand could somehow block the moment, removing from the room a word which was never his to claim.

Ms. Paul looks stricken. "Are you sure?" she asks, even though that is completely against the rules.

Eliza has a feeling that if she said no, there wouldn't be a person in the room who wouldn't let her try again.

Instead, she nods her head. She is sure.

Acknowledgments

A massive thank you to Charlotte Anne Arch, who generously gifted me with the seeds of this novel.

Thanks to Wendy Schmalz for believing in me and to my friend and fairy godmother, Alice Peck, for leading me to her. Thanks to Amy Scheibe for your enthusiasm and insight and to Chris Min for your invaluable and indefatigable fine-tuning.

I was guided in my research and writing by Neil Steinberg's essay, "The Spelling Bee," as it appeared in *Granta;* by Gershom Scholem's "Abraham Abulafia and the Doctrine of Prophetic Kabbalism" in his book, *Major Trends in Jewish Mysticism;* and by Aryeh Kaplan's section on Abulafia in his book, *Meditation and Kabbalah*.

Thanks to the many readers and editors of this book: the Fall Cafe fiction workshop; Jeff Herzbach; Anthony Tognazzini; Mark, Ellen, and Saryn Goldberg; and Daupo.

A big, wet, sloppy kiss for Lisa Rosenthal. Thank you for your advice, opinions, support, and unflagging friendship.

Jason—your love, intelligence, and compassion have made me a better writer and a better person. I love you.

Come to the heart of reading